The Hour of the Lily

By the same author

Red Omega

THE HOUR OF THE LILY

John Kruse

ST. MARTIN'S PRESS
NEW YORK

 For information, address St. Martin's Press, 175 Fifth Avenue, New York, N.Y. 10010.

Library of Congress Cataloging-in-Publication Data

Kruse, John.
The hour of the lily.

I. Title.
PR6061.R8H68 1987 823'.914 87-16145
ISBN 0-312-01129-6

First published in Great Britain by Century Hutchinson Ltd.

First U.S. Edition

10 9 8 7 6 5 4 3 2 1

BOOK ONE

1

THE SUN had not yet burned the blueness from the shadows that clung to the eastern wall of the valley when there echoed a hallooing cry. It came from the watchtower above the entrance gorge. Workers straightened in the fields and passed the call along, the mountains amplifying it till the whole fertile depression and its two walled villages rang with the curious ululation.

It reached the third village, perched on its commanding bluff at the valley's head, as a resonance that drowned even the rush of melt-waters from the Kush. This was Bab-el-Hawa – Gateway of the Winds – home and stronghold of the tribal chief. Set amid holly-oak and steep cultivation, its structure of log, pole and rock was in potent contrast to the mud and chaff of the agrarian villages below.

No sooner did the echo sound than figures stirred amongst the vine terraces, the apple and mulberry orchards. The snap of rifle breeches being charged resounded as a multiple echo – everything echoed here – as men vaulted down from level to level, agile giants, baggy-trousered, horny-footed, their cropped heads gleaming under a variety of twisted headcloths.

Pola Katyna came quickly down the donkey-steps of the street, the ragged pupils of her interrupted class trailing agog behind her. Men loped past and all around she could hear the clatter of downed utensils as women hurried out on to the roofs of the houses below, veiling themselves. Segregated by custom, they made no effort to join the male surge.

Pola was the lone exception. With characteristic determination she followed the men down on to the bluff that formed the lower bulwark of the village.

Those already there were cupping their ears against the torrent to hear the shouts from the fields below. Pola listened intently, but not even her eighteen months here had conditioned her to the peculiar acoustics of these distant conversations.

In the grey kaftan and Pathan trousers that were intended, but failed, to conceal the sinful shape of her body, with her olive complexion and high cheekbones, she could almost have passed for a woman of the tribe. But her violet eyes, their awareness and boldness and humour, told of an origin outside the strictures of Islam.

Headman Habib arrived, followed by the mullah Mahmud Abdalis. How she detested him and his barbaric beliefs. They stood together staring down into the valley – the one cleanly laundered, authoritative, the other black-robed, grey-bearded, straight and lean as a ramrod.

Vehicles were coming – ah, that was it. *Schurawi*. It meant Russian! Pola stood quite still. Had her premonition been right? Was this really it, the moment she had been dreading – when the war being waged by her people against the Afghan resistance would reach into this valley to challenge her loyalties?

A child was sent stumbling to find Ghoram Khan. Pola's favourite giant of giants, Takredi, the village blacksmith and Khan's master-at-arms, took command in his absence.

'Man the Caliph!' he wheezed through the damaged tissue of an old throat-wound.

Pola was buffeted by the sudden quite violent struggle to reach the bucket seats of the big old anti-aircraft gun. All were trained in it, but, typically, there was no set crew. Open hands slapped against necks, toes hooked up ankles. Some went sprawling. The winners boarded the platform, freed the mechanism, spun the traverse and elevation handles. The barrel swung silkily. Though captured from the British during World War Two, the Caliph was in perfect repair. Only Pathans, with their love of weaponry, could have kept it so through forty snowbound winters.

The carriage, long since divested of its wheels, was jacked up on its outriggers. Now, with a tribesman manning each jack, they tilted the Bofors – with its mere five degrees depression – forward till the aimer had the valley in his cartwheel sights. The loader rammed a clip of armour-piercing shells into the charger.

The gun was laid and ready.

But ready for what?

If it was an attack, Pola knew, these simple people were in for a shock. Though *mujahedin kaflas* filtered through from time to time with hair-raising stories, and Khan's own brother had gone off to fight and been killed, Russia's war machine was still as science fiction to these hunter-farmers. Not even Khan himself fully understood the threat, seeing the conflict still as a blood feud. Afghanistan to his mind had never been a country, just a collection of tribes.

Pola had tried to make him see that separatism could never prevail against pluralism. But the Khans, for all their deep inner hunger for women, never listened to them. Least of all in bed!

Nevertheless she had striven to bring his thinking up to date. And was never quite sure why.

Was it because, for all his fierceness, he was the underdog? Because she loved him? Love was a ridiculous word here. It savoured of courtship, shared party and social mores, family approval. She and Khan shared virtually nothing but their bodies. They were centuries apart in almost every way. Yet, mysteriously, he had drawn her, only half-resisting, into the dark place he had for a heart. So deep that, looking out, all the certainties of her past life seemed . . . well, not exactly irrelevant, but unreal.

She had been briefed on how to cope with the religious, racial and sexual intolerance that would greet her posting to so remote and primitive a place. But nothing could have prepared her for the culture shock she suffered. *Nothing*. The women here were appendages, rag-bags, slaves. No man could glimpse the face of a female who was not a member of his own family. The mullahs had hounded Pola, tried to kill her. When Khan had stopped that, they tried to force her to wear the veil. They drove her off the street, interrupted her classes, reviled her before the children. She had lived in terror of her life – and there was no escape, no communication with Kabul, no means of returning there without an order from the educational commission. And that had not come. Not even when the Soviet forces had invaded Afghanistan last Christmas, putting her in peril of sudden tribal revenge. Kabul seemed to have abandoned her.

Yet she had survived. Partly through her own courage and dedication, but mainly through becoming Khan's woman. His concubine! For a woman of her professional background, this was the ultimate degradation – ameliorated only by the fact that he hadn't forced her, that he had himself suffered for consorting with an infidel. Nevertheless, it was a bitter pill.

'*Allaho akbar!*' An open-throated cry from Abdalis brought her back with a start. God is great! The mullah was pointing, then raising his arms to heaven.

A boat-shaped armoured vehicle, with eight wheels and a gun turret, had appeared on the road below. It was followed by a jeep, then another armoured vehicle.

The gunners locked on to the front vehicle, their aimer snatching glances at Takredi, willing him to give the order to fire. The giant stood frowning, peering, while the mullah thanked God for at last delivering a detachment of the enemy to their avenging cannon. But Takredi waited, searching the sky for gunships. The sudden appearance of three lone vehicles in their territory just didn't seem right. No one, not even the *schurawi*, would be such fools!

Looking down at the vehicles, Pola saw something fluttering above the jeep. A white flag! Were they Russian or Afghan? Russian-made, of course, but the Afghan army was equipped by the Soviet. She was too far away to read the insignia.

Not that the men around her cared. The bluff was lined with riflemen, all drawing bead. So were the irrigation ditches of the fields below. A white flag meant nothing to these Pathans. In seconds they would open fire.

'Wait!' It was out before she could check herself.

The tribesmen turned to stare at her, first in bewilderment, then anger. They had accustomed themselves to her presence, but that she should *interfere* . . . ! Abdalis took a step towards her, dismissing her furiously with his hands to the rooftops where she belonged.

Pola held her ground. She had heard something he hadn't: the plop of hooves, the rattle of stones. She pointed to where Ghoram Khan was sliding his horse down the scree of the mountain. He was lost to view in the timber for some moments. Now he was walking his mount across the slimy rocks under the waterfall, now spurring it up on to the bluff, dismounting in the same movement.

He eased the carcass of an ibex he had shot to the ground, his eyes inturned as he murmured to his horse, stooping to feel a bruised fetlock. Only when he had completed his inspection did he turn towards the gun, the gaze of every man riveted on him.

He listened, head down, to what Takredi had to say. The mullah interrupted, exhorting him to order the gun to fire. Khan silenced him with a look. He raised field-glasses to his eyes and studied the vehicles.

Ghoram Khan was in his early thirties, powerful shouldered, with brooding, slitted eyes under heavy brows – blind eyes until suddenly they looked out and ate everything up and went in again. With the Kalashnikov slung across his back, ammunition belts, black turban, black moustache dragged down at the corners, he made no concessions to his rank of feudal overlord. Or to anything else on this earth.

In the silence only the impatient clicking of the mullah's beads could be heard.

Khan lowered his glasses and leaned one hand on the gun.

'Pola.'

She went to him quickly, surprised that he should acknowledge her presence in the company of his warriors.

'What are they?'

She had to think for a moment; it had been so long.

'BTR-60s. Troop carriers that can go in water. They are used sometimes for . . .' It was hard sometimes to find the Pushtu equivalent of a technical word. 'Locating the enemy.'

'Those guns?'

'I'm not sure. Quite small.'

'You do not know how far their shells can reach?'

'No.' She wanted to add 'beloved'. The mountains were still in his eyes. He looked sealed off from human contact. Then she remembered. 'There's also a machine-gun. Coaxial.' She used the Russian word. How else could she explain it?

Khan motioned the gunners and riflemen to hold their fire and turned to consult with Takredi. Pola withdrew as the headman, the mullah and the elders in their fancy turbans gathered round him, demanding to know why they could not just let fly.

Khan did not reply. She guessed he was either curious or waiting to see if there would be other vehicles.

They came on steadily, and by the time they reached the bridge it was clear they were alone. The ancient bridge, she thought, would never take their weight. But the leader was veering off, taking up a position on the river-bank. Its twin did the same on the other side of the road. She saw Khan quicken as their turrets swung and their guns elevated towards the village. She braced herself for his order to fire – those were her people down there she was sure – but still he did not give it. The jeep was coming over alone and he had guessed the move was to cover its advance.

The atmosphere on the bluff had become electric. The tribesmen shifted about, fingering their rifles hungrily. The children, herded back from the edge, climbed the nearby mulberry trees to watch the jeep attempt the perilous climb from the valley. Only Khan remained motionless, watching through his glasses.

Presently, without turning, he beckoned to Pola and handed her the glasses without comment.

The strap was still about his neck and it was natural for her to lean against him. The familiar tang of leather and horses was mingled with the smell of wild thyme from the underbrush he had ridden through. There was no answering pressure from his shoulder. The fierce intimacies of last night, so fresh in her mind, were banished from his.

She misfocused, readjusted.

A red star – yes, they were Russians all right. Three of them. The driver and the radio operator wore wavy-brimmed bush hats and belted tunics. The third man had on nylon trousers and a windcheater. Dirty-blond hair, broad shoulders . . . Pola stiffened.

The jeep shunted round the next bend. His head went back and she could see his face.

It was Andrei Pavlovich Yakushev, her husband!

2

WHEN THE jeep was close, Khan muttered to Takredi. The giant strode off down the track and held up his hands. With his shaven head gleaming beneath his *kullah*, *kamma-band* stretched tight about his middle, he looked like some great genie risen from a lamp.

The jeep slid to a stop, the driver anchoring it with difficulty at a perilous angle.

Yakushev stood up in his seat and scowled, his gaze darting to the hostile tribesmen above. He was well aware of his danger, Pola could see. She felt reluctant admiration: whatever else he was, he was not a coward. She heard him tell Takredi in laborious but correct Pushtu that they needed to come all the way up in order to turn round.

Takredi indicated a scant turning space on the bend below. Yakushev inspected it and had the nerve to shake his head.

'I insist that we—'

Khan's voice, unraised but venomous, cut him off.

'*No man wearing that uniform enters this village!*'

This brought a thunderous response from his men.

Pola watched her husband put his fists on his hips and work his gaze balefully over the opposition. He hadn't seen her yet, but in moments he would. How would she react? Turn away? Stare through him? No. She was a woman now. And very curious to know what he was doing here. For him to put his head into the lion's mouth like this, it must be of vital importance.

His gaze passed over her, then hooked back.

'Pola?' The query in his voice told her how much she had changed. He raised a cool hand to her, stepped down from the jeep and started up the track alone.

Takredi glanced into the vehicle to see if the soldiers were armed. She sensed that for two pins he'd have heaved the whole thing over the edge.

Yakushev came trudging up in his stocky way, arms swinging, eyes watchful – green eyes under almost hairless brows, something not quite right about them. The flop of blond hair made him look boyish, though he was nearing forty. Broad nose, long upper lip, thick mouth with a tuck in the corners as though he was smiling. An odd, tearaway face, conveying vigour and unpredictability.

'*Salaamat bashi.*' He made the traditional gesture as he came to a halt. His eyes had touched Pola's for an instant, now they were on Khan, summing him up, gauging the mood of the elders and riflemen around him, aware that the giant stood between him and the jeep. Aware of everything, Pola knew, yet outwardly almost challengingly at ease.

Khan stood his ground in stony silence.

Abdalis extended two fingers towards the Russian like the fangs of a snake. 'This is the enemy that threatens us and the whole of Islam – kill him!'

Yakushev ignored him. 'You are *sharif* Ghoram Khan, I take it. I am Colonel Andrei Pav—'

'I know who you are, Russian.' Khan's voice vibrated from deep revulsion. 'You have strayed far from your people. Is it that you are tired of life?'

Yakushev smiled frostily. 'Not so tired, Pathan, as to make the journey without ample protection.'

Khan looked down towards the armoured cars and spat. He scanned the sky with a slitted eye. 'I see no protection.'

'Nor will you. So long as you honour the white flag.'

Khan turned his gaze to him. 'I see no white flag.'

'You see it, Pathan. And for men of honour, as I hope you are, it has a meaning. That I come in peace. On a private matter, nothing to do with the war.'

'There can be nothing private between us, Russian.'

'I speak of family matters.' Yakushev gestured towards Pola. 'I have come for my wife.'

The two men's eyes locked. It was Khan's that flickered. Something stirred through him like the uneasiness of trees in the wind.

A murmur coursed through the gathering. The tribesmen pressed forward to stare curiously at the man who had allowed his woman to come amongst them unveiled, to become the concubine of their leader. There were jeers.

'I eat my words,' Abdalis said. 'The husband of a faithless woman is already thrice cursed. Let him take her and go unmolested.'

Pola saw Yakushev's expression change, but he kept his gaze on Khan, waiting for his response.

Khan stood in silence, his brows knit, eyes narrowed.

Yakushev waited. 'Her work here is ended,' he said. 'She must return to Kabul.'

'Must?'

'The administration *requests* that you release her.'

'She is not a prisoner.'

'Then I may take her?'

'And she is not a slave. If you want her to go, she has a tongue of her own. You must ask her.'

Yakushev turned to her without quite looking at her. 'Pola?'

Pola stood rooted. It had always had to end, but now the suddenness of it, the manner of it – Andrei, whom she despised . . . she felt the stubbornness rise in her like a tide.

'It's an order, girl. From the directorate.' Yakushev switched to Russian. 'Come on, don't make it hard for me. Just let's get your things and go.' He moved to take her arm.

'Wait!' Khan's voice checked him. 'She has not replied. Pola, speak.'

'I . . . Let me talk with him.' Pola moved away a few paces. Yakushev followed.

He said quietly, 'Listen – there's a psychological moment with these people. Delay and they work up adrenalin. This is all a bluff – I've no back-up, just the two sardine cans. So it has to be in-out fast. You with me?'

'Just tell me why.'

'Why what?'

'Why now? And why you? I'm nothing to do with the GRU. I come under the educational commission.'

'Not any more. I'll explain on the way.' He swept a hand towards the terraces. 'Where do you live in this . . . overgrown bird's nest?' He gripped her elbow.

She snatched it free, planting her feet stubbornly.

Yakushev was determined not to lose face before the Afghans. 'If we're not clear of these hills by dark there's a chance we may never make it,' he warned her.

'I asked you a question.'

'Oh, for God's sake.' Yakushev looked pained. 'Haven't you done *any* thinking while you've been here? Don't you understand any better why I had to do what I did?'

'Oh, I understand all right.'

'Sounds like it. And what was that about you being unfaithful? No, don't tell me – save it for the journey back. You think we left you in the lurch, that it? Well, we didn't. Or rather *I* didn't.'

'Who did then?'

'The education people, of course. The regime was in total chaos when we had to move in. And we ourselves were too busy to lift you out. But I kept tabs on you. I knew you were safe and—'

'You what?'

'Through air reconnaissance.'

'Liar!'

'Fact. All right, I did leave you here – but for a reason. You may not know it but you've been doing more in Bab-el-Hawa than just "subvert" their children. You've been performing a second job. Now it's time to collect your back pay, take your place behind a desk, relate to civilized company again.'

'What are you talking about? A job with the directorate?'

'Of course.'

'No, thank you. If it's with you I'm not taking it.'

'Pola, you're posted. General Dolin's orders. To the interpreters' group.'

'The "inquisition"?' She recoiled.

'You'll have your own office, lieutenant's pay. As I say, backdated . . .'

'Interrogation of prisoners?' Pola registered revulsion.

'No. You know I wouldn't do that to you.'

'What then?'

'I'll explain when we're moving.'

'Explain now, Andrei, or I won't *be* moving.'

Yakushev eyed her, gauging her hostility, debating. He glanced at Khan and his tribesmen, who stood like statues, the mountain wind tugging at their loose clothing.

'You know this country pretty well, right?'
'I've ridden over most of it with Khan. Why?'
'With Khan. So you'll have listened to tribal talk.'
It was a statement. She didn't answer.
'According to air recce there's a caravan route over the top here.'
'Is there?'
'You know there is. The *mujahedin* use it?'
She closed her mouth.
'How about arms supplies from Pakistan?'
Her lips drew into a line.
'It's all there. In your mind. What kind of arms, how many, how they bypass our picquets on the Kunar. This part of the Hindu Kush is still a closed book to us. You can open it. But more. *You know what makes these mountain diehards tick.* High command haven't a clue. The war's not working out for them. I have a plan, Pola: how we, you and I, can *make* it work out. Think what that could mean for us both. Think of the rewards!' He bared his teeth, his eyes challenging.
'This' – Pola could hardly get the words out – 'is why you left me here so long?'
Yakushev looked serious. 'I won't lie to you. It was the hardest decision of my life.'
All the same, he had made it, laid her life on the line to further his ambitions, just as he had laid her father's, and still thought she would jump at what he had lined up for her. It was incredible! He was still totally blind to the alienation he had made her feel.
Her mind spun. Khan had been caring and straight with her. She could never betray him. But against this she had to measure what refusal would mean: return to Moscow, revoked apartment, revoked work permit, penalized at every turn. She couldn't face it. Not after tasting liberty as an individual. No matter how much she had been persecuted here it was nothing to the persecution she would suffer at the hands of her own people. Unless she betrayed Khan. And she couldn't. So she could never go back. The realization was shattering. How could she, a woman of educated tastes, live out her life *here*? It was unthinkable. But so was the alternative.
All her life, when reason failed, she had followed her heart.

She did so now. Turning on her heel, she walked back to Khan.

'Get rid of him.'

One eye squinted at her sidelong. Nothing changed in Khan's expression, yet something reached out and drew her hungrily back into him. One stride placed him between her and Yakushev. He pointed to the valley.

'Go!'

Yakushev just stood, arms hanging, his expression that of a man to whom the impossible had happened.

Abdalis's head pivoted like an eagle's, his eyes flaring, the mouth beneath the beak of a nose emitting a warning hiss. 'Without the woman? No! He is here by the will of Allah!' His claw-like hand gripped Pola's arm and dragged her towards Yakushev. 'Take her, infidel! Take her and go. Hurry!'

'Be still, holy man.' Khan severed his grip with a sweep of his hand.

'She must go! Aye. Must she not go?' The mullah turned to the elders.

Fierce argument arose. Beards jerked, the crests of turbans pecked back and forth. Men at the rear jumped to see over the heads in front, then pressed forward.

'See?' Yakushev shouted at Pola in Russian. 'Are you out of your mind? Let's go, get out of here while we can!'

Takredi stepped into the growing pandemonium, dwarfing everyone as he cleared a space around Khan.

'Silence, my brothers. Have you forgotten who is master here?'

'Pola, listen.' Yakushev's voice came urgently from behind Takredi. 'This valley has become strategic. These villages are to be razed!' The giant's bulk shifted and Pola found herself staring into the intense green eyes. 'Did you hear me? *Razed*. Planes can't make distinctions. If you stay, you'll be killed!'

In shock, Pola looked at Khan, but he had turned to address the elders.

'Then I'll be killed!' She threw back her head and laughed. Yakushev opened his mouth to speak, but she drowned out his words, striking at him with laughter. It was worth dying just to watch his expression – the disbelief, the fear. She knew that she had struck his pride and ambition a mortal blow.

Khan turned back. The argument had ceased. Abdalis was stalking away towards the mosque. Takredi grasped Yakushev by the scruff of his jacket and carried him to the head of the track.

All the tension kindled by the quarrel exploded in a roar of laughter. The tribesmen poured after them. The children swarmed down from the trees.

Takredi dumped Yakushev and gave a push that sent the Russian sprawling in the dust. The cliffs rang with jeers. A stone thumped against his chest as he struggled to get up. The green eyes blazed at the thrower, then at Pola. The thick lips twisted. 'Bitch!' she read. 'I love you. How could you do this? Bitch!' He pushed his way out through the mob.

A youth tried to trip him. Yakushev rounded on him, but a rifle poked him in the gut and, as he jackknifed, cracked down on his neck. Bent double, he turned away but still would not run. Another rifle was slipped between his legs and he fell on his face, sliding heavily.

Kicking, shoving, jostling, the mob closed around him, one grabbing a leg, another an arm. He fought back furiously, sending several of them flying. They started pulling the stocky body in all directions, first jeeringly, then savagely. He had become the goat's carcass in a deadly pedestrian game of *buz kashi!*

The jeep crew watched in alarm, the radio operator talking rapidly into his handset, no doubt alerting the armoured cars as to what was happening. But they would not, dared not, open fire, for fear of hitting their own people.

Only Pola's cry and Khan's signal saved Yakushev from being torn limb from limb.

The tribesmen drifted restlessly, pausing in groups to talk, their frustrated gaze following the jeep as it slithered down the track. Some moved off to squat under the mulberry trees. Pola felt their eyes on her. There was a bad taste in the air.

She felt rage, doubt, fear, exultation, but the full meaning of what she had done would doubtless come later.

Now Habib was ordering the women and children to go home, and shouting at the tribesmen to spread out and take up firing positions. Someone was leading Khan's horse away from the gun.

Khan was taking precautions, she realized, in case Andrei ordered the BTR-60s to open fire.

The jeep had reached the valley and was making for the bridge. Suddenly anxious, Pola hastened to Khan's side. Habib waved her back, but half-heartedly.

Khan did not turn his head, but, as always, knew when she was near. He said sombrely, 'You chose badly, my Pola.'

'It doesn't matter, my love. It doesn't matter.'

'You think he was lying?'

'No. Yes. I don't care. Let them come. At least we'll be together.' It was wild talk. But her insides were still jumping.

Khan's hand strayed from his glasses to the breech of the gun. He raised one finder. The jeep was approaching the bridge now. The armoured cars would just about be starting their engines. He cared and knew little about vehicles, but guns were a part of his life. He knew that the ones carried by tanks and armoured cars were most dangerous when they were stationary. Once on the move, even with their stabilizers, they would find accuracy difficult at such a range.

A bush kicked with the spurt of an exhaust. An explosion of dust jetted from behind the second vehicle. Slowly they began to move, using their front four-wheel steering to manoeuvre back to the road, their guns still trained on the village, seeming to float a little with their stabilizing action.

The road bank was steep. There would be a moment when it was too steep for the giros to compensate. The moment was coming . . . *now*.

Khan lowered his finger and stood clear.

The air split four times before Pola could even cover her ears. The empty clip had almost been discarded and another inserted before the first shells struck.

A giant firecracker seemed to leap all around the right-hand BTR. It was hard to see through the dust whether it was hit, but the shots were perfectly ranged.

Pola's efforts to collect her senses were shattered by the gun sound like no other she had ever heard. Had the armoured cars fired first? How had it happened?

The second clip spangled orange flame around the second vehicle. Through the gathering fog and smoke she saw it lift over backwards and roll in slow motion down the bank. A great cheer echoed through the village. The smoke, she saw now, was coming from the first vehicle. It was blazing.

Even as she watched, fire seemed to spit from its heart. She heard the rush of the incoming shell and, in the same instant, its explosion just below the bluff. Earth and debris rose to obscure the aim of the tribal gunners, but they emptied another clip through it for good measure.

A gasoline fireball mushroomed out of the dust-cloud, followed by a great echo that rushed back and forth across the valley dwarfing the gunners' cheer. The jeep had stopped short, at the end of a long skid. One could almost read the consternation of its occupants. A solitary crewman stumbled clear of the blazing wreckage and collapsed on the verge. The jeep seemed to rev up, spurting towards him.

Pola stared round sharply. 'No, Khan, no!'

But he had already turned away from the gun. To kill her husband, however much she hated him, would destroy the bond between them. The two fighting vehicles must suffice as revenge for the death of his brother. *For now.*

3

THE SUN scorched down. Great raindrops fell, then stopped. To the north, lightning flickered amongst black turbans of mountain cloud. To the south, cotton balls of vapour floated in an azure sky. Spanning all this disunity was a rainbow.

Out of the tinted mist rode Ghoram Khan, his horse labouring up the slope leading to the entrance of his valley, accompanied by his two Afghan hounds Shika and Bara. He reined outside the gorge to give Shah a breather, raising a hand to the man in the watchtower above.

Black stubble darkened Khan's jaw. His eyes were red. He sat there smelling his own sweat mingled with that of his horse, silently cursing. The day was full of omens but he could read none of them.

After a cold night spent in thought beside his father's tomb, he had ridden far this morning – first to the valley of the Haqs, then to his other two neighbours. Was it weakness that had possessed him? Since when had the Khans sought help from their neighbours in the face of enemy threat? But pride – or perhaps Allah – had caught the heel that would have spurred Shah into their domains. He had sat and watched their early smoke, their pasturing and water-carrying, and thought, No; since before Tamerlane you have been our enemies. You shall remain so. And on the way back he had thought, Nor will I call on the *mujahedin*. The lion does not hunt with the tiger for good reason: they would fight to the death over the spoils.

The *mujahedin* were backed by the old fanatics who sheltered in the cities of the west and in Peshawar to the east. After many had died for them, they hoped to return, like the Ayatollah Khomeini in Iran, and set themselves up in Kabul with their mullahs. They would enforce purdah on all the women, execute adulterers and dissenters, and cut off the right hands of men caught in theft for the third time. They would do this in the name of God.

The Fundamentalists knew nothing of God. Nothing. Less than a beetle. Less than an *ant*. Khan would have no part of them. So who was left? The one who always was left when the last guest had gone and the gate been barred and the lamps extinguished – himself.

He thought of himself and his tribe and his valley as one. They would fight the invader as they had always fought – alone, survival in freedom their only goal.

But how could he resist the Russian avalanche with less than a thousand men and no modern resources?

Though he had held his breath till his lungs starved beside his father's *maqbara* during the night, the old man's spirit had not breathed into him. Even now his tribal *jirgah* was assembled and waiting for his word. And he had no word to give them.

He slid from Shah's back and went to the river's edge. He listened to the hollow voice of the water as it rolled out of the gorge, its gathering excitement as it started helter-skelter towards the Alishang below.

His river told of many things – the snows far above, the irrigation systems of his fields – but not how he could resist the mechanized might of the hordes from the north. What could they want here anyway? Pola said it was for the same reason they had cleared the Kunar valley to the east – to destroy the villages and cultivations that gave shelter to the *mujahedin*. If she said so, it was true.

His mind circled her and the problem she presented. Without Abdalis and the two junior mullahs there would have *been* no problem. His villagers obeyed and trusted him, and Pola had won much affection for herself by caring for the old and sick. But the Fundamentalist mullahs were powerful. They interpreted Allah's word, they married and buried the members of every family, attended them when they were sick, wrote letters for them when such a thing was needed. Few of his people could read or write. The mullahs had seen to that, in order to maintain their power. Reading brought knowledge and change. They opposed change. Progressive thinking was heresy. The Koran was all man could ever need. And that is what, until Pola arrived, they had taught the children. *All* they had taught.

Khan was a devout Moslem, but he was convinced that if Islam was to defeat the infidel – and that meant the rest of the world – it must master the infidel's learning, if only to reject it afterwards. And the women must be freed to take their place openly in society. He believed these things fiercely but privately – for if the mullahs suspected his views they would bring him down, as they had brought down even *kings* in the past.

Yes, she should have gone, he thought sadly. Pola should have gone with Green Eyes back to her people. That would have appeased Abdalis and gained his full support in the battle to come. His support was needed, for was this not *Jihad*? The Holy War?

But how could he have continued in life? The call of her responding body, the mystery of a mind with cities in it – long lines of shoppers, marching traffic, a terrible orderliness overwatched by an ugly power as implacable as winter – held him in thrall. These images had been stark in her eyes when she had come here, but now they were fading. He had freed the bird from its cage – the cage that would encompass them all if the *schurawi* should overwhelm them. She was a harbinger of the future sent by Allah. An angel from a dark place. A slipping of vests, a scent of foreign flowers, a fierceness yet submissiveness wherein lay all delight. No, without her he could not face whatever was to come.

Though Khan remained receptive beside the river for a time, still no inspiration came to him. He returned slowly to Shah and, remounting, called his dogs.

While they were coming, he searched the western and southern skies through his glasses. There were two rainbows now, one arching high above the other. But the blueness beyond them was virginal – no gunships to mar it. Yet.

He spurred Shah on into the perpetual shadow and chill of his gorge. It was like entering a tomb.

4

SEVENTY MILES to the south-west an Mi-4 helicopter was speeding on a deadly mission. Lieutenant-General Anatoli Gregorievich Dolin's bulk overflowed the seat beside the pilot. Behind him sat Yakushev, his right cheek grazed to the bone, every joint in his body aching. But it was nothing to the ache inside him.

The military intelligence officers of the GRU were an élite, selected from pure Russian stock, honed by exhaustive training in a military-diplomatic academy so secret that a ten-year jail sentence awaited anyone who even mentioned its existence. They enjoyed privileges accorded to no other branch of the forces, including the KGB. In return, the very highest standard of performance was demanded of them. And Yakushev had flunked.

As Deputy Head of the 2nd Directorate of Staff, Afghanistan, part of his job was the recruitment of agents. And he had just failed to enlist the services of *his own wife*!

GRU wives and husbands were supposed to be one. Complete accord, with no marital complications, was one of the many stipulations. Ideological purity with no hint of dissent on either side of the family was another. *That* was why he had been forced to denounce her father. And *that* was what had caused their split.

He had engineered the denouncement through surrogates. Yet she had found out. Who and what had betrayed him? The galling answer was his own body. It had responded to his nagging sense of guilt by suddenly and mysteriously not responding at all. He became sexually impotent.

The debility struck him in Moscow just after her father's arrest in early 1979. Pola at first did not suspect the cause. By the time she did they had both been uprooted by the sudden posting to Afghanistan, and were ensconced in the Soviet Embassy, Kabul; he as Chief Resident, she as his interpreter. Among strangers, half of them beady-eyed KGB, the paper-thin walls allowing them no privacy, the embassy was the most disastrous place on earth for her to reach her traumatic conclusion.

The suppressed rows, muffled hysterics and charged silences drove Yakushev to near distraction. With recall to Moscow staring him in the face, he resorted to crash tactics – and manipulated his wife's immediate transfer. The Afghan Schools Programme, devised to wrest educational power from the mullahs, was running short of teachers. She had a teaching degree, ideological clearance, and would have done anything, even scrubbed floors, to get away from him. She was whisked off on a training course and thence to a provincial centre for onward posting.

Not an instant too soon, by Yakushev's estimate. The Hafizullah Amin regime, then in power, was suppressing its enemies with such violence that it was plain the Soviet Union would have to intercede militarily on its behalf. And if Afghanistan became an operational front, the job at the embassy would be upgraded to a fully fledged GRU directorate, which he, as the man on the spot, might well be called upon to command. The rank for the job was lieutenant-general – a big leap forward. So thank God he had acted in time.

When, however, on 27 December 1979, the Soviet forces did invade, the directorate that accompanied them arrived with its own commander – Lieutenant-General Dolin, transferred fresh from Czechoslovakia.

Fresh? He was a died-in-the-blood fifty-five-year-old with a headful of ponderous strategies devised by the Geriatrics for war in Europe. Yakushev's hopes crashed. That he was to remain as this man's deputy consoled him not one whit. Deputies to dinosaurs often shared their extinction and this old fool understood nothing of Islam or the special demands of the theatre of war. And he wasn't going to learn. Certainly not from his deputy.

From the first day, Dolin set about finding fault with every move Yakushev made. Every lapse went on file. He was building, Yakushev realized, sufficient grounds to have him removed. He could simply have ordered it, but that, apparently, wasn't his style. Like the old party pro he was, he wanted his man trussed and ready to throw to the wolves – for the moment that he needed a scapegoat.

Yakushev understood well enough that the best response to departmental infighting was attack, while yielding minimal ammunition to the enemy. This attack, he decided at length, should take the form of an intelligence coup – one that would contrast Dolin's blundering methods with his own subtler technique. He would show that where Dolin sought to crush the resistance, he could successfully undermine it. To achieve this, though, he would need Pola's help. Could he risk bringing her back to Kabul? He decided he could.

And there he had flunked – to the tune of two lost BTRs and the death of their crews. He had played right into Dolin's hands!

Now the bastard was rubbing his nose in it.

The enormous flat-topped hat was turning. Flesh bulged over one shoulderboard as the doughlike chin came round towards him, the mouth above it press-studded in an expression of permanent distaste. Dolin pointed ahead.

They were approaching Kerala. It was, as the map had suggested, a nothing village – sprawling adobe compounds encircled by scorched fields in a parched valley. Encircled too, right now, by seven armoured personnel carriers and their complement of fifty-six Spetznas soldiers. They were deployed so that they sealed off the village and its inhabitants, who were gathered – the menfolk at least – in an apprehensive knot at the centre.

There was no reason, Yakushev knew, for this operation to require his presence. He was being made to eat crow.

The pilot put the helicopter down outside the encirclement.

Dolin waved a hand. 'You know what to do.' And sat back in the cockpit. He wasn't even going to get out.

Seething silently, Yakushev swung down and moved through the cordon towards the gathered tribesmen. They looked a ragged bunch – farmers, goatherds.

An officer wearing a camouflage tunic hopped down from one of the BMPs and saluted – a burly captain with flashing eyes and a swagger. Spetznas were daredevil, almost suicide troops belonging exclusively to the GRU, trained for drops up to 1000 kilometres behind enemy lines, for demolition and assassination. They were among the toughest in the world, and they knew it.

'At your command, comrade.'

'Order a squad of your men to collect all the women and children and shut them in the mosque. Then come with me.'

As the officer called a lieutenant to him Yakushev added, 'If in the process they flush out any *mujahedin* they're to shoot them.'

The officer winked. He gave his orders and caught Yakushev up.

'The photographer here?'

'Standing by, comrade.' The captain jerked a thumb towards one of the BMPs.

The grey-bearded *malik* was coming forward to meet them, backed by his elders. His manner conveyed a calm dignity that Yakushev would have bet a million roubles he did not feel.

'Jur hasti? Salaamat bashi.' Are you well? May you be healthy. Welcome to Kerala, etc., etc. The usual bullshit, Yakushev nodded and replied in similar vein, then watched the expression of calmness desert the faded brown eyes as the old fellow saw the soldiers making for the family enclosures.

'Have no fear, old man,' Yakushev told him. 'We are looking for *mujahedin*. To aid our search, and for their own safety, your women and children are being escorted to the mosque.'

The *malik* looked angry. 'Had you requested it, their own menfolk could have escorted them. Then there would have been no impropriety.'

Yakushev shrugged. 'It is done now. My men will not harm them.'

They wouldn't touch your filthy old hags with a barge pole, he was tempted to add.

'There are no *mujahedin* here,' the *malik* said reproachfully. 'We are simple farmers. Men of peace.'

'None here now, possibly,' Yakushev said drily. 'But we have information that in the past month you have sheltered upwards of thirty terrorists.'

Surprisingly the old man didn't deny it. 'Only as we would shelter you,' he said. 'We do not enquire the business of those in need of a roof for the night.'

'The business of fighting men is not hard to guess,' Yakushev retorted. 'You sheltered and fed them. And for more than a night.'

'Only as we would feed and shelter you.'

'You hid them from our gunships. You lied to one of our armoured patrols. Leaflets were dropped in every village, including this, forbidding such activity. The penalty was death, old man. Did you not read them?'

The *malik* stared at him, horrified. 'The paper? The paper is there.' He pointed to the outer wall of his hut, where a sheet was pinned for all to see. 'But since our mullah was called to Allah, there is none here who can read it.'

Yakushev eyed him penetratingly. Was he lying? He reminded himself that this was irrelevant.

The old man went on unhappily, 'Had we known that our custom of hospitality to all had become unlawful, we would have closed our doors against the *mujahedin*.' He added, 'But what if they had forced them open? Our position, as you see, is difficult.'

Yakushev perceived all sorts of possibilities – mainly prizing useful information from these people.

'Let us discuss your position and this difficulty. Where is your talking place?'

'It is here.'

'Call a *jirgah*.'

The *malik* clearly didn't know what to make of this. He looked towards the encircling soldiers, then to the last of the women and children being herded into the mosque. He had not expected this officer with the hard green eyes to fall for his nonsense and was deeply suspicious. He turned to discuss it with his elders.

The captain throughout all this had been watching Yakushev closely for some clue as to what was going on.

'Get the photographer over,' Yakushev told him. He removed his pistol belt and held it up for the villagers to see, then handed it to the captain. He walked away a few paces and waited.

Presently, knowing they had no choice, the villagers began stacking their own weapons – with extreme reluctance, but it was tabu to bear arms to a *jirgah*, as Yakushev was of course aware. They gathered and sat on the ground – perhaps a hundred men and boys. The youngest – a dark-eyed, mischievous-looking little fellow clutching a puppy – could have been no more than ten years old.

Yakushev eyed the youngsters pensively. They were of an age to be subverted to communism, he thought, not wasted.

The photographer marched up with his tripod and camera and began to set up in front of them.

The villagers watched him, puzzled and alarmed by this development. There was still a reluctance to be photographed among the more backward tribes. They believed the camera robbed them of more than just their visual image – a part of the soul itself perhaps.

To keep them calm Yakushev explained that this was army procedure. All such gatherings had to be recorded, so that the great and just leaders of the Soviet people could be satisfied that the prerequisites of democracy were being observed in the far-flung places of their dominion.

He could barely keep the cynicism from his tone. Suddenly he didn't care if Dolin did stack it against him. Leaving the photographer to arrange his composition, he walked back to the helicopter.

'They are ready, Anatoli Gregorievich,' he told Dolin. 'Do you want to address them?'

Dolin stared down at him as if he were mad. 'What the devil for? You know what to do. Get on with it.'

Yakushev did not move. 'It struck me that these are not collaborators as such. Too simple-minded. Perhaps we could learn a thing or two instead of always being in such a hurry.'

'Learn?' Dolin looked blank. 'Such as what?'

'We don't know what, do we, till we give it a try. But they know things, these people, about the area, the *mujahedin*. And they're scared. I'd like a chance, for once, to try and turn them.'

'Comrade Andrei —'

'We never try communication. Just' – Yakushev snapped his fingers – 'cut them off. Result is we never learn what makes them tick. A little agitprop, get them believing the rebels are a threat to their peaceful existence and, who knows, we could have them feeding us all sorts of stuff.'

'Yakushev, you're dreaming.'

'We're not rushed, are we? Why not a word with them?

Your rank and medals alone'll put the fear of God into them. It's worth a try.'

Dolin stared at him for a moment, and Yakushev caught a glint of satisfaction in his eyes, as though a suspicion had been confirmed.

'Yakushev, did they never teach you that war is fire? *Fire*. Nothing else. Not dialectic, hobnobbing with peasants, half-baked psychology. That's for losers. It's *why* they're losers. Why, probably, though I'm guessing, your good wife stands to lose her life at this moment.' He consulted his watch. 'Now I have to be at the front in an hour. So just carry out my orders. Quick as you can. Then we'll be away.'

Yakushev glanced at the expressionless face of the pilot. He had made his point. Every little helped. Without another word he turned back towards the village.

'Uh – Colonel,' Dolin said after him.

Yakushev checked.

'An army salute in front of heathen is always good practice. Shows *unanimity* of purpose.'

Yakushev did not miss the barb. Very slowly he forced his arm into the required posture.

Dolin, equally slowly, returned it.

Yakushev, his gut churning, continued towards the *jirgah*.

The photographer was removing the Polaroid print from his camera. The small boy, who had held up the puppy for its picture to be taken, was tucking it lovingly back inside his *chapan*. The photographer hefted his equipment and, tipping a casual hand to the villagers, walked away. He had performed his function simply by getting them to move voluntarily into a tight group.

Yakushev steeled himself and, before they could begin ungrouping themselves, nodded to the captain, who raised his hand, waited till his men had come to the aim, then dropped it.

The prolonged burst of automatic fire from behind them caught the tribesmen unprepared. For almost a minute there reigned confusion of sound and image such as Yakushev had never witnessed from so close. Though sickened, he knew Dolin was watching him, and kept his gaze on the slaughter to the last.

Then, retrieving his gunbelt from the captain, he finished off those still alive with his pistol. He allowed himself to evince nothing as he put the youngest out of his agony first, still clutching his whimpering puppy. He experienced less repugnance with the older ones by imagining that each was either Dolin or Khan.

5

Kifri Kebir, Khan's central village, was of a different character from his mountain stronghold. Set amid wheatfields laced with irrigation channels, encircled by walls of dried mud and chaff – never a sharp corner or straight line – it reflected the sunlight with a halation as golden as any threshing floor. Poplars, still glistening with the last rain, shimmered above secretive courtyards where this morning all the women were gathered, busying themselves, pausing to whisper fearfully, doors latched, eyes perhaps to knot-holes. For in the market-place the whole male population of the valley sat congregated, the swarming hum of their voices manifesting the emergency.

The talk stilled as Khan tethered his horse by the gate and strode pensively to the huge central holly oak. He twisted the chair placed there for him and straddled it, his heart heavy.

Already under the tree sat the three mullahs, Habib and Takredi. Facing them, the first row of elders shared the shade. Beyond them, all was glare and colour, a sea of turbans, glinting weapons – permitted today for this was a council of war, liable to be attacked from the air at any moment.

Abdalis rose, a black shadow within a shadow, and raised his arms.

'*Allaho akbar. Allaho akbar! Ush hado, Ullaelaha, illulla . . .*' His voice lifted to the mountain walls. God is great. God is great! I am a witness that there is no God but one God and that Mahomed is his Prophet!

He resumed his seat on the roots of the tree, straight-backed, his voice still journeying through the hills. The echoes died. The *jirgah* was in session.

Khan motioned Takredi to get the preliminary business over quickly. He was uneasy about the massed target they presented here.

'As my brethren know' – the giant stepped forward – 'the modern weapons we ordered from Darra have not come. Khan-master says it is because we sought to buy on credit, that others must have come cash-in-hand and robbed us of our priority. Well, if now we are to repel the infidel, we must rob them back – and quickly! We, too, must go cash-in-hand!' This elicited a running growl of approval. 'We – we . . . ' He floundered.

'Horses,' Habib prompted from behind him.

'I need thirty horses – ten from each village. And thirty men – ten from each village. We'll form a *kafla* now, today, and go to Darra and *fight* our way, if we have to, to the head of the line!'

'Well spoken!' 'High time!' 'We'll teach the dogs!' The shouts grew around him, thickening to a lusty roar. '*Ali, Ali!*'

When the noise lessened, a more practical voice put in, 'But the journey to Darra and back takes ten days. What if the infidel strikes before you return?'

The giant shrugged, then grinned. 'Just tell him, "Takredi isn't here yet" – he'll wait!'

The tribesmen loved it. '*O, Ali! Ya Timur!*' they chanted.

War fever is on them, Khan thought. They see resistance simply as a matter of courage and firing their guns – as for a tribal engagement – and leaving the rest to Allah. This time it will not be enough. The burden is on me to prepare them, direct them in such a way as to make them mighty. But how, in so little time?

Habib was addressing the *jirgah* now, reading out the list of ordered weapons and their cost.

'Fifty Sten-guns, at three thousand rupees each. One hundred AK-47 "black rifles" at the same price. Two tank-killing guns at sixty thousand rupees each . . .'

The silence had become ragged. It became utter as the realization spread that somehow *they* would have to find the required sum.

Habib read out the total. It was astronomical. He paused for a moment, watching their dismay. Then he added, 'Our master has pledged every *afghani* he possesses towards this purchase. But' – he raised his hand quickly to stem the huge tide of relief, the murmurs of '*Baba!*' Rich man! – 'but it will not be enough.

We must raise between us a further three hundred thousand rupees!'

The stunned silence that followed forced Khan out of his reverie. He glanced towards the mullahs and elders. There was a solution, but would they see it? Should he prompt them, to save time? No. This was a domestic matter, for each family to decide.

On every married woman's wrist in the valley, round every finger, throat, ankle, were the heirlooms bestowed in marriage. Even amongst these poor farmers, surprising treasures were showered upon the bride and bridegroom during the *qand shikini* ceremony, and as *runumagi* at the unveiling of the bride. But these trinkets, many of them gold, were treated as built-in security, to be traded for their worth only in the direst emergency. That emergency was now upon them. But if he, Khan, pointed that out, it would be taken as an order – and they had little enough already that he couldn't lay his hands on if he demanded it.

The elders put their heads together. Beard waggled against beard. Argument and conjecture rippled through the gathering. The rain-wet encircling walls seemed to smoke in the sun's heat. Here under the tree was where folk coming to market tethered their animals, hung their water skins. On partridge-fighting days the birds were kept cool here in their cages. Carefree times. The crowd didn't understand yet that they were gone, that they stood at an awesome crossroads. They resisted stubbornly the suggestion that they should forfeit the only things of value they possessed in the world.

Abdalis spoke, trying to sway them. A show of hands was called for. The result proved inconclusive. Time was spilling away. Khan realized he would have to intervene.

The shadow of a horse and rider fell across the village gate. The argument faltered as eye followed eye towards it. A shocked murmur grew to fill the market-place.

Khan turned to see Pola walking her horse towards the tree. She dismounted, handed the reins to one of the men and approached, her gaze steady on Khan, as if to shut out the tide of protest that swept around her.

'I have come to help,' she said quietly.

Khan forestalled Abdalis as he strode to dismiss her.

'This is an outrage! Tradition absolutely —'

'Tradition must wait on my command,' Khan said. 'I wish to hear what she has to say.' He looked at her. She wore a plain head-covering. The clothing she had donned for the occasion was voluminous, the colours faded, unobtrusive. 'How can you help, Pola?'

'I know the fighting habits of my people, what they will do, how they will come. In these matters I can advise.'

'Good. Such advice we need. But not here. This is a men's gathering.'

'Ordained by God,' Abdalis interjected sternly. 'Her very presence threatens its sanctity. Bid her begone!'

The other two mullahs ranged themselves at his shoulder, nodding fiercely.

Pola lifted her chin and said evenly, 'If tradition means more to you than survival, why are you gathered at all? To share with each other the darkness of your ignorance? You can do that in the fields. Or in the mulberry trees with the children, your mouths stained with juice.'

Abdalis's eyeballs glistened. 'You hear that, Son of Ahmed? She spits at us!'

'She mocks our institutions!' said the youngest mullah, a sallow fellow with a wispy beard.

'Begone, shameless creature!' Abdalis flapped his hands, as if he were shooing a goat.

'Wait!' Khan scowled him to silence. He looked thoughtfully at Pola. 'You know how they will come? Tell me quickly.'

Pola shook her head. 'It cannot be told quickly. If you wish it – you, Khan, if *you* wish it' – she turned her back on the mullahs – 'I will sit here with you and answer questions.'

This brought an explosion almost of ridicule from the mullahs. The gathering had fallen to utter silence now, as each strained to hear what was being said.

Khan pursed his lips. He turned to the holy men. 'If she were to answer through me, speak only when spoken to . . . ?'

'We are here, Son of Ahmed, to take direction from God, not an infidel.'

'An infidel may be the tool of God. Think, holy man. Her replies may convince the *jirgah* of the emergency we face.' Khan looked at Abdalis meaningfully.

'None would believe her. Moreover, she is unveiled.'

'Aye, unveiled.' His colleagues shook their heads, rolling their eyes at the shame of it.

'To permit her to remain would be an affront to every man present.'

'Suppose,' Khan said, 'she were to veil herself?'

'I will not be veiled!' Pola cried.

'See?' Abdalis turned his back on her. 'She spurns not only our customs but the ways of God.'

'She *breathes* heresy,' hissed the middle mullah.

'The veil, holy men,' Khan was becoming angry, 'is not the way of God.'

Abdalis said to the branches of the tree, 'You presume to tell us what are His ways?'

'The veil,' Khan said flatly, 'is the imposition of man. Conceived in greed of possession and jealousy – both sins. It is the veil itself, not lack of it, that is sinful!'

He had raised his voice. The *jirgah* heard him in astonishment. The elders looked shocked. The mullahs hissed like vipers. Abdalis raised the Koran in his hand.

'It is written —'

'Where?' Khan cut him off, reaching for the book. Abdalis snatched it away. 'Show me. Show me where it is written and I will send the woman away!'

Abdalis froze.

'Show me!'

Never before had the mullah been so challenged. He tucked in his beard and glowered, mumbling, 'It is in the Sunna.'

'It is nowhere in the Sunna,' Khan spoke out clearly, so all his men should hear. 'The veil was imposed by man. It can be repealed, when necessity demands, by man.'

There were scattered shouts of protest, but the elders were forced to nod their agreement. Each knew his Koran and realized that it was so.

'That necessity is *now*.' Khan took Pola's arm and led her to a place among the roots of the tree. She seated herself, eyes lidded.

Abdalis stood quite still for a long moment. Then he turned and, with the other two at his heels, stalked away.

Khan strode after him, spoke quietly, urgently. 'Hear me, Holy Men. Leave now and many will leave with you. They will never learn what threatens or how to resist it. Divided, our *Jihad* will fail and the infidel win.'

Abdalis hesitated, and Khan watched him wrestle with his pride. *Jihad*. It was more important than individual pride or purdah. It was the rallying cry of Islam itself.

Abdalis had two wives and six children. The fate of the valley was as much his concern as anybody else's. Bigot though he was, he was also a pragmatist.

He eyed his two colleagues mutely, shook his head, and returned to a place under the tree.

The questions came awkwardly at first, then in mounting profusion. Pola answered quietly. Khan amplified her replies in his strong voice.

The Russians would come in one of two ways, she told them – either with an obliterating air attack and no military follow-up, or in full force, with motorized infantry, tanks, guns and helicopter air support. Either way, an air strike was inevitable. They would use rockets to flatten buildings, machine-guns to kill people – *all* the people. The object, she reminded them, would be to render the valley uninhabitable, so they would probably also fire the crops and destroy the irrigation systems.

The farmers listened in growing dismay.

If the Soviets used ground forces, Pola continued, they would send perhaps a division – ten thousand men – motorized troops with battle tanks, heavy tanks, self-propelled guns, armoured cars, rocket-launchers. They would advance in roller action, the perpetual-motion technique devised for war in Europe. Armoured-car reconnaissance would come probing up the Alishang valley. The least resistance would be pinned down with heavy fire till follow-up units arrived, encircled and pinched out the enemy – by which time the reconnaissance group would be ahead again, probing, eating up the ground. The advance units did most of the fighting and, in theory, the main body never needed to stop.

This information was as new to Khan as it was to his men. He began to see that modern war was more than the pointing of a finger and a haphazard surge of men and weapons, that it was carefully devised, timed by watches, co-ordinated by voices over little radios; each vehicle and weapon was a tool designed for a separate purpose, and used in different combinations they could do almost anything. The Russians, he thought bitterly, had a whole bag of tools, while he, until the new weapons arrived, had just the Caliph, two Sterling machine-guns and a collection of old rifles. How he employed these was therefore of vital importance and must be part of a master plan, or they would be wasted. And that plan must be based upon the enemy's weaknesses rather than his own limited strength.

Pola was replying to a question about chemicals. 'Poison dust' as the man put it. He had heard rumours from the *mujahedin*.

Pola had to admit she didn't know much about it, save that chemicals were a part of the strike capability of every Soviet division, delivered by aircraft or in shells. Every tank was proofed against toxins. The soldiers carried masks.

No, she did not know if chemicals had been used in Afghanistan. How could she? She had been here teaching the children since the invasion. But she had heard that normally they were dropped from the air in the form of coloured dust, and they were deadly – blood and waste and vomit came from the victims and there was great pain in dying, and, when dead, the bodies turned black. The fall of such dust, she added, depended on the wind. Therefore, if they ever came under chemical attack, they should remember that their only direction of escape lay upwind.

A prolonged silence greeted this advice. Khan saw that at last his men were coming to grips with the true power of the Soviet machine.

He quickly ordered another show of hands on the contribution of valuables towards the new weapons.

The *jirgah* volunteered all that they possessed, to a man.

The collection would begin at once. The *kafla*, headed by Takredi and Habib, would leave for Darra tonight.

The sign, Khan realized, had come to him. Not in the manner he had expected, but just as surely. There was only one way he and his tribe could defeat the infidel.

He stood before them under the tree and outlined his plan.

6

KHAN'S *gila*, the family fortress, lay under the scowl of the cliff above his village. Five centuries of wind, snow and tribal warfare had eaten into its stones, causing sections to collapse. Some of these had been patched, some left in ruin. A sloping mud-brick tower had been added. With its scarcity of windows, outer stockade of rough-hewn rock and heavily reinforced gate, it looked a forbidding place.

In the living hall, the shadow cast by the encircling wall hid the disrepair of the scant lumps of furniture that in his great-grandfather Fazullah's day had been thought very fine. The carpets on the rough walls were still very fine – too fine for spreading on the dirt floor where chickens rutted. Old hunting weapons hung from pegs driven into the stonework. A pair of hooded falcons sat on their perch beside the enormous hearth with its blackened pots and iron spit, on which now a haunch of ibex glistened gold in the light of the fire.

Khan's wife Layla snapped the sewing thread with her teeth. With a toss of her wild hair, she levered herself up and lugged the man-sized dummy she had been making to the middle of the room, supporting its sagging weight against her pregnancy.

'What do you think?'

Pola looked up from the similar effigy she was just finishing. Though her heart was heavy, she smiled.

'I think he is either very old or very sick – or both!'

Shooing a hen, she fetched an armful of straw and stuffed it up the figure's shirt and down its baggy trousers.

Layla watched her, her full lips curling, the lapis-lazuli gem in her nostril glinting in the firelight. She made a hoarse sound.

'You are being very familiar with my man.'

Pola shot her a glance, but there was no double meaning in

the kohl-rimmed eyes. She hadn't expected one. Layla knew all about her and Khan; in such a small community how should she not? Islam allowed him up to four wives. Layla, the daughter of a tribal chief in the mountains south of Jalalabad, had expected to be one of a household of women. That Khan had been satisfied with just her had seemed strange, and she had grown lonely in the big old fort with only two servants. But since her lord and master had taken a mistress she had felt less isolated. She had begged Pola to live with them, but, mysteriously, she seemed to prefer the cabin behind the school.

'There.' Pola took the dummy from her and cast it on the pile.

Layla counted with one childishly gnawed fingernail. 'That makes seven.'

'Eight.' Pola added her own.

'Eight! I think we deserve some *chai*.'

'No, Layla. Let's get out of here and see how they're getting on.

Layla hesitated. She seldom left the house. She reached automatically for the black *chaderi* hanging beside the door.

Pola shook her head and fetched her a head-covering fringed with tiny coins. Khan had abolished the veil for the period of the emergency. He wanted all the women to be able to *see*, to *move*.

Layla shied away. 'God will punish me!' But Pola draped it over her hair and steered her out.

The mountain-sharp air was tinged with wood smoke. Sunlight glinted on the flat mica-veined rocks used to weigh down the roofs of the houses that shelved away below like a glistening stairway against the blue-blackness of the far valley wall. Sounds came of rushing water, of distant hammering, metal on metal. A team of donkeys loaded with poplar poles tottered down the street. Their drivers glanced at the two women, then quickly away. To gaze on the naked face of another man's woman still disturbed them. Things were changing too fast for them to keep pace.

Over the decades, the Caliph had become as much a statue as a weapon. Yet now it was in pieces, each part being oiled and laid out on rush matting, a score of men at work, levering, hammering out the split pins. In the absence of Takredi, now three days' march away on the trail to Darra, the Master himself was supervising the dismantling.

He glanced up briefly as the two women approached, the lines on his face very deep. He is feeling the strain, Pola thought. My country is forcing on him the burdens of being a leader in the modern world!

Layla's two children came rushing up.

'We're helping the men,' Fazi said, waving oily hands. He was nine, a year older than his sister, and a tousled ragamuffin.

Lissa stared at her mother. 'Mama, you're unveiled!' She glanced round quickly to see who was looking.

'And you're doing a man's work!' Pola said quickly to cover Layla's embarrassment. 'We're all learning to do new things. Isn't it exciting?'

Lissa's expression showed she wasn't sure. Wasn't change supposed to be wicked?

'Abdul says we're all going to get killed,' Fazi said, clapping a hand to his heart and staggering.

'Well, tell Abdul he's a *sheesha dill*!' Pola said severely, reading his anxiety.

Reassured, the boy ran off to tell his friend that he had a 'heart of glass'. Lissa chased after him.

Layla's eyes clung to Pola's for a moment, baring her agony. But now they had to move. The unloaded donkeys were being led to where the gun lay disassembled.

The tribesmen began lashing the parts of the gun to their pannier frames, trimming their balance with great care. The long barrel with its conical flash shield was lowered into a rope sling between two pairs of animals.

A second party started work on the vacant emplacement. They sank in a stout central support and constructed around it a poplar-pole replica of the Bofors. The barrel pole was accurately proportioned, with a funnel-shaped can at one end, to represent the flash shield, and a counterbalance at the other, to keep it always angled to the sky. The addition of a vane at the lower end enabled it to traverse back and forth realistically in the wind.

Finally, three of the dummies being made by other village women were brought down and lashed into the bucket seats, while the structure was receiving a coat of pitch.

Only then did Khan come over to his wife and Pola. He

stood beside them for a moment in silence, his gaze sweeping every part of the sky before descending to them moodily.

'It is time for *zuhr* prayer. Afterwards,' he pointed to where Layla's and Pola's horses were tethered beside Shah, 'we will go for a ride.'

Coveys of *sisi* leapt ahead of them with a whirr of wings, to skim away over the donkey train as it struggled up the steep track. The village from here was little more than a source of smoke, the tracks and trails that led to it, the stumps of fresh-felled timber, showing clear and white against the black overspill of mountain shadow.

Up ahead was a cave. Pola knew it from her early morning rides. Khan reined his horse and turned in his saddle, waiting till the two women rode up beside him.

Layla's face was set, her brow moist. Pola saw the quick, searching look Khan gave her.

He said, 'When the alarm is given, this is where you will bring the women and children.' The silence ate up his voice.

Pola glanced at the hole in the rock. She had ventured into it once and found that it widened surprisingly and was fully ten paces deep.

'We will need supplies, water.'

'Each family will bring its own,' Khan told her.

'How will we know when it is safe to come out?'

'I will send a man.' Khan's saddle creaked as he wheeled abruptly and Shah's white heels scrambled away up the scree.

Providing one is left alive, Pola thought. Then chided herself. Now whose heart is of glass? But she knew her Russian people too well. What they committed themselves to doing, they did too thoroughly to fail – whether in sport or war. Without the accurate information they had been relying on her to provide, they would come in sufficient force to pulverize any opposition. Khan's plan was the best possible under the circumstances. But against Russian overkill, it could be little more than the stamping of a child's foot.

She laid a hand on Layla's arm. 'How are you feeling?'

Layla nodded wordlessly. She rested her belly against the pommel, breathing deeply. The air up here was dry and sweet with the scent of herbs.

Pola clenched her eyes and wished suddenly that she had a

God. Faith in something outside them all, something through which justice prevailed and evil perished, from which miracles might be expected.

But her conditioning was too strong. She knew that even now computers were bleeping at Soviet army headquarters, professional faces conferring over their readouts, technicians readying the death-dealing machinery. While below them, twenty-three donkeys . . .

Pola and Layla huddled in their saddle blankets while waiting for the pack-train. It was excruciatingly cold. Khan panned his glasses minutely across the mountain ocean, in which his valley was but a small green trough.

When at last the donkeys caught up, Khan remounted and led the way along the crest of the ridge. It was the old caravan trail, worn by centuries of traffic, easy to negotiate though its sides in places were almost sheer.

After half an hour they came in sight of a work-party. They were preparing the fresh gunsite on the edge of the cliff.

Khan dismounted and gave orders. While the Caliph was being unloaded, Pola moved to the edge and looked over. Far below nestled Kifri Kebir in its pattern of fields. Further along, Shirāt was clearly visible at the inner end of the gorge. In the other direction, Bab-el-Hawa could still be seen, tamped like a swallow's nest under the mountain eaves. This was the one place, she realized, from which the whole valley was visible.

'Tamerlane . . .' Khan was beside her. He scrubbed the rock at her feet with the sole of his *chupli*. 'Maybe on this very spot. In the year eight hundred.' He stared away blindly.

'Khan—'

'That was your year 1398.'

'Beloved—'

'He looked at our valley. He wanted to attack it, but it was winter. Snow. All this was snow. He did not know how to get down.'

'I just want you to know that I regret nothing. That I would make the same decision again.'

Khan continued, 'Eventually his army slid down the far end of this ridge on their shields.'

'Their shields!'

'They lowered him in a basket attached to ropes. He was lame, you know.'

'I didn't know.'

'By the time they entered Shirāt we had all gone. The valley was deserted. We knew the way up on to this ridge. We were all here – above them. And they could not get back up to attack us.'

'So that is where you got the idea from!'

He nodded. 'It worked once. Why not again?'

It was not a question. Pola knew she must be careful. She said, 'Tamerlane didn't have gunships.'

'Gunships are vulnerable to fire from above.'

She hesitated. 'Beloved, I have been thinking. Suppose you did not fire at all – that you just stayed hidden?'

'Hidden?'

'Or, better still, we all just melted away into the mountains, and came back when they were gone?'

Khan looked at her, puzzled. 'We are men, not ibex.'

And that was that. Practical solutions of the sort that won Vietnam for the Viet Cong did not work in the Kush. There was an Aryan pride factor, a feud factor, a religious crusade factor, everything but a plain common-sense factor! You could never make a Pathan into what he was not.

She asked presently, 'How did it end?'

'Tamerlane? He left part of his force to occupy Shirāt and went on down the Alishang to conquer the other valleys. We came down at night and massacred his garrison to a man.'

'And he didn't come back?'

'He came back.' Khan raised his glasses to his eyes and peered. 'But we had blocked the gorge with an avalanche. He never got in.'

There were vapour trails in the sky far to the north-west. He watched them intently for some minutes, Pola straining her eyes beside him. But the trails came no nearer.

She relaxed and told him what he needed to hear. 'It is a good plan. Your men are strong and fighting for their families. And they are in defence, which gives them an advantage.'

'And we are Allah's chosen. He will guide our every bullet.'

'Then it should be enough,' she lied. 'You will win.'

A smile came to the grim face. 'We, my Pola. *We* will win.

You helped us. This makes you one of us, separated for ever from your people.'

Pola stood very still. She thought she had accepted this, but the spoken word gave it fresh finality.

Faintly then, so faintly it might have been the beating of her own heart, she heard the pulse of rocket fire. She shivered, dragging the blanket tighter about her.

Nodding at their lengthening shadows, the thirty weary horses entered Darra, Pakistan, their riders dazed by the gathering bustle around them. It was a poor place, a shanty town, but after the remote silence of the Kush it seemed to them like a metropolis.

People stared at the dusty giant astride the lead stallion. Fingers beckoned them from *chai kanas*. *Nimbu pani* sellers paced alongside them, clattering their drinking vessels. The strangers must be weary, in need of refreshment! Come here! Come there! But the riders never faltered, following their ears unerringly towards the whine of lathes, the ring of anvils.

The street looked like any other – twin rows of ramshackle open-fronted shops under sagging corrugated sheeting. But here there was a pall of forge-smoke, and the vendors were dealers, the customers exclusively men. And the object of their negotiations was always a weapon – a brand-new Luger 9 mm handgun, or the popular AK-47 automatic rifle. It could equally have been a Soviet paratroopers' assault rifle, or a PKMB 7.62 machine-gun, or a mortar, or an anti-tank gun. Anything up to 50 mm could be reproduced to near-perfection by the workshops behind the premises – with ammunition to match.

'Tell me which one,' Takredi wheezed, squinting at the lettering above the doorways. He could not read.

'Over there.' Habib pointed to a shabby open front.

Khan's master-at-arms lowered a leg to the ground and stood off his horse. He unhitched a pair of bulging panniers, tossed them across his shoulder as if they contained straw, and turned towards the shop.

Outside, a small wall-eyed man in a black waistcoat over a none-too-clean *dhoti* was watching a bearded tribesman aim a shiny new Lee Enfield at a nearby chicken.

Takredi inserted himself like a cliff between them.

'We are from Ghoram Khan and we have come for our order!'

The dealer swivelled his master eye upwards to encompass him, then along the impressive line of armed horsemen. Cupidity vied with guilty recollection in his expression. His lips peeled back from brown stained teeth.

'In a moment, sir. Cannot you see, I am with a client?'

Takredi collected the two sides of the man's open waistcoat in one fist and lifted him off the ground. He carried him into his shop and dumped him on his desk, flinging the panniers at his feet with a jingle that drew the dealer's eye like a magnet.

'We want our weapons *NOW*!'

7

'Spassky, RO Intelligence, yes?' Impatient.

'Oleg? Andrei. What in hell's wrong with your line? I've been trying to get you all day!'

'Rebel action or signals inaction – take your pick.'

'Did you speak to General Rossakov?'

'About? Ah yes, your wife. Yes, of course. Look, Andrei, we're virtually on the move. I—'

'Just tell me – what did he say?'

'Nothing, but he took it in. I stressed it again at final planning yesterday and he's got it in writing in our information enemy troops summary. So he knows, *Andrei, rest assured.'*

'But as OC strikeforce he must have issued an order of some sort, some measure to preserve her safety.'

Hesitation. 'Not in my hearing.'

'Didn't you attend Command Group Orders?'

'Of course.'

'And still he gave . . . no . . . ?'

'Andrei, you know Command Group – they're into strategy and timings, not— Listen, I'm convinced *it'll be taken care of.'*

'For shit's sake why didn't you call me? We've got the whole of the Spetznas standing idle. A para drop on the village to neutralize their gun, grab her, hold her safe until . . . I mean, we could have tied it in as part of the assault. Rossakov would probably have jumped at it!'

'You should have put that to him through General Dolin.'

Yakushev was silent. He had considered asking Dolin but pride wouldn't allow him to.

'Got to go now. I'm sure it'll be all right, Andrei.'

'You couldn't have a word yourself with – who's commanding the advance regiment?'

'Vassilyev. He's gone, Andrei. Hours ago. I'm with the main body, just moving out.'

'Get on the blower.'

'Can't, old comrade. Radio silence.'

'Radio—' Yakushev couldn't believe his ears. 'What in hell's name for? The tribes don't monitor us. They haven't a set between them.'

'I know, but that's how they teach it at Frunze so that's what we do.'

Yakushev made a despairing sound. 'All right, listen—'

'Can't old—'

'A second, Oleg. When action starts and the silence is off, get on to Vassilyev, tell him about Pola if he doesn't already know, ask him to warn his—'

'Right, I'll try – must dash. Out.'

The connection was severed.

Yakushev scraped back his chair and fumbled for a cigarette, his ears replaying the background rumble he had heard over the telephone. It conjured in his mind the image of a huge, unstoppable tidal wave of mindless machinery.

THE WOOD embers split and rolled, bringing the walls of the cabin to fitful life.

Khan came awake with a start that brought Pola to uneasy then relaxed consciousness as she saw his naked shape move to stoop over the fire. She watched his body grow golden as he tended what was left of their protection against the cold mountain night – the heavy-shouldered but lithe, marvellously hinged horseman's body with, just beneath the skin, seemingly the restless boughs and twigs of a willow tree. The face as dark against the pale skin as a miner's.

Now he opened the top half of the door into the walled yard and raised his face to the sky. Always the sky. Past his head, she could see a saffron rent in the night. Dawn was just a frontier away, coming up over Pakistan and the Tribal Lands.

She thought of the *kafla*. Just two more days, if all had gone well. Knowing Takredi, perhaps less. They would all be exhausted, the horses nearing collapse under their vital burdens. It really began to look as if they would get their weapons in time. At least it would give the tribe a fighting chance.

'You'll catch cold, my love.'

'I must return home.' Khan closed the door and reached for his clothes.

'You've done all you set out to do. You should rest now while you can.'

'She is alone. She sleeps little, fears much.'

Pola said softly, 'Of course.' She stretched her arms till her fingers touched the dry mud of the wall. The coarse weave of the blanket brushed her nipples. She felt it all the way to her loins. The sight of his naked body always stirred her indescribably. She wanted him inside her again, suddenly and excruciatingly. The thought of Layla lying alone in the shadowy old fortress inhibited her. Khan was not sleeping with her now that she was in her seventh month. He knew that the violence of his passion was a danger to the child. But at dawn it was his custom to kneel with her and pray, so that the child would be born a true Moslem. Dawn, though, was still a dream away. Pola's body ached, and life was now – *now*.

'Beloved . . .'

Dressed in just the loose *shalvār* trousers, he was tying the end of his *kamma-band* to the latch of the door, preparatory to winding himself into it. He did not respond.

She held out her arms mutely.

He came slowly, sat on the *charpoy* and leaned over her on one arm, kissed her breast and looked into her eyes very closely and twisted a smile. 'No.'

She caught the charm around his neck as he made to pull away. It was a bullet that had once passed through his body. He froze and gently pried her fingers away.

'Do not touch it. You are a *kuftara* and will drain it of its power.'

A witch? He was joking, but she knew he took his superstitions seriously. Just how seriously she could never quite be sure, as so much of what he did and said was prescribed by custom.

He sat quite still for a moment, listening. She inclined her own ear, her eyes questioningly on his. But presently he relaxed and slid his legs into the bed. He lay there looking at her without touching her.

After a while she asked, 'What do you see?'

She watched him search for an answer. 'A lily.'

'Those ugly black-tongue things amongst the rocks?' She laughed.

'Amongst my father's books there is a translation of a foreign poem.'

'About lilies?'

'I learned it as a boy. It begins . . . "Thy dawn, O Master of the world, thy dawn. The hour the lilies open on the lawn . . ."'

'Ah, *those* lilies.'

'"The hour the pale wings pass beyond the mountains, The hour of silence when we hear the fountains . . ."'

Pola closed her eyes. The soft gutturals of his voice washed over her like music.

'"The hour when dreams are brighter and winds are colder, The hour when young love wakes on a white shoulder."'

His voice stopped. She felt his finger on her lips. It lingeringly traced her smile. Then suddenly his lips were on hers and he was clinging to her, clinging in a kind of agony. She held him fiercely, and slowly the agony went away and mastery returned, his whole body changing, hardening. He turned on to her, becoming as rock between her thighs as he pushed back her hair and gripped her head between his hands, his face a blur above her. She could hardly breathe. She dug her nails into his back. He winced and laughed.

'So fierce? Like a Pathan. You sure you're not a Pathan?'

'Do they scratch? What do they do? Tell me what they do!'

He considered. 'They do all things. Like a horse they respond according to the rider.'

She laughed. 'You mean you whip them?'

'You like that?'

'Me? No. Sometimes Andrei would strike me. I put a stop to it.'

'He let you order him? A weak man.'

'Not really. He has two sides. Strangely, it was the weaker I fell in love with.'

'There is a mother in you.'

'I need to give. To feel I am needed in more than just the one way.'

'Do you feel that with me?'

'No-o-o. But the one way is so beautiful with you, it is enough.'

'You think that is all I saved you from Abdalis for?'

'It was in your mind.'

Khan came near to a chuckle. He eased his weight on to one elbow and slipped off his *shalvār*. He began to caress her gently, watching her response to every lingering contact.

'You are wrong. I needed someone who would open me. Who would talk with knowledge and meaning. Not as Layla, about just house and children.'

'I know. You were very lonely, my love.'

'Alone, not lonely.'

She giggled.

'What is funny?'

'I'm sensitive there.'

'And here?'

'No.'

'Here?'

She sighed and laid her head back, rolling it slowly. The rafter poles marched, first this way, then that in the firelight.

'You are like moss by a warm river.'

'I melt when you touch me.'

'A sea-flower . . .'

The breath hissed between her teeth.

'You have a good place for me there.'

'Always, my love. Always it is ready for you.'

Fierce and gentle, he was over her again suddenly and there was a moment of smooth fire, then he was deep, deep inside her.

Why did she count? Because of the steps, wasn't it? The steps leading up from the square near the Kitai Gorod, where they were always mending the road, her black strap child's shoes climbing the twelve outside steps, a pause to switch hands with the carrier bag containing her exercise books and gym things, then thirty-four inside steps to the apartment that was home and love. It was cramped, but it didn't matter. In winter they shivered, but it didn't matter. There was a special warmth there that she would never know in her life again. Mama still alive. Papa . . . No, she must not think of Papa. If she did, she would fail.

The willow tree weaving beneath her fingers, think of that. The thrusting inside her, think of that. There was another warmth here. The past was gone. The future – may it never come! Just *him*, the rafters, the firelight . . . the shimmering glass of Lenin's portrait . . . each time the door of the busy courtroom opened, the picture above the judge's chair chattered against the wall. Papa . . . She fought it, she fought it, but his dazed face forced its way through each barrier of random images she erected. Throughout the trial he never lifted his head, but now, as they started to lead him out to the van that would drive him to the sanatorium and ultimate death, one hand seemed to catch in the cage-wire separating him from the court. He swung himself free of them and pressed his face to the mesh, concentrating, fighting through the sodium aminate that clouded his brain, to give her one last smile – clear, transcendent and loving. They had wrenched his hands away, but his face was turned towards her still as they forced him down the steps, a grey shadow now, diminishing, diminishing . . .

'What is it?' Khan had stopped moving, concern showing through the opaqueness of his eyes. He stroked her hair quickly, as one would to quieten a terrified animal. 'What is it, Pola? What have I done?'

She was crying. She couldn't speak or stop. She twisted her head from side to side till the bedclothes roared in her ears.

She felt Khan stiffen from head to foot. His head jerked back. No breath came from his lips. The next instant he wrenched himself out of her. The bed covering went with him as he lunged for his clothes. He was shouting at her.

She checked the movement of her head. It was only then that she heard the rifle shots. Two – then one – then two more; the full clip of a Lee Enfield, repeated by rifle after distant rifle.

The *signal*!

8

THE SOUNDS of battle were coming from everywhere, chasing around the mountain walls: gunfire, the thudding beat of machine-guns, the rev-rev of Kalashnikovs, interspersed with the familiar thrashing echoes of tribal Lee Enfields. But not an enemy was in sight.

Khan crouched beside the Caliph, on the ridge, elbows on a rock, glasses focused on the dawn mist that hung above the Alishang. He could see flashes on the hillsides of the Haq valley, but the weapons producing them were hidden from his view by the end wall of his own valley.

His men in the watchtower could see what was going on. So could the work-party whose task was to lever rocks down into the gorge to block it – as had been done against Tamerlane. He could hear the crashing of the boulders even now. But that was two miles away. Without a telephone or little radio, or the flashing of a lamp that Pola had called 'Morse', there was no way they could convey to him what they saw. All he could do was try to interpret the sounds, build up his own picture.

And to concentrate was not easy. Pathans in battle are seldom silent. His men, concealed along the ridge, were shouting to each other, arguing the origin of each echo.

'I tell you, they are tanks!'

'Nay, the sound is too heavy for tanks. They have brought up cannon.'

'I heard a cannon once at the Kabul Army Display – and it was not like that!'

'He is right, Softbeard. With cannon there is a wait between the gun sound and the explosion sound. They are tanks.'

'Many tanks!' shouted a more distant voice. 'The Haqs have rolled down rocks and the road is filled with tanks, stopped one behind the other like a chain of caterpillars!'

This fitted Khan's own picture. The Alishang road was narrow, flanked by boulders. A column of vehicles, once stopped, would be trapped there with no room to deploy.

Caterpillars? The men were laughing.

'Imagine the butterfly from such a caterpillar!'

'They are called gunships,' shouted a wag. 'Praise Allah that you hear none!'

'Such butterflies fly only by day,' asserted an old hand. 'The day has but just begun. They will come.'

Aye, they will come, Khan thought. *Bismullah* that they come quickly! That it was happening before the arrival of the new weapons was bad, but, now the infidel was here, he wanted his teeth into them. The women and children and aged were hidden safely in their caves. His gun crew, a camouflage net trimmed with camel thorn stretched over them, hungered for a target. The two machine-guns and riflemen were concealed along the ridge under their rock-grey blankets, not a white turban anywhere, rifle muzzles freshly blackened. The bonfires were all lit, misting the fields and villages below. The hillside timber was burning, the smoke crawling away thickly, fogging the outlines of his own village. All was ready. He was impatient to see now to what effect.

'A fire!' someone shouted. 'The Haq village is burning!'

Khan raised his glasses. Yes, it was their village, all right. And to judge by the meteor-shower of explosions in and around it, it was being pounded to dust.

His watchtower loomed large in his binocular field. Suddenly he saw it vanish in a dab of smoke. There was a moment of hurtling timbers, then nothing but a dark smudge fading into the atmosphere. The explosion came as an afterthought.

A running bellow of anger coursed the ridge. Hardly had it died than the crash of rocks into the gorge ceased, to be replaced by the rattle of small-arms fire from the crests where his men had been working.

Khan knew then that the tide of men and armour, rolling as Pola had described up the Alishang, had at last begun to approach his valley.

Mortar bombs and rifle grenades pitched on to both crests of the ravine – bright sparks with slapping echoes. But he was sure it would take more than that to dislodge his work-party from among the rocks. And for as long as they remained there, no infantry would dare enter the gorge.

But now the screech of tank sprockets reached them faintly through the gorge. Khan felt a first pang of uneasiness. Suppose the way through had not been adequately blocked? His defences were not designed to repel ground attack. The women and children were safe from the air. But from soldiers . . . Soldiers would see that the figures populating the villages were dummies, and know that a trap had been laid. Soldiers could *smell* women. They could follow tracks, hear a baby cry . . .

Khan strode to the Caliph and checked its sighting. The cross-wires of the cartwheel were centred truly on the dark fissure of the gorge opening.

'Fire, Master?' The aimer breathed *nan* and *pilau* round at him as he munched a hurried breakfast.

'Be ready.'

The man stuffed the food into his *kamma-band* and wrapped his greasy fingers round the fire-grip. His two layers balanced their handles for instant action. The jack-men readied themselves to change tilt. The loaders hefted their clips of shells expectantly.

Now Khan caught a new sound. With all the firing it was hard to be certain, but it had sounded like the distant mutter of rotor blades. He called to the compulsive talkers to be silent.

The mutter died. Though all inclined their ears, the moments stretching into minutes, it did not repeat itself.

Perhaps, Khan thought, he had caught a freak echo from fighting in another valley. Even so, this changed—

A loader yelled in his ear, stabbing a finger, not towards the gorge, but in the opposite direction.

Khan turned just in time to see twin rocket paths etched against the timbered slopes at the Bab-el-Hawa end of the valley. A double explosion blasted a hole in his village's smoke overlay. A second pair of rockets streaked in, shattering the dummy gun emplacement.

'*Illah!*' Heads popped up amongst the rocks.

Khan was dizzied by the rapid succession of rocket trails that followed, coming from a 'V' in the hills facing the village. He could see no aircraft – just the fiery streaks as his village, his ancestral *gila* was ripped apart.

He sprang clear as the Caliph swung through a hundred

degrees, the jack-men winding frantically to keep it in the vertical plane. 'More, more!' The aimer was watching the lateral bubble. 'Up on the right, Ibrahim – up!'

Now they came – four gunships, in pairs – through the 'V' and down, tight above the smoking treetops, camouflaged, hard to see, like trout in a sunlit stream. They spun towards the village, raking it with machine-gun fire – no doubt, in all the smoke, dust and chaos, taking the dummy population for real. It was working. His plan was working!

They skimmed the rooftops, veering away to right and left at the end of their run, to circle, level off and come in again.

Khan had never seen a helicopter attack before and their speed and manoeuvrability dismayed him. They were not going to be the sitting targets he had imagined. He warned the gunners not to fire. From this range it would be like trying to hit dragonflies over a pond with a stone-bow.

The flight made two more rapid passes, at the end of which Bab-el-Hawa was no more than a smoking scar in the hillside, his *gila* a pile of rubble.

Rage seized him – and awe. Allah! With equipment like that he could drive the infidel back across the Oxus.

Now they were re-forming. No, three of them were. The fourth was climbing above them. But all were turning towards Kifri Kebir, the three below fanning out to line abreast. Smoke from the bonfires burning in the fields misted their shapes. The fourth continued its ascent, rising, rising . . . Khan had the sudden presentiment that it had spotted them on the ridge. But presently the ship levelled off and proceeded towards them in level flight above the valley.

The Caliph's crew panned with it, the jack-men winding, the aimer yelling. How much to lay off? Khan couldn't help. Air speeds, projectile speeds and angles of coincidence were beyond his brain to calculate and his language to convey.

'Aim ahead by one ring!'

The traverse man jerked the gun one ring of the cartwheel ahead of the helicopter. Khan felt the familiar space open up inside him and his breathing diminish. Six hundred paces and closing. He kept his hand raised. Firing too soon could spook their quarry.

Now he could see that the beast had eyes in the top of its head – twin windows narrowing towards the snout. The pilot, he realized, had only to look up to see the gun silhouetted against the sky. So fire now? No, he would be looking down as the first rockets were spurting from the pods of the other three gunships, sizzling towards Kifri Kebir, their tail-ends glowing like hot coals.

Khan shut his mind to the explosions, concentrating on the overwatcher. Range, four hundred paces. Suddenly the gunship stopped dead over the doomed village and hovered.

Khan beckoned the traverse man fiercely back on to target and shouted an order to his riflemen. He gave the aimer a full three seconds to get it all right, then told him to fire.

Momentary blindness and deafness came with the rapid percussions. The ground trembled. Empty shell cases clattered out of the chute. Khan regained his vision in time to see the gunship spinning round, tailless, under its rotor. Equipment, ammunition cases, then a man shot out of the open fuselage in an arc. As the rotation gained speed the machine began to fall. It plummeted down into the valley and vanished from sight.

The cry of '*Ali!*' from the gunners was drowned by rifle fire as all the tribesmen along the ridge showered the unarmoured topsides of the remaining gunships with every round they could cram into their breeches. One burst into flames. A second went out of control and pitched into a wheatfield. The third banked parallel to the ground, corkscrewed rapidly away cross the river and went into a vertical climb up the far wall of the valley.

The Bofors emptied clip after clip after it, the elevation man winding crazily, the aimer cursing his slowness, the shells stitching a seam of explosions up the valley wall, two per second, but the ship's rate of climb was fantastic.

Everyone knew that it was coming for the Caliph. Fire poured towards it, but the ship was head-on to them, and, at half a mile, presented a minimal target. Even as it climbed, rockets leapt from its fin-pods, machine-guns blazed from its bow. The rapidity and density of its firepower was awesome. But the crest of a ridge is hard to hit. Rockets whizzed past to self-destruct above the next valley. Cannon fire hammered into the cliff below the gun. Machine-gun bullets cracked and howled amongst the rocks. Through it all, bellowing at each other, the loaders rushed back and forth. As one passed Khan his chest seemed to explode, showering him with blood and tissue. The aimer thumped against a windbreak, transformed into a crimson huddle of clothing. Khan grasped the fire-grip and hauled himself up in his place. The Caliph barely stopped firing.

But now the gunship was level with the crest of the ridge, now above it, starting its final run straight at them – now it was a whitish flash that turned orange with black edges, out of which hurtled great chunks of armoured fuselage and weaponry that exploded twice more before the whole lot drifted earthward like the dying embers of a firework display.

'Ali! Ali!' The ridge came alive with dancing figures.

'A fine shot, Master!'

Khan found himself the centre of a noisy crowd. He shouldered himself clear of them and panned his glasses round the landscape.

He could see nothing else in the air. No enemy was visible in the region of the gorge. So, with luck, they might think their ships had been downed by ground fire. The tribe's position might still retain the element of surprise.

But not if they behaved like children at a New Year merrymaking. He turned on them sternly, ordering them to remove the dead and get back to their positions.

On the caravan trail a mile to the east, Takredi had heard the firing. He and Habib had hurried on ahead of the horses and now stood on a shoulder of rock, peering up through bleary eyes at the razorback occupied by Khan and his men.

The firing had stopped. Suddenly they could see nothing. But both had recognized the rapid thumping of the Caliph and were in no doubt that their valley was under attack.

Takredi shouted back to the *kafla* to hurry. Habib threw himself down to rest. He was bearded now, his neatness gone. None of them had washed or prayed or slept more than three hours in twenty-four since leaving Darra. They had lost two horses from exhaustion and one in a rockfall. The remainder seemed to be plodding along in their sleep.

Takredi, though he had lost much weight, seemed the only one with a vestige of vigour left. He paced the crest, anxious for his master, cursing the delay. As he did so, a fluttering movement far along the slopes of the razorback caught his eye.

He thought at first it was the wing of an eagle beating rapidly as though about to land on its nest. Then the wings drew clear of the rockface and grew a body – but not an eagle's. He wheezed a warning to Habib, threw himself flat on the ground and pulled his blanket over him.

The gunship came on almost silently, the wind against it. Another appeared behind it, then another . . . Four M-24s were heading straight towards them.

Habib shouted back to the *kafla* to stay below the crest. But if the ships had sighted them, they gave no sign, and presently began to rise vertically up the ridge in a row, as though hoisted on invisible ropes.

Takredi watched them grow smaller and then vanish behind the outcrops above. He bellowed and bounded down towards the horses. He told half the *kafla* to break out as many of the new weapons as they could carry and follow him. The rest were to follow with the horses and remaining weapons as fast as possible.

Even as he smashed open a box containing a replica RPG-7 rocket-launcher, he heard firing begin again above. While the others were festooning themselves with weapons and shouldering ammunition boxes, he assembled half a dozen projectiles as the dealer in Darra had shown him, stuck them in his *kamma-band* and strode off up the track.

Before the rest of his party got started, he was high above them.

It had begun as a distant whine which grew suddenly to an immense thumping. Khan and his tribesmen stared round to see the four helicopters spaced along the ridge, rock-steady behind them. At first glance they were all huge eyes and stubby projections. Khan shouted to the traverse man to free off. The man sat there hypnotized. Khan freed off the ratchet himself.

Flame stabbed from the nearest machine, and kept on stabbing. One of the jack-men screamed and went backwards over the cliff. Men everywhere were either hurling themselves to the ground or being mown down. Though he threw all his weight against the fire-grip, Khan could not get the gun round against the forward tilt of the platform. It swung back and hit his leg. He pitched heavily to the ground. There was a wink from a wing-pod and a sound beyond sound. Fragments of rock struck his face and body.

Through the dust he felt more than saw the Caliph lift, tail over barrel, slither forward and then crash back. Its rear jacks clawed at the cliff-edge for a moment, then both gun and platform toppled into the abyss. Camel thorn raked his naked scalp – his turban was gone. He was under the camouflage net, pinned to the ground.

Khan saw in his mind's eye glowing bullets hurtling to shatter him. He saw his father, Layla with Pola's face, his children, and Death. Death was a yawning darkness – an end, not a beginning – no Allah, no houris, no peace. Fibres burned into his eyes. He clawed at them. They were part of the net. Now he could see through them – straight into the clustered eyes of the nearest monster. There was a bulge where its mouth would have been, with what looked like a thick four-barrelled shotgun protruding. It was panning back and forth, the barrels rotating, splitting a torrent of fire and bullets.

Khan grasped the foresight of his Kalashnikov and pulled it round off his shoulder. The beast was armoured and bullet-proof, but it had to be vulnerable *somewhere*. The strange shotgun? The breathing-holes of its motors? He chose one of its four wing-pods. They were like fat wasps' nests. Each hole was where a rocket came out. If he could shoot into a hole where there was a rocket . . . !

He switched to semi-automatic and took aim. But the beast wasn't steady. Nor was he. All of him was shaking. He lowered his head for a moment, breathing deeply. When he looked up again, the ship had gone.

Freezing air beat against his back, flattening him to the ground. The beast was above him. But only for a second. The next, it was spinning down towards the valley – perhaps to inspect the wreckage of the ships they had shot down. Raising his head, he saw its companions further along the ridge also changing position, backing off the crest to hang in the sky like sentinels, their guns almost silent – just a burst now and then when they spotted a sign of life.

He bellowed, 'This is Khan – who are left?'

Voices answered, muffled, from mouths pressed against the earth. A few only. But along the ridge there would be more. What should he tell them? What *could* he tell them.

'Allah!' a voice whimpered, close by under the net.

Khan could not see who it was – just the severed stump of an ankle, the sinews twitching.

Something cold and slimy fastened over his wrist. He saw a clawlike hand, crimson with blood. A face appeared. Piercing black eyes without a trace of fear in them glared into his as mullah Abdalis wormed his way under the net beside him.

'Allaho akbar.' The sleeve of his robe had been torn away. The flesh of his upper arm lay open to the bone, but the holy man evinced no pain.

'God is great,' Khan echoed dourly. 'But He is not with us.'

'He is with us, son of Ahmed. Have faith.'

The mullah peered balefully towards the helicopters for a moment, then fumbled inside his robe. He brought out his beads. Closing his eyes, he laid his forehead against them.

Khan could smell the mosque on his clothing. Lying so close, he could feel the man's power – a dark power, no love in it. But something else. Something awesome, utterly unquenchable.

'Allah!' moaned the unknown man again.

'There is one who needs your ministrations,' Khan muttered.

'Let him call. God answers the dying. It could benefit all of us.' The bearded lips moved in prayer against the dust. One thumb clicked each bead deliberately against the next.

Now the whine came again, but higher pitched this time and from above. Another helicopter was approaching, farther along the ridge. It was smaller than the gunships, with a high tail-bar and lacking the stubby wings. It tried to set down, but had trouble. At the last moment it spilled away off the crest and circled and came back for a second attempt.

Khan watched it hovering and then endeavouring to land gently, but its rotor seemed to slip through the air. It came down heavily, rocking on its four wheels.

A cargo door slammed down to form a ramp and soldiers in steel helmets pounded down it. They carried assault rifles with bayonets fixed.

As they spread out across the ridge, a second transport came in – much closer. It had the same trouble in landing. More soldiers rushed out. They deployed also, and both groups began to sweep the crest, yard by yard, shooting into every body, dead or alive, then bayoneting it.

'You still think God is with us, holy man?' Khan growled.

'He is with us.' The mullah's conviction was absolute.

The nearest troops were within fifty paces, moving steadily towards them. Khan relied on the din from the overwatching gunships to screen his voice.

'Each take a man! Wait till they are close!'

'Ali!' came the pitifully thin reply.

The mullah kissed his beads, put them away and checked the cartridges in the magazine of his rifle.

The soldiers came on warily, more than a dozen of them, hulking fellows in long belted overcoats and jackboots. From this distance their faces appeared oddly flat. One of them fired a short burst and paused to bayonet the body. With a yell, a wounded tribesman came to his feet only paces from him and fired a single shot. The soldier's head snapped back. His helmet flew off. Before he hit the ground, the tribesman's clothing burst into tatters and he vanished, riddled, amongst the rocks. The other soldiers barely paused.

Khan could see their faces now. Yes, they had high cheekbones and slit eyes. Hazaras? No, not in Russian uniform. But Mongols of some sort. He had picked his man – the most brutal looking. He put the Kalashnikov to automatic and brought the high post of the foresight up to cover the fellow's barrel chest. He felt Abdalis gather his legs beneath him.

The man in front of them uttered a last howling 'Allah!' It was amputated in mid-breath by a hail of fire, the net coming alive as tracer streamed into it. Abdalis leapt to his feet with a cry of '*Allaho akbar!*' and let fly. Khan jerked the trigger, but his gun climbed wildly as metal tore into his leg and a searing pain shot through his neck. There was a thump. Abdalis convulsed and, tangled in the net, fell across him. .303s began firing from the rocks. Soldiers were dropping. Their comrades rushed forward at the crouch, spraying everything in sight. Khan emptied his magazine across them, back and forth. Arms flailed, guns clattered. Fighting to stay conscious, he reached into his *kamma-band* for his second magazine. It was gone! The .303 fire was petering out. He could see just two soldiers left. One of them was reloading, knocking the curved magazine against the underside of his gun in his haste. The other had seen Khan. His muzzle swung towards him but his burst of fire was drowned by a heavy thumping. The bullets went wide as the man seemed to struggle with an invisible adversary. The tails of his topcoat whipping. He ducked and ran as a third Mi-8 transport almost fell out of the air on to the ridge where he had been standing.

Takredi, the breath sawing in his throat, was staggering up the final outcrop below the crest when he saw this last troop carrier making its descent. Khan-master was up there, he knew, and in bad trouble. He could hear the gunships, but they were out of sight round the curve of the mountain. There was no sign below him of the *kafla*. He was on his own.

He dropped to his knees and took out one of the bulbous missiles and tried to remember the instructions. Screw the warhead and sustainer motor tightly together – yes. The booster charge? Ah, that was already inside. So . . . just stick it in the tube. *Click* – it was in!

He put his eye to the sight. It took him a moment to discover it still had the cap on, another to realize that the little squares and numbers were utterly beyond his ability to comprehend. There was an iron sight – praise Allah! – like a rifle. But where was the foresight? He levered it up. By this time the helicopter was almost down.

He tucked the weapon against his neck, took aim and pulled the trigger in the forward grip.

There was a rushing sound as the projectile leapt from the tube, its fins shooting open, bright flame spurting from its rear end. It raced towards the helicopter, straight as a pigeon – but low. It burst against the hillside, shattering a cluster of rocks.

Within moments Takredi had another projectile out, screwed it tight and clicked it into the muzzle. He aimed up by as much as he had missed and fired again.

The helicopter had just stopped rocking on its wheels. The cargo door slammed open. The first troops were in the very act of bounding down the ramp when the PG-7 missile hit the armoured fuselage. Its charge punched a hole through the plating, blasting the interior with hot metal and a copper slug that ricocheted amongst the personnel. Something exploded – maybe ammunition. Then the fuel tanks caught and the whole machine went up in a fireball, hurling flaming bodies in every direction.

Takredi stared for a long moment, his mouth hanging open. The thump of gunship rotors pounded his ears. He flattened himself against the rock and dragged his blanket over his head.

The blast carried everything with it. Khan felt himself lifted over backwards by a searing breath of enormous force. His mind braced itself for the ground impact, but there was nothing. He was floating, falling into space, the strands of the net rasping his flesh, tangling around him, stones, weapons, a black shroud of something and empty shell cases falling with him. He clutched at the mesh convulsively, nearly tearing his arms from their sockets. The stretch of the mesh pinched out his fingers till he lost his grip and continued to fall, his head swinging downmost. There was a heavy drag on one knee. He flexed it automatically and everything inside him seemed to suck into his head as he came to a stop, bouncing with the give of the net. A support pole hit him. Stones bounced off his body. But they were moving, he was not.

With his arms below his head, back arched and shirt over his face, he felt gravity dragging him towards the valley a thousand sheer paces below. He could see nothing, hear nothing. Only the sensations of his body told him that the back of one knee was hooked through the mesh. The other leg seemed to be gone, dead. His neck was on fire, beating like a drum, his brain crushed against his skull with the pressure of his blood.

He tried to push up his shirt. He glimpsed the rockface. It spun away from him. The sky rotated . . . mountain tops – again the rockface. He gripped the mesh again and tried to claw his way up it. The black shroud thing was imprisoned in the folds of the net above him. It was Abdalis's body. The shirt fell back over his face. The net began to slip. He felt it going in jerks. His head cracked against something. He fingered it blindly. A rock. Some wiry growth on it. He could see a part of it. A saddle. The net was going. He tried to pull himself in towards the saddle. The strata crumbled in his grasp. He swung outwards sickeningly. The net slipped further. As he swung back again he gripped the wiry growth. Slowly, slowly, so as not to uproot it, he pulled himself in above the rock. As he did so he felt his consciousness going. He fought it, but the redness then blackness was soaking down inexorably into his brain.

9

BEHIND THE camouflage screen of uprooted bushes and camel thorn that Pola and the women had woven across the entrance, the cave was dim and claustrophobic. Even with legs tucked under bodies and infants hugged close, there was little room to move. Pola had tried to organize a space at the back where the children could relieve themselves. But with the mothers abstracted and the younger ones afraid to leave their sides, it hadn't worked out, and the atmosphere was becoming more fetid by the hour.

Bab-el-Hawa itself was not visible from the cave mouth, but the women had no doubt as to the fate of their village. Their grief vented itself in a wailing and caterwauling that had gone on and on till Pola longed to hit them all on the head. The noise level made it impossible to think straight or keep the children intelligently occupied, or even interpret accurately the course of the battle from the echoes.

Those echoes were dying now. The Bofors had fallen silent. The predominant remaining sounds were from the weapons of her own people. The women had lapsed into a will-of-Allah resignation. Convinced that the battle was lost, they were waiting now for death. Well, that was something Pola had no intention of doing.

Though it would be suicide to leave the cave in daylight, she decided that if they had not heard from Khan by nightfall, she would lead an expedition deep into the mountains. Where in the mountains? The *aylag*, the summer pasture, was the most remote place she knew. A few shepherds camped up there through the summer months, minding the sheep and goats. There was only one crude *kana* for accommodation, but they could add to it. They could live off the herd until . . . until what? That was something they would all have to decide. But later. The most important thing now was to convince these women not just to sit waiting to be slaughtered like animals.

There was a loud whining followed by a heavy battering noise. Then, through the camouflage screen, she saw something huge lifting past the entrance of the cave.

Women crowded to the screen in time to see the undercarriage of a helicopter climbing out of sight, then reappearing much closer, losing height, swinging from side to side, the engines racing.

Gradually they could see the whole of its fuselage. There was a red star on it, a stencilled serial number, some bulges like protruding eyes, the outline of a cargo door. Pola recognized it as an Mi-8 Hip transport. They had a low hover ceiling and at ten thousand feet it was probably working beyond its capability.

The downdraught from its rotor snatched at their camouflage screen. Pola clutched and hung on to it, calling on the other women to help. The control-cabin door was level with the cave. Through its window they could see the young Russian pilot fighting with the controls.

The blast was tearing the screen to pieces. There was nothing they could do to stop it. In moments they would all be exposed. Pola shouted that everyone should let it go and get right back into the darkness of the cave.

Some did, others hung on. The Mi-8 landed heavily but temporarily on the narrow bluff outside, the pilot gunning his turbo-shafts to gain sufficient rotorage for lift-off. He glanced out of his window, gave a slight start and spoke quickly into his intercom.

What happened next was bizarre. The transport hopped round on its axis like a great vulture. Pola saw something like a penis swivel under its belly. A blaze of machine-gun fire issued from it.

Those who were not already scrambling to the back of the cave now did so in a screaming rush. Crushing against the rock, they fought tooth and claw to preserve themselves and their children against the mounting weight of bodies, those on the outside struggling to bury themselves behind the others, some crawling between legs so as not to be caught in the withering hail of bullets. Pola fought as wildly as the rest, mainly for air. All she could see was flailing silhouettes against the glare of the cave mouth; all she heard was bullets thumping into flesh, and the shrieking and screaming.

The wall of bodies between her and the entrance thinned with terrifying swiftness. A woman pressing against her clutched at her, open-mouthed, as she was hit. Pola recognized Layla and felt churning agony in her own side as the bullet ploughed through into her. Layla went down, dragging Pola with her. Senses spinning, Pola glimpsed below her a face, a child's face, its mouth gaping, eyes bulging. Lissa? She tried to hold herself off her, but there was no strength in her arms. Other bodies piled on top of her. Her breast crushed down on the open mouth. Small hands dug into her frantically but she could not move. The child squirmed horribly as she suffocated.

A distant double slam. The multiple thump of army boots on ramps, their echoes and vibration as they entered the cave. Pola felt consciousness drifting away from her. Her side had gone numb. The weight on her began to lessen. Bodies were being pulled away. Assault rifles began to spank deafeningly. Now there was light. She saw a white-bearded face. It receded suddenly as the old man was dragged clear and a rifle thrust into his mouth. His whole body bounced as the gun exploded. The woman next to her was heaved on to her back. Layla's dead eyes stared into hers as a bayonet plunged into her throat, then into her pregnant belly. The sound was indescribable as babies were wrested from dead and dying arms and their skulls dashed against the walls.

The soldiers were cursing, exchanging talk as they worked. Asiatics, exclaiming lasciviously as they uncovered girls and younger women and dragged them clear of the carnage by feet or hair. However badly injured, their clothing was shredded. Some of them were mere children, but the soldiers began slaking their lust on them. The screams were chilling.

Pola felt her ankle seized. She was dragged, her head bumping on the rock. She lost consciousness. She came to feeling she was being split up the middle. She was naked, her legs being dragged wide apart. A slab-faced Mongol threw himself down over her with a hoarse cry. He thrust his fingers up her to prize open her seized muscles before driving his member into her. It was like a stake being driven up her vagina. She tried to scream. Nothing would come. She repeated, 'I'm Russian! I'm Russian!' But no sound issued from her lips, only gasps, as his brutal thrusting drove the breath out of her, agony shooting through her side. Blood was pumping from the welter of torn tissue, glistening thickly across her belly. But the sight of it only seemed to stimulate the soldiers more. Others were gathering. The man kneeling on her arms thrust his member into her face, seeking her mouth. She twisted her head away weakly. He caught her face and prized her lips apart. The other was emptying himself with a savagery that arched her spine. Then he was gone with a wrench and there was another and others waiting. A field-dressing had been wedged between her teeth to stop her from biting and a penis was down her throat. She felt herself suffocating, her senses sliding. Her insides were mangled, her vagina numb, but the thrusting went on, and on. She was bleeding from inside now. Her mouth was foul with semen. She choked, vomited, choked. Her mind went away and then came back and it was still happening. She wanted to die. She prayed for death. Without ever having had a god, she prayed – *Allah, be merciful, let me die!* But the thrusting just went on. Man after man emptied himself into her.

Someone shouted an order. The man inside her withdrew with a violence that wrenched at her womb. Her legs and arms were released. She lay there, limbs akimbo like a dummy, no longer capable of movement. Consciousness had retreated to the innermost part of her mind, but it was still there. It watched from behind fluttering lids as an assault rifle was swung over her face. A remote part of her felt it settle between her eyes.

It came at last then, the blackness. But not before the whole universe had disintegrated into a jigger of white light.

10

Takredi clambered wearily to the crest of the ridge. With the sun a red ball low behind him, he stood and stared down into the deep lake of shadow that had been their valley. Apart from a few walls still standing the villages were mounds of rubble amid blackened fields. The river had backed up from the blocked gorge and was creeping with glassy fingers along every familiar path, completing the picture of devastation.

The Russian steam-roller had taken hours to pass. It sounded as if its advance units were now attacking Nīlāw, twenty miles to the north. The Alishang road was still thronged with supply vehicles, and heavy-lift helicopters had been ferrying up cargoes all afternoon, creating a fuel and ammunition dump right outside the gorge.

The gunships had been like angry hornets for hours after Takredi had blown up the Mi-8 transport, combing the hillside and timbered slope beyond yard by yard, their undercarriages practically scraping the ground. He had managed to roll under an overhanging rock and tamp himself in there with his blanket. They had tried to flush him out by sheer terror tactics, but he had refused to be drawn.

They had flushed out someone, though. He had listened to the rocket and machine-gun fire for half an hour, and his fear that they had found the *kafla* was brought to almost certainty by the heaviness of the return fire. But eventually that fire had been silenced and the gunships, still intact, had circled back to guard the transports as they took off the soldiers. The shudder of rotors had diminished gradually, and Takredi knew at last the attack was over.

Now his thoughts were of his wife and children first, and secondly the master. He turned towards the cave.

He had not gone far when three men from his village rose

from behind some rocks. They looked more like animals than fellow tribesmen, their eyes white and haunted in smoke-blackened faces, two bloody from wounds. They had found a bag of food and were wolfing it. They were the men left below to light the fires, he knew. They offered him some *nan*. Takredi had not eaten since before dawn. He chewed off a hunk of the bread and swallowed it without bothering to spit out the grit of baking. There was water. He lifted the whole goatskin and sent the warm liquid gurgling down his throat.

'Do not go to the cave,' one of them warned him, and told him what they had seen there. Takredi read from their eyes the horror of it. He sat down and wept.

The sun went down and a chill like death settled over the Kush. Takredi hoisted himself up.

'We must collect the other women and children from where they are hidden.'

The men shook their heads. 'We encountered Naki Jan and four others returning from above the gorge. They say they watched the helicopter soldiers land in the valley. They found both hiding places.'

Takredi did not have to question them further. It was there in their faces.

After a long moment, he said, 'What will you do?'

The men shrugged hopelessly. 'Go to the *aylag*.'

'Go then.' Takredi turned away from them along the ridge.

'And you, brother?' they called after him. 'Will we see you there?'

Takredi did not reply. It was almost dark by the time he reached the gunsite. He circled it slowly, turning bodies with his foot. A pulverized rock and cordite smell was everywhere. And something else. Almost a presence. The huge expenditure of energy had left a discharge in the atmosphere that no breeze could dissipate. Takredi shivered and peered about him uneasily. There were Jinns about, he could almost see them. Feeding on the dead.

'Master?' he wheezed as loudly as he could. Why was there no sign of him?

He saw the camouflage net stretched over the precipice. It was held by a single stake. He stepped over it and moved away.

He searched among the bodies further and further afield, then came back.

'Master?'

An echo reached him. It had the semblance of a human sound, but it was the Jinns, he knew, mocking him. Allah, he could *feel* them pressing about him. He tried not to breathe. If they entered him, they would steal his mind. Just one more breath, he thought, very quickly, then he would go.

'Master?'

BOOK TWO

1

THE SUMMER died and the dust settled, and in the sharpening light of winter the snows crept down from the mountains. Where the war had waxed it waned. The circulation of supplies slowed, Soviet outposts withered and the rebels came creeping back, now into the Kunar valley, now into Ghazni and Kandahar. They closed in like hungry wolfpacks around Kabul.

Assassinations became a nightly occurrence in the city and Afghan officials began paying protection money to rebel groups to buy safety for their families. Government offices were barely functioning, taxes were not collected, industries closed down. The Afghan army had dwindled through desertion from 90,000 to 30,000 men. And even these could not be trusted. They were being replaced by Russians everywhere. Five thousand more troops had to be drafted in from the Soviet Union. But only five thousand. With forty divisions around Poland and forty-three facing China, the USSR could spare only conscripts, mere children. The 'children' had been told they were coming to defend Afghanistan against imperialist aggression. But, finding *they* were the imperialists, and so despised that they could only venture from their enclosures in armed groups, they swiftly became demoralized. They huddled together and wrote disenchanted letters home that were burned by their officers, and smoked hashish, for which they traded ammunition and even arms. Hepatitis was rife. Even *Krasnava Zvezda*, the Soviet army newspaper, admitted that they were having a 'very, very difficult life', working for the most part as labour gangs, destroying cover along the main routes to thwart the incessant guerrilla ambushes, clearing airfields and constructing new ones.

Yet, despite the apparent stalemate, the Soviet Union *was* working slowly to a plan.

Afghanistan was gradually being built into the Soviet system. Absolute economic dependence on the USSR was advancing. Three million tribespeople had been deliberately driven to take refuge in neighbouring Pakistan and Iran, overloading those countries' economies and destabilizing them, while at the same time ridding the Babrak Karmal regime of one-third of its rural opposition. Yakushev's agents were busy courting the Baluchi population of West Pakistan, identifying the Soviet Union with their struggle for independence. Fresh Mig-23 and SU-27 air squadrons were flown into Baghram air base. And, in December 1981, Marshal Solkholov, a vice-minister from Moscow, arrived to take over supreme command of the Soviet Forces, Afghanistan.

So imperceptibly as to cause not a ripple at the SALT talks being held with Reagan, or amongst the vast army of nuclear disarmers who, whether they liked it or not, were becoming the Soviets' fifth column in Europe, the Russians were gathering themselves for a major strategic move.

Its codename was '*Zhatva*' – 'Harvest'.

Yakushev looked out of the window in his office in the inadequately heated girls' school that housed the GRU directorate. Beyond the brown hills that grew like termite mounds out of the city, he could see the retreating snows of the Kush. Almonds were blossoming along the river. The war was entering its third spring.

For him, too, it had been a long, hard winter. That he had survived it at all in the face of Dolin's constant provocations was to his credit. But survival by compromise was not to his taste.

His plan, though handicapped for lack of Pola, was still valid. In fact more so since the advent of Solkholov, who, instead of abandoning his predecessor's overkill tactics, had actually escalated them – which Dolin thoroughly approved of. Yet if the old fool had stopped to think, he would have realized he was flying in the face of his own intelligence reports, for they showed that, in response to these heavy elimination methods, the seven main resistance groups, till now mutually hostile, were at last beginning to co-operate.

And as 'Harvest' featured increasingly in the Soviet planning sessions, so a rebel code name was beginning to emerge. In Pushtu it was 'Sausan'. In Russian 'Liliya' – 'Lily'.

So far the word was a mere whisper in the bazaars. The agents who reported it did so simply in passing. It was only when collating their reports that Yakushev noticed its frequency. He had the word checked for linguistic or religious connotations, but drew a blank. Never mind. It always occurred in relation to the unification of the whole resistance movement – and that excited him. For the more centralized the opposition became, the more vulnerable it rendered itself to destruction from within. No one at group intelligence seemed to have matched his deductions, and he kept his findings to himself.

There was a knock at the door. Sergeant-Clerk Goriansky came in and stood to attention.

'The staff-car driver is here, Colonel.'

Yakushev shook off his thoughts.

'Bring him in,' he said.

A young, slim, straight-nosed, straight-backed Afghan in high-necked khaki uniform stepped forward and saluted.

Yakushev told him to be at ease and sent Goriansky back to work.

'You're . . .' He glanced at the note on his desk. 'Corporal Zahir?'

The man started to unbutton his breast pocket to produce his paybook, but Yakushev motioned him to forget it. If only they were all as smart as this, he thought. But then this man, selected from hundreds, had been exhaustively screened by both GRU internal security and Khad, Afghan intelligence, before becoming General Rossakov's driver.

'You say you have been contacted by the *mujahedin*?'

'By a man, Colonel. Perhaps of the *mujahedin*, I do not know.'

'What did he want?'

'Information, *seb*, about the general's movements.'

'How and when did he approach you?'

'Two hours ago. Outside the Shara Ra Road Post Office.'

'Well, go on.'

'I was waiting by the car while the general's servant mailed a package. A lorry stopped in front of me and backed up very close. This man was sitting in the back facing me – a very big man.'

'Where was the general?'

'Visiting the Harbiya Military Academy.'

'So you were without security protection?'

'The security jeep was guarding the general. I just had my own gun. I was polishing the car. The man said I would wear a hole in the paintwork. I told him it didn't matter because under it were six more layers of paint. He seemed astonished. I put him down as a man of the fields, with not much intelligence. He asked me how much the army paid me to keep the car so polished. I told him I was paid to drive it; the polishing was done in my spare time. He asked me, wasn't it difficult to find my way about? I said no, I had a map. He said he had never seen a map of Kabul and could he look at it? I thought, this man must be the local idiot, and was about to refuse. But he got out of the lorry and, *seb*, he was *enormous*! A giant!' The corporal raised both hands wide above his head with a grimace. 'So, well, I showed him the map. He—'

'Just a minute.' Yakushev felt a small kick of excitement. 'Describe him to me – his face, his voice . . .'

'His face, a pumpkin. His voice, like that of a man who has shouted too long at a game of *buz kashi*.'

Yakushev uttered an involuntary sound. He took out a cigarette, tapped it furiously and lit it.

'Go on.'

'We spread the map on the car and leaned over it. He traced the roads with his finger for a moment, till it came to rest on a building. "This," he said to me, "is where your family are living. Your wife Rana, your two little ones, your father-in-law and your two mothers-in-law."'

Yakushev saw the sudden fear the corporal must have experienced reflected again in his eyes.

'And it was the correct building?'

'The very house, *seb*! Then he said to me, "Mark with a pencil where you will be driving your officer tomorrow, marking also the times you will be at each stop."'

'What did you do?'

'I thought quickly. I told him I did not know yet where I would be driving tomorrow.'

'You should have shot him!'

'He was too close, *seb* – too big. He would have crushed me with his hands before I could pull the trigger.'

Yakushev inhaled from the cigarette. He understood the young man's trepidation only too well. 'All right. What then?'

'He asked me when I would receive tomorrow's schedule. I told him not until later tonight. Before or after the hour of curfew? he wanted to know. I said after, thinking it would be too late for us to meet again. The man went to the lorry and spoke to someone, and for the first time I realized there was another person in the back.'

'You couldn't see who?'

'He must have been lying below the level of the tailgate. When the giant came back, he said that as soon as I had received the schedule I was to copy it and keep the copy. I was to wedge the original, using a piece of rag, behind the outside spare wheel of the duty officer's jeep. If I didn't do it, he said, or if I told anyone about it, my family would be put to death.'

Yakushev smoked in silence for a moment. Clearly the man hidden in the lorry was familiar with army routine. The duty jeep was the only vehicle in the pool *certain* to leave the cantonment during the hours of darkness, when the DO went on his rounds.

'Did you get the lorry's number?'

'I have it here.' The corporal handed him a slip of paper.

Yakushev couldn't help being impressed. 'You did well. Return to your duties. I will send for you later.'

The corporal hesitated. 'Colonel, if I do not follow his instructions . . .'

'You will, you will. We are going to catch this fellow.'

'Yes, *seb*. But if they are *mujahedin* we are unlikely to catch them all. My family will remain in extreme danger.'

'You may have to move them into the compound; we'll discuss it later. Dismiss.'

The Afghan stiffened his body, clicked his heels and turned about. He marched from the room.

Yakushev got up. He turned on the coffee machine. Without question it had been Khan's giant. So he was still alive. Good. He had a score to settle with him. But he hadn't been acting on his own account. Simply as a frightener. Setting up the general as an assassination target for someone else. Who was that someone? Khan?

No, he thought, that would be *too* much like reunion night. There had been rumours that Khan had survived, but Afghans believed what they wanted to believe. Mythmakers abounded in every market-place. There was even a rebel leader known as Khan – a very active one, too, with a host of successful raids to his credit – but Khan was a common name, common as Boris.

And yet . . .

The general was Chief Soviet Military Adviser to the Afghan Army General Staff. But the posting was recent. Last year, as a field officer, he had commanded the combined force that stormed Bab-el-Hawa. A coincidence?

In almost any other country the answer would have been, yes, a coincidence. But what was the old Hindu saying he had heard quoted the other day? 'O gods, from the venom of the cobra, the teeth of the tiger and the vengeance of the Afghan – deliver us!' And hadn't he felt deep anger himself against Rossakov for having failed to warn his commanders of Pola's presence in Bab-el-Hawa?

He had felt the same about the colonel – what was his name? – commanding the advance regiment. Yakushev's friend Oleg of RO Intelligence swore he had contacted the colonel the moment radio silence ended, but from all reports the bastard had done nothing about it either. It seemed that no one dared burden the advance troops with additional orders. Yakushev had a mental image of Pola, vulnerable, terrified, being crushed to death by a robot machine. He had never learned what really happened. Her body was never found. There was rumour of a filled-in cave but, though he had searched, he never found it.

Back it came, fleetingly – the sudden empty chill in his gut. He knew it now for guilt. If he had been more understanding, used his powers of persuasion, *loving* persuasion . . .

His trained senses were trying to tell him something, dragging him back from this emotional cul-de-sac. Something about the advance regiment commander – what *was* his name?

'Goriansky!'

The partitioning of the old classrooms was thin. A moment later the sergeant-clerk entered, a pencil protruding from his wavy hair, his knobbly features attentive.

'Cast your mind back. The clearance of the Alishang. Who was in command of the advance regiment?'

'Colonel Vassilyev.'

'That's it. He died, right?'

'Not in the attack, Colonel.'

'No. A rebel ambush, wasn't it?'

'Near Charikar. Last November, I think.'

'Something strange about it.'

'Yes. He was travelling in regimental convoy. The rebels killed only him. They blocked off his vehicle from the rest, shot his driver and radio operator, then slit him with a knife, crotch to chin.'

Yakushev nodded sombrely. He lit another cigarette and exhaled a plume of smoke. It was beginning to tie in.

'Work forward a bit. The lead battalion, the one that actually stormed Bab-el-Hawa – you don't happen to remember *that* commander's name?'

Goriansky thought. He shook his head. 'The village itself, though, and the heights above it, were captured by two companies of 14th Airborne Support.'

'You're right. Yes. Do we have a record of who their officers were?'

'I can look it up, Colonel. But the 14th are not here now. They were repatriated. What was left of them.'

'Ah, yes, they were pretty badly mangled.'

'I was referring to the Salang Tunnel bombing.'

Yakushev stared at him.

'They returned home by road?'

Goriansky nodded. 'Their convoy took almost the whole brunt of the cave-in.'

At length Yakushev bestirred himself to hand Goriansky the slip of paper bearing the lorry registration number.

'Check this out with the police, see who it belongs to. Probably stolen, but . . . Then I want you to invent a tour schedule for General Rossakov for tomorrow. Doesn't matter where you say he is going. Just make it look official – get the transport office to stamp it.'

He sat staring out at the snow-capped peaks of the Kush long after the clerk had gone. The wavering cry of a *muezzin* calling the faithful to evening prayer reached him above the mutter of the generators. Like a wild bird across the marshes.

They were relentless. You had to admire them for that. With the patience of hunting beasts, noses raised to the wind, they had sniffed out the identities of those who raped their valley and were putting them to death.

It was so much in the Khan ethos. *Could* he be alive?

Yakushev reached for the internal phone. It shook slightly against his ear as he waited for Department 3 – Spetznas – to come on the line. Suddenly all his frustration, guilt, bitterness had found a focus other than Dolin.

2

THE CHECKPOINT at City Exit 5 showed as a splash of arclight on the dead straight, curfew-empty road to the airport. One had an intimation of the Bimaru Heights looming darkly above, from where, in 1504, Babur the Tiger first cast a hungry eye on the fair city of Kabul. The eyes of the present conquerors were not hungry as they stepped from behind the plane trees to intercept the duty officer's jeep, merely apprehensive. They had been in the army just long enough to know that inspecting officers were fickle, motivated by forces ideological as well as military, and sometimes alcoholic, and their reports were influenced by pressures from above as well as actual defaults on the ground.

The jeep halted at the barrier. They straggled into line, weapons at the port, chins tucked well into collars. Their NCO commander saluted.

The GAZ light truck that had been following the jeep at a distance, and in total darkness, pulled in unobtrusively under the trees two hundred metres short of the roadblock. Yakushev elevated his bottom to the back of his seat, steadying the night-glasses on top of the windscreen. The eight Spetznas cut-throats and their captain behind him craned forward, straining eyes that showed luminously in their blackened faces. In their camouflage jerkins, armed to the teeth, they exuded a collective primal energy that matched Yakushev's mood.

He barely watched the DO run his eye over the assembled guard, then check the entries on the NCO's clipboard. Nor did he follow him through the glasses as he and the NCO strolled towards the two armoured personnel carriers that stood glinting in the shadows, perhaps for a word with their crews, more likely for a quick swig of vodka. The nights were still cold here one mile above sea level. Yakushev's gaze remained riveted on the jeep's rear end.

Between the twin rubies of its tail-lights the spare wheel showed as clearly under the arcs as an archery target. He had not shifted his eyes from it once in the past ninety minutes; not while speeding through deserted streets, nor crossing bridges, nor while the jeep halted at any of the four previous checkpoints. So far nothing and no one had passed between him and those glowing rubies. Not a wink had advised him that covetous hands were removing the schedule, wedged, as per the giant's instruction, behind the spare wheel. After this, there were only three more checkpoints to go. The time was 0315 hours. Getting towards the end of curfew. The odds were lengthening against a successful operation, and his temper was shortening.

Perhaps, he thought, the GAZ trailing the jeep had scared the rebels off. But what had been the alternative? A damn great gunship with searchlights, clattering about overhead? As it was, he had had to order the second Spetznas squad to remain centralized in Pakhtunistan Square, rather than following them around in a motorcade. Whoever had thought up this drop method had known his stuff.

One of the twin rubies winked suddenly, sharpening his attention. The guards had been stood down and one of them was sauntering in the roadway behind the jeep.

A Russian? Yakushev found he had not seriously considered the possibility. Yet it was not impossible. The cost of procuring drugs created criminals everywhere in the world. And, sometimes, traitors. Only last month he had had to bag four conscripts of the 107th Motorized Rifle who had held up a bus on the Jalalabad road and robbed the occupants. Russian boys mugging Asiatics was bad propaganda. And there had even been looting during house-to-house checks.

The other rear light winked as the guard strolled on. The magnification of the glasses made him look closer to the jeep than he really was, Yakushev realized. But as the youth turned and came back he was distinctly nearer.

'Go on, lad, don't be shy!' growled one of the cut-throats.

'Quick, now's your chance!' They were hungering for action. The suspension squawked as they shifted to get a clearer view.

'Still!' Yakushev snapped. He was watching the guard's arms. His hands were in his pockets, his weapon slung behind his shoulder.

The guard sauntered on to rejoin his comrades. His hands had not left his pockets.

There were groans and curses from the men in the back.

The DO and guard commander were returning now. Salutes. The DO boarded his vehicle. It turned in the roadway and came back past the GAZ, gathering speed.

Only then did Yakushev let the glasses swing. Damn. A Russian would have made it so simple. They were conditioned to fear authority. There would have been no need to be subtle. Just grabbed by the scruff of the neck by the Spetznas and shaken till his teeth broke in his mouth and he would have spilled the lot. With these black-faced tigers itching to take you apart, who wouldn't?

The GAZ started up and U-turned after the jeep, following it without lights at a distance – back past the barracks, the US and Italian embassies, and down around Pakhtunistan Square. The huge coloured fountains were switched off at this hour to save electricity. The reserve squad's GAZ was parked out of sight in the link road behind the Ministry of Finance; he just caught the glint of its reflectors as they passed.

Presently, the blue dome of the Pol-i-Hesti Mosque loomed ahead. The river rushed by beneath them, brimming with melt-water. The twin rubies doubled their intensity briefly as the jeep braked at the Maiwand junction. There was a roving picquet included in the nightly round and it was based nearby.

Yes, there it was, waiting punctually beside its mother vehicle – a BRDM armoured car with twin mounted machine-guns. The six soldiers came to attention as the DO stopped alongside to receive the NCO's report.

Apparently there had been no rebel bombing attempts on the local electricity company, no collaborators nastily executed in the maze of alleyways, because in less than a minute the twin rubies were moving on, the indicator beneath one of them flashing the left turn into the Shor Bazaar.

The street was narrow now, tortuous. Yakushev felt movement behind him as the cut-throats changed position, settling their backs to each other, so as to keep a wary eye on the upper windows and flat roofs of the crowded buildings. Though the traders who populated this rabbit warren resented it, they often had to shelter the guerrilla bands that slipped into the city for a night or two before putting a rocket through a window of the Soviet Embassy or assassinating some member of the ruling Khalq or Parcham factions.

But tonight all seemed to be darkness, each house turned in on itself, barely a thread of light or murmur escaping to the outside world. The shop-fronts, which by day extruded their wares half across the street, were roller-shuttered.

The milling crowds were gone, though the daytime smells remained, pungent, disgusting. Slops and refuse glistened along the centre channel. Skeletal dogs skulked with their noses to it, staring glow-eyed at the jeep's headlamps before sliding away.

The GAZ had closed the gap slightly. The rubies ahead glared and dimmed with the more frequent braking. The buildings beyond them began looking oddly misty.

The jeep rounded a bend and there was the fire – no flame, but grey smoke coiling from an alleyway and filling the street.

The rubies were bright red as the DO's driver braked before easing into it slowly, then began to fade.

The GAZ driver accelerated so as not to lose them. Yakushev leaned forward, gaze fixed unblinkingly. As he watched, a shadow was cast on the smoke. The left-hand ruby went into eclipse as the shadow moved across it, then shone again. For a moment both rubies were clear, but Yakushev was convinced he could see the shadow between them, close up against the back of the jeep and keeping pace with it. Then the right-hand ruby blinked off and on as the shadow flitted past it and away through a narrow gap in the buildings.

'That's it!' Yakushev twisted in his seat. But the officer had already tapped a shoulder. A man was off the vehicle and running on silent, plimsolled feet before the GAZ had stopped. Through choking smoke Yakushev saw him race towards the gap, which he could discern now as the mouth of an alleyway. Two more men went after him as back-up. Their prearranged brief was not to shoot or alert their quarry but to track him to his destination and report back.

Images flashed swiftly. In a lane to their left a bonfire of rags was burning, unattended. Ahead, from the same side, came a burst of automatic fire. The leading Spetznas was driven head-first into the corner wall of the alley. Even as he dropped in a bloody heap his two comrades swerved into a doorway. Chips and dust spattered around them as the hidden gunman switched his aim. The captain snapped an order. The GAZ leapt forward and now all that pent-up energy exploded into violence. The flashes were coming from a rust-hole in the roller-shutter of a shop-front. The mounted machine-gun and every assault rifle aboard the GAZ blazed fire as it sped past, perforating the shutter, ripping it apart. There was an amputated cry from within, a clatter, then silence.

The GAZ stopped. The men swarmed off it, rushed back, kicked the shutter in and sprayed the interior with more fire, before leaping inside.

Yakushev straightened up in his seat. Heart thudding, ears ringing, he triggered the R–105D and called the reserve squad. Holding the headphones to one ear, he glanced across at the doorway. It was empty. The back-up men had sped on after their quarry.

'Cypher S-seven?'

He activated the mike. 'We have contact – Shor Bazaar South. Circle to the Gardez road and come in from the east. Contact me when you reach the TB Centre.' He signed off.

'Just one in there,' the captain called as he stepped out through the shutter. 'Old fellow with a red beard – dead.'

He turned to his men and sent two of them down a parallel alley with orders to try to outflank their quarry; the remaining two he sent down another lane. He turned questioningly as Yakushev came along past him.

'Better just check!' Yakushev grimaced and hurried through the smoke to where the jeep had stopped. The DO was standing beside it, his face a picture of alarm and indecision. His machine-gunner had the 7.92 trained dead on Yakushev as he came out of the fog.

'You checked behind the tyre?'

'Yes, it's gone,' the DO said. 'What was all that firing?'

Yakushev eyed the stocky machine-gunner. 'You get a look at him?'

The soldier scrubbed his jaw and admitted, no. Yet the figure had been within centimetres of him.

'What do you want me to do?' The DO sounded plaintive,

as though all this had been designed to sabotage his duty schedule.

'Bugger off,' Yakushev said. He added a word of thanks for his co-operation but the fellow's manner annoyed him. He looked back at the captain. He was standing in the smoke, head inclined, listening, straining his ears in the heavy, almost shocking silence that follows a burst of shooting. What else could he do? The Russian army used no walkie-talkies, and back-packs were impractical on an operation like this one. He was out of contact with his men.

Yakushev lit a cigarette. The jeep was already on the move. His hand was shaking – adrenalin, not fear. The houses all around remained in darkness, not a door had opened. Two years of occupation had taught them to keep their noses out of it.

The rebels had planned it well, he thought grudgingly. The captain's men wouldn't catch a whiff of their quarry; the old gunman had seen to that. The courier would be in his bolt-hole by now, head down. He'd lie like a mouse till the soft padding feet of his pursuers died away. Then lie some more. Then, when curfew ended, he'd step out, chirpy as a cricket, and deliver the schedule to whoever, wherever . . .

Yakushev's gaze was on the departing vehicle, and just as the rubies were disappearing, a familiar figure flitted across them. It *could* have been someone else – a lover, a thief – but he knew intuitively it wasn't.

With a shout to the captain to recall his men and follow, Yakushev sprinted up the street. He tried to gauge where the figure had vanished. There was a narrow passage. He turned into it and ran as silently as he could, which wasn't easy with the echoes from the adobe walls. It was all walls in this slum end of town, enclosures, tin sheeting, junk. He was trying to pick up an echo from the man ahead, but was getting nothing.

He paused to listen, mouth open, concentrating his senses. Dolin would throw a fit if he knew his deputy was playing hide-and-seek with the rebels. Well, to hell with Dolin. There was something he had to ascertain. Something important to both him and the directorate.

There wasn't a whisper of movement ahead. Had he misjudged the turning? Or had his quarry stopped, too, to listen?

Yakushev started forward, then froze again as a faint sound

reached him. A chicken had clucked rapidly, then was silent. Nothing more. Yet it conveyed a picture – that of a hen scuttling away from advancing feet. Someone beyond the wall to his left was on the move, which meant that, if he was right and it was the courier, he *had* taken the wrong turning.

There was nothing to do but head on down the slight incline. Presently the passage was met by another, coming from his left. He paused again to listen.

For a space there was absolute silence. It was broken at last by a muffled, scraping sound, as of someone dragging or pushing something heavy aside. A moment later a dark shape appeared on top of one of the walls. It dropped almost soundlessly into the alley and remained crouching invisibly in the shadows, perhaps peering and listening. Then it darted, quick as a cat, across the lane and drew itself up the far wall, rose to full height and walked along it.

From its size and agility, Yakushev guessed it to be a boy. The youth clambered on to a higher intersecting wall and, balancing easily, catwalked away between the buildings.

Yakushev, exultant now, sped on down the passage. The walls opened out and presently there was a drinking tap and trough facing on to an open space in front of a tiny mosque that he never knew existed. Its minaret was no more than a stubby square tower with a wooden balcony, its entrance a heavy studded door. Its walls ran back less than twenty metres, gaining in height as the path descended and stopped at a crude rail above a drop.

Yakushev heard a brief disturbance some distance behind him – perhaps the Spetznas on their way. He concealed himself again and waited.

The sounds behind him were not repeated. A chill wind reached him across the city, the foretaste of dawn in it. He felt exultation. He knew now it was going to work. Now anxiety had left him, he could enjoy the experience, the thrill of using his body and senses, instead of arse and brain.

A shape grew noiselessly to full height against the Milky Way, stood there for a second or two, then dropped to the ground. Yakushev, in a kind of high, watched the boy cross to the entrance of the mosque. There was no grating of a latch, just the protest of hinges. The figure vanished inside. Now it came – the seating of the stout metal tongue, muffled by stealthy fingers, followed by the patient nudging home of one bolt . . . two.

Yakushev came to his feet and, in shock, found himself surrounded. They were all there except the GAZ machine-gunner, exuding their extraordinary power. Not a word was spoken. They raced towards the mosque, dividing into two groups, each taking a different section of wall. The leaders were up it like a circus act, lowering their rifles to pull up the next, and the next. Now crouching and running down the sloping inner roof.

A sudden long, ripping burst of fire broke the silence. A cut-throat threw up his arms and vanished from sight, his weapon clattering. His comrades scattered and rolled, pouring fire into the inner courtyard, lobbing grenades. The air trembled with detonations. A man screamed.

Yakushev, galvanized, stared back up the alley. Had the captain contacted the reserve squad and told them where to come? The mosque should be surrounded *at once*, the rebels sealed off from all escape. He realized *he* should have stayed back to give that order. Well, too late now. He dashed to the fence to see if the mosque had a rear exit. But the drop made it impossible to find out.

He doubled round to the other side. A pitched battle seemed to be under way in the inner court. Yes, in this far wall there was a low, stout door. He drew his gun to cover it, but he was too exposed here. There were steps leading to the space below. He went down them till his head was at ground level.

Even as he turned to cover the doorway, it was dragged open and two Afghans staggered out, one pouring blood. Yakushev strove to get his gun up, missed his footing and fell backwards into empty darkness.

He landed on his back, the impact driving all breath from his body. There was a stamping and hissing around him. Something sharp caught his cheekbone as a creature leapt over him. His eyes raked the sky as his lungs fought to drag in air. Up there was a window, its frame lit by sporadic flashes. With each flash came the roar of an explosion. He heard a rush of bodies down the steps behind him. Afghan voices swept past him and away, jabbering urgently.

Yakushev managed at last to draw breath. The stink of goats caught in his throat. He felt around for his gun. As the sounds of battle began to abate, a flash revealed a figure squeezing itself through the window above. Dammit, where *was* his gun? It was a long drop to the ground but the figure landed with scarcely a sound, no more than a metre from him. He didn't run like the others, but crouched there for a moment, collecting himself deliberately.

Yakushev prepared to launch himself in attack. At that moment a grenade flash lit the man's face. Yakushev froze, and squeezed his eyes shut. When he opened them, he saw only rooftops and mountains. The man had gone.

He fumbled frantically around him for his weapon. Even as his fingers encountered it, he swung it up and loosed off a hail of bullets after the departing figure.

But there was no departing figure. Had be fallen? No, just vanished into the darkness, any sound he might have made drowned by the roaring of the gun and clatter of the terrified goats hurling themselves against the tin sheeting that encircled them.

There was a tumbling rush, a bright light, and the weapon was kicked from his hand, another rammed into his kidney. He yelled before the Spetznas soldier could shoot.

Two more came down and gathered about him. He was hauled to his feet. Disjointed words apprised him that they had killed four, lost three but captured the boy. The captain's leg was half shot off and he would bleed to death if they didn't move fast.

Yakushev just stood there, dazed. They pulled him up the steps. He couldn't focus. The features of the man he had shot at remained burned into his retina by the flash of that final grenade. He saw the jaw, as shiny and blue-brown as the horn of an anvil, the moustache like two daggers, the eyes secret, fed not by what they saw but by something terrible within. The rest was a suffering of scars and shadows, the whole mounted on powerful shoulders, one of which had been ripped open and glittered with blood.

All he could think of was that he was alive. Pola's lover was alive!

3

YAKUSHEV'S ACTIONS were swift yet measured. Within twenty minutes personnel carriers were racing through the streets, depositing men at every intersection in the south-eastern sector of the city. Checkpoints were doubled. That this happened to coincide with the end of curfew, when picquets were changed anyway and civilian traffic – lorries, buses, carts, caravans – were getting on the move, created considerable chaos.

When Yakushev walked into his office the phone was buzzing.

'Colonel?' enquired a harassed Afghan voice. 'Excuse me, this is – *crackle*—'

'Who?' Yakushev cried. The generators outside were roaring and the gunships at the airport were beginning their warm-up chorus.

'Corporal Hamad, *seb* – the general's servant. He—' The voice broke off and another came on the line, unmistakably Dolin's.

'Yakushev, what the devil's going on?'

Yakushev started to tell him.

'I can't hear you!' He heard a struggling noise the other end, then a window slam shut. Dolin's comfortable apartment in the squash club faced on to the Spetznas' camp road. 'Start again.'

When Yakushev had managed to explain it all over the terrible line, there was a grunt. Then silence for a moment.

'So you reckon that Ghoram Khan and Khan the rebel leader are one and the same?'

'Undoubtedly.'

'And you say you've caught this – this courier?'

'He was wounded in the fighting. He's only a kid. He's with interrogation now, at the fort.'

There was a click in his ear. He thought Dolin had rung off. But he was still on and his anger seemed to have subsided. Perhaps one of the girls from army signals was with him, running her fingers through what hair he had, because he muttered briefly, 'All right. You seem to have it in hand. Carry on.'

Thanks, Yakushev thought, for the waste of six valuable minutes. He hung up and rattled the bar. Presently he was through to the fort. It was still dark outside. They had had the boy only a few minutes, and Major Tablian reminded him of this plaintively in his oily Turkoman accent.

'He's in a bad way, Colonel. One arm practically severed. Barely conscious.'

'Then make him conscious. I want to know where Khan would go. Was that mosque his city hideout? If not, where is it? Who shelters these people? Kids get around, hear a lot of tattle. I want every damn thing you can squeeze out of him, and I want it now, Tablian. Call me the moment you have it.'

He rang off and went to the washroom to bathe the cut on his cheek. His old zipper jacket stank of goat shit. He took it off and beat it about, and for an instant relived that final grenade flash. If Khan's attention had not been focused on the steps above, he would have seen him crouching there, virtually at his feet. What would he have done? Yakushev wondered. It was an intriguing question.

He imagined a silent, grunting struggle to the death – himself at the disadvantage. But life wasn't so obvious. Khan had refrained from killing him at Bab-el-Hawa because he was Pola's husband. There had been a kind of bond then, with her alive. But now . . . No, there was still a bond, but subtly changed. The bond between hunter and hunted. Having felt the power of the man crouching over him, Yakushev was by no means certain who was which.

Anyway, Khan knew now that the driver's schedule had been a trap and a fake. His plans *vis-à-vis* Rossakov were therefore void for the moment. And he was wounded. All of which suggested that he would hardly stick around for a slice of *nan* and breakfast coffee.

The big imponderable was: could the cordon contain him long enough for Yakushev to organize a house-to-house search?

Beneath the south-eastern outskirts of Kabul runs a long-forgotten storm channel. Within sight of the arcs of a main checkpoint meanders a stream sufficiently overgrown by willows to conceal a number of stooping men for a distance of almost a kilometre. In a culvert under the continuing road are stored inflated goatskins for the support of any fugitive hardy enough to cross the icy torrent of the river without recourse to the guarded bridge. Beyond that lie open fields and the occasional ruined hamlet, lifting abruptly, after twenty kilometres, to a 3,000-metre peak capped with snow.

By these means, Khan and Takredi were clear of the cordon within an hour. One more kilometre brought them to a lonely farm building, half an hour before sunrise. As they circled the wall, dogs began to bark.

Coming to the solitary door, Khan eased the gun off his good shoulder and sank to the ground with his back to the adobe. Takredi watched him with concern as he waited. His master had lost much blood. The chill wind had dried the clothing on their bodies. It was not a good combination.

The dogs were whining and sniffing behind the door. Gradually other sounds became audible – the snap of kindling, the rattle of a pot lid.

They had not been expected back so soon. Had things gone right, Khan and his party would have remained in the city for another day, or until the *schurawi* general had been slain. Now . . .

Now they would have to reorganize and, later, try again, Khan thought – perhaps at the cost of more brave lives. He mourned individually each of the four friends he had lost. Each was irreplaceable.

Nevertheless, he would try again for the general. *And again.*

He gazed at the fresh-sprung blades of wheat that encircled the farm. The winter snows had flattened the furrows; they badly needed reworking. This was what he should be doing, not . . . He knew no word for the process he was caught up in. The image was of a wheel with teeth, turning in his gut. It was powered by other images, of his loved ones – images conceived in joy, remembered in anguish from which there was no relief until revenge was complete. When the last *schuwari* had been slain or driven from the land. His reason told him this was impossible, that the Russians would just pour in more and more men. But the rein of reason had snapped long ago.

The door was opened at last. His dogs rushed out and cavorted round him. They were followed by the hard-bitten old farmer.

'Are you well? Are you harmonious?' the old man enquired automatically as he handed each a bowl of green tea.

'We are neither,' Takredi growled. 'My master is wounded. Even camels are not left to catch chill when their blood is warm.'

'This is not a caravanserai.' The old fellow peered uneasily at Khan's shoulder. 'Nor a hospital. The bullet – is it still embedded?'

'The bullet is gone,' Khan said.

The farmer looked relieved. He did not wish to become involved. He had lost his two sons to the Russian bombing and was now forced to work his fields by night for fear of the gunships.

'You want heated water?'

'Just bring us our clothing, old man. In mine there is a salve.'

The fellow grunted and went in, closing the door behind him. His women were all he had left. He guarded them jealously.

The tea was sweet and warm. The dogs, excited by the smell of blood, had begun to pester. Takredi stamped them away. They had been brought along to aid their disguise. The homeward journey by day was always a problem across this open terrain. For this reason, he and Khan and the other five survivors had parted company after crossing the river. Possessing neither spare clothing nor horses, the others would make their ways back to the stronghold at Mir Shiklama in ones and twos. It would attract less attention.

The farmer returned with their riding clothes and went back inside immediately, for the sight of nakedness, even of a limb, was considered sinful.

Takredi found the Russian field-dressing. He broke the capsule over Khan's shoulder, front and back. He hissed through his teeth when he saw the lacerated flesh.

'They were using the new bullet,' Khan said thickly.

The new Soviet bullet was tail-heavy and turned over on impact, causing much damage and suffering.

The giant spat. 'They were Jinns – each visage daubed as with the smoke of hell! Would that you had let us stay!'

'There was nothing to be gained, old friend.'

'Nothing but the joy of proving who was master! And could we not have done with their coloured jackets?'

'How would you have squeezed into one?' Khan forced a smile, then frowned. 'I am worried about young Abdul. He fell, but I fear was not dead.'

Takredi spread the gauze and then the plaster over the larger wound. 'What can he tell them?'

Khan had no answer. It was hard to remember precisely what one let slip in trusted company.

When they were ready, the farmer led out their horses. The giant rolled the two Kalashnikovs in their discarded *chapans* and strapped them behind the saddles. He helped Khan mount, then straddled his own enormous mare.

Finally the farmer handed them up their hunting rifles.

'May Allah reward you,' Khan said. 'And preserve you.'

They turned their horses towards the mountain, which was silhouetted now against the true dawn. Takredi whistled the dogs.

'May you never be tired,' the farmer grunted, fetching a leafy branch of willow. 'May you live for ever.'

When he had brushed out their prints as far as the harder ground, he went in and shut the door.

Yakushev sat with his eyes clenched against the sunrise and tried to hear what his master inquisitor was saying over the bad line. Why *were* the lines so bad?

'Just an outsider? What are you trying to tell me – that they picked the kid out of a hat? . . . That's better. A cousin of one of Khan's lieutenants. What's his name?'

He scribbled 'Ahmed Feizl' on his pad. 'Keep going.'

Something was bothering Tablian, he could tell by his tone, but his next words had Yakushev sitting up in his chair.

'When you say, a lead to Khan's hideout, do you mean his hideout in the city, or . . . his *group* hideout? Give it to me!'

There was a knock. The door opened. Yakushev made a blind gesture for whoever it was to come in and sit down.

His excitement waned somewhat. 'I'd hardly call that a lead. A day's march in which direction?' He scrawled it down. 'East of the Gardez road. No place name, village? Dammit, we need more than that, Tablian. Now you get back in there and squeeze him dry, do you hear? Pump more stimulant into—' Yakushev broke off to catch what the other was saying. 'Dead? What do you mean, he's dead! . . . *Who* took off the tourniquet? . . . I don't care where you had to go – you didn't leave him alone, surely? . . . What the hell's the use of a guard *outside* the door? . . . Well, obviously he wasn't, if he managed to get his tourniquet off . . . If he hadn't the strength to do it, who are you suggesting did? The place is guarded like the Kremlin. Look, I think you'd better get your ideas together and call me back!'

Yakushev hung up, furiously. He fumbled for a cigarette, lit it and rotated his chair to face his visitor.

Bloodshot eyes surveyed him knowingly from under a tubular felt hat that was pulled down over his ears like a flowerpot. Hair and beard like a bramble thicket, black-rimmed fingernails, dust-whitened ankles. Even the smell was right. Sometimes Yakushev felt that Pavel Ivanovich took a dissident delight in the role he played. He was a walking insult to the army he purported to serve. He had started with Spetznas but his flagrant indiscipline had proved more than even they could swallow. Had it not been for his undisputed genius, he would long ago have been shot.

'You sober enough for a mission?'

'You mean drunk enough.' Pavel grinned and shrugged. He held out the begging bowl suspended about his neck. 'Could always do with a top-up, *seb*. What have you got?'

The creature was a lieutenant. Yakushev could never understand why he put up with his insubordination. It had to do with the total lack of rank-recognition factors, he supposed.

The only way Pavel could be reached without blowing his cover was by three short blasts of the city air-raid siren – in itself a pretty weird procedure.

'Where were you?'

'Uh – converting the girls of the Hollywood.'

'You seem to live in that whorehouse.'

Pavel nodded sadly. 'They do take a lot of converting. Divine benediction seems to turn them on. If the only way to their souls is through their cunts, what can a wandering holy man do but resign himself to the journey?'

'Well, mind you don't resign yourself to VD, or the journey will be back to Moscow.'

'Allah forbid.' Pavel clutched his rosary to his brow fervently.

Yakushev shot him a look, but refrained from comment.

'What have you heard? About Ghoram Khan, for instance.'

'Khan? Oh, he's gone.'

'Gone? Already?'

'So they say.' Pavel yawned.

Yakushev suppressed his frustration carefully. 'Do they say where to?'

'They don't say things like that.'

Yakushev looked at the lieutenant's tattered patchwork coat. Known as a *muraqqa*, it consisted of ninety-nine pieces, symbolizing the world's illusions. It was stained with God knew what. Pavel's pupils looked suspiciously small. He was probably on drugs and clearly hadn't slept. Yakushev reached for the telephone.

'Air recce,' he told the operator, then, to Pavel, 'Did you hear what the inquisition gave me just then?'

'Yes. East of the Gardez road.' Pavel scratched his crotch. 'Big place.'

'Here—' Yakushev reached in a drawer and brought out a length of string. He handed it and his pencil to Pavel. 'A day's march. Thirty kilometres.'

He watched the extraordinary figure support himself on his stave to the wall map and lay the string against the scale. As Pavel started to describe a quarter-circle a familiar voice came on the line.

'Gorsky,' Yakushev said. 'Do you have an Antonov handy?' He had to wait a moment while the other checked. 'Well, hold her. I've got a man going up.' He replaced the instrument.

Pavel had turned to cock a look at him. 'On an empty belly? You know how it turns my gut.'

'Fill it before you go. With *food*.' Yakushev joined him at the map, careful not to stand too close. He inspected the quarter-circle and said, 'You may have to drop. It's up to the pilot. You'll need an R-140.'

'I'm wearing one.' Pavel tapped the small of his back.

Yakushev was surprised. 'Isn't that a risk? What happens when you have to strip? Like in the whorehouse?'

Pavel looked shocked. 'To reveal one's body is against God's law, Master. Besides, what holy man needs to strip to find his staff?'

The Antonov 2-P was a stubby biplane renowned for its short landing and take-off and slow-flying qualities. Designed originally as a crop-sprayer, it was adopted by the Soviet army in 1948 and had been employed ever since as a transport and paratroop trainer. In Afghanistan it was used almost exclusively for spotting.

Pavel and the pilot sat abreast, each leaning outwards to gaze down through his bubble-shaped side window. The ruined buildings – casualties of the Soviet drive to create fire-free major supply routes – looked deserted from this height, but Pavel's educated eye could detect, here and there, subtle signs of continued habitation: the pale spokes of fresh tracks, the dark stripes of recent irrigation, the shadow, perhaps, of a grazing donkey. Despite the constant harassment, the peasants were as hard to dislodge from their patches of land as crabs from pubic hair.

Which reminded him – Pavel scratched his crotch thoughtfully – he really must look in on the MO.

Wherever he spotted signs of reoccupation he marked them on his map for closer inspection. Within the quarter-arc of their search he was looking primarily for a grouping of seven men – the number believed to have survived the attack on the mosque. They might be holed up in one of these ruins or, hearing the approach of the aircraft, pretend to busy themselves in one of the fields, or camouflage themselves amongst a larger group, possibly at a bus stop. They might even be aboard the multi-coloured bus he could see making its way along the river valley towards Mohammad Aghah. But, if so, the road patrols would take care of it. He was only concerned with the country to the east of the river, and as far north as the Kabul–Sorubi power line.

Assuming the fugitives were on foot, they could not have travelled much more than seven kilometres. That gave them another twenty-three to go. So there was no mad rush.

Pavel was grateful for the respite. It was pleasant in the cockpit, warmed by the sun and the single engine.

To keep himself awake he took a swig from the quarter-bottle of vodka he had filched from the canteen. Doze off, and the pilot would put in the dirt for him. Everyone did if they could. The Soviet system could not abide a maverick. Why should he get away with what I can't? was the general attitude. The same attitude that women in the early milk queue took towards some wretched mother with a baby and husband to feed and a job to get to, who was trying to gain a few places in the line. The party and the KGB, of course, mistrusted all 'illegals' and deep-cover agents because they couldn't monitor their every breath. The GRU wasn't a lot better, despite the fact he was risking his life for it. Yakushev was about the only one he even vaguely got along with – because the colonel had his own problems, and he used people blatantly, which at least made for a realistic relationship.

No, when his mother died and they couldn't take it out on her, he would simply disappear. He of all people could do it. Vanish right off the Soviet monitoring screen. But until then, he had to give of his best to every assignment. Otherwise they would ship him back to the biggest prison camp in the world – Mother Russia.

They were cruising on the seven-kilometre curve and he had seen perhaps a dozen souls, none of whom matched even remotely what he was looking for. Now two horsemen swung into view below them.

Pavel trained the glasses on them. They had long rifles, carried across their thighs, not slung on their backs, and dogs. He watched them rein in and gaze up as the plane came over. He watched to see if they would make a hostile move with their guns, for the aircraft was vulnerable at this altitude. But, no, they spurred their beasts on, unconcerned. Antonovs were a familiar sight and known to pose no threat.

Hunters, he decided, making for the uplands.

He was about to dismiss them when he noticed a minor phenomenon. Though they were riding over even ground, the shadow of one appeared considerably larger than the other.

It was not a point of great significance – *unless* you had been fully briefed as to whom you were looking for.

Pavel was tempted to tell the pilot to circle, but this would have alerted the quarry – if they were the quarry. So he made a careful note of their direction and let the plane fly on.

They proceeded north as far as the power lines. Pavel saw

nothing on the way that aroused his suspicions. As the pilot made the turn Pavel asked him to gain height and, on the way back, cut his engine.

He watched ahead as the plane coasted in a silent shallow dive, and presently made out the two horsemen. He noticed that they were no longer moving in the same direction, but were heading east-south-east, on a course that would take them round the shank of the huge mountain.

'Now, comrade, start your motor.'

No sooner had the nine-cylinder radial clattered to life than the horsemen changed direction again – towards the uplands.

The pilot asked, 'Now what?'

'Lose three hundred and hold your course,' Pavel said. 'Slow as you can make it.'

He checked the horsemen's tracks back as far as he could see. There was no doubt at all that they were trying to disguise their direction of travel. Then he turned the glasses hard on them, studying them from the lower height. By the time they had diminished astern he was sure one of them was the giant. The chances were, then, that the other was Khan. To hell with the other five. Who needed them?

He marked their position on the map and told the pilot to proceed along the course on which the horsemen were heading, and to maintain height until screened from them by the shoulder of the mountain. He radioed the directorate briefly, to put the sighting on record and inform them he was going down.

As soon as they were lost to the horsemen's view they descended and began looking for a landing spot. It was that or jump. Pavel was not particular, but the pilot prided himself on his short touch-downs. The lower slopes were eroded and impossible. Below them were overgrown fields incised by deep watercourses raging with torrents from the snows above. Also impossible. But between the fields ran a track, more or less straight. Flat log-and-mud bridges carried it across the *Kwars*. The pilot brought the plane down on the track.

Pavel got rid of his parachute and lodged the vodka bottle in the pilot's pocket. He pulled the R-140 and his water gourd round to the front of him and hugged them. The Antonov skipped along, raising a long corkscrew of dust. It hopped the first bridge, ran across the second with mere centimetres to spare. As it slowed convulsively, Pavel had the door open. He threw out his staff first, then faced aft and dropped in a honeypot to the ground. He rolled heels over head for fully ten metres. By the time he had come to rest the plane was again airborne.

Masked by the dust, he crawled into the grass and wild flowers and lay watching it rise to an innocent height before flying back the way it had come. Only a close observer would have guessed it had deposited a man. He raised his head and looked carefully in every direction. There was not a soul to be seen.

He nudged the R-140 round again to the small of his back, and adjusted the throat mike under his beard. He thumbed the switch in his pocket and listened to the static that issued from the dual-purpose microphone. No damage that he could detect. He switched off and retrieved his staff.

He estimated that at the speed they were travelling it would take the horsemen about four hours to reach here.

Now he could take his nap.

The GRU officers' mess was located in what had been the school sports hut. The kitchen was an added structure, in which the cooking was done by high-pressure flame fired horizontally into a brick hearth structure with such noise and ferocity that the Russian serving staff and Afghan cooks refused to light it. So breakfast of a morning had to wait upon the arrival of the one man who could handle its eccentricities – the mess sergeant – and his rising habits were governed by the amount of vodka left in the glasses the night before.

Hunched over a mug of tea – for at least the samovar was working – Yakushev watched the sergeant's belated efforts disinterestedly through the huffs and puffs of the service door. Breakfast was a running meal and he was first in, physically weary but mentally restless. A lot was happening. To judge by Pavel's radio report there was a success story on the cards. But within the huge sphere of the directorate's activities, which drew intelligence from agents not only throughout Afghanistan but also in Iran and Pakistan, Khan was a drop in the ocean. As was every other piffling guerrilla band – *unless or until* they began to operate in unison. This was the spectre that interested him. He thought again of the code name 'Lily'.

Dolin always made a point of getting in ahead of the rush. He hung his hat on the rack, rubbing his hands together as he strode forward. Seeing Yakushev was his only companion, his manner tightened somewhat. He took his seat at the head of the trestle. An over-application of talcum made his chin look even more dough-like than usual.

'Did they get your man?'

'Good morning, General,' Yakushev said pointedly, before answering negatively.

'Cereal, two eggs,' Dolin told the sergeant, who came hurrying out of the kitchen with a jug of hot water. Dolin watched him open the private tin of Swiss instant coffee that stood beside his plate, dole in a spoonful and pour the water on to it. When the ritual was complete, Yakushev said:

'Did you call Tablian?'

Dolin's eyes popped towards him. 'Tablian? No?'

'He says you did. Around six.'

'Then he's lying.'

'Ah.'

Dolin cut a slice of the army bread and reached for the tin of butter. 'Finish it.'

'Nothing. Just, he had a 'phone call, purportedly from you and urgent. He left an interrogation to answer it, but there was no one on the line.'

Dolin shrugged. He wasn't interested. 'The lines get worse every day. Tell Zotov to take his finger out.'

'He claims it's either tracked vehicles or chafing from the wind. I've got him going over the whole system.'

Dolin grunted, blew on his coffee. 'This Rossakov thing. I want you to double his security.' He added dourly, 'I'm dining with him tonight. I don't want to catch the one with his name on it.'

Yakushev left to avoid the main influx. He stood outside and smelled the cantonment smell – vehicle exhausts laced with sewage. So someone *had* taken off the boy's tourniquet. But how? His gaze roved the shabby residential villas, the tentage gleaming tautly in their trampled gardens. The Soviet enclave lived within a paranoia of barricades, new ugly walls, mountains of wire. An outer ring comprising four army camps bristling with weaponry added belt to braces. The fort where prisoners were interrogated was contained by the ring. And yet someone had been able to penetrate it. His gaze came to rest on Major Zotov bouncing along in a signals jeep. It swerved and drew up beside him.

'You were right and I was wrong,' Zotov cried. 'There are traces of wire-tap all over the place – bared cables, clip-marks. No apparatus that I can see. They must listen only at night and clear off before reveille. But who? And how? I mean, with picquets and sentries almost standing on each other's boots. And they'd have to understand Russian, Andrei Pavlovich, think about that. Will you notify camp security or will I?'

Yakushev told him he would take care of it. As he walked back to his office he found himself staring hard into passing army faces, wondering if indeed they belonged to genuine Soviet citizens. Several were from the Asiatic republics, indistinguishable in feature from northern Afghans. It opened his mind to a whole fresh set of possibilities.

Suddenly everything seemed more threatening.

Pavel sat up and drank sparingly from the gourd, his gaze working up the mountain facing him. On his map it was marked as simply a spot-height – 3400 metres – but the locals called it mysteriously, 'Sword of the Two-Sworded King'. Pavel looked around for the other 'sword', but the feature sloped away to the east, breaking up into a series of valleys and ridges. The nomenclature, he decided, must be historical rather than geological.

Behind him was a ruined hut, wild flowers springing from its crevices. The plain beyond stretched away interminably, spangled with scrub. In the shimmering distance he saw the black tents of a nomad encampment.

He brought his gaze full circle to rest on the sloping shoulder of the Sword, and saw two distant specks. If they weren't liver spots, his timing was perfect.

For a while they seemed to be heading directly towards him, and Pavel began to wonder if he would have to move. But at length they changed direction and he realized they had detoured so as to make use of the track. He was about a hundred metres off it, so there was no problem.

One of the men sat his saddle wearily, one shoulder slumped forward. That must be Khan. The other was unmistakably the giant. He looked all about him as he rode ahead, then behind, then at the sky.

Presently the giant reined his horse, pointing to the ground. Pavel hoped that the plane's slipstream had erased the tyre marks from the loose dust, but no such luck. They were old pros, these two. He watched the giant look up and all around again, even more carefully. He stared towards the ruined building several times, then, for an instant, directly – or so it seemed – at where Pavel was hiding.

The Russian's heart skipped a beat. But he had chosen a spot where his felt hat would almost exactly match the rocks around him. He did not move a muscle. And the giant's gaze roved on.

Slowly the riders resumed their journey. Their very postures now had a searching look that showed they were reading every sign. Marvellously primitive. Pavel could not help feeling a pang of admiration.

He remained without moving till they had receded into the distance. Even then, he hesitated to follow. The other five must be around somewhere. But there was no sign of them yet.

Keeping the horsemen just in sight, he strode along with his staff, flattening himself on the ground whenever they halted. From time to time he triggered the R-140 and spoke a map reference or described a landmark – not transmitting, simply recording, for the body-radio was designed for use in the very presence of the enemy, or in circumstances where transmission was impossible. It recorded and accumulated messages for later transmission. And it possessed other, even more sophisticated functions.

The sun had long passed its zenith when the riders ahead quit the trail and turned up into the high country behind the Sword. They topped a barren hill and disappeared.

Pavel, sensing they must be nearing their goal, put on speed. To lose them now would be a disaster.

Arriving at the hill, he followed in their hoofprints very cautiously, stopping before the crest when his eyes were level with the valley beyond. He stared in awe at the jutting cliffs, their vertical ramparts rooted in detritus slopes angling down to a valley floor as flat and white as a salt pan. A thousand streams wound away like blue and silver serpents. The lake below him, like none he had ever seen, swept out, like a great brimming chalice, fifteen metres above the valley floor. Its rim was of rock, tufted here and there with grass, through which the spillage filtered in sheer waterfalls to feed the serpents of the valley below.

Standing in the shallows, fetlock to fetlock with their own reflections, Khan and the giant were watering their horses.

Two rifle shots rang out sharply, then the sound turned to kicked tissue paper and ghost steam trains rushing and shushing away between the cliffs. Pavel ducked. As he raised his head gingerly he saw that the giant had fired them in the air, and now, from high along the valley, came two answering shots.

Pavel peered to see where they had come from. But the scale was too vast to discern human movement.

The reflections trembled and shattered. The horsemen were on the move again, skirting the inner shore of the lake. It seemed to take them an age to reach the point where the rocky rim began its great outward curve. There must have been a precipitous path winding down to the valley floor, for the horses slithered nervously as they descended from view.

Pavel cast a wary look behind him, then he was up and sliding down the long slope to the lake's edge.

From the shore he peered again towards the cliffs. Those on the western side were caught in dense afternoon shadow, but now he could just detect in one of the nearer bastions a honeycombing of caves. And there was the fine thread of a trail winding up the detritus towards them. Was this where Khan and the giant were making for?

To get a clearer view, he moved out to the near rim of the chalice. It was amazingly narrow and, on its outer side, sheer. Rather than venture along its crest, he waded through the shallows a little way, poking with his staff to ensure a footing. His *chuplies* crunched in crystalline scum. The lapping waters, he realized, deposited minerals around the edge, where they congealed to rock, raising the rim. And as it grew higher, more meltwaters rushed down to keep it ever brimming – and ever building.

From here he could see all of the honeycombed escarpment, even tiny figures gathering at a cavelike entrance. He knew then that he had found Khan's stronghold.

The horsemen were invisible still, beyond the lake's far rim, and would remain so for some minutes. Pavel sat with his feet in the cold water and got out the map. Pinpointing his position, he calculated the four-figure map reference of Khan's fortress. He recorded it all on the R-140's tape, ready for transmission the instant he was clear. He put the map away and prepared to make his way back.

Standing up now, Pavel was just able to see the horsemen. They were picking their way along the mineral tidemark, heading towards the track that served the fortress. From this distance they merged into a single dark punctuation mark against the whiteness.

As Pavel watched them, a nagging suspicion grew to certainty in his mind.

They *were* one. One horse and one rider!

His mind leapt to a chilling conclusion. He turned.

The other, the giant, was standing, legs splayed, arms akimbo, on the shore behind him!

Pavel stared at him, for a moment incapable of movement. Then he waved. Poking for a foothold with his staff, he waded back towards him. It was the natural course for a humble seeker after God.

The fellow must have doubled back along the valley, hugging the shadow cast by the lake, he thought. Seen near to, he was a monster – eyes slitted with malevolence, rifle in hand. No sign of his horse. He must have left that below.

'Are you harmonious?' Pavel cried.

As he drew closer he spread his hands helplessly. 'I am here by the will of Allah.' He added, 'Though I know not where is here, nor here is where.' He stopped in front of him and touched his begging bowl. 'If you are in need of a prayer, but a portion of *nan* will ease it from my lips. For a loaf, I will recite the *sura* of thy choice.'

The giant did not reply, but looked at him carefully, at his face, his tattered clothing, as if seeking a flaw.

Oh shit, Pavel thought. Did he see me with the map? He flicked the bowl with his fingernail, allowing its emptiness to ring for a moment before he whined:

'I am lost and starving, Brother. Know ye that in the forty-seventh *sura* it is written: "You are called upon to give to the cause of Allah. Some of you are ungenerous; yet whoever is ungenerous to this cause is ungenerous to himself."' As he spoke his fingers became subtle snakes, insinuating themselves through the layers of his clothing.

The giant dropped his rifle, took one stride forward and reached for him.

Pavel was under his arm and behind him in a flash. His staff cracked across the back of the huge skull and, as the giant swung round, he drove it hard into his gut, then his throat. Another crack to the skull had his adversary reeling. Pavel swiped sideways with all his might, aiming for just below the ear. The stave struck true, with such savagery that it broke.

The giant stood for a full instant, like a tree at the last stroke of the axe. For good measure, Pavel scrabbled inside his garments as he watched the tree topple slowly forward, stepping back a pace to make way for its length. Alas, too late! The great arms shot out and seized his ankles. The world somersaulted and he was dangling upside down in the air, being shaken like a sifter.

Out fell the map, followed by the small-calibre automatic he had been groping for and, finally, his Spetznas combat knife.

The giant uttered a kind of hissing bellow. The ground leapt and hit Pavel a dizzying blow, then began to pummel him, the sun stabbing between his lids as the brute dragged him by one heel along the shore.

Pavel twisted, kicked at the hand gripping him, kicked at the back of the nearest knee and strove to hook up one great ankle. He struggled to climb up his own body and wrap himself around the tree-trunk legs. All to no avail. He spread his arms then, desperately clutching at passing rocks and stones, seeking a missile. Suddenly one was in his hand. He hurled it at the giant's head. Missed. He twisted sideways, groping for another.

There was no fear – no time for it. Survival, now, was all. He glimpsed the lake's rim bumping towards him. A round, heavy stone came into his hands. At the same instant icy fingers penetrated his clothing. Water lapped up round his face as he was dragged through the shallows. He curled his body, the rock raised in both hands. His head went under. Water burned into his sinuses. Waves engulfed the cliffs. The sun turned green. The stone was gone. He was choking. He jerked frenziedly to kick himself free. But the grip on his ankle was like a manacle.

Now the water was rushing past him. Air came suddenly but his lungs could not capture it against the centrifugal pressure. He was being swung in a circle, faster and faster, the blood sucking into his head to swamp his senses.

He was still kicking and twisting as the manacle unclamped and he sailed into space. He had dreamt of it often – the void below, the utter inevitability, intestines a chill vacuum, the ground growing up at him, doubling its rocky fists to crush him . . .

4

HAVING MADE sure that the spy was dead, Takredi rode back along the trail for a distance, to see if the dog had been leading a pack.

He peered, he sniffed, he listened, but could detect nothing that was not integral to the wilderness. Nevertheless, he sat down cross-legged beside the trail, as an animal sits, open to everything – the whisper of the torrents, the gentle weaving of the wild flowers against the mountain's shadow, the swoop and settle of birds, the crawl of insects. He was remembering that morning when the *schurawi* had materialized out of the mists of the Alishang to devastate their lives. They must never be caught again.

The map troubled Takredi. In it, the 'holy man' had marked the position of their stronghold. And he had been waiting *ahead* of them, as Takredi had ascertained moments after seeing the wheel marks of the aircraft. He had wanted to kill the man as he lay in hiding. But Khan had been curious.

Curiosity, Abdalis had once said, was the Jinn's lure; Hell lay at the end of its beckoning. But Abdalis, Khan told him, had been wrong about many things. If Khan said so, it was true.

But *ahead* of them. Did it mean that the *schuwari* had forced the boy to reveal the whereabouts of Mir Shiklama? Had, in fact, the boy *known* its whereabouts? Takredi could not be certain.

Soon the remaining survivors began to appear along the trail. They had encountered no one and observed nothing untoward. Reassured that attack was not imminent, Takredi walked with the last pair to where he had left his horse.

Taking the lower path, along the valley, they had to pass where the 'holy man' lay. It appeared to Takredi as if he had somehow transmogrified horribly to a mound of bubbling grey lava. As they drew nearer the bubbles divided, hopping this way and that, some hoisting their bodies into the air for a few wing flaps, as though lifting ragged garments. The dead man's coat of '99 illusions' was revealed as but the skin of a carcass. Buckled round what was left of the intestines, he thought he saw a belt. Something was attached to it. A box?

He was curious, but he would not touch the body because a man who has died in a state of uncleanliness, without the reading of prayers, is believed to remain at the scene of his death as an *urwah*, an evil ghost. Takredi moved past quickly, his face averted.

The three of them had not gone far when a soft bleeping sound issued from the carcass. The vultures froze in their rending to cock umbrella-handle heads. But it was too like a bird-sound to offer any threat and, anyway, it soon ceased. They continued feeding.

In the Signals office, Yakushev tapped the operator's shoulder and wagged a finger in front of his eyes. Enough. If Pavel was in a position to answer he would have done so already.

It was the third time of trying, though. Yakushev turned to the signals major with a worried frown.

Zotov shrugged off his concern. 'He could still be screened. These mountains are the devil, and that integral aerial has always been a pain in our arse.'

'He could also be in a position where he can't reply, close to the enemy,' Yakushev argued.

'Then wouldn't he shut us up? Two flicks of the pressel – he knows the routine. We'd hear the transmission surge and stop bothering him.'

'Hm.' Yakushev was unconvinced.

'If he's screened he could shift into the clear at any time. Leave it to us. We'll put him on call. Say, every half-hour?'

'No.' Yakushev wasn't sure why he objected. He wasn't thinking too well. No sleep. A day of inspecting possible entry loopholes to the enclave, of listening to negative search reports, of mulling over the files and screening reports of Afghan personnel employed within the cantonment. He hadn't even had time to shave. 'No, I'll—'

Before he could finish a padded door opened and the cyphers officer, Colonel Yuri Mostin, came out of his penetralium. He shut the door carefully behind him, for the equipment and files in the room were top-secret. Other than his operator, no one in the directorate, including General Dolin himself, was allowed access. Few people were even allowed access to *him*. He could not travel except under heavy escort, nor be in the presence of non-Russians for even a moment, no matter how closely guarded he might be. He alone had direct cypher dialogue with GRU Moscow, which made him Moscow's watchdog over the directorate. This in turn gave him power beyond his rank, and he knew it.

He nodded to Yakushev and raised enquiring brows towards his major, who explained the problem.

'Is your agent's report long overdue?' Mostin asked.

'You don't lay deadlines on a man like Pavel,' Yakushev said.

'Well, lay one now,' prescribed the monarch. 'Just bleed him. The process is silent. Whatever his situation, it's no skin off his nose.'

'What if he's screened?'

'Shall we find out?' Barely waiting for an answer, Mostin pointed to the big X4 high-gain transmitter. The major handed the operator the code. The man tapped it out on his key.

In the high valley, darkness had driven the vultures off to roost. Now the first of the night scavengers materialized, picking his way delicately across the streams, following his sharp nose towards the scattered remnants of the Russian agent.

A grey dog-fox was the next link in the chain of demolition. With teeth that could grind more finely than the sharpest beak, he attacked the stubborn meat clinging to the rib-cage.

No sooner had he begun than, with a click and hiss, the micro-recorder went into re-wind almost under his nose. He recoiled and cantered off a short distance. He stood listening for a moment, then returned haltingly. He twitched once as the spools stopped and went into playback, but hunger drew him on till he was once again tugging and scrunching as though nothing had happened.

He even gave the gory box thing a lick as it silently transmitted the voice of his host.

5

YAKUSHEV SAT on the rickety bed, pulling on his socks, gazing absently at the photo of Pola. Whenever he thought of Khan she seemed to include herself, uninvited. Perhaps to enjoy the vicious pang of jealousy that racked him. Well, it would soon be done now. Would her image desert him when it was over and Khan was dead? he wondered.

The servant entered with hot water. The water heater in the one bathroom was defunct, and anyway they couldn't all shave in there – there were five of them in the small villa.

He watched the dark, narrow hands fill the tin basin. Astonishing how alike they all were in khaki, without their beards. Straight-nosed, strong-jawed, lean. Unreadable. You thought you knew where you stood with them, but you didn't.

'*Seb.*' The soldier bowed and left silently.

All exhaustively screened. Yet Yakushev, given his own way, would have fired the lot and replaced them with Russian conscripts. More secure, certainly – but it wasn't politic. Wasn't socialism.

It was two days since he had learned the whereabouts of Khan's stronghold, and so far he had shared the intelligence with no one save his immediate staff and Colonel Goldanov of Spetznas. His reason for this was security, though he recognized possessiveness in it too. Khan was *his*.

The attack was to be conducted his way. If it ever got off the ground – there were obstacles – it would be a showpiece of economy and impact. The precise opposite of everything devised by those dinosaurs at Front.

Khan commanded a force, so Pavel had believed, of around a hundred and fifty men. Against them, he and Goldanov proposed to field no more than two companies – sixty cut-throat troops. No bombing or softening up. Simply a pre-dawn para drop to the crest of the escarpment. Ropes over the edge. A rapid swarm down into the caves. Surprise, together with blinding lights, riot gas and sheer fury, would destroy all resistance within minutes.

There would be no prisoners. Spetznas usually shot them, together with their own wounded. Any interrogations would be done on the spot, the prisoner's testicles gripped in one hand,a knife in the other. Simple, expedient, terminal.

Boots sounded on the stair. Goldanov – the professional villain, honest villain – came in. He had the lower front room.

'Dined at brigade last night. They're all tooled up and ready to go, whenever the met boys give us the word.'

'And a certain other party,' Yakushev reminded him evenly.

'Yes.' Goldanov grinned. He had a black patch over one eye and a scar chasing down from it clear to his collarbone. The air in his huge chest hissed in his flattened nose. 'I've been thinking. Better let him think it comes from me.'

'What a good idea,' Yakushev said, having already thought of it.

'The way you two get along, if it had been you who dreamed up the defence of Stalingrad he'd have ordered a retreat.'

'With me bringing up the rearguard.' Yakushev did not smile. 'No, by all means, you do the talking.' He eyed Goldanov's jigsaw camouflage of pockets and sub-pockets down the legs. 'Suppose I have to put on a uniform?'

'Better. You know what he says about that old jacket of yours – that you get more like Pavel every day.'

'Wishful thinking.' Yakushev went to the wardrobe. 'Pavel being dead.'

'You reckon? You don't think Khan took him prisoner?'

Yakushev leaned sideways to glance out of the door. He shot Goldanov a warning look.

The big man clamped shut his mouth and nodded. 'Must watch that. Well—' He slapped his thighs. 'See you down there.'

'Down there', was what had been the school principal's office. Walls varnished and grained to resemble wood, kicked furniture imported from some administration committee room. Lenin, humourless as ever, separated from Babrak Karmal by a local calendar depicting a massed rally of Afghan children with floral hoops, obediently making like little Russians.

Dolin sat with his back to a sunlit view of the cantonment, his face in shadow.

As Colonel Goldanov outlined the proposed action the shadow seemed to deepen. Dolin sheafed through the transcript of Pavel's report and yesterday's low-level air photos showing the honeycombed cliff, its approaches, the valley. He frowned up at Yakushev, then put his spectacles on and peered closer.

'Looks deserted.'

'Well, they'd have heard the plane,' Goldanov said. 'But see that misting? It's smoke.'

Dolin grunted.

Goldanov continued his exposition.

Yakushev remained as still as a man facing a house of cards.

Dolin glanced towards him again, curiously. Yakushev thought, damn, he can tell. It stinks of me.

At length, when Goldanov had had his say, Dolin leaned forward slightly, his hands on either side of his blotter, eyes closed, like a man trying to master a stutter.

After a few moments he opened his eyes.

'First, may I ask, why this conspiracy? Why have you suppressed this information and developed your own plan?'

Yakushev could see no point in further silence. 'To avoid any chance of leakage, spooking our man.'

'Leakage? Why should there be?' Dolin cocked his head from one to the other. 'You're referring to this telephone business?'

Yakushev confirmed that he was.

'It hasn't occurred to you that it might have been the KGB simply checking up on someone?'

'Look, General,' Yakushev tried to keep his tone relaxed, 'there are other indications that we are not whollly secure. But can we leave them for another time and concentrate on this?'

'The elimination of your *bête noir*? Ah yes.' Dolin's smile was faintly mocking. 'Do, uh, I detect in all this careful preparation a personal vendetta?'

'Departmental, General.' Yakushev did not bat an eye. 'Khan disregarded our white flag at Bab-el-Hawa, he destroyed two of our BTRs and eight men. Nine, if you now include Pavel.'

'I see. So you are just righteously indignant on our behalf. Good. Nice to see solidarity.' Yakushev could have hit him. 'So you both feel strongly that we should keep this in the family.'

'I think we should take a crack at him,' Goldanov said. 'We, the GRU.'

'It'd be good for our image and morale,' Yakushev said. 'Show Front' – he almost said 'the geriatrics' – 'what incisive action is all about.'

'Laudable.' Dolin even permitted himself a chuckle before leaning back in his chair, his face becoming bleak. 'Unfortunately we are not at liberty to do that without Front's permission. And, quite simply, we won't get it.'

There was a moment's dead silence.

'You don't know that,' Yakushev said.

'I know Marshal Solkholov. And I know Front is furious about the threat to Rossakov. When they find out it was Khan, they will want him made an example of. I mean obliterated. And *seen* to be obliterated.'

Yakushev stared. 'You mean . . . a chemical attack?'

Dolin returned the stare. 'We finished testing our NCB capability in 1981, Andrei Pavlovich.'

'Maybe so, but the marshal has used it since on three separate—'

'There are no records to show that.'

'Nevertheless—'

'So close to Kabul,' Dolin talked him down, 'I think we can be assured he will employ conventional forces.'

'Then why not ours?' boomed Goldanov.

'Because he regards you as far too specialized to waste on such an operation. And so do I. You are the ace up our sleeve, Viktor Alexeivich.' Dolin paused a moment. 'You force me to say this prematurely, but Spetznas are earmarked for a vital role in Harvest. Special training commences at the end of next week. I will elucidate no further at this juncture, except to say that I will convey this intelligence,' he indicated the report and air photos, 'to the marshal when I see him later this morning. But I will make *no* mention of Spetznas in this context. Clear?' He slipped the material back in its envelope and put it in his briefcase. 'Now I must get on.'

Goldanov the ruffian had magically become Goldanov the lamb. He spread his hands mutely towards Yakushev, bared his teeth apologetically, shrugged beefy shoulders and left the room.

Yakushev did not move. Though the Spetznas' role in Harvest was news to him, he had prepared himself for this outcome. He drew a second envelope from his pocket and deposited a dozen close-typed pages on the desk.

Dolin frowned, as if surprised he was still there.

Yakushev smiled faintly. 'I don't let go that easily, General. *Departmentally*, we still have a role to play in this. An important one.'

'Yes?' Dolin's tone was terser now that Goldanov had left the room.

'Security-wise. In the light of recent events, I'm drawing up a separate report. My staff and I have prepared some necessary revisions to the general handling of classified information, especially limiting the circulation of information concerning forthcoming military operations to, as far as possible, word of mouth; excluding junior commanders, non-Soviet personnel—'

Dolin blinked. 'Why on earth—'

'Khan,' Yakushev said distinctly. 'We found him. Now we're not going to let the bastard slip away by telling him in advance what we are planning.'

Dolin froze. 'Are you suggesting Front has been infiltrated?'

'I believe so. So have we.'

Watching Dolin's pen turn rapidly over and over in his fingers, Yakushev sensed that he was torn between the emotional desire to dismiss such a notion out of hand, and his responsibilities as head of the directorate.

'Other than the telephone business, give me one concrete example.'

Yakushev leaned forward. 'Less than an hour ago, when we were at breakfast, General Rossakov's driver was found dead in his staff car. Right here in our compound, General. Strangled with the seat-belt. His tongue cut out.'

6

''Twas Ramadan, ere the sacred moon arose . . .'

The heart of Mir Shiklama was a maze of interconnecting caves and rockfalls giving access to black holes through which the breath of deeper caverns fanned. Stalagmites peopled the gloom with dwarfs and *jinns* and *dayoos*, while, far above, stalactites hung their limy swords. Cloak upon shoulder, spear upon helmet, smoky legions seemed to march with each burst of flame as camel thorn was tossed on the firepits. Roasting goats glistened on the spit. Crowded Pathan faces showed ruddy against the sombre rock, teeth and eyes bright.

They were gathered for the first night's feast of Ramadan, the sacred month. All were parched and ravenous after the day's fast. The sentries outside would report the moment it became night. Then they would eat. How they would eat!

Habib had procured the goats. Neat and businesslike as ever, he now supervised their roasting, while Khan's youngest lieutenant played the sitar; the men clapped and Takredi clowned.

With a veil across his face, he relaxed his massive pectorals till they wobbled like breasts. Slowly he danced, torso gleaming, arms weaving. It was sinful. Abdalis would have forbidden it. But the men loved it.

Khan watched the strangeness and wished Pola were there to witness it, for her wonderment was enhanced by intelligence and, when showing her his land, he had drawn deep pride and pleasure from it. The eerie splendour of his stronghold now seemed like a link with God's own strength. Through it flowed a supply of fresh water. In a storage cave were stacked tins of Bulgarian mutton, East German beef, milk, cheeses taken from ambushed convoys. In another were captured weapons maintained by a gunsmith with a charcoal forge and bellows as efficient as any in Darra. The approaches could be defended by a mere handful of men, and a concealed escape hole emerged to the rear of the escarpment.

Above were other more remote, more silent chambers, one with a 'window' looking sheer down to the valley. It was there he would have taken Pola to his bed of goat and ibex skins, with none to watch their love-making but the bats.

With an effort he brought his mind to the Russians and General Rossakov, and ended the mood of reminiscence. His shoulder was almost healed. It was time to celebrate this holy month with something big. Deal the *schurawi* a major blow.

Suddenly the sentries came in from outside to announce that it was night.

Silence spread raggedly throughout the cavern. Takredi ceased his clowning and put on his *chapan*. The sea of eyes turned towards Khan.

He sank to his knees.

All sank.

He went through the motions of ritual cleansing.

All cleansed.

He raised his face to the stalactites and spoke above the hissing and sizzling.

'Allaho akbar, Allaho akbar, ush hado, Ullaelaha, illulla, ush hado, una, Mahomeder, rassul, ullah, Allaho akbar, Allaho Akbar!'

When the last echo had died, he rose to his feet and signalled for the feast to begin.

Khan was waiting beside a road in the hills, his hand against a tree. Above him was a bird. A stork. Its huge nest straddled the uppermost branches. Ants marched up and down the trunk, taking guano from the nest. They made a tickling path across his hand.

Someone was coming, he knew. His heart was filled with promise, but there was a darkness as to who it could be, a sweet darkness, graceful and sacred.

The shadows grew long. The ants had found a way up his leg now, passing under his clothes and along his arm on to the tree. But the road wound away, empty still.

He waited patiently for her to come, for the darkness, he knew, was woman. But instead she sent a milky arch of stars and then the dawn. She sent a sudden horse that was gone in a frenzy of dust. She sent another night with a white moon. The moon waned. The bird flew away. The ants now used his body as their regular path. Deposits of guano mingled with the juices of the tree on his flesh, turning it to bark, his arms to branches. Though he had grown into the tree, he still waited. And still she did not come.

Winter came and took his leaves. Followed by spring. The bird came back and nested in his arms. And now, at last, someone was coming.

Heart bursting, he strove to distinguish who it could be. The shape materialized slowly along the road. It was a man with an axe.

'Master! Master, wake up.'

Khan's fingers fastened round his Kalashnikov. It was dark still, save for Takredi's lantern.

'What is it?'

'I – I am not sure, Master. But you should come.'

Khan raised himself and swiftly wound his turban. He followed the bobbing light down sloping passageways, stooped under a squeeze of roof and slid after Takredi into the main cavern.

The fires had long died to a glow of ash and the feasters had departed to sleep elsewhere. Habib and a remaining few squatted amongst the debris, their gaze fixed on a stranger who crouched in silence by one of the beds of embers, a *piala* of tea in his hands.

Khan approached him. He did not look up.

'*Zendeh nabashi?*'

The man made no reply.

With a puzzled glance at the others, Khan lowered himself to the ground near him. He wore simple pushtun clothing, the headcloth pushed back on his high forehead, and a beard ran round under his chin in a prophetic fringe. His face was older than his years, sweat-streaked and grey with exhaustion, as though he had run a long way.

Khan waited for him to finish the evidently needed refreshment.

The runner laid aside his cup and placed a hand over his heart, rubbing it for a moment as though it pained him. When he spoke his voice was rough from exertion.

'Allaho akbar.'

He scratched something in the dust, then folded his arms across his crouched knees and raised yellow-flecked eyes to Khan's.

'This is a prophecy and an instruction. On the third morning of Ramadan you will prepare your men for battle.'

Khan felt the small muscles harden all over his body, as a porcupine raises its quills.

'No man, coming as a guest,' he said evenly, 'speaks imperatives to his host.'

'If a host is he who provides,' replied the messenger, 'I come from a greater host and you are his guest. He gives to you freely of his bounty, asking nothing in return, save that you listen.'

'There is only one such Host,' Khan said. 'Mohamed is his prophet.'

'Save that you listen,' repeated the stranger.

Khan frowned at him for a moment. 'Speak.'

'I bring you foreword of what will happen and what you will do. Open your mind's ear well, for there is much.'

Whereupon he closed his eyes and recited in a monotone, with a slight singsong lift at the end of each passage as though chanting from the Koran.

Khan listened with at first scepticism, then dismay, doubt, growing conviction, and finally a surge of primal energy. He viewed the reactions of his men. They appeared dumbstruck.

When the messenger relapsed into silence, Khan asked: 'What then?'

'There is a veil,' murmured the stranger. His eyes opened and came round to Khan across his folded arms. 'But all veils are for lifting. Be comforted.'

Khan looked away, debating. He shook his head. 'You tempt belief. But how can I be sure this is not . . . ?'

The messenger rose abruptly to his feet, as though insulted, bowed his head to all and made to leave.

'Wait!'

His exit was barred by the sentry.

The stranger turned slowly. 'Detain this servant, doubt him, follow him, and no further veils will be lifted. You will die here, as a tree dies without water.'

A tree . . . ! Khan started. It was undeniably a sign. With one word the man had stilled his disbelief.

He motioned the sentry to let him go.

He turned to his men, who were gathered about the messenger's scratchmark in the dust, trying to decypher its meaning.

It was in the shape of a broad, pointed leaf. Growing up out of its centre was a stamen.

7

YAKUSHEV WAS astounded by the sight before him. If Solkholov had set out to epitomize all that was ponderous in the Soviet approach to war, he could not have devised a more telling demonstration.

The wide bed of the valley shimmered with one whole division of tanks. From his vantage point, seated in his jeep on the high ground overlooking the lake, he could have counted all 325 of them, plus the 400 BMP personnel carriers, the battery upon battery of SAU howitzers, the rocket-launchers, the full range of support and command vehicles, not to mention the gunships spinning overhead or the Mig-27 penetration bombing that had preceded the attack. It was as if the whole Moscow May Day parade had been diverted through the Hindu Kush.

Apart from the astounding overkill, it was psychologically naive. A short, sharp Spetznas assault would have dismissed Khan and his force with a snap of the fingers. But this overvalued him. Whatever the outcome, he would gain hero or martyr status which could only advance the rebel cause, in terms of arms from Egypt and China and sympathy from the rest of the world – to which the Kremlin was becoming increasingly sensitive.

Khan, he mused, given a sense of gallows humour, ought to be tickled pink at the VIP treatment he was getting. If he was still alive. The first-light bombing had struck deep into the cave system, and now the rocket and artillery fire was stripping away the outer layers of the escarpment – so it was possible he was already dead. Yakushev wasn't sure.

Munching a sandwich to stop himself from smoking, he steadied his glasses on the gaping pockmarks. He could see no sign of movement, but the distance was more than a kilometre, and they would hardly be dancing about. But they were there. Oh, they were there all right. He'd made quite sure of that.

Last evening's air photos had shown definite occupation – smoke, figures – and high-altitude surveillance this morning had revealed no mass exodus through the surrounding hills. Technical facilities had, by means of photo enhancement, located a tunnel exit on the rear slopes of the escarpment and that was now covered by mortars and machine-guns.

Yakushev had insisted that this assault be organized in as near sterile security conditions as it was possible to achieve.

He panned down the detritus slopes to where the leading tanks, dwarfed by the scale of it all, were just coming into line. Would they attempt the climb? Forty-five degrees. A gradient of one-in-one. Yes, they would! He was impressed.

They began to claw their way up the detritus, firing from the short halt in the manner and formation prescribed by the Frunze Military Academy – for war in Europe. Up they went and it all looked great. But the pounding of their 125 mms, plus supporting rocket and artillery fire, was bringing down huge rocks that set the scree sliding to build up a barrier that the tanks, surely, would never surmount.

Indeed platoon by platoon they came grinding to a halt, more than 300 metres short of their objective, which was the base of the vertical cliff above. Brilliant.

Now it was up to the infantry. Was this what the rebels were holding their fire for? he wondered.

The personnel carriers closed up behind the tanks and anchored with difficulty on the shifting scree. Out poured the riflemen, and deployed into skirmishing line. The tanks and supporting weapons fell silent as the men began their long climb. Now there were only automatic grenade-launchers, machine-guns and mortars to keep the rebels' heads down – anything bigger would start the rocks falling again, crushing the men to strawberry jam.

Yakushev scanned the caves above them, inclining his ear to catch the first burst of defensive fire. The enlarged orifices looked like a great skull grinning from the bedrock; sinister, through all the smoke and dust. He felt himself tighten. Something was not right.

Intuitively, he panned along the cliffs beyond. Then across

the valley to the opposing wall. Just one heavy mortar cunningly sited . . . half a dozen defiladed machine-guns . . . could wreak havoc from the rebels' considerable altitude advantage.

But could see nothing that was not a part of nature. Not from this angle anyway. He panned back to the riflemen – all four thousand of them – clambering amongst the boulders, seeking ways up, not always succeeding, backtracking, bunching. They were trained to advance in line, but that was impossible here.

Khan *couldn't* be that low on ammo, he thought – not after all those supply columns he had ambushed. No, there was another explanation. Explosives?

The final thirty metres were supposed to be covered at the double, to the Soviet battle cry of 'Urrah!' Yakushev strained his ears but the crashing echoes drowned all lesser sound. He saw rather than heard a section of rock collapsing. A man fell with it, limbs flailing, as tiny against the rockface from this distance as a plummeting bird.

Well, for whatever reason, Pola's 'bit of rough' had lost the boat now; the leading squads were *there*, struggling up over the debris, charging into the grinning jaws of the skull.

Yakushev listened intently for sounds of resistance from within the caves. There were a few thumps, but those could have been the troops tossing grenades ahead of them in the darkness.

More and more riflemen closed on the objective, till they were clustered in their hundreds under the brow of the cliff. Yakushev froze in the act of lighting a cigarette, suddenly aware of their vulnerability. All covering fire had ceased, nor could it be reactivated without putting every rifleman at risk. The formation of the slope made it impossible for them to deploy. They were as tightly packed as a football crowd.

Suddenly men appeared in the 'eye-sockets' high above them. Yakushev's heart missed a beat. But they were Russian – the leading squads. They began tossing out what looked like bodies, Afghan bodies, about a dozen of them. Then they beckoned to their comrades below to come on in, the caves were clear.

Yakushev activated the jeep radio link and tuned in to the rifle battalions. As the follow-up squads began pouring into the cave system, for all the world like a guided tour, he listened to the company reports.

'Deserted,' they said. 'Not a rebel in sight.' 'Nothing but a few dummies.'

God is Great . . . God is Great . . .

The army commissary in the Kabul enclave was housed in an old mosque. The motif proclaiming God to be Great circled the building in endless defiance of the Soviet flag flying on top. A Russian guard stood to attention as Yakushev strode angrily past him.

This was a pit-stop – a throat cleanser after thirty kilometres of eating supply-column dust before returning to his office. He ordered beer. He could have gone to the directorate mess, but he needed time to think before risking a confrontation with Dolin.

The total evacuation of Mir Shiklama, especially the dummies, signified just one thing – that despite all his precautions, Khan had been warned of the attack. Well, there was one silver lining: he had eliminated so many possibilities that he must be close to discovering the source of the leak.

The beer was American beer – an example of indiscriminate bulk buying that would get looked into when he had the time, but delicious for all that.

'After all your efforts – how could it have happened?'

Yakushev turned and realized that one of the little plastic tables was occupied. Zotov of signals was on his own, shoulders hunched, swigging vodka.

It was just what Yakushev had come here to avoid, but Zotov was a comrade. He waited to collect his change, then sauntered across.

'Ask me that in twenty-four hours, Nikolai, and I'll give you the answer.'

'He was my uncle.'

'Who?' Yakushev pulled out a chair.

'Rossakov.'

'You've lost me.'

'Rossakov – my uncle,' Zotov said impatiently. 'My mother's brother. Used to give great parties. Took me fishing at Silver Pond. When my dad died he was like a father to me.'

'Was? Was? You talk as if . . .'

Zotov stared up at him, his narrow, bespectacled face working. 'You haven't heard? What did you think I meant when you came in? I thought everyone knew by now.'

'What happened?'

'They got him. That's all. They got him.'

Yakushev stared at him savagely. 'How, dammit? I scrounged him a bullet-proof car!'

'He was out of the car.'

'Where were his escort?'

'All around him. He was at the Harbiya Military Academy. He and Babrak Karmal were taking the salute at the passing-out parade. A sniper shot him.'

'From where? The parade ground is enclosed.'

'They waited till the gates opened for the march around town, then picked him right off the rostrum. It must have been some distance, because no one seemed to know where it came from. The whole place went crazy. The parade broke up. About three hundred cadets in ceremonial gear and white gloves rushing about the place looking for the bastard. But he just vanished.'

It was chastening. The timing. The ease. The effrontery. Yakushev was in no doubt as to the identity of the assassin. There wasn't another rebel in the country who, given the choice, would have shot Rossakov and not Babrak Karmal.

Khan must have had *days* of warning, Yakushev decided as he threaded his way between the tentage, sandbags and wire. Yet he had plugged every conceivable hole. It only left the grey areas. The telephone system was still a question mark. Afghan personnel . . .

He stomped up to his office and got out the file copy of his orders. His staff spotted his arrival and came crowding in.

'Yes, I've heard. Post mortems later.' He ordered them out. After thirty seconds he called back Goriansky.

He indicated a deleted passage, over which was scrawled a correction in red ink. 'What's this?'

'General Dolin amended that, Colonel. He said the instruction went directly against protocol.'

'Protocol? What protocol?'

'Well, if we don't trust Afghan intelligence sufficiently to keep them posted concerning our forthcoming operations –

this is what he said – they won't inform us of theirs, and we could double up on the same objective and waste time, or worse.'

Yakushev suppressed his anger. For security operations that might make sense, but not for military ops, because Front planned *all* military operations. Dolin was up a tree. 'I'll have to talk to him. Do you know if Khad *were* warned?'

'Yes, they were.'

'How?'

'Memo to their liaison.'

Yakushev hit the file with his knuckle. 'Goriansky, *word of mouth*!'

'Yes, I know, but General Dolin said he didn't have time to speak to Major Jangalak personally, and it was internal, so I was to stamp it READ AND DESTROY.'

'Who delivered it?'

'I did.'

'And did you watch the major destroy it?'

'I . . . well, no. He sat there reading it. I didn't like to stand over him.' The sergeant stared down at his boots.

Yakushev exploded. 'Do you realize—' He mastered his fury. 'Fetch me the file copy.'

He followed the clerk along to the busy main office and took the memo from him. He carried it up two flights of stairs.

Though totally restructured by the GRU and KGB, Khad intelligence was ostensibly an independent body and maintained a liaison office at the headquarters of both organs. In the school building, that office occupied the old arts and handicrafts classroom tucked away under the roof.

Damp etched black fingers on the rafters, formed ghostly continents on the walls. A pile of buckets stood telescoped in a corner, ready for a future deluge. The windows were whitewashed against sniper fire.

Major Jangalak had scraped a hole in the whitewash and was gazing out as Yakushev entered. He had been accommodated in here to keep him out of earshot of signals and cyphers – a customary precaution with outside liaisons. He turned almost with a girl's grace.

'My dear fellow.'

He was lean, lank-haired and, despite the deep pockmarks, conceitedly handsome. The tailoring of his uniform made the

Russians look like Chinese peasants. He indicated the ornate samovar kept on his filing cabinet.

'Forgive me, my friend, it is not lit today in respect for the holy month, but I can send down to the canteen . . .'

'Not just now, Ali.' Yakushev throttled back with an effort. He laid the memo on the desk.

A waft of aftershave reached him as Jangalak leaned forward to study it. Yakushev had always found him correct and efficient, but there was an 'Anyone for polo?' air about him that smacked of reaction. The son of a politician who had served under King Daoud, the Afghan was a survivor of the old ruling class and he had converted to Marxism-Leninism too abruptly for Yakushev's suspicious mind.

The leak, he thought, *could* have originated here.

'When this came in, what did you do with it?'

'The actual memo? Burned it. As per instruction, my friend. Then I passed the information on to General Naqaswar.'

'How?'

Jangalak looked surprised. 'Word of mouth, naturally. Also as per your instruction.'

'At your HQ? In his office?'

Jangalak nodded, his gaze becoming speculative.

'Anyone else present?'

The Afghan thought back. 'No . . .'

'Any doors open? Clerks coming and going?'

'Not that I recall.' Jangalak frowned, then smiled. 'By the way, before I forget: there is dancing at my cousin's house tomorrow night. You and the general, and Colonel Velikov if he is back, will be welcome.'

'Men dancing . . .' Yakushev made a dismissive grimace.

'Women, my dear fellow. See how socialism is changing us? Hazaras from the north. Very colourful, I'm told.'

'Shall we stick with this for a moment?'

'I see.' Jangalak distanced himself slightly. 'What is your complaint, my friend? Presumably it has to do with either the death of your General Rossakov or today's fruitless operation?'

Yakushev eyed him sharply. 'How do you know about that?'

'A cloud of dust.' The Afghan waved a hand towards his peephole. 'Heading back towards Baghram base. The day still young. Too young for your force to have met with opposition. I presumed the bird had flown.'

'More than flown.' Yakushev watched him. 'It was he who shot Rossakov.'

Jangalak looked amazed. 'At the same time as you were . . . ?'

'At exactly the same time.'

'But Mir Shiklama is – how far? – thirty kilometres?'

'Go on.'

Jangalak did not reply. He saw now the reason for this visit.

'It suggests, Ali, that Khan was not only warned of our attack in time to evacuate Mir Shiklama, but managed to learn that Rossakov was scheduled to attend the academy parade – *and* he must have reconnoitred the ground in advance, because it was a complicated shot. Now do you see what I am talking about? A foreknowledge in the region of five days, maybe more.'

'*If* it was Khan who performed the assassination.' Jangalak moved quickly to defence.

'If it wasn't him personally, he'd have been there.'

'He was identified? How can you be sure?'

'I'm sure, Ali.' Yakushev fixed him with a knowing eye. 'And so, dammit, are you.'

The Afghan was silent.

'Now listen – *our* security was 98 per cent on the attack, 100 per cent on Rossakov's movements. All I want to know is, can Khad say the same?'

He drew back and watched the dark-rimmed eyes.

For a moment they held his, proudly dismissing the possibility. Then uncertainty began to flicker, behind it pain – the pain of a man loyal to something he fears has erred.

Yakushev was convinced then that Jangalak was not the cause of the leak.

The Afghan passed back the memo. He locked the drawers of his desk, reached for the riding crop he affected.

'Where are you going?'

'To tell General Naqaswar.'

'Tell him what?'

'That you believe we have been infiltrated.'

'Sit down, Ali.' Yakushev offered him a cigarette, knowing he didn't smoke, simply as a gesture. 'Flouncing out like a ten-day bride isn't going to solve a thing. Tell me – what has convinced you that the leak could be amongst your own people?'

Jangalak looked past him.

'Irregularities? Poorly screened personnel?'

No answer.

'You're not alone, you know. It's happening here, too. I've watched it coming and not recognized it. So, it seems, have you. Let's talk it out into the open.' He lit a cigarette, nodding to the chair facing him.

Jangalak lowered himself slowly as if on to a bed of nails. His country's intelligence service had lost face before the Russians. His Pathan pride was bleeding.

Yakushev inhaled deeply. 'You know why so many of our people go down with hepatitis? Too many poplar trees. Work that out. Roots get down into the sewage pipes. Little tendrils probing for moisture. Invisible to begin with. Then suddenly you have a great back-up of shit and everyone gets sick.' He added, 'That's infiltration.'

Jangalak frowned, only half listening.

'For "water" read "sources of intelligence",' Yakushev explained. 'Same little tendrils, probing, getting a grip, syphoning off information. This morning the shit backed up on us. Same as Zabit Halim's attack on Khabul airport last month. Those gunships he destroyed hadn't been on the pad an hour. Brand new. Coincidence – or more shit? Our search-and-destroy strike on Banow – where were the *mujahedin*? They were slaughtering our rearguard. Who gave them the time and place? And I could cite a dozen other instances.'

Jangalak was beginning to listen.

'Yet back in January they couldn't have handled it. You could have fed them the whole of our future strategy and they would have thrown it away by fighting each other for the honour of being first into the attack. Now, no. Something has happened. Do you agree?'

'I agree,' Jangalak said tentatively, 'that they are becoming more practised.'

'Come on, Ali. Forget your pride. Forget your racial affinities. We're your comrades now, your future. If ever they came out on top you'd be locked in the past for ever, your wife back in purdah, thieves with their hands cut off. Earn some of those millions of roubles we've poured into Khad. You hear things. Far more than we do. Let's have some of it. Remember that rumour we discussed? The Lily? What more have you learned about it?'

'My people are very fanciful, my friend. They wish, so they invent.'

'What do they wish? Tell me. A combined front against us bloody infidels, right?'

Jangalak smiled ruefully. 'Pathans don't know the meaning of the word "combined".'

'Well, someone is teaching them. How would they do that? What element would unite them?'

Jangalak inclined his head in thought, brown fingers with ash-grey, moonless fingernails tapping his swarthy brow. At length he said, 'I can think of only one thing that would make them all bury their differences. Fear.'

The unexpectedness of the reply somehow gave it veracity. Yakushev leaned forward.

'Fear of what? Death? Torture?'

A curl of Jangalak's lip dismissed such trivia.

'Of God.'

Of God! *Of course*, Yakushev thought, swinging his shoulders with each slow, hands-in-pockets stride as he hugged the outside shadow of the school building, back and forth, his adrenalin flowing. God is their one common denominator. Closed-circuit television to every heart!

He was on the right track at last. He and the Lily were in the same business. The intelligence business. They fielded agents, gathered and collated information. As he used Spetznas, the Lily used men like Khan and Massoud and Zabit Halim. They must have a communications network and a central directorate. Khad would find out where. Khad, now, were going to find out a lot of things. They were going to take their long narrow fingers out of their Pathan arses or he would drag them into the post-mortem concerning this morning. Then it would be goodbye independence, goodbye roubles, with the GRU and KGB vetting them even when they went to the latrine. That was the deal he had struck with Jangalak, and it was *his* deal. Dolin and Front would share no part of this till he had milked it dry. And he knew just how to do it.

'Oh, there you are, Colonel.' It was Goriansky. 'Signals say they're monitoring a clash between the rebels and our own people just north of Sorubi. I thought you might be interested.'

'Why? There something special about it?'

'It's Khan again.'

Yakushev cocked a dour eyebrow. 'Do you think he's a magician? Sorubi's at least seventy kilometres from here.'

'I know, but signals can hear the tanks talking and one of their commanders reckons he's recognized him, says he's been in action against him before. And they say the giant's with him.'

Yakushev hurried into the building.

8

As a herd of goats climbs a hillside, each picking its own path, the fifty rebels filtered up through the steeply terraced fields, their gaze fixed on the crest of the ridge beyond which lay safety. But, reaching the topmost terrace, Khan planted his feet and turned his glasses back on the village.

'Wait, my brothers!' Takredi wheezed.

The order was passed from mouth to mouth till all were halted, some throwing themselves to the ground.

'We should hurry, Ghoram,' Fareed gasped. A bullet had opened his cheek and his beard was a crimson birds' nest.

Young Feizl leaned the PKMB machine-gun against an almond tree and flopped amongst its fallen blossom.

Khan steadied the glasses on the leading tank as it blundered jerkily between the ruined houses, its gun erect so as not to get a muzzleful of adobe. Behind it, he could make out, when his hands stopped shaking, a second and third rampant gun zigzagging, disembodied, above the walls. Following, invisible for their dust, would be the six BMP troop carriers, each with its complement of eight riflemen. A formidable force. But Khan's blood was up. A new power was with them. There was no end, now, to what they could achieve.

He ran his gaze along the road, which wound with the river, away and up into the rugged hills in the direction of Do Rish. Steep country. Almost a gorge.

He turned to look at where the crest of the ridge bared its teeth against the sky. No more than two hundred paces. A few minutes' climb only, should things go wrong.

Khan called to the men, asking if all had sufficient ammunition.

'They may have called for gunships,' Fareed warned.

Khan ignored the caution. All had their blankets. If air support appeared they would simply vanish into the hillside.

And if the carriers disembarked their troops, it would be fifty against fifty, with the height advantage theirs.

And if the troops were Afghan – their brothers?

They *had* no brothers.

'Take ten men,' Khan said to Fareed. 'Go to where the road bends out of sight and block it. Remember,' he added, as Fareed swept the flies from his wound and rallied himself to obey, 'the rocks must be higher than a man's hip.' Experience had taught him what obstacles a T-64 tank could and could not surmount.

He told Feizl to take the machine-gun round the shoulder of the slope and place it to cover the shoulder and the roadblock below.

As the youth grinned and heaved himself up, Khan told Takredi to get the rest of the men into firing positions.

The giant ambled off, content that the memorable day was not yet ended.

Khan took cover, pulled his *patu* over his head and watched again through the glasses.

The T-64s were out of the village now and slowing as their commanders raked the hillside with their optics, trying to relocate their fleeing enemy. They were furious inside those steel blisters, he knew. And with good reason.

Even at a distance of five miles, the pall of black smoke overhanging the Golbahar–Sorubi road was still visible. It looked as though a steam train had just puffed its way across the open land beyond the village. It was too far to see the seven aviation-fuel tankers smouldering along the highway, and far too far to witness the havoc wrought at Baghram and Golbahar by the severance of their power supply from the Sorubi Dam, but the spectacular fireworks display as his group had felled the live cables across the passing convoy would console him for many a lonely night to come.

The force chasing them now had been the convoy's escort, front and rear. Khan had allowed the vanguard to pass before blowing the pylon charges. The two tanks and three carriers had turned in pursuit as fast as the terrain and exploding lorries would allow, which, thanks be to Allah, had been slow enough for the men to get clear and on to high ground. But now vanguard and rearguard had united and were hungry for retribution. Such hunger, though, Khan well knew, was often at the expense of caution.

But so could be his own hunger, he reminded himself. He was in a state of high emotion after their success. Lying in their hide under the sacks of vegetables in the back of the truck, he and Feizl had watched the gates of the military academy open at exactly the appointed moment. Feizl had fired the shot, as Khan's shoulder could not have withstood the jolt of the Lee Enfield. Just one shot – the nose of the bullet having been filed and incised so as virtually to explode on impact. Rossakov's chestful of medals had seemed to disintegrate. His belly, seen through the glasses as he lay on the rostrum, had looked like a nomad tent with the wind under it. Then the 'borrowed' lorry had jerked to life under them and whisked them away.

They had abandoned it where the Afghan army truck was waiting, by courtesy of the Lily. Manned by Afghan deserters in uniform, it had driven them out of the city without challenge. They had avoided the two checkpoints near the airport by going across country, and shot their way through the one at Sorubi. Takredi, Fareed and the rest of his force, having left Mir Shiklama two nights in advance, journeyed direct to Do Rish, where they set up the new base. Then fifty of them had come on down to the Golbahar–Sorubi road and were waiting beside it when Khan and Feizl arrived. They had already laid the charges around the pylons, and there was nothing more to do but rest and watch the hands of the clock and wonder whether the Lily's information concerning the fuel convoy was as accurate as the rest of its forecasts.

It was. Khan knew for sure then that he was dealing with experts. Inflicting maximum damage on the enemy was an art. His first strikes after the razing of Bab-el-Hawa had been from blind rage – and costly. But he had learned a great deal since then. To destroy a bridge with nothing crossing it, to blow up enemy trucks or buildings that did not contain vital supplies, was a foolish waste of the explosives he and his men extracted so painstakingly from unexploded enemy bombs. Sometimes it hurt the Russians more to hole a water tank than a battle tank. These things he learned, and now it was like a song to him to know that the Lily understood them too. The powerlines *and* the tankers was a piece of inspiration.

The tanks were still rotating their optics, having failed to sight either Feizl or Fareed on their way along the hillside, and now they and their men had passed beyond the curve on the slope. They had blind spots, these mechanical Russian dogs – some at close radius, some when their guns were at certain angles. Their automatic loading devices sometimes loaded the loader's arm into the breech of his gun. They were so cramped inside that only men the size of small women could be used as crew. They strangled themselves with their cleverness.

The danger now was that the dogs would continue sniffing along the road and reach the defile before Fareed had had time to block it. It was the moment, then, to attract the enemy's attention. Khan called to his men to open fire on the tanks.

The range was too great for accuracy, but rather than waste their bullets, they were aiming for the external fuel tanks. These were resistant to small-arms fire, he knew, and the fuel inside them was low-octane diesel, almost impossible to ignite, but . . . what was there to lose?

He kept his glasses trained on the tank cupolas to observe their response to the bullets as they began to careen off their decks.

Almost at once the beasts pricked up their remote-controlled machine-guns and began pumping fire back up the hillside, blindly. The armoured carriers, strung out along the road, responded too, their short turret guns swinging and lifting. Infantry weapons appeared through their side ports. But these, he knew, would never gain the elevation. He and his men had captured several BMPs: they were too cramped to allow the soldiers to crouch low enough to shoot steeply upwards. But the turret guns could just manage the angle, and presently the *rush-bam!* of their finned 73 mm projectiles added itself to the din.

Khan looked at his watch. He would give Fareed seven more minutes.

The lead tank was revving up now. It was going to try to gain enough elevation to use its big gun.

He watched it cock one track against the near bank – the dog taking a piss. Yes, that should do it, but how would it ever reload? The three-man-long 125 mm would have to lose elevation before the automatic loader could breech the next shell, and the height of the bank would never permit it.

Sure enough, the gun fouled the bank. Khan smiled grimly as it backed off and manoeuvred in an attempt to cock its leg higher.

But now the personnel carriers were shifting, backing along the road. They tucked themselves in under the bank and he heard their ramps go down.

A stream of tiny heads showed in his glasses as their troops climbed out. They were spreading out for an assault – from a flank, so the tank machine-guns could support them as far in as possible to their objective.

Here came the first squad – Afghans in field khaki, no helmets, just peaked forage caps, light machine-guns and mortars fanning off to the sides to give covering fire. But what could they see? Just rocks, a flash or two.

He shouted to his men to cease fire. Without even a flash to direct them they would be lost on the vast slope.

Three minutes to go.

The squads of eight were veering off course. Their officers kept stopping to peer up through their binoculars. There was a hiss. A mortar bomb splatted just below his position, showering him with debris. He looked up and saw another one wobbling at the peak of its trajectory, but it phutted down and didn't even explode. For no reason, the image of Pola came to him, as so often it did in battle. Just her expression, the light in her eyes. *Phutt-phutt* – two more duds. He scarcely heard them. His wheat crop would have been standing ripe and golden, the women rhythmically bending with their sickles, his children running, calling. Pain seared through him. Pray Allah there was a place of caught echoes where they would meet again. Where time stood trembling and still.

Time . . . Yes, it was time.

Khan leaned shut the door of memory and shouted the order to retreat.

He waited, hearing it passed from rock to rock, then secured his glasses and rifle under the drape of his *patu*, rose and started along the slope.

The hillside came alive with loping, clambering figures. Below them the guns swung. Behind them the troops shouted and changed direction. The rocks sparked, mortar bombs shattered – but wildly, the targets too sudden, the range too great and increasing, the slope curving away, the outcrops rising, the rebels diminishing beyond them.

In moments, it seemed, they had reached dead ground. Khan looked back and saw the tanks already on the move, gathering speed along the road to keep them in sight. But would the BMPs follow? The question was vital because his object was to lure the T-64s clear of any covering fire. The soldiers, after starting to give chase, were straggling to a halt. Khan delayed to see what they would do. Their officers were clearly issuing fresh orders. Now they were turning back towards their transport.

It was perfect. The time it would take them to climb in was all he needed. He changed direction downhill, shouting to his men to follow.

Now at last they perceived his strategy. Whooping and laughing, blankets and clothing flying, they bounded down the slope, riding the loose scree towards the defile where Fareed and his men could be seen rolling rocks on to the roadway. There was Feizl covering them with the machine-gun in case things went wrong. The T-64s were audible but not yet in view. It was going to work!

By the time the lead tank arrived there was not a resistance fighter to be seen. Its hatch was up, its leather-helmeted commander searching the hillside for sign of them. Seeing the defile ahead, he ducked down and pulled the hatch shut – an automatic precaution. The tank swung into the first narrow bend, the driver slowing to allow the gunner time to elevate his gun so as to avoid impact with the rocky walls.

From above, the beast looked massive and impregnable, covered with wartlike protuberances, white-light and infra-red searchlights, mine plough and snorkel attachments. The thunder of its 1000 h.p. engine rose as it geared itself around the second bend, then dropped away completely as the driver came in sight of the blockage.

The second tank came jerking round after it, to halt abruptly when it saw the other had stopped.

The third monster hung back warily, its engine snorting.

Even as the leader lowered its bulldozer blade to clear the rocks, Khan gave the signal.

With rifles slung, small bags of mud in their hands, his men landed lightly on the decks of all three. They carried these bags always for this purpose; in waterless country they would have been filled with their own excreta. In seconds they had slapped mud over every optic and viewing block.

Takredi crouched in front of the leader's hatch, Khan behind it, the breath from the exhaust vents warming his backside, ready. The moment the hatch was raised even a fraction, he would drag it open. The others stood by with grenades at the ready, forefingers through split-pin rings.

The rear tank responded first, gnashing into reverse and backing blindly. It mounted a verge and slumped backwards off the road, tossing the rebels from its decks as it became bogged down, bows tilted, tracks clawing the air.

The front tank was the next to engage its tracks. A grating sound came from under the gun as the driver's hatch swung open. It took Khan and his men by surprise, but only for an instant. A horny foot stamped on the driver's head, shoving him sideways under the glacis as three grenades were tossed in. Two more followed. The hatch was swung shut and all jumped clear.

Two dull thuds sounded inside the tank. The third triggered a tremendous multiple explosion that blasted the whole turret out of its mounting, upending it on its gun for one awe-inspiring moment, like a twenty-four-foot steel lollipop. The rebels scattered as it came slamming down across the glacis. The roar of ammunition exploding in its racks was now deafening, the gaping hole in its deck belching fire and metal like a cannon's mouth.

Khan clambered away up the rocks in time to see grenades being dropped down the open hatch of the second tank. His men leapt clear. The driver's hatch swung aside. The driver was halfway out when the grenades blew. He convulsed and hung slack. There was no accompanying blast of ammunition and a man with another grenade ready started to climb back, but Khan signalled it was enough. The third tank commander must have alerted the BMPs by radio. It was time to go.

Their eyes flashing with exultation, voices raised in self-congratulation, his force swarmed up around him. Smoke billowed from the hull of the beast below but the explosions had ceased and Khan was able to make himself heard. He ordered them straight up and over the ridge, to head for Do Rish. Every man for himself. Feizl would cover them until . . .

The man nearest him sank to his knees. He rolled over on to his back and slid head first down the rocks. Someone just managed to grab his ankles before he fell to the road.

Khan and the others stared down at him and then around, uncomprehendingly. A weapon clattered, then another, as two more men prostrated themselves quite slowly. What was happening?

Suddenly his force was sinking to the ground all around him. He saw Fareed shaking his head, striving to get his assault rifle up, as if to fight off an invisible foe. Instead he sat down suddenly and foolishly, then keeled over backwards.

Khan felt his own senses start to swim.

'Master!' Takredi's face loomed close. The giant caught him under the arms as he reeled. 'There are devils! This place is haunted!' And with that Takredi tucked him under one arm and started to lug him to safety. The rocks streamed past, misting before his eyes, then swung up and hit him as Takredi let go of him and subsided to all fours. Khan felt no pain, just a great weariness, and faint amusement to see Takredi crawling about like a drunken bear.

But with a stupendous effort, the giant heaved himself to his feet. He groped for Khan's limbs, got hold of an arm and pulled it over his shoulder. With his master's feet dragging like a rag doll, he hauled him away up the hillside, now pausing to spread his legs against the whirling in his head, now staggering on, lungs heaving, breath sawing, his progress becoming slower and slower.

Finally he came to a halt, head back, eyes sightless, mouth agape. Khan slid from his grasp and fell in a huddle. Takredi flexed his huge muscles as if to fight physically what was happening inside him. He reached down once more to take hold of his master. A great expiring sound, like the last groan of a felled tree, came from his throat. He pitched forward . . . and lay still.

The hillside above the defile was like a killing ground. The entire rebel force lay sprawled across the rocks and each other in attitudes of death.

The bluish fog issuing from the turretless tank swirled up dreamily around them, like steam from a witch's cauldron.

9

Perhaps it had once been the residence of a wealthy merchant. Certainly its interior appointments were grand, if on a bijou scale. Filigree arches encompassed a central space with a fountain – silent now, to save electricity – where coloured bulbs illuminated the water, conjuring exotic silhouettes from the plastic ferns and lily-pads.

Under the arches were alcoves containing divans lush with rugs and cushions. On the dais once designed to accommodate the players of stringed instruments, was a record-player and amplifier, the speakers cunningly concealed behind the Baluchi tambourines that decorated the carpet-hung walls. Their stretched and painted skins added reverberance to the hard-rock music that thudded deafeningly from them.

Paying scant attention to the incessant beat, eight girls lounged in one of the niches around a board game, gossiping and eating sweetmeats, with no regard at all for their already full figures. They wore a seductive mixture of Western and cheap Afghan finery, with built-in quick release. They were idle girls with doe eyes and soft pouting lips.

They cocked their ears to the sound of shooting bolts and voices. In rushed a little man with a beaked nose and thin moustache, wearing a white *karakul* cap and jacket.

'This way, my flowers.' His eloquent hands drew them in like a hypnotist – six more girls, cleanly dressed for the occasion, kohl-rimmed eyes agog.

They were met by the proprietress, a ship of a woman in a sail of glistening damask, amulets and necklets and rings winking from the folds of her flesh.

'Show your faces, my pretties.' The little man fussed round his wards, flipping aside their head-dresses and veils to expose youthful features, flawed only by here a wandering eye, there a cheek vaccination, and overall a certain dullness of wit. He turned to the woman.

'Here they are, Madame Geneifa, Soul of your Mother – as ordered.'

The house girls had turned to watch, giggling and nudging each other. By a mere glance, Madame Geneifa cast upon them and their thumping music a spell of instant silence. The ship sailed slowly past the country cousins, looking them up and down, peering especially at their lips. When satisfied that they bore no visible sores, she said: 'Strip.'

The order was greeted blankly. Their mothers would not have commanded it. In their villages, a doctor needing to make a physical examination of one of them would have had to do so by proxy, through one of the family. That they were whores was irrelevant.

'Come along, come along.' Madame Geneifa stamped her foot impatiently. 'You are in the big city now. None of this provincial nonsense. There's a war on and you are front-line soldiers!'

The response was hardly soldierly, but presently their bodies were begrudgingly, even fearfully uncovered.

'Right now. Legs apart and open yourselves.'

This seemed to come more easily to them, and Madame Geneifa passed again along the line, peering now at their thighs and sexual parts. Two showed first-stage ulceration of the vulva, one the remaining blemish of same. The other three had second-stage rashes about their thighs.

Madame Geneifa straightened with a grunt.

'You are satisfied, Soul of your Mother?' the agent enquired, one hand mating on the back of the other.

She said, 'Passably,' though in fact she was delighted. His selection had been, as ever, unerring. How did the little rat *diagnose* them? was what she wanted to know. Not by getting them to undress, that was obvious. And not by fornication, of that she was sure, because all were in the highly contagious stages of syphilis.

She told the girls to get dressed, which they did hastily, pink from embarrassment.

'Now these are your duties.' Madame Geneifa paced the tiled floor like a general. 'You will walk the bazaar and have intercourse with the Russian soldiery – in alleyways, vehicles, where you will – but on no account will you ever return to this address. Is that clear?'

She gave the agent a little money for them, to tide them over till they got started. One asked to use the toilet and was refused. Madame Geneifa's own live-in girls were clean, and the last thing she wanted was for the Soviet army doctors to close down the House With No Doors. Should that disaster occur, the Lily would have her head.

'Your receipt,' the agent murmured, handing her a slip of paper.

She glanced at it and raised an eyebrow. Folding it, she posted it in the heaving gorge of her cleavage.

When the agent and new recruits had departed she went to her office, locked the door and translated what was written on the paper into classical Arabic. It was the scholarly version of her own mother tongue, and as remote from the disciplines of the GRU and KGB local monitoring staffs as any code.

On the hour, she unlocked a drawer in her commodious and deceptive desk and tapped the message out on a Morse key.

The tiny impulses passed up and along a cable which followed the rooftops to join a power-line crossing the street to the minaret of the nearest mosque; up, then, inside the tower to an internal aerial and thence away, across valley and mountain, desert and snows . . .

A spatulate thumb touched the pressel switch of the big new Japanese transmitter-receiver. The static died in the headphones and they were laid aside. It took the operator but a moment to interpret the classical Arabic, for was it not the language in which the Koran originated, and was he not a learned priest? He rose and glided along the ancient hall, to a low, bare room where seven men sat at a slate table. Before them were spread maps and writings, an abacus and a great leather-bound copy of the Koran.

The operator spoke his message, his breath white at this high altitude. Two of them got up, one tall and powerfully built. A third followed suit. His beard was chased with grey, his turban and robes black, his posture like a ramrod. It was Abdalis.

'Let me be the one to convey the message,' he said.

No objection was raised. The three passed along into a stone antechamber. There were braziers on the wall, not yet lit. They stepped out of their shoes – Abdalis grudgingly – on to the cold flagstones.

The powerfully built one stood before a curtained doorway.

'Does it please the Soul of Aminah that we enter?' he enquired in the voice of the mosque.

There was silence, then a voice groaned uneasily, as if to itself, 'Does the wind speak words? Have I not enough to haunt me?'

'It is I, Dhost,' the mullah said more loudly. 'We bring a message.'

'Dhost!' screeched the voice. 'Are you with message as I am with child? Does it crave food and drink in a belly empty from fasting?'

The mullah had no answer to this.

'Give your message birth, Dhost,' the voice said wearily. 'But pray that it please me.'

Dhost hesitated. Abdalis spoke out. 'May we enter?'

Hearing who it was, the voice changed. 'Come like a dog to the foot that kicks you, have you? Then come, dog, if you must.'

The mullahs trooped into near darkness. An incense burner glowed on a low surface, its perforated light conjuring dim shapes. If there were windows they were covered. The eye had to win each object from the gloom. Stone rang but hangings deadened. Curtains? A dais? On it, a softness of cushions. And something else. A pyramid of blackness, darker than shadow, that the senses gradually imbued with human shape.

The mullahs planted their feet gratefully on a rush mat and bowed their heads, except Abdalis, who maintained a defiant manner.

The pyramid did not move. It was a *chaderi*, enveloping all of a figure seated cross-legged on the dais, leaving not even a hint of flesh.

'Well? I am waiting!'

Abdalis took a stride forward. 'Ghoram Khan and fifty of his men have been captured,' he announced, peering hard at the veiled face. They are held at the Kollola Poshta, awaiting interrogation.'

'Why do you stare so, dog? Stand back or I will lay on you a mounting torment!'

It took a strong man to resist such venom. Abdalis only just qualified. He stood conjuring his reply for a moment, then said cunningly, 'Is it an accident, O Great Soul, that the 74th *sura* of the Koran, from which those two last words were taken, continues: "This is no more than borrowed magic, the words of a mere mortal"?'

'In the *sura*,' hissed the figure, 'that question was asked by a sinner – a sinner who "pondered and schemed".' A finger shot out from the robe, directed at him. '"Confound him, how he schemed! Confound him, how he schemed!" cried Allah. "I will surely cast him into the fire of Hell!" As *you* will be cast, Abdalis, ere this sacred moon has waned. That is my prophecy.'

Even Abdalis flinched under this onslaught. Dhost, his face a thundercloud, grasped his shoulder and hauled him behind him.

'Forgive him in the light of the day's fasting, Soul of Aminah. Tell us how we should respond to the message.'

'Respond? Respond? When your sword falls into a cleft, do you need instruction how to redeem it? You send for ropes, for your lightest and most agile man. And you waste not a moment, lest the enemy be upon you! – *Not a moment*. Begone!'

As the mullahs turned from the room the figure screamed after them, 'And before he eats, put the dog through his beads, that he may cleanse his mouth and soul! Each day the same, till Allah's Judgement overtakes him.'

The curtain twitched three times and they were gone.

The figure quietened, rocking slowly back and forth, as if in thought.

Once it murmured, 'O, my beloved.'

Behind the coarse mesh of the veil, the eyes were troubled. Violet eyes.

10

MIKE MCCABE, ASC, had free-fallen into Afghanistan from five thousand metres, rescued his camera gear in its shock-proof boxes, buried the chutes under a heap of rocks and sat on a hilltop till dawn revealed a caravan of men and donkeys winding up the southern foothills of the Kuh-e-Baba mountains towards him.

The same patient plod, he noted, weapons across the shoulders of even the youngest. Typical purveyors of the world's most popular secondary occupation – justifiable homicide. If there was such a thing. And there wasn't, in McCabe's book.

He had chewed-looking brown hair, grey eyes with a friendly crinkle under them and a good mouth with a tuck in each corner. But the crinkle and tucks could vanish to a bleakness, and did so increasingly now, in his late thirties, as his love of mankind diminished.

They escorted him down to what appeared to be a nomad encampment surrounded by feeding flocks beside a fast-flowing river. But under the black tents, concealed from air observation by their very visibility, lived almost a hundred resistance fighters of the Afghan Islamic and Nationalistic Revolution Council – a large group with its headquarters in Peshawar, Pakistan. McCabe met the unit's leader, Bishr Khazim, and its doctor, Ayesha Salimar. A woman, by God! How the Islamic chauvinists were changing. Ayesha was the widow of Colonel Omar Salimar, who led his whole battalion to desertion from the Afghan army in February of 1981 and was killed in July by a KGB agent while obtaining a T-72 gunsight from a Russian sergeant in return for hashish. He was acquiring it for the CIA, with whom he had established a connection. Ayesha still maintained that connection. It was because of this, and her excellent English, that McCabe had been directed to her.

She was aged around twenty-eight, with a wealth of dark hair that cascaded forward from her forehead and then was tucked back, revealing a face of beauty, seriousness, intelligence, determination, and private grief. The nose was delicate, with nostrils slightly flared, the eyes large, the irises dark brown, the whites so white, so clear against her olive skin, that when she looked sideways McCabe couldn't take his gaze off them.

The rest of her was small-boned, spare, graceful, in modest khaki shirt and slacks. She wore a black band around her upper arm and a black scarf that she pulled up over her head when meeting Moslem strangers.

McCabe crinkled his eyes at her and swept a wary look round the camp.

'What happens when the planes come?'

'So far, they do not.' She had a quick, husky voice.

'But if?'

'We show no activity. Our herdsmen stay outside with the animals. We are looking like nomads. Why should they waste bullets?'

'Wasting bullets is what war's about.' McCabe rolled a cigarette between his fingers. He nodded. 'Just like to know the form.'

'You say "form"?' Yes. The form, for a stranger, is very important.' She darted a look at him and away.

'You speak incredible English.'

'Thank you.'

The sun was behind the fat-tailed sheep and lambs by the river. She watched them. She was nervous, conscious of his gaze on her.

'Whatever you are wanting to know you must ask,' she said suddenly.

'You're here as a doctor, right?'

'Also a fighter.' Her eyes lifted to a Kalashnikov hung on the ridgepole.

'How come you're not veiled?'

She smiled. 'It is not necessary. We are all one family here. I am their sister.'

'The men aren't shy to be tended by a woman?'

'Yes,' she admitted. 'They are all a little shy. It is nice. I scold them. I say, we are beginning a new world where men and women are more equal. They do not believe me. But it is nice.'

She sat reading a letter from her mother while he wolfed the bowl of *gaimac* and about a quart of green tea. She had apologized for not joining him, but this was the month of Ramadan; he knew what was Ramadan?

McCabe said he knew indeed. It was the month you got no work or sense out of anyone. They were all too shagged after the night's celebrations.

The heat smote the dark brown wool of the tent, but the flies were up, promoting a breeze. Silhouetted against the outer brilliance were sleeping forms as far as the eye could see. It looked like a rest camp, but he guessed it was either the effects of Ramadan or they operated by night only. But wherever the war was, wherever the Russian machine was pulverizing villages and people and driving three million of them into exile, it sure wasn't here.

Ayesha was blinking at the letter, as though she was thinking about something else. After a space she looked up.

'Are you well now?'

'What did they tell you?'

'Oh . . .' She shook her head, her eyes zigzagging. 'Simply that you have been in a lot of wars.'

'That I went nuts?'

She didn't understand what nuts was, so he explained.

'No, no.' Her startlement was genuine.

He passed her a pack of capsules. 'I'm on these. Says it all, huh?' He watched her open it and check the colour coding. 'I got blown up.'

'Just your head? No other damage?'

'You can give me a check-up if you like. *I'm* not shy.'

'You know that the mission will be very demanding?'

'Don't worry about it, Doc. I'm in the peak of middle age.'

She frowned. 'I'm not sure that I should go with you. Not because of these.' She handed the pills back. 'Simply I am needed here. And what you are here to film – may I be frank? – is almost impossible.'

'I thought you were going to say too dangerous.'

'It will only be dangerous if we *find* what we are looking for.'

'We?' He put out a hand but she moved her wrist back. 'Seriously, Doc – I *mean* seriously – this is no job for a woman.'

'If you want to unpersuade me—'

'Dissuade.'

'Then to say such things is not the way. It is like a challenge. I think at once, how will he manage without an interpreter?'

'I'll get by. I always have. Do they understand Arabic?'

'No.' She blinked at the ground for a moment. 'We will see. Bishr Khazim will hold a *jirgah*.'

'Get-together?'

'Yes. Your mission will be fully discussed. Then I will make up my mind.'

That night, when the feasting had ended, McCabe lay in his sleeping bag and listened to the camp dogs scrunching the bones, to the snores of those who hadn't gone on the harassing raid, to the rush-rushing of the river. The smell of it did fresh things to the air. It was a shot in the arm after the Mojave Desert, the terrible daytime heat, the strafing of the Ethiopian planes – Russian-piloted SUs. Only three weeks ago! It seemed like a century.

He examined his feelings about the mission. To define his attitudes on anything was becoming increasingly difficult as the years went by. Nothing was clear-cut any more. Not that it ever had been, just youth had made it appear so. In those early days he had set out confidently to say things on film that now seemed unworldly, to say the least. Serving up the horrors of war to the general public as a kind of aversion therapy had been one of them. He had genuinely believed that with his little aerosol he could spray a meaningful message on the living-room walls of the world.

Ah, love! How did the poem go? 'Ah Love! could thou and I with fate conspire/ To grasp this sorry Scheme of Things entire,/ Would we not shatter it to bits – and then/ Remould it nearer to the Heart's Desire?' Well, nothing wrong with ideals. You had to have some damn good reason for toting a freelance camera through Vietnam, Laos, Angola . . . Of course, he had remoulded nothing. The square-eyed public had simply gawked at their TV and wondered how in hell he had filmed them without getting his balls shot off. Since when, the world had become steadily a more, not less violent place. The industrial powers saw to that, with their supplies of killer weapons to primitives who, left to their own devices, could barely have put together a bow and arrow.

The super powers were the guilty ones, he had grown to realize. Yet they were also his market. How did a man of conscience come to terms with *that*? They paid him handsomely for his horrors, showered praise and awards on him. It was all one steaming great paradox. Sinister too. He could almost swear they were using him to provide a shop-window for their lethal wares!

So, once disenchanted, why had he kept going? Probably because there was nothing else he knew how to do quite so well. Certainly because, as the only son of an American publisher and an English actress, born in the USA, educated and domiciled in the UK, he had early come to regard himself as neither fish nor fowl, a loner – and there weren't that many lone occupations. Certainly not combining self-reliance, mortal danger and creativity, far from the urban sprawl and all its loathsome trivia. And, hell, though he had gone to war in the first place to register his protest, though he still abhorred it, he was hooked on it. That was the more honest truth.

All of which had nothing to do with his present mission. Or everything. How did he feel about it, was the question. The answer was, angry. At himself, for having suddenly ditched his independent status and taken on a commissioned assignment. All his working career he had gone where and when the spirit moved him. Maybe his instinct had preserved him. He could move with the fall of the cards, pull out if the signs weren't propitious . . .

That the bastards had propositioned him while in the throes of post-traumatic stress was no excuse. The fact remained that he had betrayed his most sacred principle for a mess of potage. And he was superstitious enough to see in that his possible epitaph.

The *jirgah*, as with all the group's daytime activities, was held under the sprawling flies of the tents. The squatting warriors craned their necks in curiosity and, presently, disbelief, as their leader made known to them the purpose of the visit of this man from *Englestan*. To have been dropped from an aircraft was a rare distinction, yet clearly the man himself was expendable, a pawn, for he did not strut his importance. His boots were worn, his camouflage jacket patched at the elbow, and he treated their leader as an equal, eye to eye, not gazing over his head. From the receptive way he sat, the soles of his feet drawn decently under him, he might almost have been one of them. They began to feel sorry for him.

McCabe had noticed they were almost all Pathans, though Bishr Khazim, surprisingly, was a Tajik – a wiry, swarthy ex-police officer with a left arm he had to move about with the other hand as though it didn't belong to him, and a racking cough from the black tobacco he chainsmoked. No sooner had he declared the *jirgah* in session than he beckoned a bearded fellow with piercing blue eyes to sit with them.

'This,' he told McCabe through Ayesha, 'is Wakir – our only man with experience that could be of use to you.' He turned to him, stifling the grunt of pain the movement caused him. 'Tell the *feranghi* where you are from.'

The man pointed south. 'From the village of Banu Kala, beyond the road to Kandahar.'

'Tell us what happened there, and when.'

'Last year, in the month of Jumada al-Ula, the *schurawi* came.'

'How did they come? Tell us the story.'

The man looked away, his blue eyes growing distant with memory, his lips stiffening. Ayesha translated in her husky voice.

'I was grazing my flock on the hillside above the village. It was late afternoon, the sun descending. Far away I saw two planes. They came slowly – not with the rush of planes that attack, but' – he hummed through his nose – 'of planes that observe. Such planes do not bear weapons. I watched them without concern.'

McCabe interrupted, twisting his finger in the air. 'They had propellers?'

The man confirmed that they had propellers.

'L-19s,' McCabe said aside to Ayesha. 'They sprayed chemicals?'

'They dropped dust.'

'What colour?'

The man had to think. 'First, the colour of half-ripe barley. As it fell on my village the people began behaving strangely.

Among them I saw my wife and youngest son, wandering stiffly as dolls. They fell down, pulling at their mouths as if to open them. I ran down the hillside towards them, to see vomit coming from betweeen their teeth and down their noses. All seemed afflicted the same way. But before I could reach them there was an explosion above. The second plane had fired a rocket. It burst above the ground, leaving the air red like sunset. I saw that it was more dust and turned and ran back up the hill. I began firing my rifle at the planes, but soon they were too far away. I watched the dust settle. It tinted everything. My family and friends were jumping on the ground, as the chicken jumps when headless. Now as the dust settled they began to bleed, not slowly as from a wound, but the blood bursting from their bodies as if they were being crushed by unseen boulders. The blood formed in pools round each, spreading, joining, till my whole village was stained with crimson shadows. I could hear choking and crying and, though my heart ached to go amongst them, my head warned me that it would be useless, that someone must live to tell others of this horror – also to carry the torch of vengeance!

'Alas my people took a long time to die. Their agony was pitiful. The stench of their waste, Allah forgive me, reached me where I stood. As the sun bent its face towards the mountains the bodies of the dead began to turn black.'

The man lowered his head between his knees, adding brokenly, 'I wept then. Not so much for their deaths, for Allah bequeaths death to all of us, but for the shameful manner in which the *schurawi* forced them to die!' He lifted his head and in a loud voice cried, 'For this I pledged my rifle and my loyalty to you, my brothers, and have killed already four *schurawi* with bullet and grenade, and one prisoner with my bare hands! And I vow, *inshallah*, that I will kill more, and more!' He came to his feet shouting, '*More!*'

The others seized on it, overacting to impress the stranger, leaping up, faces contorted. In moments the gathering was in an uproar.

Bishr Khazim did not intervene. He smoked, even beating time with his good fist as the shouts compounded into a chant.

The incredible whites of Ayesha's eyes flashed as she glanced towards McCabe.

McCabe did not respond. He watched, as from an island.

Presently, when the noise had abated, she leaned towards him.

'Did you know about the dust?'

He nodded moodily. 'It's known as T-2. "Yellow rain".'

For an instant he relived the NATO briefing in London, the sobering statistics of the Soviet chemical capability, the ruddy features of Colonel Schuster as, carefully expressionless, he demonstrated the horror-movie protection mask, suit, gloves, boots that were to be issued to him.

The men were murmuring amongst themselves. Ayesha inclined an ear for a moment.

'Forgive me. They are asking why you have undertaken such a thing – to risk your life in so horrible a way?'

McCabe shrugged and shook his head.

She persisted, the question this time her own. 'Is it from anger at what they do to us?'

'Sorry to disappoint you but emotional involvement isn't part of my game. Kills objectivity.'

'Then—'

'A camera's not a gun, sweetheart. It's for opening eyes, not shutting them.'

He watched her try to fathom that one. 'Now ask Wakir why he thinks his particular village was picked as a chemical target. I mean, it doesn't happen every day, right?'

'No. We think they are very careful to keep what they do secret,' Ayesha said bitterly.

'So let's try to figure it out. I'll get my map.'

But Bishr Khazim had one, dog-eared to the point of distintegration. He opened it gingerly, one-handed, on the ground. Smoking and coughing, he indicated a spot two hundred kilometres south-west of Kabul.

'We are here. Here is the Kabul–Kandahar road.' He ran his finger down the curve of it to a point sixty kilometres short of Kandahar and then off the road southwards. His yellowed fingernail cut a niche midway between the road and the Pakistani frontier. 'Here is Banu Kala.'

McCabe ran a practised eye over the contours. The village occupied a depression on top of an island-like feature surrounded by undulating, probably arid country meshed with small roads.

'First, what did they do up there – were they farmers?'

Wakir answered. 'Farmers, yes. And fighters, when the call came.'

'Call?'

'From Abu Haroun, the leader of our group.'

So they weren't quite the innocent victims Wakir had implied. McCabe had suspected as much. 'Then what?'

'All from the neighbourhood would assemble in Banu Kala. We would plan – we would march – we would strike!'

'Strike where?'

'At this season, while the snow-water is strong – at the bridges.'

'Whereabouts? Show me.'

Khazim forestalled his man, rubbing his finger along the highway east of Kandahar. 'While the *schurawi* were mending one bridge they would blow up another, causing repeated delays to military traffic and supplies. That is the reason you seek – why Banu Kala was so exterminated.'

McCabe cocked a brow at Ayesha. 'Is he suggesting the Russians resorted to chemicals out of revenge?'

'No. Their mountain, he says, was too steep for tanks, and its crest had a natural fortification, providing shelter against gunships.'

McCabe looked at Wakir. 'So the Russians tried conventional attack first?'

Wakir said they hadn't.

'Then how did they know the place was attack-proof?'

Khazim was clearly not interested in how. He had supplied the explanation. He lit a cigarette from the last stub and looked away through the smoke.

McCabe studied the map again.

'Attack-proof? was nonsense anyway. An air strike followed by a company of paratroops . . . And, hell, with all those roads, they could have ringed the place with every deep-penetration firework in the book. No, they had resorted to chemicals for some other reason. Maybe political. Or simply topographical. He half-closed his eyes.

Up through the blur emerged two salient features – the proximity of the Pakistan frontier and the web of small roads, more here than almost anywhere on the map – linking the numerous villages, obviously. He traced a few of them and found that a fair proportion extended to and across the frontier into the Pakistan province of Baluchistan. Old caravan roads, possibly. He counted seven devious but distinct routes starting in and around Kandahar and ending up in the Baluchi city of Quetta. Banu Kala stood within striking distance of them all!

He looked up slowly.

'Ask him, how's the Baluchi situation these days? They still agitating for independence?'

Khazim snorted. 'It is all they do. If they want freedom from Zia they must fight for it, like men.' But the unexpected question had aroused his curiosity. 'Ask what is in his mind.'

The question, McCabe said, is 'What's in the Russian mind?'

'Concerning the Baluchis? They support them.'

'How far?'

'They train their revolutionary leaders.'

'Suppose the Baluchis were actually to rebel – how far then?

Khazim replied slowly, 'He is asking if they would aid them militarily?' He gave it a thought. 'Who can tell? But he is asking more than that. Much more. He is saying that in such an event Kandahar would become their prime base and all that lies between it and the frontier would be strategic.'

'Right on.' Pretty sharp, McCabe thought, for a policeman. 'It would explain Banu Kala, tell him. Why no noisy military attack. They wanted no attention drawn to the area. So they just struck it quietly off the map.'

Ayesha stared at him for a fraction before relaying this.

The deep lines of Khazim's face twisted into an expression of almost comical wryness.

'Tell our friend he is like an Afghan. He builds a whole mountain of conjecture, then points to it as God's truth.'

Ayesha chuckled dutifully as she translated, but her manner was thoughtful.

To show there was no disrespect, Khazim added, 'But suppose that were the explanation, what then?'

'I'd want to know if there were any other such strongholds left in those hills. Stubborn pockets that could qualify for the same treatment. If there were, that's where I'd make for.'

Apppreciation dawned on the leader's face, though plainly he considered his reasoning unnecessarily inventive. He glanced at Wakir questioningly. Wakir shook his head. He had no means, he said, of knowing the situation there now. Khazim frowned at the tip of his cigarette for a long moment.

Ayesha, however, gave McCabe a reassuring smile.

'We will find out,' she said.

11

FOR SOME reason Yakushev had changed into his uniform before driving up to the Kollola Poshta. His staff officers had looked at him differently this morning, as though his number had come up in a lottery. In the streets, too, there was an atmosphere. People just standing in small groups. The mosques were lit up with millions of electric bulbs for Ramadan, but the vibes around town were not festive. How word of Khan's capture had got out he could not imagine, but there seemed no doubt that it had.

He supposed he should have been full of vengeful anticipation. Instead he felt vaguely uneasy. Yakushev mistrusted handouts. He had the nagging feeling that there was a bottom line to this fortuitous gift that, at the last moment, would rob him of his long-awaited satisfaction.

Though ten per cent of all Soviet tank, artillery and mortar ammunition was charged with chemicals, their use was controlled by the Ministry of Defence through Military District, and their issue to units in the field limited accordingly. They were stored on all the bases, of course, but there was little sense in wasting valuable space in, say, tank ammunition racks, by carrying a weapon so infrequently employed.

Blue-X, however, as opposed to T-2, was a clean weapon – one might almost say, benign. It rendered the enemy unconscious for up to twelve hours, and with no apparent after-effects. In dealing with concentrated groups, in zero wind conditions, it had a practical application, with minimal human rights comeback. Hence two shells per tank platoon – to be carried in the commander's own tank – had become routine ordnance. And it was into this low statistic noose that Khan had unwittingly placed his head.

They were coming up to the fort now. Its battered towers

and ramparts loomed in the morning sunlight. The feeling of height, of being on an island, the view across the city magnificent.

His driver found a slot between the parked army transport, dislodging a ragged fellow selling tea from a samovar on a barrow. A blast of the horn barely shifted his customers. Like the groups in town, they just stood. Dark, unreadable eyes watched Yakushev alight and stride towards the entrance.

Stepping in through the postern, he stabbed his signature in the guard commander's book and ducked up narrow curving steps to the gallery that encircled the big inner yard.

The shadow of a tower with a machine-gunner on top slanted against a splash of sunlight on the far wall. All below was in shadow. Six towers, six machine-guns covered the fifty-odd prisoners squatting down on the cobbles. Recent intakes were brought here for questioning before being sent to the camps. Yakushev did not allow his eye to linger and seek out anyone he recognized. The gift was too precious to unwrap yet.

Commandant Yenkov of the GRU POW Division lifted his ample bottom off his chair as Yakushev entered the tower office.

'Comrade Andrei Pavlovich, come in, come in!'

He was bald, straight as a Prussian, but an ineffectual chin explained his posting to this cul-de-sac. With him were interrogators Major Tablian, looking like a little Turkoman bushy-haired cut-throat, Captain Suchev of the huge eyebrows, Captain Morianov, all Stalin moustache and shining glasses, and big, flat-faced Rahman Tul, the Azerbaijani.

'How is he?' Yakushev scanned their faces to detect the first shadow that would mar the day. But all was smiles.

'Fully conscious, has been for hours,' Yenkov said bluffly.

'In passable shape?'

'First-class, comrade. Not a mark on him.'

'Yet,' someone added, and got a titter.

'And your security this time?'

Yenkov's expression lost some of its ebullience. 'I separated him from his men. Put him down in the cells. Non-stop surveillance. Anything he could hurt himself with removed.'

'Is he shackled?' Yakushev had it in for the man, after the tourniquet business.

'Why, no.'

'He could dash his brains out. I want him secured in such a way as to make that impossible.'

Yenkov muttered, 'Very well,' and reached for the telephone.

'Not now – it's too late. After his first interrogation. But don't hang up. There's the beginning of a crowd outside. I want them cleared. Put a roadblock with sentries on the approach road.'

Yenkov gave him a sulky look and spoke into the instrument. Yakushev turned to Tablian and asked for the full count of prisoners.

'Fifty-three.'

'Including the giant?'

'He's there.'

'Not loose, I hope?'

Tablian's smile and reassuring gesture showed that he thought the colonel was being over-twitchy. 'The combat troops had him trussed like a chicken when they delivered him. We've kept him that way.'

Yakushev's look of relief was short-lived. He turned and moved to the arrow-slit window, suddenly realizing that Khan must have learned a lot about him through Pola – their marital rift, his impotence, the reason. It could all – plus the fact that the Afghan had been his wife's lover – be bared by this interrogation.

'Smoke, Colonel?' Tablian tapped his arm with a packet of Winstons. When Yakushev refused, he lit one himself, with a sly glance from under his lids. 'Tell me, what do we want from Khan before we put him against a wall? Just a general debriefing or something specific?'

'Specific.' Yakushev fastened on it. Of course. That was his solution. They wanted, he said, the location of the rest of Khan's group and his sources of information.

'For the Rossakov assassination?'

'All his recent actions. I'll break it down on paper before we start.'

'We?'

'I'll be with you on this one.'

'Good, Colonel. We'll crack him together.'

Suchev said dubiously, 'Have you seen him? He's a cut above the usual *mujahed*.'

'We can go straight to sodium pentothal,' Tablian suggested.

Yakushev suppressed a start. Here was another pitfall – Khan spilling his guts at random.

He said, 'No drugs.'

The team froze. Morianov's glasses flashed.

'Colonel, you get nothing from a Pathan without drugs, you know that.'

'Well, that's how I want it.' Yakushev looked round at each of them pointedly. 'I want him in full command of his faculties.'

He watched them infer his meaning. An uneasy breeze seemed to stir through them. Feet shifted. GRU interrogators were firstly linguists. Trained at the Military Institute of Foreign Languages, their education also included ethnic psychology and the use of mind-altering drugs. Physical torture had been at the very bottom of their syllabus, regarded as retrograde and Tchekist.

Torture, said the institute, was messy. It degraded not only the subject but the interrogator and should be used, therefore, only when scientific methods were not to hand.

And they were to hand, as Tablian reiterated.

Yakushev remained emphatic, as he outlined his alternative. He could see they were strongly opposed to it, that at best they considered it a long, crude haul.

He made it clear that a hypodermic followed by a bullet was tantamount to an act of clemency.

Yes, they could see that. Nevertheless, attrition was not their job. And what would happen if Khan did not respond as the colonel anticipated?

'Then we switch,' Yakushev had to concede, 'to your method. Drugs.'

'With consequent loss of face,' Tablian pointed out, 'which will strengthen his resistance.'

'So my order and your brief,' Yakushev's tone brooked no further protest, 'is to make sure it doesn't come to that!'

They fastened Khan's wrists behind him and propelled him roughly from the cell, up darkened steps that stank of urine, through more enclosed darkness relieved by a naked bulb, into a startingly white room lit by fluorescent tubing. It had been whitewashed from floor to vaulted roof. He was thrust into a heavy chair in front of a table and his wrists untied and clamped to the arms. Two soldiers remained to guard him. The rest withdrew.

Apart from dryness in his mouth and heaviness in his limbs, Khan felt normal. In his head, though, there was a worrying darkness. He knew neither where he was nor what had happened to him, whether his men were alive or dead, if it was day or night, yesterday or tomorrow.

The soldiers pointed their guns like overgrown children. The room had a curious, evil smell. There were cabinets filled with what looked like medicines, and metal boxes with dials. One had a light that flickered. He noted with instinctive uneasiness that the stonework surrounding the door had been pierced to permit the entry of a thick electric cable. This went to a control panel on the wall. Out of the panel came smaller wires that served the lamps, of which there were several on metal stands, and the boxes, and the other table with straps and terminals. Or was it a bed?

He was afraid, but he was not fear's victim. More its challenger. To resist the *schurawi* utterly and in all ways was the aim of his every breath. To hurt them with his own pain, by resisting it, would be a victory worth two in the field. That he could do it, he had no doubt. Even here, alone and caught in the sterile world of the godless, he could do it.

He went away from the evil room into his mind in search of strength.

First Pola, then Layla met him. And there played his children, with quick glances to see if he was watching. His father stood, luminous, in a sunlit wheatfield. Old friends came near, their eyes creased in trust and pleasure. 'Are you harmonious?' Shah's robustness galloped beneath him. His dogs sped like arrows. His river sang. From these things that had nurtured him, he fed now.

The chair scraped opposite him as Yakushev settled himself, ostentatiously businesslike, elbows thudding on to the table, hands interlocking. The soldiers were going. The door slammed shut. They were alone.

At first, Khan did not recognize him. When he did, it came as a shock – but, curiously, not an unwelcome one. A known face, however hostile, was preferable to an unknown in these circumstances.

He looked older, Khan thought. Closer to the edge of some inner precipice.

'Cigarette?' It was a token offer, an excuse to take one himself, light it, break the deadlock of their gaze. Yakushev blew out smoke.

'How do you feel after your . . . ?' He didn't expect an answer. Just another token. Feeling his way to a start. This urbanity would have a purpose.

After a short pause Yakushev said, 'You've had a good run, I won't deny. Due in part to our own negligence, I won't deny that either. But I was close to you that night, you know, as you jumped from the mosque. If I'd had my gun your luck would have ended there.'

He took a puff of the cigarette, eyeing Khan severely. 'I won't dwell on the inconvenience you've caused us in the past eight months. It has been considerable. Yet quite pointless. We're still here, and will remain. Regardless of anything you or your friends get up to.'

He paused again to survey his prisoner. Khan remained expressionless.

'You doubt that? Listen, I will explain something. We are committed – pledged, you understand – to certain things that make our withdrawal impossible. I will confide in you. Among them is your gas. You know in north Afghanistan there is gas?'

Khan didn't. He knew about the jade and precious minerals they were taking, but not about the gas.

'We are piping it to our own country,' Yakushev went on, 'to replace our own from Siberia that we are selling to Western Europe. Much money has been spent to make that possible. Rather than see that money wasted, we will kill every reactionary, raze every village and drive their occupants into exile, till only those who support communism remain. Then the country will be run by the people for the people – and not just the few, as in the feudal past.' Yakushev added, 'You could have shared in that.'

He broke off and balanced his lighter on the table. He looked up sidelong. 'Perhaps you still could.'

He waited for Khan to respond.

Khan thought, after all the blows I've struck against his people and the regime? Does he think I'm a fool?

'Are you interested to know how?'

Khan gazed past him.

Yakushev was unperturbed. 'If you talk to me, man to man, answer my questions straight – no lies – it is possible – I say, *possible* – that I can save your life.'

Khan shifted his gaze to his fists and balled them.

Yakushev sighed. His voice took on almost an injured tone.

'Deep down we are reasonable men, surely? We both loved the same woman. It seems incredible that we cannot arrive at some other mutuality.' He leaned forward, blinking earnestly. 'Must every page in the history of the relations between our two countries be written in blood?'

Yakushev stood with his back to Khan, fiddling with one of the machines. He had changed the subject a number of times – expressing grudging admiration at the shooting of Rossakov and wonder as to how it had been achieved. He had talked of the truce with Massoud in the Panjshir, said that the other leaders were becoming disenchanted, that a united resistance was a myth fostered by the West, who pretended sympathy but declined to help for fear of encouraging the Islamic revolution, which threatened their oil supplies. He paused frequently for Khan to comment, but he would not be drawn.

Khan was not interested in Soviet strategy, only in Yakushev's. He could not fathom it. So he just waited.

Now, apropos of nothing, Yakushev said quietly, 'Were you with her when she died?'

Khan did not bother to mask his surprise, as the Russian's back was still turned.

'At least you can tell me that,' Yakushev murmured. 'How it happened.'

Khan hesitated, wondering if this was a trap. He decided he didn't care if it was. It was his first chance to hit back. His voice seemed to jolt from the vaulted roof.

'She was murdered! Defiled first by many Mongols – Russian Mongols – then murdered!'

He wanted to see Yakushev reel, but the Russian stood quite still.

'They would not do that. Their officers would not have allowed it.' Yakushev turned. 'I asked you, man to man, for the truth and you lie to me.'

'Why do you think we killed them in the Salang Tunnel?' Khan growled. 'A dangerous operation costing much time and several lives. They defiled all our women, then killed them and our children.'

'Lies! Propaganda!' Yakushev strode to him, but his face was white.

'You train your army as beasts and send them among us. Only when they kill your own wife do you show concern.'

'Pathans invent and then believe – it is well known. Your imaginings feed the Western press. You—' Yakushev broke off, perhaps suddenly conscious that he was wasting rhetoric on a doomed man. 'Even suppose it were true,' he changed tack completely, 'she had her choice. She chose to stay with you. I warned her of the danger. But no, she stayed.'

The Russian was absolving himself now, Khan thought. The blow had hurt him all right. He let him simmer.

'Well, I'll tell you some truth,' Yakushev said through his teeth. 'I loved her. And the thought of you and her turns my *gut*: you will die for it. After I've taken what I want from you, you'll be shot!'

Khan regarded him impassively. Here it was. He had brought it to a head himself, and so, in a way, gained the upper hand. Was it not up to him the way the interrogation went? He could make it easier on himself and them, or hard – whichever *he* wished.

Why should he spare them?

Absurdly young Russian soldiers erected the retractable barbed wire barricade, while their sergeant herded the loiterers back along the fort approach road with his Kalashnikov.

The Afghans, some of them black-marketeers, pockets abulge with packs of American cigarettes, others with plugs of hashish wound under their headcloths, moved away – and edged back the moment the NCO's back was turned. The ragged fellow selling *chai* re-established his barrow close enough to the barrier for his small boy assistant to ply the sentries with refreshment. He was a familiar sight outside

Kollola Poshta and the sergeant did not force him further back than was necessary.

He had a cheerful villain's face, with meeting brows. His clothing, though frayed by much beating against river stones, was spotless, as befitted his trade. He was known as Masr.

Masr's home was in the village that clung to this hill overlooking Kabul. It was an old village, perhaps older than the city itself, and as a boy he had collected arrowheads and musket balls from around the foundations of the fort and sold them to tourists. He knew more about the Kollola topographically than even the curator of the museum. And, after adopting this pitch four months ago, he knew as much about its military comings and goings as the commandant.

He knew now, from the number of ten-ton lorries remaining parked outside, that yesterday's unprecedented intake of rebel prisoners was still on the premises. He had heard from the local mullah who their leader was and, for two ounces of hashish, had coaxed his whereabouts in the building from one of the guards.

Though he gained little financially from these observations, it was reward enough to receive the solemn reassurance of the mullah that he was helping to fulfil God's scriptures.

The lights were a barrage of brilliance. They burned through Khan's lids as through paper, their heat enormous. There was movement around him, a dragging sound, the scuff of army boots, grunting. Though curious as to what was happening, Khan could not open his eyes against the light.

There was talk – short, anxious questions, reassuring answers, all in Russian. The boots began to shuffle away. The room, drained of most of its human content, became ominously silent.

Khan kept tight rein on his imagination and waited. So huge was his resolve, there was no room left for fear. He held his head proudly erect.

The lights swung to one side. It was not they that moved, but himself, as unseen hands shifted his chair. After a moment, in the lesser glare, he opened his eyes. They remained blind for some moments. Then Yakushev grew on his retina, to his left now, still seated at the table. Beyond him stood two men in white coats over army shirts and trousers – one small and bushy-haired, the other hulking, with the round head of an Asiatic. Within the margin of the light he glimpsed two more.

'The major has something to show you,' Yakushev said, raising his hand towards the small man, as a singer might divert applause to his musicians.

Tablian held up an iron rod. One end was slightly bulbous, from the other issued a stout flex. He plugged the flex into the control panel and turned a calibrated knob in the handle. Yakushev tapped out a cigarette.

Khan stared into the distance.

After a while, he noticed that the bulbous end of the metal was turning red. Yakushev leaned over and used it to light his cigarette.

Khan affected to see nothing.

Slowly the metal passed through white heat to incandescence. Then the major came forward, holding it in Khan's line of sight. At a metre's distance its heat reached his skin. At half a metre, it was scorching. Tablian brandished it tauntingly closer to his face.

Though it taxed his willpower, Khan remained rigid, his grip crushing the arms of his chair. The moisture in his eyes evaporated, forcing them shut. The incandescence glared through his lids. With a light flick, Tablian dabbed him on the tip of the nose with it.

The flesh ignited. Pain exploded in Khan's membranes. Water burst from his eyes. The flame went out and smoke arose. Mucus began to pour from his nostrils and eyes like water from a tap. The agony went on, though the iron had retracted. Twisting its thermostat to zero, Tablian plunged it, shushing and bubbling, in a bucket of water. The team watched Khan's response closely.

Nothing. He had neither recoiled nor uttered a sound.

'Now listen to me,' said Yakushev. 'That was nothing. A mere demonstration. You know what I want – straight answers to straight questions.' He peered. 'Can you hear me?' He waited.

He signalled Suchev and Morianov. They turned Khan's chair to face him.

'Answer me, Khan, answer me. You want us to proceed with the iron or shall we talk?'

Khan gradually mastered the continuing pain. He opened streaming eyes. He snorted mucus and spat.

'Do what you like with me,' he said thickly. 'And be damned.'

'With *you*?' Yakushev laughed. 'So that you can play hero?' He gave the lamp rig a kick. It spun on its castors to illuminate the far end of the room. The men behind Khan twisted his chair now so that he faced the 'bed'.

On it, he saw for the first time that spreadeagled, face down and naked, his limbs and body strapped beyond possibility of movement, was Takredi!

It was a terrible shock. Khan thought at first that his faithful friend was dead. Then he saw he was breathing.

Yakushev watched him keenly. Rahman Tul was filling a hypodermic from one of the bottles in the cabinet.

'Now give me your attention.' Yakushev flipped open a memo pad.

This changed everything. The whole edifice of resistance Khan had built to his own pain had been shrewdly bypassed. He watched the Azerbaijani jab the needle in Takredi's neck and slowly empty it. Did it contain poison? What—

'Your attention!' Yakushev snapped.

Khan's chair was jerked round again to the table. Yakushev read aloud his first question. Khan scarcely heard him for the thudding of his pulses. His mouth had gone like chalk. Yakushev repeated his words, hammering their meaning at him. The bulk of his force – he wanted him to betray where they were located. Khan's gaze kept returning to Takredi. He saw that his eyelids had begun to flutter, his muscles to twitch.

'Think, damn you!' Yakushev kicked him on the knee. 'You can save him. A straight answer. Where are they? Their location.'

Set the gunships on them to save the agonies of one man? How could he do that? The small officer was taking the iron from the bucket and moving to the torture table. The Asiatic was slapping Takredi fully awake. The giant's eyes came open. He stared full at Khan. He tried to jerk up but found he was powerless. A groaning bellow began and died, as awareness came to him.

'Look at me!' Yakushev kept hustling. 'Listen. You have no

choice. Just tell me where they are. And hurry – we've a lot to get through.'

They were trying to confuse him. Khan sat doggedly, filled with dread but showing nothing.

Yakushev stabbed an exasperated finger towards Tablian. The Turkoman held up the iron, as a conjurer might, to make Khan fully understand what he was about to do. Rahman Tul dragged Takredi's buttocks apart. Tablian inserted the iron and thrust it up his rectum.

Every eye then focused on Khan.

'The iron is cold,' Tablian explained. 'But you've seen how quickly it heats. It consumes from within. The agony is unique. The incandescence finds a new area of pain with every centimetre of increased penetration. But not all at once. With careful control of this knob, your man can be made to suffer for . . .'

'As long as you resist,' Yakushev finished the sentence. 'But talking then, of course, will be too late to save him. To save his life, you must talk now.' The notebook in his hand was shaking. He put it down. He peered at Khan to see if he had got the message.

When Khan still did not respond he glanced uncertainly at Tablian. 'Do you think he's still with us?' His gaze jerked to the two behind the chair. 'Wake him up. I think he's in shock.'

Suchev shook Khan by the shoulders. Morianov got the bucket of water and emptied it over his head.

Khan emerged from the deluge motionless.

Suchev tested the pulse in his neck. His eyes narrowed behind his glasses. 'High but steady. Keep going, Colonel.'

'I'll give you the first question again.' Yakushev's delivery seemed to be losing confidence. He cleared his throat, and waited. The room went quiet.

Khan's lips trembled under the dagger moustache. But it was another voice that spoke.

'Have strength, Master!' Takredi wheezed urgently. 'Don't tell them. See them dead!'

Rahman Tul took a stride and struck him. The giant, in rage, exerted his mighty strength. Straps and structure started to creak.

Khan's lips had drawn tight again. His moment of weakness had passed. Yakushev watched the straps anxiously for an instant, but they remained firmly anchored. He snapped at Tablian, 'Get ready,' then leaned across the table.

'This is your last chance,' he told Khan. 'Your last chance. After that . . .'

Khan believed him. But in the tone of the Russian's voice he glimpsed his goal – and took strength. Searching Takredi's eyes, he saw in them the same implacable resolve as his own. Every muscle in the giant's body was clenched. The knuckles of one balled fist showed greenish white. He was ready.

Khan returned his gaze to Yakushev. He breathed deeply and strained towards Yakushev, as if to speak. Snorting more running mucus from his nose, he spat full in the Russian's face.

Yakushev was too incredulous even to recoil. How could he have so miscalculated? He had exhausted the potential of this ploy, now he must retract. But to do so would harden Khan's resistance, as Tablian had pointed out in the office. He had questions about the Lily. Vital questions. The answers were all but in his grasp. A twist of the thermostat, he was certain, and they would be his. He could not let himself be beaten. He told Tablian:

'Do it.'

Tablian did not move. A protest seemed to begin in his throat. It was stillborn. He shook his head.

Yakushev's hand groped in cold fury towards his gun. He remembered he wasn't wearing it. He took a pace towards his inquisitor, his face working.

'Do it, I say – *do it*. It is an order.'

Tablian still did not move. Then suddenly, afraid of the repercussions, he relented. He gave the thermostat a twist.

And it began.

12

IN THE directorate mess that night Yakushev's chair was vacant. Voices were raised to counter the drumming of rain on the tin roof. Yakushev heard it as a rushing torrent in the gutter above his office. Plastic raincoats crackled around him as he tried to catch up on the day's business, checking through reports, signing Goriansky's pile of letters, his signature growing ever more illegible. As the other officers said good night, he was sure he detected veiled disgust in each voice.

He hadn't touched the sandwiches. Opening the top of the window, to evacuate the fog of smoke, he watched it trickle out into the roaring wet. It was more than smoke he wanted to clear. He had changed every item of clothing, showered and scrubbed himself, but he could still smell burning flesh.

Only occasional footsteps rang now in the halls. There was a tape just in from Teheran that he must listen to, and an 'Eyes Only Top Secret' sealed envelope to read. He chose the envelope but froze as Khan's graven face interposed itself. He had never moved, not in all those forty minutes, by so much as a twitched muscle. Despite those hellish sounds. They could as well have been roasting an ox. Indeed, the giant's outer flesh had begun to get a blistering glisten, when Tablian said a blood vessel had burst in his brain.

Yakushev hissed and tried to dispel another image – of himself shaking Khan, shouting in his ear that just *one* had died, that there were fifty more of his men waiting up there in the yard and did he think he could sit and watch each one of them die in the same way?

He would *have* to talk.

Khan must have heard him, though he gave not a sign. Then Yakushev had hit him, again, again. It was like . . . like nothing. Just a series of sounds. He had bloodied his fist.

He knew that he had gone a little crazy because he could not have carried out his threat. Even now there could be repercussions. There had been an extraordinary atmosphere when he left the fort. Tablian couldn't or wouldn't speak. Suchev looked ghastly, with vomit down his front. Morianov kept asking, 'Why, Colonel? Why did we do it? *What have you not told us?*' They would insist tomorrow on resorting to medication, with its consequent threat to himself.

He could order Khan to be shot, of course. In which case the bastard would carry his connection with the Lily to the grave – triumphantly. Afghan intelligence still had not identified the informer in their ranks. There was no other link. Khan was his one source. And Khan was not going to give in.

Well, nor was he. There *had* to be a way of getting inside his head without the aid of sodium compounds. Yakushev slit open the top-secret envelope as though it were Khan's skull.

It was several moments before he could bring the two lines of typescript into focus.

YOUR EYES ONLY AND DESTROY

D-DAY HARVEST SCHEDULED 5 JUNE 1982

Yakushev jerked forward to consult his calendar. Two weeks. The Baluchi rebellion would begin in two weeks. Headed by their Moscow-trained revolutionary committee, armed and supported by the Soviet Union, it heralded the final stage in the USSR's drive to the Indian Ocean via the oil-rich Gulf of Oman.

Yakushev lit a cigarette, held the flame to the letter and thoughtfully watched it burn. If the Lily should gain access to this gem of intelligence what could they do, he wondered. Passing it to the Americans was their obvious move.

He suddenly spat on the blaze and beat it out. Intact, still, at the top of the page was the distribution list. It was exclusive: tank, infantry and air army commanders, their RO Intelligence units, KGB, Dolin, himself. Well, you couldn't get much more secure than that.

Or could you? That was his second thought as he reignited the fragment. Who could tell how deeply the Lily had infiltrated Front's command structure? There was now only one absolute way of safeguarding such a secret.

Hunched against the rain, Masr strove to keep his footing on the rocky slope below the fort. It was not guarded, for the walls above were considered proof against everything short of aerial or artillery bombardment. The village with its lights and Ramadan feasting lay behind him. Below sprawled the outskirts of the city – villas and gardens mostly, incised by shining rivers of road. Music, voices lifted to him, but eerily, as the distant jangle of a fairground might reach a shepherd grazing his flock.

Masr had broken his fast with a little food and drink before leaving his family gathering, for the night could require his utmost strength. He carried a coiled rope, knife and flashlamp, and wore his darkest clothing in deference to the machine-gunners above, who had been known to make the curfew law a pretext for pouring forth streams of glowing bullets at the least suspicion of movement.

To say that he was scared would have been to ennoble his state of mind. The uncinching of the boy's tourniquet had been easy compared with what the mullah had now instructed him to do.

Below, he could just make out the paler stones of the ruined structure nestling amongst the rocks. It was believed to be the tomb of a saint. When Masr was a boy, tribal leaders had brought their rifles here to be blessed before setting off to make war on their neighbours. But Masr discovered that this was not its original purpose.

Before the Russian invasion, when the fort was occupied by Hafizullah Amin's secret police, he had put his secret knowledge to use by ferrying messages back and forth between political prisoners held here and their families. Those were the days, he thought uneasily as he slithered down to the 'tomb' and began to remove an apparent fall of stones, lifting each one and stacking it silently. He had never in his life earned so much money and that had made it an adventure, the issues straightforward. Now war and ideology had intruded. And he had been requisitioned by the Lily.

Uncovering the ancient door that sealed the mouth of the tunnel, he prized it open.

His cigarette a firefly in the window, Yakushev threaded the tape on his deck, jacked in the headphones and listened.

Identification serial, point and date of origin . . . He strove to concentrate on the clipped tones of the directorate's foremost 'illegal' in Iran. The situation there was highly relevant to Harvest because the more preoccupied Khomeini and his forces were with their revolution and the war with Iraq, the less likely they were to interfere.

His agent's first words conveyed the extraordinary information that the present lull was due to the Ayatollah's indecision whether his next offensive should be on Baghdad or Damascus, a thousand miles to the west. Yakushev knew attacking Syria would surely bring in the Saudis and the rest of the Arab world. For Harvest it would be an absolute godsend. He began to take rapid notes.

So deep was his concentration that the sulphuric sting in his nose of a struck match was the first intimation that he was not alone.

Boris Repin, in a belted raincoat with shoulder-wide lapels, appeared almost completely square. His head was an only slightly smaller square stuck on top, in which the high mounded cheekbones provided the only roundness. Perched straight on his head was the tiny-brimmed felt trilby hat that was all the rage just now in the KGB.

He blew out a cloud of smoke, leaned over and deposited the spent match in Yakushev's overflowing ashtray, beaming into his face.

Yakushev removed the headphones and killed the tape.

Repin affected sadness. 'May I not have a listen?'

'You're up late, *tovarich*.'

'Not too late, I hope.' Significantly.

'For coffee?' Yakushev parried. The KGB were bad news, whatever they wanted. They and the GRU were cloak-and-daggers drawn. How had he got past the guard?

Repin squinted down his squashed nose at Yakushev's notes. 'Don't mind if I do.'

Yakushev got up, then hesitated. He removed the notes and spools of tape and dropped them in the filing cabinet next to the coffee machine. The sharing of *any* information between the two organs was a matter for negotiation. They existed in permanent opposition, components of a system that, having created organ A, created organ B to prevent A from becoming too powerful, then created C, and so on – the object always to protect the state.

'Interesting stuff?' Repin was referring to the tapes.

'Black, or with this powdered goat's piss?'

'Uh – put like that – black.' He paused. 'What does Ghoram Khan have to say?'

Yakushev suppressed a guilty start. So Repin had wrongly deduced that he was listening to the interrogation tape. But what could be his interest? He was instantly on his guard.

'Sugar?'

'My word, yes please.' Repin moved up close, as if to watch this rarity being administered. After a moment, he said quietly, 'What does he know that the others don't?'

He watched Yakushev sidelong. When he did not reply, he enquired, 'Or was it just some bad news from home upset you? Some girl turn you down?' He sauntered a pace and turned. 'A row with Dolin?'

Yakushev sighed. 'Boris, have you been celebrating Ramadan?'

'There is nothing up your nose?'

'Only you.'

'Then the question remains. You're not a sadist, it would be in your file. Yet not even we use the "barbecue". Ergo, Ghoram Khan must have something extremely vital to impart. One is naturally curious to know what.'

Yakushev cursed inwardly. He poured the coffee, watching his hand to make sure it was steady. Someone had shot off his mouth. Morianov? He had for some while suspected the glassy-eyed bastard of fielding for the opposition.

'Since when,' Yakushev asked, 'has the KGB concerned itself with *mujahedin* strategy?'

Repin phrased his reply carefully. 'There could be other strategies involved.'

'For example?'

The KGB man sipped noisily. 'Mm.' He stooped to peer at the make of the coffee machine. 'American.' He managed to imbue the observation with just the right note of censure. He wandered away round the office, cup in hand. 'For example, the very strategy of interrogation is in itself a study. Like statistics, opinion polls, history even, it tells us more about the collator than the collated.'

Yakushev laughed. 'Such as you and your almost pathological misinterpretation of the facts?' But he felt a chill. 'Listen – like you, Ghoram Khan has listening posts in a number of sensitive places.'

Repin turned, interested. 'What kind of places?'

'Soviet army places. I'm looking for those ears. When I've squeezed the details out of him, I'm going to cut them off.'

Repin was watching him, weighing his manner. 'Russian ears?'

'Maybe. He hasn't talked yet.'

Repin looked sceptical. His eye went to the filing drawer.

'That tape is from Teheran,' Yakushev told him. 'I repeat – Khan has not talked. I'm surprised your informant didn't tell you.'

Repin lidded his eyes. He remembered his cup of coffee and slurped some more of it. 'Russian ears . . .' He looked thoughtful. Then raised his speculative gaze to include Yakushev.

Damn, Yakushev thought. Nothing alerted the KGB's suspicions more than volunteered information. He should have said No to the suggestion of Russian ears, because that made it KGB business. Repin's next remark confirmed his fears.

'When you've finished with him, Andrei Pavlovich, we would like a go. So be a good comrade, don't burn his arse off.'

Two cups of coffee and six cigarettes after Repin had gone, Yakushev was no nearer a solution to this sudden new threat. Hell, the Tchekists had been quick off the mark! But too quick. They had revealed their hand. He would see to it now that they never got to Khan. And Khan must never be subjected to medication, not with Morianov on the team.

What alternatives did that leave him? Coercion out, drugs out, killing out. If only, he thought, I could start again from scratch. Shift him and— And he had it. Shift him right off the map!

He knew where, how he could be induced to talk, everything.

He took a deep breath and reached for his topcoat. He was back on his horse. He had Repin to thank, for holding the bridle.

The *charpoy* had been relocated in the centre of the dungeon floor, its supports bolted to angle-irons driven between the paving slabs. Khan lay on the boards, one ankle shackled to the bed. He had no covering against the dank and sunless cold. They had brought him nothing to eat or drink. His only means of relieving himself was on the straw-covered floor.

Other than the convulsive shudders that racked his body every minute or so, he lay like a dead man, totally withdrawn, mourning Takredi, suffering his torture again and again. Guilt constricted his heart like a snake. Was there so much of value he could have told them about the Lily? Would not his men camped at Do Rish, had they known the circumstances, have gladly faced Russian attack? Had it not been, after all, out of personal pride and revenge that he had sacrificed his faithful friend?

Time passed unheeded, like the throbbing of his nose, the chill, the rush of rain outside the high, small window, the sporadic shifting of the guard's feet on the flagging.

If he raised his head he could see him through the bars – a blond youth hunched in a military topcoat and synthetic fur hat. He was seated on an ammunition case, his paperback angled to the solitary overhead bulb, the AKMS propped against the wall beside him.

Behind the guard, open stone steps rose by way of an arch, then a spiral, towards yard-level above. Other cells lurked in the darkness of a passageway with no exit. This was a place of suffering, of last despairing messages scratched on the walls, of bars burnished to a silken lustre by centuries of clutching hands.

Water dripped somewhere with regularity. The paperback flicked as the sentry turned a page. He sat with not a cough or sniffle. Clear young lungs. Lineless cheeks. Rapt in his reading.

A sigh began in the throat of the spiral stairs, maturing to swift footfalls that came through the arch on to the open steps without pause – there to stop abruptly.

Masr stared down at the sentry in shock. Never in his experience had there been a guard down here.

The Russian looked up. He reached for the Kalashnikov and stood up, pocketing the book.

Masr, seeing it was too late to withdraw, raised both empty hands with a disarming smile and came on down.

'Tea?' was all he could think of to say. He had picked up some Russian from his driver customers. 'You want tea, I fetch.'

Khan, aroused by the stranger's voice, slowly lifted his head.

The sentry stared at Masr, puzzled. He did not raise the gun. The approach was so innocuous as to offer no threat. Besides, this man with the continuous eyebrow seemed vaguely familiar.

Masr waited, smiling, for recognition to dawn. The youth said something, clearly demanding to know what he was doing down here. Masr chuckled and gestured, as though trying to explain. He raised a finger. Wait. He came closer, delving under his soaking jacket, apparently to produce a pass.

Watching dully through the bars, Khan saw the Afghan's other hand join the first and together plunge towards the boy's chest. More than the action itself, which appeared inept, it was the fearfulness and urgency of the newcomer's expression that alerted him to what was happening.

The Russian's topcoat was thick and buttoned double at the point where the knife struck – and it failed to penetrate. He jerked out a cry, mainly of surprise. Masr struck at him again and now he let out a half-scream and staggered back, crossing his arms to protect himself, the gun becoming part of his shield. Masr, panic-stricken, began stabbing him all over to silence him. Some of the blows must have penetrated because the boy doubled over, pushing him away and fumbling now to gain a lethal grip on his gun. Masr rushed back with a clumsy sideways hook of the curved blade. A red shower burst over him. The gun clattered. The youth fell against him, mouth open, arms clasping at him for support.

The Afghan shook off the grip in horror. The Russian slid to the floor and lay on his side, groping to staunch the crimson flood welling from his throat. He looked up at Masr, his mouth working, no words coming out. Masr fell on his knees beside him, crying for Allah to forgive him.

Khan had levered himself up and got his legs off the bed. Marshalling his energies he exhorted his rescuer not to give way to his emotions and to get the keys quickly. He pointed to where they were hanging. Masr regained his self-control with an effort and fetched them. His hands were shaking so much he could not find the right one.

Then he had it and the gate swung open. Khan took them from him and unshackled himself. A wave of nausea overwhelmed him as he stood up. He was forced to sit down again.

The Afghan was staring back at his victim, who was holding out his arms towards them imploringly, the terror of death in his eyes. Khan gripped the Afghan's shoulder and pulled himself up. Staggering to the gate he stooped to retrieve the sentry's weapon, and fell. Masr helped him to his feet and heaved him towards the stairway.

'How will we get out?'

'The well.'

The sluggish return of his circulation made each step a bed of needles. They had barely mounted to the archway when the thump of boots marching in unison sounded above. Masr clutched him to a stop. They listened. A guard detail, by the sound of it. But bound for where?

The next moment Masr was hauling Khan backwards so quickly that they both almost plunged to the floor below. The boots were coming down.

Khan spread his legs and checked the gun. It was cocked, with the selector on safety. He flipped it to semi-automatic and aimed it at the archway, but Masr pulled him sideways into the darkened passage. Khan glimpsed a series of open cell gates. Masr steered him into the end dungeon, got out his flashlight and shone it around. But where was there to hide?

An overpowering smell of straw drew his beam to the cell opposite. It was used as a store, stacked high with new bales.

The guards, followed by their officer and commandant Yenkov, came down the steps. Yenkov was saying in his blustering voice, '. . . the very strictest security, you understand? Not one word of his transfer must—'

His sentence was cut short by exclamations from the guards ahead and their sudden rush down the final flight.

Hidden amongst the straw bales, Khan and Masr heard the echoes of dismay, the confused scutter of boots. Incredulity gave way to sharp orders. Some of the boots rushed back up the steps, others came along the passage. A light flashed. Cell gates screeched on their hinges. The light grew brighter. Khan readied the Kalashnikov, gripping the magazine so it shouldn't rattle. The light blazed in amongst the bales. Someone shouted, '*Niet!*' Away went the boots, turning into a trot. Lights and sounds diminished, sucked away up the steps.

'Now!' Masr had Khan by the arm again. 'Before they have time to call out the guard!'

They went up the steps, Khan's circulation almost normal now through the surge of adrenalin. They emerged under cloistered arches in time to see the last two searchers hurrying away towards the gatehouse. The arches supporting the upper gallery had been bricked up to a height of two metres, and the top of each arch sealed with wire mesh. Through these half-moons glared brilliant light from the arcs overhanging the enclosure.

Masr pulled Khan to the wall. So long as they clung to its shadow they could not be seen by the machine-gunners above. Even now questions and answers were echoing back and forth between the towers and gatehouse. In minutes this walkway would be alive with soldiers.

Masr hurried Khan towards the end furthest from the main gate. Reaching the corner of the building, he paused to peer round it. Praise Allah, the next leg was clear. Midway along it was the well, long disused and capped with heavy boards. But he pointed warningly to a patch of arclight spanning the way immediately ahead of them. The wall was interrupted by a mesh gate giving access to the courtyard. For an instant they would be in full view of the far guntower.

Masr edged forward, leapt and was gone. Khan made to follow. Glancing through the mesh, he checked.

A metre out from the wall the rain beat a glittering fringe around the cobbles of the yard. Huddled in the space between it and the brickwork, to gain meagre shelter from the eaves, were dozens, even scores of prisoners. They crouched with their sodden *chapans* over their heads, in misery.

Khan knew instinctively that they were his men.

Masr had reached the well and was beckoning urgently. But Khan delayed, loath to desert his brothers, yet knowing he must.

'Khan?'

A bedraggled face was peering uncertainly through the wire. Khan could not distinguish the features but the voice was as familiar as his own.

'Feizl! Praise Allah you are alive!'

'How are you free? What is happening?'

'There is no time to talk – the guards are coming.'

'Let us out – we will take care of the guards!'

'No, the gate is locked and you are at the mercy of many guns.'

'Turn off the lights, they will not see us!' Feizl jabbed a finger through the wire. 'The switches are in that box.'

'Listen,' Khan said. 'I will come back with others. We will find a way to free you.'

'We may be gone from here, or dead,' Feizl began hopelessly, then broke off, inclining his ear.

Khan heard it too – the distant bark of orders, the clatter of weapons.

'Go with Allah,' Feizl cried. 'Hurry!'

Khan moved back for one glance around the corner. At the far end of the walkway he saw a squad of Russian soldiers emerging from the guardroom at the double. He made a rapid calculation and knew that to reach the well ahead of them would not be enough, that the soldiers would be there before he and Masr could descend to the bottom and take cover. A delaying factor was vital. He had the gun, but it alone, with one magazine, was not sufficient. Feizl's expedient leapt to mind.

The metal box on the wall was not locked. Inside were three switches. Khan struck them up.

The arclights died, plunging both yard and cloisters into blackness. He groped his way back to the corner, aware of startled shouts from the guntowers and of Feizl's voice bellowing to his men in the quadrangle, but concentrating on the silhouetted shapes of the advancing soldiers against the guardroom light. They were slowing now, for they were facing into darkness, their leader pacing backwards for a moment as he shouted something towards the gatehouse, perhaps to switch on the walkway lighting.

Khan's prolonged burst whacked audibly into their young bodies. Only two made it into an adjacent doorway; the rest lay strewn, some with vaguely quivering limbs, along the paving.

He triggered a shorter burst at the doorway, then turned towards the well, but had not progressed two paces when the gate to his left seemed to explode. Torn off its hinges by sheer weight of numbers, it swung back on its padlock, hurling him aside. Bodies collapsed in a pile in his path. Others scrambled over them.

Pandemonium ensued as fifty groping, shouting, rain-soaked men came crushing into the walkway with but one thought in mind – to escape from the yard before the machine-guns opened up. And now they did, the tower gunners raking the compound, turning it into a crackling, careening deathtrap of random tracer. But already most were through, filling the cloister, uncertain which way to move or what to do next.

His way to the well blocked, Khan thought furiously that events must have robbed Feizl of his sanity. He strove to take command but his men could neither see nor hear him. Vital seconds were slipping away. He did the only thing possible – he fought his way back to the control box and re-lit the arcs.

The uproar died raggedly as face blinked into wild-eyed face. The guns fell silent when their crews saw the empty yard. For one eerie instant it was like a deafness. In the space of it, Khan bowed to an inevitable decision and seized his men's attention.

'Follow me!' He shouldered his way ahead of them towards the well.

Masr had removed the boards. He stared in horror at the advancing horde. His first response was self-preservation. He swung his legs over the parapet, grasped the top rung and was gone. Even as he vanished from sight Khan spotted a flurry of movement and saw a second Russian squad rounding the corner beyond the well. He never paused, opening fire at them as he ran. The soldiers plunged to the paving, guns flashing. The air filled with snapping, luminous metal. Thumps and cries sounded among the men at his heels. His AKMS clattered to a stop, empty. He tossed it away. He was almost at the well. A visible object came whizzing over the top of it. The blow to his solar plexus was like the kick of a mule. He hit the paving with not a breath of air left in his body. Lungs in vacuum, he watched the canister that had hit him roll in front of his face. It burst into a cloud of smoke. Feet were thudding past him. He heard the hollow sound of bodies slithering, almost tumbling down the well. Someone grasped him under the arms and started to lift him, then, with a cry, collapsed on top of him.

The smoke was everywhere. It burned his eyes, then his lungs as, finally, he managed to suck in breath.

His last conscious observation was the peculiar revving of fire, like someone trying to start a motorcycle in a tunnel, as the guards emptied their automatic weapons down the well.

13

GOD KNEW where they were. They had literally been blown off course by a wind so strong that they dared not trust themselves to the ledge-like track that led down from the Jabal-os-Sanda pass. With ice still underfoot at 3,000 metres, the horses would have gone over for sure. They had backtracked and followed the leeward slopes of the *jabal* and wound up in a maze of geological french pleats so tight it was taking them an hour to negotiate country a crow could cover in a few wingbeats.

It was McCabe who called the halt. His legs, after the Mojave, weren't up to the gradients yet. And to cap it the Afghans were fasting, and he had felt it bad form to grab more than a surreptitious snack and a few gulps of water since dawn.

'Let's get a little science working here,' he gasped, planting his hips against a rock. He crossed his ankles and lit a cigarette.

Wakir, the blue-eyed survivor of the chemical attack, brought his five colleagues and the three horses to a stop.

Ayesha rotated on her heel for a moment, then came back towards him. Her manner was freer in the mountains, but a direct look was still a rarity, and somehow precious. She stood back to allow Wakir precedence over the map McCabe had pulled from his thigh pocket, warm and limp with sweat.

Wakir, not good with maps, beckoned her to deal with it. Her hair hung loose from the scarf as she traced where she thought they were with a long, unpainted fingernail.

McCabe traced where he thought they were with a square, grubby one.

'If I'm right and we climb to the top here, we should see a wide, flat valley and a road.'

'*If*, Michael. And we would be back in that terrible wind.'

'But a *road*, sweetheart. One of those marvellous, easy-to-walk-on, directional things.'

'In Afghanistan?' She sounded amused. 'But you want us to go up there and look?'

McCabe gauged the climb and grimaced, but nodded. 'I want.'

The escort and horses remained on the track while Wakir accompanied McCabe and Ayesha up the rugged slope. He was the obvious choice for guide, since they were making for his home ground – the area McCabe had suggested was strategic.

To McCabe's surprise, Bishr Khazim had taken his suggestion seriously and straight away sent off a man to investigate it.

Exactly how one investigated such a thing in a wilderness with few villages and no telephones, McCabe was intrigued to know. He was even more intrigued when, two days later, the man returned exhausted and frostbitten with a message handwritten on the back of what looked like a printed notice.

Khazim studied it, then told McCabe that he was right, those hills were indeed strategic to the Russians, though the note did not appear to explain why. Moreover, there was still one rebel strong point there that the Soviet forces had tried time and again to remove without success – a mountain village overlooked by a fortress known as Hisr-y-Bala.

'You are advised to go there with all speed.'

'Advised, who by?' McCabe naturally wanted to know.

Khazim looked at Ayesha. He thought for a moment, then handed her the message and moved away.

'He is unsure how much to tell you,' Ayesha explained, and tried to make a joke of it. 'Policemen are trained to extract information, not give it.' Her smile faded. 'But we, the resistance, are in a strange situation. If you had not the approval of the CIA I would not tell you what I am going to now. You will please keep it amongst yourself.'

'Amongst myself. Okay, sweetheart.'

And she had explained to him about the new, anonymous secret leadership. She showed him the Lily insignia at the bottom of the message.

McCabe thought that anywhere else he would have written it off as a figment of the local brew. If it was all so hush-hush, he asked her, how had they managed even to communicate with the Lily? She confided in him the two methods by which they were permitted to make contact, if absolutely necessary.

'And this?' McCabe tapped the reverse side of the message.

For the first time Ayesha showed reticence.

'That is simply a leaflet. One that is being circulated in the towns and villages.'

'Saying what? Will you read it to me?'

She hesitated. 'It is what you would call propaganda. For Believers. You are of the Book, no?'

'Book? The Bible? Of course.' He knew that to say he was an atheist would alienate her and the whole group. Other beliefs were tolerated; never disbelief.

'Then I think you would not understand what is expressed.'

'Try me.'

She was reluctant, even embarrassed. She began to translate, her tone reserved.

'"*I swear by the Declining Day, man's lot is cast amid destruction.*" That is from the Koran,' she explained. 'A traditional opening.'

As she continued, the reserve faded from her voice. He could see that, though she was familiar with its content, the rhetoric of the message still had the power to move her. Couched in the apocalyptic imagery of the Koran, it exhorted the reader to prepare himself to die for his God, '*So that His Prophet can be reborn, to lead all Islam to victory against the infidel schurawi.*' There was a lot of repition, dire warnings to those of little faith, then: '*Lo!*' the message ended, '*the Child is already in the Womb! Deliverance is nigh!*'

Oh boy, McCabe thought. Threats, contrived allegory, overtones of hellfire – wasn't that Islam in a nutshell? But he said, 'You're right. I don't understand it. What does it mean?'

She groped for a moment, then said distantly, 'It is something one cannot explain.'

In short, gobbledygook. And he was supposed to submit to its guidance.

'Tell me. The CIA – do they know about the Lily?

She nodded. 'Indirectly. But there is no communication. The Lily is quite independent.'

Hm. He was not sure whether that was a good or bad reference. Then he thought, what choice have I? It's all a crazy pig in a poke anyway.

And now here he was, helping them to live out their fantasy, just cresting the ridge in the last wink of the dying sun.

Not a breath of wind met them. But the view below was so unexpected that the three of them stood for a full minute, just staring in silence.

'Well,' Ayesha said at length, 'you were right about the road. But we cannot use it. Let us go back.'

McCabe told her to hang on. He sank to the ground and steadied the glasses on his knees.

'It will be dark, Michael, by the time we get back to the horses. There is camp to be made, prayers to be said, food to be prepared. None of us has eaten since dawn.'

'I'll catch you up.' It was not to be so swiftly dismissed, this, his first glimpse of the Soviet presence in Afghanistan.

The valley was deep. The sun had been off it for some while and lights were coming on in the hutments. Uniformed figures moved between the buildings, while a fitful brilliant blue star showed where oxyacetylene welding was in progress.

Panning slowly, McCabe counted a platoon of tanks, two SA-6s with ground-to-air missiles angled to the sky and, between them, a radar vehicle – one of the Straight Flush type, to judge by all the lumpy tracking gear on top. Well clear of the buildings, facing on to the runway, were open-ended bunkers stacked with fuel and ammunition. And, yes, there were the tractors and flatcars.

Within easy reach of a crew hut were four gunships, one of which was being serviced by a bowser. Further along in the dispersal bays were parked four camouflage-painted SU-24 fighters, a couple of prop jobs under wraps, and an Antonov. And beyond them he made out the familiar double snow-shoe dishes of a B-15 Flat Face radar truck, standing way out on its own.

There were no arcs on, no runway lights. It was a forward landing field under active conditions, blacked out against possible guerrilla attack. McCabe totted up five sandbagged heavy machine-gun emplacements dotted around the perimeter, two of which were within a stone's throw of the road.

But forward of what, he wondered. In this war where there was no front line. What was its purpose, tucked away here, north of the Kandahar road? There was an airbase at Kandahar, seventy-five miles away, and another at Ghazni. Between them their gunships could protect the road, no sweat at all. So what else was there? As if he didn't know. Why, nothing but a dusty plain stretching south, give or take a few barren mountain ranges, to the – up it cropped again – Baluchi frontier.

McCabe hoisted himself to his feet. The others were still waiting. They had scarcely started back together when he halted, turned and raised the glasses again.

'Michael, please.' Ayesha could not conceal her impatience.

Something was bothering him. He re-examined the installation below carefully for a clue as to what it could be.

The two prop jobs . . . Why *two* props when they had the Antonov for spotting?

McCabe swung to high magnification. But the distance, coupled now with the reduced light entering the lenses from the narrowed field, provided, if anything, less detail – just two amorphous shapes against the paler tarmac. The wraps were stretched from engine cowling to wingtips to tail, masking all but the undercarriages. To see more he would have to be lower and closer.

Even so, hell, what else could they be?

L-19s. Chemical strike aircraft.

14

McCabe had outlined his plan to Ayesha on the way down and got a silent reception. If he could have put it directly to Wakir he was sure he could have swung him, but there was no way he could do that. And Ayesha had become suddenly surprisingly, an obstacle. She knew Wakir's limitations as a decision-maker and was using her superior intelligence to protect him from making an error. McCabe admired her for it, but it was frustrating.

He waited till they had eaten.

He soaked up the last of the *pillau* with a hunk of *nan*, watching her face, waiting for the process of digestion to coax the blood from her brain and sap her resistance. The men were relaxing, belching appreciatively, wiping their beards, but they didn't matter at this stage. She was ladling out tea from the stewpot, her hair beautifully awry, the firelight in her eyes. She looked disconcertingly alert. Whereas he felt liable to drop off any moment.

He lit a cigarette to sharpen his mind. 'Any more thoughts on what I suggested?'

She did not reply till every man had received his bowl of tea.

'My opinion, Michael, is still the same. To take such a risk now could end our mission before it begins.'

'Well, for my money, the film begins here.'

'With respect, that is not what we agreed.'

'Sweetheart, we need any opening. A sequence shot on that airfield will give us exactly what we want.'

Ayesha tucked her legs under her and sipped her tea.

She said, in profile, 'Our position is this. We are not here to make art at the risk of our lives. We are not film makers. We are resistance fighters, interested only in the benefits your film will bring to our cause.'

'Well, I *am* a film maker,' McCabe retorted evenly. 'And I'm not here to support causes, never have been. I'm here to make a simple visual statement in the best way I can.'

Her eyes flashed. 'You are not for our cause?'

'And not against it,' he reassured her. 'If what I turn out benefits you, okay. But in return I must have your co-operation.'

'What are you saying?' Her fierce gesture encompassed the expedition. 'That we do not co-operate?'

'Keep your hair on. Your beautiful hair. My dear Ayesha.' He smiled at her till she regained her composure. 'And let's hear your objection.'

'Our purpose is to film a chemical attack, no?'

'Yes, but that's the climax. This is—'

'In our opinion,' Ayesha said, 'that climax will, by itself, provide all the shock necessary to—'

'Our?'

She looked away. 'All right, my own.'

'Shock necessary to do what?'

'Win sympathy and support from the important people you say will see it. The United Nations, heads of Western governments, United States Congress. That is what you said, no?'

'Sweetheart, do you know who makes up the UN? Half of them are pro-Soviet. They're going to resist this film tooth and claw. The other half are bombarded with shock every day of their lives – by the media – news pictures of terrorism, torture, disaster, space fiction, hard-sell advertising—'

She looked bewildered. He was introducing concepts beyond her experience.

'They're *inured* to shock, sweetheart. To convince them, we need more.'

Frowning, Ayesha swilled out her tea bowl and turned it over on a rock to drain.

He went on, 'Look at it another way. Suppose we never get the chemical strike shots? At least we'll have whatever footage we manage to grab here. *Could* just save the day.'

Ayesha scraped the remains of the *pillau* into a plastic bag. When she had spun the bag and knotted the neck, she looked directly into his eyes.

'Michael, these men are brave and honest and we are both in

their care. Nevertheless, though it must not appear so, in such matters as we are discussing they are in mine. Bishr Khazim has made me responsible, and I have very strong doubts about what you require yourself and us to do.'

'Yes, well I'm not used to having women – even beautiful doctors – wipe my nose for me.'

'No, you are not.' She eyed him with understanding, her manner softening. 'I can see you are not. Perhaps that has been part of your problem.'

'What problem?'

'I don't know. You – you are so uncommitted. I do not criticize, Michael, please. I simply remark it.' Then she shrugged and half-smiled into the darkness. 'But you always get your way, no?'

'I try to. When I know what I want is right.'

'That was Omar's weakness. Rest his soul. My beautiful man.'

Ayesha poked at the embers for a moment, her hair hiding her face. Then she looked up and laid her gaze on him as she might have laid a consoling hand on a patient.

'All right, Michael. I will *ask* the men.'

McCabe sat up with a start. Something had brushed past him. The men were on the move, loading the horses. The fire was out. Everything looked greeny-grey in the fixed smile of the moon. His wristwatch showed a quarter to three. The hills were sort of wide-open silent, taking every *clink*, magnifying it.

He spilled a little water on his toothbrush and scrubbed it round his teeth. Habit of a lifetime. Second habit – he lit a cigarette. Ayesha materialized from the direction of the horses, unscrewing a Thermos. Her jasmine smell was so strong he guessed she had just poured some perfume on her hands and wiped it round her face.

'Everything you want is on the one horse.'

'You're a marvel. Did you sleep?'

'One learns to do with very little. Careful, it is quite hot.' She held the plastic cap with the tips of her fingers.

McCabe drained it in three gulps. She poured some more. He grimaced. Green tea was like gnat's piss but the sugar was a pick-me-up. Shivering, she handed him half a *nan*, baked the night before.

'Are we legal?'

She chuckled. 'Eat while you can. Anyway, you are not yet a Moslem.'

'Yet?'

'Perhaps I will convert you. It would be excellent therapy for your ailment of uncommittedness.' There was just a trace of censure in her voice.

'You'd have a job.'

'I think so.' She sighed.

She seemed to be in a strange mood. He gouged out the tip of the cigarette and tucked it away in his shirt pocket before taking a bite of the *nan*.

'Something on your mind, Ayesha?'

She shrugged. 'The men were eager to do it for you. I never openly oppose them.'

'As you do me.'

'We are modern people, Michael.'

'All the more reason we should stick together.' He waited, but she refused to be drawn. 'Anyway, what's the betting their decision was nothing to do with you, me or the mission, just a chance to fire their guns, right?'

The faintest chuckle. 'You are learning quickly about Pathans, Michael.'

'The men maybe. But you're a Pathan. You're not so easy.' He handed back the Thermos cap and gave her wrist a squeeze. 'But a lot more rewarding.' She withdrew her hand quickly, but not before the contact sent a tingle up his arm into his chest.

She hurried ahead of him towards the horses, as if afraid he might touch her again.

Just short of the crest the party divided. One man and two of the horses would wait here. The rest of them continued over the ridge and picked their way down the forward slope. The moon had set. No glint of light from the airfield or hutments below.

McCabe and Wakir moved ahead to select the fire-point. The Afghan's surefootedness in the darkness was marvellous. It was he who found the natural breastwork of rocks. Range from target: approximately five hundred yards. The others came down to them and McCabe unloaded what he wanted from the horse.

'And this please, Michael.' Ayesha swung the duffel bag containing the protective clothing towards him.

McCabe started to protest, then didn't. It was a hell of a fag to lug the bloody thing, but if she wanted it . . . He sat down and lit a cigarette, taking care to shield the flame. She seated herself beside him, drawing up her knees.

He unpacked the two walkie-talkies and handed her one. 'You know how to work this?'

She fumbled for a moment and he guided her finger to the switch and her thumb to the pressel.

'Press while you talk, then straight off, okay?'

'We could do with some of these.'

'You'll get them.' He clipped its twin to his breast-pocket, then looked up, gauging the sky. He could feel the thudding of the ground as the camera horse was led back over the ridge. That left Wakir, Ragajeet and Selim. They returned to the firing point and began to select their positions. They were armed with old .303s. Wakir had had to borrow his from one of the drivers because Kalashnikovs were useless at this sort of range. They were made for slaughter not marksmanship.

McCabe felt his inner focus becoming sharp. Danger did that. The Milky Way was like a chandelier, the hills all around in cold storage till the sun broke. A lot had to happen before then.

He slipped his arms through the harness of the pack containing the battery and spare mag. He stood up to buckle it. Ayesha stood up with him. She lifted the duffel bag on to his shoulder. Thank God it was light. He tucked the stock of the Arriflex under the other arm.

'Tell them no jumping the gun, huh?'

'I have told them.'

'Tell them again.' He peeled off the field-glasses, handed them to her. 'You'd better keep these.'

'Won't you—'

'I have the big lens to watch through. Stay cool now. And – what is it you say? – live for ever.'

'You also.'

He picked his way cautiously along the slope. The quality of the darkness had begun to change. Still not a glimmer from the Russians but he could just make out the runway. He dislodged a stone. It sounded like an avalanche in the stillness. Have a care, McCabe, he warned himself. He spoke into the walkie-talkie.

'Testing.'

There were moments of silence before the reply came.

'I hear you, Michael.'

'I interrupt something?'

'We were at dawn prayer.'

'Oops. Sorry.'

'It is strange. I have never talked like this over such a radio.'

'I thought you were modern. Say something modern.'

'I can only say something old. The men are jealous of us, you and me.'

'You're kidding.'

'The way we talk so much together. I tell them Western people always talk man-to-woman like this. They do not believe me. They say I wear the black of mourning and it is not proper.'

'Keeping their sister in line, huh? Hard on you, because I have a feeling you miss talking, that you talked a lot with Omar, am I right?'

There was a slight pause. 'Yes,' she said in a lower voice.

'Well, do your thing, I say, and to hell with them.'

She was silent. Then, tentatively added, 'I have been thinking, to sit on your fence and make cold judgement on film, excluding yourself from the marching columns, it is . . . how can I explain? Do you not understand that mental breakdown is the soul fighting the mind?'

'You recruiting? Allah wants me for a sword-in-hand fanatic, that what you're trying to say?'

'He just wants us. That is enough. All of us.'

'Full of hate, I can imagine.'

'And love, Michael. Both. If you cannot hate you cannot love. But I am psychoanalysing. I am sorry. Forgive me, please. It is just that I feel you are in – is the word "limbo"?'

'That's the word. Though when I look around me I think maybe that's not such a bad place.'

'We will argue that. I will let you go now. Be careful.'

There was a click. He was alone again, trying to pick his way without falling.

Coming parallel to the end of the runway, he could see no sign yet of the ruin he had spotted last evening. Nor of the *kwar*. The ruin was down on the flat but the *kwar* had been just about here.

He slowed right down. Stumble into that with the unprotected camera and goodbye mission.

He checked himself right on the edge of it – a ragged fissure, dry of course. He didn't climb down into it, just turned downhill and followed its erratic descent towards the valley. Ten minutes later, it levelled off and cut under a log bridge with a packed dirt surface. He moved up on to it and found himself on the road, which he crossed on tiptoe.

From here he could make out the nearest gun position. How far – two hundred yards – three?

Straight across from him now he could just see the ruin. Hm. Suppose they kept a picquet posted there? Or there were chickens roosting! That had happened to him in Somalia. Chickens stay on in a place long after the folks evacuate. The shindy they made in the Mojave had brought down a stonk from the Ethiopian 110s. He could still taste the chickenshit.

He didn't make directly for the ruin but followed the fissure. It passed close to the building and was deep enough to provide cover on the way back.

Before the Russians came, the building had been a farm. Now it had no roof, no windows, just piled rubble inside crumbled adobe walls. One had a hole blasted through it that faced towards the runway. McCabe placed his camera there. The weight of the butt supplied a nice counterbalance to the 1000 mm lens as he sighted it on the parked aircraft.

The range was in the hundreds and the shapes too dim still to make out, but the big bottle brought them in dark and close.

He checked his watch. Four thirty-four.

'You there?'

Clickety-click. 'Yes, Michael, where are you?'

'On station. Wakir and Co ready?'

'It is too dark yet for them to—'

'Are they *ready*?'

'Ready – yes.'
'Right. Stay tuned, sweetheart. For the breakfast show.'
McCabe lengthened focus to take in the ammunition bunkers. They were at extreme range, almost sideways on to him. One was stacked high, he couldn't make out with what. Rockets? No colour yet, but it was coming. He set his direct-light meter for the ultra-fast Eastmancolour and held it up.
No reading.
He lit a cigarette. The smoke told him there was a light breeze.
He panned back for another look at the aircraft. His heart gave a thump. No doubt now. They were L-19s.
'We're in business.'
'You mean we must start to shoot?'
'Not quite. I'm waiting for a reading. Got the glasses?'
'Yes?'
'Now we don't know exactly what we're looking for. The red powder is dispensed by rocket, but there must be a dozen types there, so we'll give that a miss. Go for the green. It'll be in – and I'm guessing – pressurized tanks. Probably streamlined, like wing fuel tanks. Long and flattish. What can you see?'
There was silence the other end.
McCabe took a last drag on his cigarette and flicked it away. He looked through the camera at the nearest gun position. The machine-gun had a ground cape draped over it. No heads visible. Unmanned? No, they wouldn't leave the gun there. Very faintly then, he saw an exhalation of smoke rise above the sandbags to drift away.
Let it be hash, he thought.
'There is a stack of things like cigars, on their own.'
'Streamlined one or both ends?'
'Both, I think.'
'Sound like drop tanks for the SUs. Look for something with a rear nozzle.'
More silence.
'Would they have – do you say, fins?'
'No fins.' The last thing they would be was jettisonable.
He was watching the light-meter. He had a reading. Only a hair off zero but the needle was beginning to climb.
Suddenly he thought, this is crazy. Pressurized tanks would

be reinforced way beyond the penetration capability of small-arms fire.

'Michael, I can see nothing.'

'Try for something fatter. A drum. With possibly a cone nose to eliminate wind drag.'

'There are many drums.'

'Flat ended?'

'. . . I think so.'

He was getting a clear f.2 from the meter now. Suppose they carried the stuff *inside* the fuselage? In a sort of sealed hopper with gravity ejection? Hell, they could dish it out by ladle, for all he knew. He didn't want to confuse her.

'All right. Try for the drums. The olive ones will be aviation fuel. Look for some with different colour coding. A small batch, maybe under wraps against satellite photography. You might just see their ends showing.'

But they could be underneath at the back, or stored in a hut, kept in a pit with the lid on, in refrigeration . . .

'There are some yellow ones, separate, Michael.'

'Give them a blast.'

F.4 now. He set the stop on the camera.

'You mean, tell the men to open fire?'

'Give them a good look through the glasses. Make sure they understand the target. Let them shoot when ready.'

At five hundred yards, he knew, it would be pretty approximate stuff, dependent on the quality of the coarse gunpowder refills supplied by the Darra gunsmiths, the casting and alloy of the bullets, and on the men's skill.

He panned to the bunkers to watch through the camera. No sense in rolling yet. He had just eight minutes of film in the mag, and the shot, once started, had to be continuous to avoid any charges of fake.

He couldn't see the drums. Couldn't see bugger-all really. Weird. There was always something weird about the very early morning. Unpeopled. The dim grey glare of diffused shapes with no key-light.

The rifle shots sounded, dull as hammered stakes but with tin-tray echoes that thrashed through the hills and back . . . and back.

He was right, there was nothing to see. As if the cutting room had dubbed on the wrong sound-track. The still shapes of the field remained undisturbed while the shocks echoed back and forth.

The machine-gunners would be uncovering their guns now, panning around, looking for where the fire was coming from. But unless they could locate the actual tiny flashes, the echoes would keep them guessing.

Now one post started pumping out shots blindly. Then another.

Suddenly there was a whoof of flame from one of the bunkers. Then a whole great sheet of it. The sound of explosions followed.

A penetrated drum, he guessed, ignited by the spark of a ricochet.

'Switch,' he told Ayesha. 'It was fuel. Try another bunker.'

A black and gold mushroom was rolling into the air. He could hear the machine-gun bullets thumping into the ridge.

'If they get on to you, stop firing and lie low, you hear me, sweetheart?'

'What? Yes. We are shooting at the middle heap now.'

The firing went on. Suddenly there was more flame. Then a really heavy explosion. Then more. Fragments blasted into the air amongst grey smoke that turned over in the breeze like ocean surf.

Hopeless. All they were achieving was sabotage. Figures were coming from the huts now, some running, some standing helplessly. The machine-guns on the other perimeter were firing into the hills on *that* side; the echoes still had them completely foxed. Maybe he should tell Ayesha to pull out now, before they got un-foxed – retreat across the ridge as planned and move along the far side to meet him as he came up the fissure and over the top.

'*Michael!*' Her voice sounded so loudly that he jumped. 'Something is happening!'

It was indeed. A weird greenish pallor was showing through the smoke and flame. It was creeping like dry-ice across the runway.

McCabe checked the stop, pointed the camera at the nearest SU fighter to feature its red star, pulled the focus in sharp and pressed the tit. He listened for the correct soft flutter, then directed his entire psyche through the optic.

First, setting the scene: a Soviet airfield – *ta-ra*! Don't rush it, give them time to read the serial coding on the fuselage. Now pan slowly to reveal the L-19s . . . hold for recognition . . . ten seconds . . . twenty . . . give the experts time to note the wing pylons and decide if they're carrying spare tanks or toxic aerosols . . . then continue pan, lengthen focus . . . And there it was – a cloud now, greeny-yellow, billowing as well as creeping . . .

'Are you filming it?' Ayesha's voice held awe and excitement.

The exploding ammunition was spreading the stuff. A siren began to wail somewhere.

Suddenly something huge lifted into picture above the inferno. A gunship. Her exclamation reached him as he panned up with it. His concentration wavered.

He said, barely moving his lips, 'Pull out, Ayesha. *Now.*'

'All right. But you must go too – as soon as you have what you need.'

'I'll be there before you.'

There was a mistrustful pause.

'When I see you move,' Ayesha said, 'we will move.'

Two more gunships appeared briefly in frame as they lifted above the eddying green dust. The Lee Enfields and machine-guns had fallen silent. A part of him guessed why and he panned to the nearest gunpost – in time to see a flailing arm, as one of the crew struggled into his protective suit. His companion was pulling on a rubber hood. He let the camera run on them.

'Michael, do you have it? Are you ready to go?'

Both the crew were hooded now, but they hadn't resumed operation of the gun. They had their backs to it and were watching the toxic cloud apprehensively. Beautiful. A picture worth a thousand words.

'Michael, you must please settle for what you have got. There are three helicopters now. One has risen to a high position, the others are making circles. And the dust is moving your way! Have you on the clothing? Michael?'

McCabe was panning from the gun crew to what they were looking at. He had shot five minutes of film. Three left.

'Michael, answer me. Say you hear me.'

He opened his mouth vaguely to reply, but something was happening along the runway. He lengthened focus. A lorry . . .

'One of the gunships is coming close to your ruin – can you hear me?'

Yes, he could feel rather than hear the thumping of its rotors. But the lorry was growing along the tarmac towards the bunkers; there was something strange about it. A bulbous shape on the back. A concrete mixer?

'It is over you now. Say you are receiving me. Say something!' There was some frantic clicking. 'Hello – can you hear me? Hello!'

The gunship was over him all right, but he was tucked well down and the truck was getting near the bunkers now – taking a helluva chance with the exploding ammunition because, though obviously chemical-proofed, he didn't think it was armoured. He could barely see it through the green haze.

Ah, it was turning short. As it came into profile he saw that the bulbous thing was an aircraft turbojet, its huge nozzle pointing rearwards. Between it and the driver's cab was a thousand-gallon tank.

He knew then, from the briefing pictures, that it was a TMS-65 decontamination truck. It could double as a smoke generator or for melting snow on runways.

Ayesha's voice was rapping in his ear but he heard not a word. The truck was beginning to spray. *Fantastic.* Neutralizing chemicals gushed from the spray-ring to be atomized by the hot breath of the turbo. The vibration was gone, so the chopper must have passed on. Sudsy liquid was swamping the bunkers, the runway. Thirty seconds of film left. But he had enough.

'Okay, sweetheart, cool it – I'm moving.'

He cut the motor and disconnected the battery. As soon as the chopper had gone he would slip out.

His reassurance had stemmed Ayesha's flood of words. But she was still talking. He heard her sudden sharp intake of breath as she said one word, '*Allah!*'

Her tone alerted him. He looked out and saw the gunship about a hundred yards away, low above the great swirl of dust whipped up by its rotors. Even as he looked there was a wink from one of the wing pods.

Ayesha's despairing cry was the last sound he heard.

15

THERE WERE men throughout the ruin, like maggots in a skull. In their quiet seething was preparation – oil for every weapon, cartridges for every magazine.

Abdalis sat alone at the slate table, sulking over his Koran, his curiosity tugging at him but not moving him. At length the Book thumped shut and his shadow rose to the ceiling, then preceded him into the hall.

His colleagues were in the antechamber, the whorls of their turbans showing like whipped cream with walnut centres against the curtain to which their ears were inclined. Abdalis joined their eavesdropping from a dignified distance.

Audible through the curtain was Dhost's deep voice.

'Our agent Masr and all the prisoners were killed, O Soul of Aminah. Ghoram Khan alone is said to survive.'

'The fool!' The Lily sounded outraged. 'He is headstrong, Dhost. Was it not written clear, the means of his escape?'

'Most clear.'

'Then if freedom still eludes him, he is the hostage of his own deeds.' In the darkness of her chamber she was pacing back and forth before the dais, belly distended.

The mere gleam of a cheekbone and glisten of a beard that was Dhost remained silent. He knew her well and was waiting for her pacing to slow a little. As, sure enough, it did.

'And now he has vanished, you say?'

'They drove him away secretly by car but an hour later,' Dhost informed her. 'Not one of our watchers has seen him since.'

'Nor our listeners heard word of him?'

'Those few that are left since the unbelievers doubled their security measures – no.'

'Then good riddance!' The Lily stamped her foot and

resumed her march. 'The moving finger writes, Dhost, and having writ moves on. He deserves no further consideration. We will exclude him henceforth from our plan.'

The mullah again said nothing. He watched the shadowy feet sweep by him once, twice, thrice, before they again faltered.

'Your disagreement deafens me, Dhost. Out with it! Convince me why I should not strike him from our list of chosen ones?'

'He still has a vital role to play, O Immortal Soul. That of the Judas ram.'

'Why should we not find another? Convince me, convince me.'

'If it is not he who kills Colonel Yakushev, Allah's justice will not be done.'

The Lily shrieked, 'You dare confound me with my own prophecies, Dhost?' Her voice dropped instantly to the softest purr. 'My good Dhost. Then tell me, what is your suggestion?'

'It would do no harm to try to find him.'

'And, on finding him, have to devise for him another plan of escape? And, on devising it, have him again fly in the face of it? You take me for a fool?'

'You asked for my suggestion.'

The amorphous shape came slowly to rest. It stood in silence.

'Very well.' Having decided, her tone became singsong, even dismissive. 'Alert all our watchers and listeners and hunters, especially those close to Yakushev. Give them three days to locate Ghoram Khan. If they fail, we must leave him to his fate and revise our plans.'

'You are a Saint of Mercy, Soul of Aminah, Mother of Mahomed,' the eavesdroppers outside heard Dhost exclaim. They drew swiftly to one side, in case he should emerge.

Abdalis added with a sneer, 'Only where it concerns her beloved.'

The youngest mullah frowned. 'Were she to cut off Ghoram Khan's head, you would swear the blade was paper. If she were the woman you claim she is, would she ever have suggested abandoning him?'

'She is cunning,' Abdalis coiled his hand like a snake, 'and knows we are listening.'

'What does it matter who she is?' the red-bearded one demanded bluffly. 'She is touched by God. Who can deny it?'

'I,' said Abdalis. 'She is a walking heresy. Her claim to carry in her belly the resurrection of Mahomed is vile heresy! All prophecies agree that he will be reborn of man.'

'Such promises, I fear,' murmured the oldest mullah, with a droll twist of his mouth, 'are all a man will ever conceive. Anyway, why debate? Faith is what is demanded here.'

'Faith in a Russian whore?' Abdalis glared till his eyes resembled bullets.

'In God. And that we are all instruments of God. Including her.' The old man raised a gnarled forefinger. '*That* far, my belief in her is absolute.'

'And mine!' cried the youngest.

There were murmurs of agreement all round.

'If she is who you claim,' the old mullah went on, 'then she is using us, and –'

'Precisely!' Abdalis cut in.

'*And we her*.' The old one stepped close to him. '*For the unification and liberation of our land*. If to do so, we must play charades and crawl, so be it. Dhost shares my view. All are agreed but you. When is a chain not a chain, Abdalis? When does what it raises come crashing down, I ask you?'

'When it is struck asunder by the wrath of God!' Abdalis thundered, and strode away.

16

KHAN'S FIRST view of the Choukha as he regained consciousness was of a pitted ceiling running with slime from the condensed breath of scores of bodies. They lay without bedding on the stone floor, jerking and struggling for warmth and space like stranded fish. A door and a window opened on to a caged balcony, equally crowded. Dawn showed beyond the steel mesh, green and icy. Hands crawled over him like fleshy spiders.

Takredi's bursting face, the veins like whips, eclipsed his mind's vision, then the attempted escape, his men flailing, dying in the hail of fire. He couldn't forgive Feizl for his precipitate action. That he had died with them was Allah's justice, though no comfort.

His own chest and throat burned from the effects of the riot gas. His nose pulsed like a living creature. The pangs of thirst and hunger consumed him. Where was he? Where else but caught, still, in the toils of Yakushev's vengeance!

'Up! Up! Up!' The thud of blows. A rising chorus of howling jeers. 'Up, filth!' Guards with clubs were beating a path along the balcony as the day's work details were established amid pandemonium. When they found Khan, they marched him away.

The balcony ran the full length of the building. There were others above and below. The internal cells had long ago burst at the seams, their occupants merging to live in chaos and near-anarchy. The building looked as if it had been a barracks. The name 'Salamanca', in English, chiselled in the stone, denoted the floor above. Inscribed in English. The building was a remnant of the British occupation one hundred and fifty years ago.

They took Khan below ground to the old ammunition store

and beat him on the soles of his feet with a barrel stave. They asked him no questions. Directing the torture was a swag-bellied man wearing an open-necked shirt under a double-breasted grey uniform. He clicked a string of amber beads in his hand, watching the delivery of each stroke through wrap-around sunglasses, gauging its effect against the new prisoner's power of resistance, while crippling him as he had been instructed.

Khan, suspended by the ankles, his head on the floor, was shocked, blow by blow, from outrage to fury. He strove to arrest his swimming senses long enough for one clear look at the man whose raised finger signalled each explosion of agony. He memorized the bulging chins, as smooth and distended under the short black beard as the throat of a frog, and marked him for vengeance.

He did not know yet that this was Governor Yasir, only that such bellies in today's Afghanistan were a sin and that somehow he would seek this man out, *inshallah*, and slit him from crotch to chin!

The beating went on and at last Khan went away from his body. When he came back he was lying in a corner of the ablutions. Men were defecating over the open holes. Some lay groaning nearby, too dehydrated to move away from the path of the constant traffic. Agony yawed in Khan's ears. The soles of his feet resembled distended crimson bladders. Next to him some men were bellowing at two confused cockroaches. There was money on the ground. One shoved Khan's legs aside to allow the beetles wider range. The pain jarred Khan into angry life. He came to his knees and elbowed right and left till he had cleared a space for himself. Breathless, he drew his feet under him and turned towards the door. But walking was impossible. He fell forward on his face. Shouts and blows were rained on him as he dragged himself on one hip out on to the balcony.

He pushed his way to the parapet, thrust his face between the pilasters and drank the air. The image of Yakushev glowed and faded in his mind. No man could do this to the son of Ahmed. *No man!*

The prison faced east across the city. A sheen of mist spun by the low sun lay over the buildings, through which the hills of Sharara and Kollola Poshta and Tape Bibi Mahro rose like islands. Beyond were the mountains and, behind them, the true mountains that had given him birth.

The sight of them steadied him. He anchored his swimming mind to them and asked himself why Yakushev had sent him here. Why *here*? Did the Lily know? If not, how could he contact them? But his prime need was food. He had not eaten for days.

He asked the old man squatting vacantly beside him how and when the food came.

'What they call food,' the old fellow snorted and spat, 'does not come. It is dished out in the yard at noon.' He looked at Khan's feet with knowledgeable and dubious eyes. 'If you can get there.'

Khan tore the tail of his shirt into bandages. He bound each foot as tightly as he could bear. Gripping the parapet, he tested his weight on them. To stand was still impossible, but he did not stop trying. The sweat sprang from his brow.

Such beatings were commonplace, to judge by the bloody rags and scars about him. Others had had a hand severed at the wrist – the penalty for stealing. There seemed to be no medical supervision. Sores and diseases festered untended. Yakushev had flung him into a human cesspit. It was the ultimate degradation. At last Khan balanced himself gingerly and let go of the parapet.

He lay where he had fallen, scowling towards the source of laughter – a slit-eyed fellow with a shaven skull and single tassel of hair on top. A Mongol. He of all the prisoners in this section was well fleshed, even powerfully built. Khan had already guessed, by the fawning, the coming and going around him, that he was operating a trade. Hashish? Tobacco? And had noted the man watching him, sizing him up.

Now Khan returned his gaze. Slowly the mockery died in the flat eyes as they perceived the calibre of the new arrival. Then someone moved between them and the moment passed.

His name was Said Mechiti, the old man informed him – a notorious Khalqi cut-throat who had fallen foul of his political masters. In here, he worked for another master. 'See his feet? Not a mark on them. He is protected. Beware!'

Who by? Khan wanted to know.

The old man raised his eyes and a finger towards the floor above, but did not explain.

Khan did not press him. His fight was with the Russians, not this riff-raff. But if any of them stood between him and survival, he would have to kill him. That included Said Mechiti.

When the noon gun boomed from the ramparts above distant Baber Shah Park, Khan came to his feet in the general surge and dragged himself along the parapet, elbowing aside all who got in his way. He half-fell down the steps, crawled, got up and tottered to join one of the three food lines forming in the yard.

The queuing was torture. He sat and crawled alternately, defending his place with blows. The guards looked on impassively. They wore holstered pistols secured to their bodies by short lanyards, and carried clubs. A knot of them stood around the food table. At their centre stood Yasir, legs splayed, belly out, beads clicking between his fingers.

Catching sight of him, Khan willed himself to his feet. He moved forward, revealing his agony by not a tremor. As he came in front of the table he raised his gaze to meet the governor's, holding it until he saw growing recognition. And something fiercely satisfying – chagrin. A flat loaf of *nan* was slapped in his palm, a ladleful of rice dumped on top. He looked down to take the watery mug of tea, then back again at the man he had vowed to kill, before turning away.

Now, he realized, he had to *walk* back.

Each step triggered the reflex to fall to his knees. The bones in both feet were fractured, he believed, and the flesh was bloody and raw. But with head erect, shoulders as casual as he could make them, he managed to reach the building and enter it before he collapsed.

The mug clattered to the steps. *Nan* and rice were scattered amongst passing feet.

In a trice he was surrounded. Greedy hands became shovels. Khan watched them as from a distance, nausea in his throat, watched them freeze then withdraw as a solitary pair replaced them – broad and hairless and spatulate. They scooped the rice and bread into the tail of a shirt.

Seen close to, the Mongol's skin was as poreless as fine tanned leather. The black sultana eyes were on Khan's, his every move a challenge.

Khan summoned what reserves remained in his body to seize

the muscular throat. But he was too weak. With a supreme effort, as in a dream, he raised his hands, only to find the throat elevated beyond his reach. Face grimacing, Said Mechiti was being lifted to his feet by the tuft of hair on his head.

Khan perceived another face. In contrast to the Mongol's it was all gleaming teeth and savage young energy.

For a short space the two men faced each other, one bow-legged like a wrestler, the other exultant, untamed as a rearing horse. But no explosion of violence came. With a laugh, the youth turned and hauling Khan up, took him on his back. 'I am Hafiq.' He indicated the food still jealously contained in the tail of Said's shirt. 'Bring it.'

With no great effort, he carried Khan bodily up the steps, the Mongol following – past the rows of faces that had paused to watch, past 'Kandahar' to 'Waterloo', on the floor above. Shouting to the prisoners thronging the balcony to make way, he strode its length to a door at the end – the only intact door Khan had so far seen. He kicked it open.

The small room was as run-down as the rest of the building, but it did contain *charpoy* beds, matting on the floor and basic furniture. There was even a makeshift shelf with books. Two prisoners – one portly, with a pink, shining head, the other stocky and hirsute – turned in the act of setting their food on the table.

'Who is this?'

'Ghoram Khan!' Hafiq lowered his burden to one of the beds with a chuckle.

'Here?' The plump one looked astonished. 'They don't put resistance fighters in the Choukha.'

'Well, they put this one. Mazloumian recognized him.'

Hafiq motioned Said to leave the food on the table. He slapped his shoulder jossingly as he turned away, but the Mongol pulled him round and pointed warningly to his abused topknot.

'Next time I will kill you.'

Hafiq roared with laughter and took him by the throat.

'What's going on?' A heavy-featured, thickset man of forty or so had entered behind them. His face was pock-marked, and there were purplish shadows of ill-health under venomous eyes.

Hafiq let go, grinning.

'Nothing, Master,' the Mongol muttered, and left.

Three more prisoners entered. Hafiq jammed the door after them. Questions and answers flew back and forth for several moments. Khan could tell from their Western clothing and manner that, with the exception of his saviour, they were educated men.

The one called Mazloumian brought Khan a mug of tea and identified himself. He had Levantine, good-humoured features, with eyes that stared earnestly when he spoke.

'You are lucky I have a memory for faces,' he said. 'There was an article on the resistance a few months ago in a French magazine. It carried your picture.'

Khan's hands shook so much that Mazloumian had to support the mug. Khan contrived to keep his wits, aware of the others watching him – a strange animal brought to their den – as they added tinned meat and *dahl* to their meagre rations. There was a small hoard of canned and bottled groceries on the table. The pink-skulled man was tending a battered samovar. Only the tall, aloof prisoner delayed eating his meal. He brought water to the boil on a primus while sorting through what looked like a medical box.

He came over and without preliminaries cut the makeshift bandages from Khan's feet. He bathed them, then dabbed them with colourless fluid that burned like fire. His swift movements suggested a great deal of practice at this work.

Khan swallowed three mugfuls of the tea. He leaned back gasping and closed his eyes.

'Would you rather eat later?'

He opened them again. He was ravenous.

The pock-marked man watched Mazloumian mixing Khan's rice into a *pillau*.

'Go easy on that.' His own mouth was bulging. 'We are not even sure he is who you say he is.'

'You have my word.'

'Words come as easily to an Armenian as planting a spy does to Yasir.'

Mazloumian said evenly, 'Give him a little time, Tamim. He will confirm it himself.'

The tall one said over his shoulder to Hafiq, 'Where are the pieces of wood we used for Mahmud?' He glanced up at Khan, only briefly questioning, before tearing a further strip off his shirt tail. 'We will have to get him another shirt, Tamim.'

'Anything else?' the pock-marked one asked sarcastically.

'Yes, we are running low on surgical spirit.'

Hafiq guffawed. He brought him two bloodstained off-cuts of plywood. The tall man pressed them each in turn to the soles of Khan's feet, positioning the toes carefully before binding them firmly.

Mazloumian turned to Tamim. 'You think Yasir would cripple one of his spies like that?'

'He might. If not, then tell me what a rebel leader is doing in Choukha? Yasir won't let them near the place. He knows it's a tinder-box.'

'He took in Hafiq,' the pink man reminded him.

'Hafiq was a mistake. He was arrested for looting and the police were too slack to check his record.'

'They must be blind,' murmured the tall one drily, as he completed the splinting. 'Anyone but a fool could see he is a one-man war looking for somewhere to happen!'

This got a chuckle.

'Then praise Allah for fools!' Hafiq cried, thumping his chest. 'For without my protection where would you be?'

'And without ours, where would you be?' Tamim licked his greasy fingers. 'Brains can always buy muscle.'

'Only brains who amass profit from the weak.' Hafiq stood over him, showing off before the new arrival.

'Watch your tongue, wild man.'

'Who poisoned Allah's children with hashish and poppy!'

'Are the Russians Allah's children? I've blunted their fighting power more than you with your pop-gun.'

Mazloumian said, 'Only since the Lily commandeered your distribution.' He brought Khan's food and sat down beside him.

Khan struggled to attentiveness. So they had heard of the Lily.

'What I am trying to say,' Tamim glowered about him, 'is that I am the survivor here and you my parasites. And why? Because *I trust no one*. And I say something is wrong here. For Yasir to take in Ghoram Khan – if this is Ghoram Khan – someone must have brought pressure to bear. I want to know who and why. So as soon as he is ready to speak I want to hear his story.'

Though Khan ate ravenously, he forced his mind to listen. He needed to know and understand these men. They were the power within these walls and if he could he would use them.

The tall one, he learned, had been head surgeon at the Aliabad medical centre. His name was Sadiq Anwar and he had apparently been imprisoned for saving the life of a prominent dissident who had been gunned down by a Khad execution squad. That meant he was for the resistance. Good.

Mazloumian, he discovered, was a lawyer. He had been sentenced to eight years for refusing to divulge details of a client's defence to the government prosecutor. Khan did not understand about defenders and prosecutors but his stand sounded honourable and he, too, supported the resistance. If he hadn't, Khan would not have been here.

The pink man and the dark stocky one were 'politicos', the former, Gulbadin, a deputy minister of agriculture in the ruling Parcham party, the latter an ex-provincial schoolmaster activist for the Khalq party under the ill-fated Hafizullah Amin. Ideologically these two were bitter enemies, but after almost a year together in the Choukha they seemed to have buried most of their differences, perhaps to resist the domination of the criminal Tamim. Khan mistrusted all politicians, and both parties had collaborated with the Russians, so of the three he would sooner trust Tamim. And anyway, this clearly was Tamim's enclave. As a long-term prisoner, he probably only tolerated the others for the outside money they could contribute. Tamim was the lynchpin.

Food in belly, Khan leaned back and looked at him speculatively. 'The guards do not trouble you here?'

Tamim had a nasal voice, close to a sneer. 'They know which is the camel's head and which its tail. I have trained them to fetch and carry for me. Like the dogs they are.'

'Yasir?'

The sneer deepened to malevolence. 'Yasir is Yasir.'

'A jumped-up army sergeant,' Mazloumian supplied. 'With too much to lose to be corruptible.'

'Unless you happen to have a younger sister.' The corner of Tamim's lip curled to reveal gold teeth. 'A virgin of fourteen, preferably. Who is not averse to his disgusting habits. I knew him before. I had . . . certain dealings with the House With No Doors. He was always in there. Still is. Every weekday afternoon. Three to five. Can you imagine that on top of you? The girls there are terrified of him.'

Hafiq spat. 'For that, *inshallah*, I will kill him.'

'No,' Khan said. 'He is mine.'

Hafiq swung round to contest his claim. But meeting Khan's stony eye, he bestowed a courtly gesture.

'So be it. Age before beauty.'

Tamim said grudgingly to Khan, 'You have the *authority* of a leader, I'll grant you. But, Hafiq – you're a judge of a fighting man – is he or isn't he?'

Hafiq took a rhetorical pose. 'Would I have yielded Yasir to another if my father were not my brother and Afghanistan our mother?' He was paraphrasing an old poem.

'Be serious, ape.'

Tamim pinched his pock-marked nose. 'All right. So he is Khan. Let us examine now why he is in the Choukha. Who put you in here, Khan, the police or the military?'

'The Russians.'

This caused a stir.

The surgeon said, 'So Yasir had no choice. That explains it.'

'But not the purpose. Why here and not in a camp? Or dead?'

'To await interrogation?' Mazloumian hazarded.

'I have been interrogated,' Khan said.

An awkward pause followed his words. Each knew what that must have entailed.

'Did you—' Mazloumian began, then checked himself. There was more silence. 'Then I see it! Twice I have had clients sent here by the police. *Between* interrogations.'

'For softening up?' Tamim thumped his forehead. 'Of course. Yasir is renowned for it.'

'You mean the Russians still resort to violence?' the surgeon cried. 'With all their drugs? Why? Why would they do that?'

Tamim shrugged. 'Does it matter? They have done it, and now we know why he is here.'

Majid's eyes darted to Gulbadin's. He said quickly in Dari, the Persian tongue affected by the intelligentsia, 'If that is so, by helping him are we not opening ourselves to . . . ?'

Gulbadin mirrored his alarm. 'Mazloumian, you should have consulted us before having him brought here.'

Mazloumian stared at them. 'Are you serious? What would you have done – turned your backs on him?'

Sadiq Anwar gave them a distasteful look. 'Ignore them. They think of nothing but their bellies and skins.'

They were all speaking in Dari, assuming that Khan would not understand. As it happened, he had gleaned a working knowledge of Persian from the books of his youth. He could follow them – just – and was finding it very revealing.

'Do you know why we are in this mess?' the lawyer demanded angrily. 'This war, the Russians crawling upon us like locusts? Because of men like you in the seat of power – your greed for privilege. At least,' he indicated Tamim, 'he makes no bones about what he is. He makes no claim to be a patriot.'

'Don't group me with them, Armenian,' Tamim retorted. 'I support my country in my own way. Look to yourself.'

'All right, I was born in Iran and did not support the Shah. But since coming here I have made this my land. I tried to bring dignity and justice to its courts. What did I find? My way was barred by corruption. It permeates this system like rot in a tree. Both parties the same: vested interests, exploitation. Worse – the violence of Amin against the provinces. Which you supported.' He pointed at Majid. 'That is what caused the insurrection that brought in the Russians. Only men like our friend here stand between us and total domination. And you talk of turning him away for fear of losing a few privileges!'

'Simplistic rubbish!' snapped Majid. He was about to launch into a counter-attack but Tamim cut him short.

'Enough! Let us be practical. For once – and I say "for once" – our politicos have a point, Mazloumian. Khan *is* a danger to us. So let us hear what your plea for the defendant is leading up to, Armenian.'

'I am not leading up to anything. Simply—'

'Yes, you are. A lawyer is a fox. He deviates, he backtracks, but always he has one true direction in mind.'

Mazloumian fell silent.

'Let us hear it.'

'He is all camel wind,' Gulbadin said.

Hafiq had had enough. He had not understood a word. He planted himself between them.

'If you are going to argue, do it in a man's tongue, so all can understand!'

Tamim nodded absently. He eyed Mazloumian and waited.

'The obvious answer to all our problems,' the lawyer said at length, reverting to Pushtu, 'is that we help Khan escape.'

Khan awoke from a nightmare to hear them still arguing. His feet throbbed. Through the window he could make out spinning-tops of wind-cloud. Their golden hue told him the sun was sinking.

'I do not understand,' Tamim was saying, 'what is wrong with smuggling him out on the trash lorry or one of the supply vans.'

'Because someone has to go with him.' Mazloumian sounded exasperated. 'He cannot walk. And there is not room for two to hide on the service transport.'

'I will be that second man,' Hafiq said. 'So think of a good way, Armenian.' He grinned at Khan. 'We will go together – you on my back.'

'Your job is here,' Tamim told him curtly. 'Guarding us in this room.'

'Find someone else. What did you say – brains can always buy muscle? Promote Said Mechiti. I will go with my brother.'

Tamim pointed a warning finger. 'Desert me, you spleen of a goat, and I'll see neither of you gets out!'

Hafiq went dangerously still.

Mazloumian said quickly, 'Shall we get the plan agreed first and decide that later? We are going to need outside help. Perhaps a horse or transport for Khan. If it is at night, there is the curfew to be thought of, and patrols. So the help will need to be armed. Does that make sense?'

Gradually heads nodded, Tamim alone abstaining. 'The guards will need plenty of . . .' Tamim rubbed forefinger and thumb slyly together. '*Who* is going to pay for all this?'

'I thought you were all so eager to get rid of him.' Mazloumian eyed the politicos.

Gulbadin, after a quiet word with Majid, said, 'If it is only a matter of a guard or two, I expect we can cover it.'

'And the outside help?' Tamim again.

Mazloumian spread his palm towards Khan. 'The resistance. His people. Better still, if he can contact the Lily, they will organize it.' He turned to Khan. 'Is that possible?'

Khan shook his head.

Mazloumian looked disappointed. 'Not even indirectly? Well then, the resistance. A small force. You must know someone.'

Khan thought of his men still at Do Rish. 'What would they have to do?'

'I don't know yet. Protect you. Smuggle you out of the city. Perhaps a diversion?' The lawyer's whole manner suddenly grew luminous. 'An attack!'

Tamim sighed. 'Armenian, you are a dreamer.'

'No, listen. A small fighting force. Breach the wall – openly – a big bang! Open fire on the guards. Start an exodus. The perfect diversion – pandemonium! Prisoners escaping, pouring out into the city. Khan and – and whoever – slip out of a side gate and—'

'What side gate?' Tamim demanded. 'You are talking out of your arse. You think Yasir would not know who organized all this?'

'Yasir is dead,' Khan said, suddenly aware that the plan could work. 'Before I go, I will kill him.'

'Crawling on all fours, I suppose?' Tamim raised his eyes to Allah.

Khan looked towards Hafiq, who slapped his thigh and rolled out a laugh. 'We will kill him together – you the hunter, me the horse! Allah, this is a good plan!'

'I will write a message,' Khan said. 'Who will take it?'

'One of the guards.' Mazloumian glanced at Tamim. 'Young Abu?'

Tamim flapped his hands, disclaiming all involvement.

'How long will it take your men to assemble?' Sadiq Anwar asked Khan.

'A few days.'

'*Days?*' The lawyer stared at him. 'Why so long?'

'They are in the hills.'

'How far in the hills?'

Khan hesitated and was silent.

'Time is of the essence,' the lawyer stressed. 'If you are here only in between interrogations, Yasir will waste no time. And no effort,' he added uneasily, glancing at Khan's feet. 'How far must the message travel?'

Khan groped in his mind for a noncommittal answer. Even as he did so, he realized that the messenger would have to be told his destination. Could the guard really be trusted? Could even the men in this room be trusted?

He tried to think of an intermediary. Someone in or close to the city who could receive the message and carry it on personally to Do Rish. He could think of no one.

It came as a shock, then, to realize that his own survival was not the be-all and end-all, that it would always be subordinated to the safety of those who put their trust in him.

He sat dully under Mazloumian's pressing, puzzled stare, unable to answer.

The next morning, the guards came – and despite fierce argument from his mentors, dragged Khan down to the ammunition store, stripped the dressings from his feet and beat them again. Yasir watched more closely this time, concentrating less on the physical than the psychological impact of every stroke.

Half an hour later Khan was returned to the room. But the room, not the ablutions. When he could think again clearly, which was not for some hours, this troubled him.

17

YAKUSHEV HAD contrived to spend the day within reach of his telephone. Impatient now, he stretched the sheet of paper between his thumbs and stared at the printed Afghan text, scarcely seeing it.

'So what is it?'

'*Chabnameh*,' Ali Jangalak said. 'Night letters. They are all over town.'

Something in his manner was different. Yakushev wondered if somehow he had heard about the barbecue episode.

'*Mujahedin* propaganda?' Yakushev turned the paper and peered at the design – was it the printer's logo? – below the text. Its significance came to him slowly. He jerked a sharp look at Jangalak, who nodded.

'You were right, my friend. The Lily is not a myth. You were right.'

He was smiling and nodding, happy to concede the point. Not at all like him.

Yakushev said drily, 'You've just come to that conclusion? How long ago did we talk about it? How many things have happened since to confirm my words, culminating in Khan's attempted escape last night?'

'I was sceptical, I admit. But this is proof. Actual proof.'

Yakushev turned back to the leaflet. 'No wonder it's taken you people so damn long to find that infiltrator.'

'Since you mention last night's episode at the Kollola . . .' Jangalak said. 'With this evidence that the Lily is getting bolder, General Naqaswar thinks that they may try for Ghoram Khan again. He asks whether Khad can help assure his safekeeping.'

'Does he think we're so inefficient?'

'You are satisfied then that he is absolutely safe?'

'If it is any of his business, yes.'

Jangalak did not bat an eyelid. 'He says, if you are having trouble with his interrogation, he is holding a man who once lived in Bab-el-Hawa. He thought, if you would like us to put them in together . . .'

'Who told him we were having trouble with Khan's interrogation?'

'He said, "if".'

The level dark eyes appeared innocent of guile. Yet Yakushev had the distinct impression that he was probing to find out Khan's whereabouts. 'We need no help, tell him. But thank him.'

'I think he is concerned that—' Jangalak persisted, but Yakushev's raised finger silenced him. He had begun reading again.

Jangalak watched him expressionlessly for a moment, then sat down and crossed his legs. Manicured fingernails drummed on the desk-top until Yakushev's sidelong scowl stilled them.

'What's this crap about the Prophet being reborn and the child being already in the womb?'

The Afghan shrugged elegant shoulders. 'We are a poetic race.'

'You telling me they'd print it if it didn't mean something?'

'The object, I imagine, is to instil fear and mystery.'

'Fear. Yes, you said that before. Fear of God.' Yakushev gave the text more scrutiny. 'You have any more copies of this?'

'We have confiscated, so far, almost a hundred.'

'Run one over to your doctors of holy law – what are they called?'

'The *Ulema*.'

'See if they can detect a hidden meaning. It may be a reference to something in the Koran.' A thought occurred to him. 'Ramadan wouldn't be anything to do with the birth of Mahomed, would it?'

'No. It celebrates the month of his coming to prophethood.'

'Anyway, do it.' Yakushev got up and stood jingling the small change in his pockets. 'Distribution by hand, of course. Have you pulled in any of the recipients?'

'There are never recipients of *chabnameh*, my friend. The letters simply appear and are passed round.'

'Nothing "appears", Ali. There's a first man in every chain.

Find him. He'll lead you to the distribution agent, he to the supplier, and so on up.'

Jangalak flared an incredulous eye at him. Only a Russian could prescribe a near-impossibility in such bland terms. But today he made no protest.

Yakushev continued, 'I'll get our technical services to analyse the paper and printing. My guess is they were run off in Peshawar across the border, but that won't stop us. We'll reach out a long arm and interrogate the printer's balls off.'

Jangalak nodded. He was waiting for a chance to speak. 'Colonel—'

The telephone made a sound like a bee under a cup.

Yakushev reacted as though it had stung him. 'That's all. I want action from Khad this time, Ali. We have a deal, remind the general.'

'Of course. That was why—' Jangalak had a lot more to say, but Yakushev practically propelled him out of the door.

He picked up the phone. 'Hold on.' He put it down and checked outside to make quite sure Jangalak had gone. He came back, convinced that the caller was Yasir at last.

But the voice he pressed to his ear was Dolin's.

'Get yourself up here, please.'

The tone was level, but Dolin's 'please' evoked the image of wind across ice.

'I've just had a call from General Organskiy.' Dolin was packing files into an attaché case. 'Concerning Ghoram Khan. He wants access and we've got him hidden, is that right?'

His sidelong glance held curiosity, even suspicion.

'Hidden from them, correct, General,' Yakushev said easily. Though inwardly he cursed. The whole world, suddenly, was interested in Khan. Organskiy was head of the KGB directorate. Repin's boss.

'Any particular reason?' Dolin enquired of his filing cabinet.

'We haven't finished with him.'

Dolin reached for the sugary-looking triptych of photographs of his family, folded it reverently and laid it on top of the files.

'You off somewhere, General?'

'I'm going with the marshal to Kandahar again. Two days.'

'Problems?'

'Nothing that concerns you.' Dolin looked directly at him. 'Why *would* the KGB be interested in Ghoram Khan?'

'I don't know and I don't particularly care.'

Dolin kept looking. 'When you get what you want, can they have him?'

Yakushev hesitated. 'It depends on what we get.'

'And what's that likely to be?' He was still looking.

'His sources of information.'

'Nothing more specific?' Dolin paused for a second or two, then bent to close the case. 'I understand you barbecued one of his followers. That's not like you.'

More like you, Yakushev thought, but said, 'No. It . . . wasn't my intention. Just the way it worked out.'

'Well, that was what alerted the Tchekists.'

'So I gathered. I suppose Harvest has got them on edge. Like it has you,' he made the pause fractional, 'and me.'

Dolin stilled dangerously. After a moment he bent to lock each desk drawer carefully. When he straightened, the covers were off his guns.

'Well, if their paranoia has any basis in fact and there's something – *anything at all* – that could have a bearing on Harvest that you're not telling me, I'll have your balls, Andrei Pavlovich, make no mistake.'

'I'm fully aware of that, General.'

Dolin waited. 'Well, is there?'

'No.'

The general grunted. He moved to collect his enormous hat. He put it on, facing Yakushev, at pains not to fingerprint the patent leather brim.

'Personal vendettas are messy things, Colonel. More important, I dislike intensely having the KGB on my back.' He picked up the attaché case. 'So my suggestion to you – no, my order – is that you remove the cause of it. Cut your losses. Have Khan shot.' He picked a signal out of his in-tray. 'Understood?'

'Understood.'

'Having done that, you will feel freer to pursue matters like this.' He handed the signal to him. 'You can study it later. Briefly, a British war cameraman is under interrogation at Air Army RO. Seems he got some guerrillas to shoot up the T-2 canisters stored on Forward Air Strip Q8.'

Yakushev looked amazed.

'A gunship stopped him with a rocket. He's concussed and it's making interrogation difficult. They've got his film, no problem there. The problem is going to be what to do with him. He has no proof on celluloid, but he still has a mouth, and the moment the international press hear he's under arrest they're going to clamour for his release.'

'I can stop that.'

'In the short run possibly. But they're a clannish lot. They'll make him a *cause célèbre*, world headline material. The big danger, though, is that word of what he was up to will leak. Result: publicity and accusations re our brutal use of chemicals against defenceless villagers. The Americans will make a meal of it. And all at this very sensitive time. You follow?'

'Then the press mustn't even hear of him.'

'Precisely. Only one problem. Preliminary lie-detector tests suggest that he was sent in by the CIA. They could sound the alarm themselves.'

'Only if they know what has happened to him.'

Dolin stared at him. 'You mean that until they're sure he's been captured they're going to keep their mouths shut? That point had escaped me.'

'Were the *mujahedin* with him captured as well?'

'Another good point. You'll have to find out.' Dolin moved to the door, slightly mollified. 'Anyway, the thing for you to aim at is, this Englishman never happened. We have no knowledge of him at all. Certainly until after Harvest.'

'I'll get on to Air Army.'

'That's all,' Dolin opened the door. 'That and Khan.'

Belly first, meaningful gaze last, the general vanished along the hall.

Throughout the beautiful spring afternoon and evening Yakushev worked and smoked and waited for Yasir's call. Shoot Khan? He could not disobey. But Dolin had not specified a deadline. That gave him until the old man's return – two clear days in which to outwit and break his old enemy.

He sent a signal to Air Army RO Intelligence telling them what to do with the British cameraman when they had finished with him, and advising them to observe strict security silence concerning his capture. He himself could muster little interest in him. He would make up his mind whether to put him through a GRU interrogation when he had received a copy of their transcript.

Ali Jangalak. He thought about him for a while, weighing their past conversations, and came slowly to a decision.

The sun set in magnificent colours. He could see the chains of light outlining the mosques from his window. Soon the *muezzins* would be calling the faithful to prayer over their tinny public address systems. Until then the bazaars would be teeming. Then the gauzy smoke of a thousand fires would appear as each family prepared its feast.

Night letters . . . *Fear of God.* Only in such a culture could the Lily come to flower, he thought. West versus East. Spacemen versus angels.

It was not so unequal a contest as it had at first seemed. The angels were providing him with quite a challenge.

Unlocking the top drawer of his filing cabinet, Yakushev released a folder taped under the roof of the fitment and opened it on his desk. In it he had recorded everything relating to the Lily's existence. There was no other copy.

The penalties for withholding such information were harsh indeed, but he was confident that, in retrospect, his lone venture could appear heroic – if, of course, he was successful.

He mulled over the entries thoughtfully, planning his moves. But Yasir never called.

18

FOR MCCABE, time had ceased to have meaning. It was marked by short periods of consciousness and pain, nothing more. In one, he seemed to be lying in a plastic bubble surrounded by astronauts. He saw his precious camera glistening in a mist of aerosol sprays and wondered vaguely if that meant that he himself was contaminated. Later there was a bed and his head was a cannonball on raised pillows.

In his line of work he was only too familiar with the symptoms of concussion. But how about the rest of him? In the leaden darkness behind closed eyes he called the roll, starting with his toes and flexing each bit in turn, till he was sure that all of him worked. Well, reasonably sure. One could lose a leg and still think it was there, he seemed to remember.

The Russians stood over him and talked to him in their own language – *at* him, like men knocking on a closed door. *'Is there anybody there?' said the traveller.* He let their own echoes answer them. Closed weekends. Back Monday.

Monday already? Or perhaps they couldn't read. This time one was speaking in English, with an accent like bees scraping honey off their wings. '. . . . whole lot to explain!' American bees. But the overtones were international: he was in trouble. Big trouble. And he remembered perfectly well why.

The needle came out of the blue, sudden as a wasp under your shirt. They had kept piling pillows under his head and he had struggled to get rid of them, and suddenly – *zing* – he became a different man. They weren't going to wear his act, they wanted him singing. And here he was talking about sister Lola, how they had tried to build a houseboat on the lily pond out of packing cases and nailed the plastic underneath and wondered why it wasn't watertight. The faces around the bed took on a greyish tinge. Their perspective went wrong. He could hear a helicopter lifting off somewhere so clearly that he could distinguish the different pitch of each turboshaft, but the faces at the front seemed to be behind the faces at the back, and that worried him.

The one who spoke English smelled of tobacco. The finger he pointed at him was stained bright orange and was longer than his arm. He was haranguing him, accusing him of sabotage, demanding to know who had put him up to it, who his conspirators were and from what base they operated. McCabe One wanted to explain it all to him very carefully; McCabe Two said, Not on your Nelly!

Nothing seemed to resolve itself. They went away, only they were still there, their uniforms bluish in the failing light. He talked a lot, trying to keep the nonsense flowing, but he caught a few words of the truth popping out here and there and it scared him badly. He was an old pro, dammit, and Ayesha and the President were depending on him.

He tried shutting every orifice, like a crewman in a tank – the eyes first, the mouth next, then the ears. The ears were the hardest. He twisted them against the pillows and set up a roar, from side to side, side to side. He was shut in now. Impregnable. But for how long?

The hell of it was, he had always been responsible just to himself and the viewing public. He had never had anything to hide before.

The medical hut in Somalia had been full of napalm cases, half of them kids. Carson had found him stretched out on the dirt floor amongst them, minus his camera gear, sound equipment and his wits, after the ambush explosion. He hadn't known Carson from Adam, but Carson knew him. He was from the US State Department, where they knew everybody who was somebody, and McCabe was somebody all right. Somebody they wanted.

Big, soft Carson had flown him by helicopter, raving like a lunatic, to Mogadishu, to a US missile cruiser anchored in the bay, where the MO had pumped him full of dope. When he woke up he was two days out to sea. He had stopped shaking and was *compos mentis* enough to be coldly furious. So bloody well what if he was in post-trauma and needing medication? Did it make this any less of a kidnap?

Carson was earnestly reassuring, evasive and clearly stalling – until . . . He raised a pudgy forefinger, relief oozing from every pore. The ship was slowing. McCabe just had time, he said, to shower and shave.

Fifteen minutes later, a marine marching ahead of them, he escorted McCabe to a forward hold, where portable screens had been placed around a little table behind a stack of missiles.

Presently, McCabe heard a thump on the deck above and a helicopter came down on the elevator, its rotor still swinging. Out of it, who should step, for Pete's sake, but Philip Habib's one-time aide and co-negotiator, Jakobus Hirsch!

'I'm here, Mike, as an intermediary,' were his first tired, slightly accented words. 'The President called me in Riyadh. He said, 'Jake, go see that young fella who makes the other war news guys look like they never left the hotel . . .'

Hirsch listened to McCabe's complaints sympathetically, then ignored them. How did he *get* to some of those places without political clout behind him? How come he never used a crew? How many major awards was it now? Was it true he was tortured by the Cubans? Gradually Hirsch worked the topic round to Laos. Had he been up amongst the hill tribes? Had he encountered any of the Hmong refugees? Well then, perhaps he had picked up a few . . . disturbing stories?

Hirsch watched his expression oddly, then moved on. McCabe had made a film comparatively recently in the Yemen, wasn't that so? Well, had he ever gotten to the village of el Kwama? Bombed by Nasser in June 1973? No? But he had heard what happened there, surely?

McCabe had the sudden feeling he was trapped in a maze without a ladder.

Again Hirsch, after examining his expression, rolled the ball past him. So he had decided to retire? Well, the world would lose a great talent, but, of course, if he felt he must . . . and had enough put by . . . He *did* have enough put by? Hirsch supposed.

No, McCabe misunderstood him. By 'enough' he meant sufficient to stake him in some new career. 'Making out' was for the birds. A whimper. How could a man of his calibre start a new life on anything less than a resounding bang?

Then Hirsch leaned forward and said distinctly, 'Private commission. Off the record. Government funded. Half-hour film. Very limited distribution. We'd own the copyright. If you didn't want your name associated with it, it need never appear on the screen.'

McCabe stared at him. And made his first mistake.

'Film of what?'

'I think you know. The truth. As only your camera can convey it. Shot so it can be *seen* to be the truth. No possibility whatsoever of fake. Uncut negative.'

The next moment Carson was scribbling under his nose. 'We would pay you this for the copyright.'

Copyright of what? McCabe still wasn't sure what the hell they were talking about. They had to be either desperate or crazy trying to hire a guy in breakdown! He peered past the Schaeffer felt-tip held phallus-wise. Zero after zero after zero! He couldn't focus. *Was* it a double image?

McCabe woke up suddenly to find himself in a plane droning through the sky. He felt peculiar, and his forearm itched, but his mind was receiving, so far as he could tell, accurate messages.

He was fully dressed in his tattered Pathan clothes, lying on a stretcher between two rows of tip-up seats. These and the circular portholes told him he was in an Antonov 2-P biplane. Sitting stoically on the foremost seats were two airborne infantrymen in camouflage tunics and fur hats. They held AKMS assault rifles with folding stocks at the ready, but their attention was directed outside the aircraft to the ground below. Beyond them, the backs of the pilot and co-pilot showed in silhouette against slowly moving slopes of snow.

His first thought was, shit, Had he talked and told them all that about Hirsch and the President? More important, had he let slip what he had learned subsequently – that the prime purpose of the film was to shock the hard-heads in Congress into voting the finance necessary to set the US on the road to chemical rearmament?

He groped for some stray, telltale image, as one does to recall a dream, but all he came up with was Ayesha's voice yelling to him to pull out. Jesus, had he blown her and the guys as well? If so, they'd be dead. But there was still nothing concrete. It was weird how he could remember nothing and yet was so alert.

He was scratching again. He pulled back his sleeve and peered at five puncture marks. Four were old and greyish but the fifth was pink and fresh with a yellow centre.

So that was why. Before putting him aboard they must have injected a stimulant. That meant they had finished with him.

The pilot pulled suddenly off the runway and shut down three hundred metres short of the buildings bearing the big sign 'Kabul'. There was a wait.

'What's going on?' McCabe was up now, gazing out at the distant host of parked Turbolev transports. They looked like a school of stranded whales.

One of the men spread pink, almost Dayglo, hands. The other stared past him, hostile and bored. There was some talk between the pilot and the tower. It petered out. Neither he nor his mate moved.

McCabe wondered apprehensively whether he had the strength to face all the red tape that was sure as hell about to come his way. Ending up in a civil court maybe. A commie court. The Gary Powers syndrome. Embarrassing. Worse. Blown up out of all proportion, then used by the Russians as a bargaining factor. His release for one of theirs. If the US had one of theirs. If not?

A GAZ light truck pulled up alongside and the one with Dayglo hands wrestled the fuselage door open. Three hard-looking characters came aboard. They wore airborne jackets with the yellow security flash. Two clipped handcuffs on him while their NCO took charge of a webbing zip case containing, presumably, the paperwork. They had him down and inside the closed back of the truck within two minutes. Outside the airport in four.

Two rode inside with him and their alertness suggested they had a dedicated interest in seeing that he got to where they were taking him.

'You speak English?'

If either of them did, he wasn't letting on.

McCabe made the cigarette sign.

Neither smoked.

He gazed through the plastic back window. His headache was coming back. Now take it easy, he warned himself. Don't flip. The road streaming behind was dead straight and lined with trees. Following was an ancient taxi, empty except for the man at the wheel. Its bodywork could only have been painted by someone on an acid trip. No wonder the driver wore dark glasses.

They crossed the river amid heavy traffic and turned right. Radio music howled past them from every shopfront. No sign of the Russian presence. But then you never saw the puppeteer, just all the little Babrak Karmals dancing. As they stopped for a herd of goats now, he realized the taxi was right up behind them.

Now they were crossing the river again. 'Harton Bridge'. Ayesha said she had been born around here somewhere. Would he ever see her again?

Now left. The taxi was still following.

McCabe began to take a serious interest in it. But almost at once the truck turned off up a steep slope and the cab went straight on. Moments later they nosed to a halt before a massive keyhole gate.

19

The Choukha lacked much of the refinement, even elegance, that characterized the Raj cantonments of the 1840s. Some effort was made, however, to bring the administration wing up to standard, as it would house the officers' mess, where local dignitaries were customarily entertained.

The long room with its view across the city, where regimental officers once dined in gleaming protocol, perhaps to the skirl of bagpipes, was now Yasir's office. That its pastel colouring and ornate plasterwork were long gone, its crystal chandeliers torn down in the belief that they were made of diamonds, was of no interest to the ex-army sergeant. The proportions of the room suited his ego. He could pace its length and imagine himself a monarch, with the power of life and death in his cruel fingers.

McCabe watched his knock-kneed walk as he paced out his territory, beads clicking, belly a sagging prow in his uniform. McCabe was in shock. He had just been inducted, stripped, deloused, head-shaved and robbed of his watch and every other personal possession. He had glimpsed the horror of what was to be his environment. His headache was back, and his double vision. He had kicked up such a shindy that he had been brought before the Governor, where he had demanded to see a lawyer, or the American or British resident, or a member of one of the non-aligned diplomatic missions, or a representative of any of the press associations, including Tass – *anyone*. The bastard hadn't understood a word he said.

Now they were waiting, God knew for what. At worst, he knew, he should have been put in a holding jail to await arraignment. But this place, he could tell at first glance, was a long-term prison where, in a country like this, people just vanished without a trace. The only way to get noticed was to make enough splash before going under. Keep splashing. It was his only hope.

The tall door with the classical architrave opened. A prisoner was thrust into the room and the door closed behind him. He stood there awkwardly, his eyes dark with fear. He had rounded features, not the sharp, lean ones of a Pathan, and wore what had once been a hacking jacket of good cut. But the long shirt hanging beneath it and the tattered trousers spoiled the effect.

Yasir made him wait, as he made everyone wait, while he contemplated the view from one of the high sash windows through his dark glasses. The newcomer eyed McCabe with uneasy curiosity, his gaze then straying to the selection of whips, canes and bludgeons that shared the rack with Yasir's absurdly braided hat. The rack was made from the bent hooves of mountain ibex and, apart from the desk and two chairs, was the only appointment in the whole of the room.

Yasir swung round suddenly and barked a string of sentences at the prisoner, the walls amplifying the utterness of his authority.

The prisoner blinked and turned to McCabe.

'You are English?'

Thank *God*! McCabe's hand flew to his throbbing brow. He poured out his complaints, reasserted his demands.

The prisoner seemed to have a tolerable command of the language because he translated everything he said unhesitatingly into Pushtu.

Yasir listened, his thumb snapping his beads together with mounting impatience. He interrupted increasingly.

'He says there is no mistake,' the prisoner told McCabe. 'His orders were that you be held here incommunicado.'

'He can't do that.'

'I am afraid he can. He says—'

'Look, tell him I demand the right under the—'

'You have no rights. I am sorry,' the prisoner cut him off. 'I am a lawyer and I tell you that under the present martial law you can be held here indefinitely without trial or communication.'

'You're a lawyer?'

'I was, yes.'

'Then tell me what the hell I do. There has to be *some* means of appeal, for Christ's sake!'

'I – I cannot think for you now.' Mazloumian eyed Yasir apprehensively. 'But my advice is accept the situation and I will find you a way of getting word out to – to whoever we decide. Please do not resist at this point. It will only bring you punishment. The punishment here is very severe. Trust me – please.'

McCabe fell silent. He felt as if he would burst. He looked daggers at Yasir, but flapped his hands.

The wraparound glasses studied him with hostile intensity for a moment and McCabe had the distinct impression that his submission had saved him from being flogged for temerity. The glasses switched back to Mazloumian questioningly.

The lawyer mumbled a few propitiating words of explanation.

Yasir's gaze bored into McCabe once more. His lips curled like snakes around a short sentence as he turned away.

McCabe needed no interpreter. The governor wanted him out of his sight.

McCabe lowered himself to an unoccupied *charpoy* and clutched his pounding head. He had scarcely glanced at the six prisoners lounging around the little room. His mind was filled with the degradation he had just witnessed on his way through the prison.

'I think he is sick,' Mazloumian said to Sadiq.

'Is this a hospital?' Tamim hauled himself up from his bed angrily. 'Who is he anyway? Why have you brought him here?'

'He is from *Engelstan*,' Mazloumian said meaningfully.

Tamim, startled, took a second look at McCabe.

'He is a news photographer,' the lawyer explained. 'Jailed, I don't know what for – perhaps illegal entry – but he is desperate to make contact with people outside, to let them know he is here. Desperate, you understand?'

Tamim understood. Desperate meant 'at any cost'. His manner changed.

'Gulbadin, give him some tea.'

Mazloumian made brief introductions. McCabe tried to pay attention. Hell, they looked pasty. All but the wild-looking one and the one with bloody rags round his feet and a vivid burn-mark on his nose. The latter lay motionless; only his bloodshot eyes moved.

McCabe asked no questions. He kept his mouth shut and his brain as alert as possible, and waited. He had been a prisoner before.

'Who do you want to contact?' Tamim asked him through Mazloumian.

McCabe listed the alternatives.

'It will cost you money, you realize?'

McCabe shrugged. 'No problem. Once the contact is made.'

'Not before?'

'You think I have it stuck up my ass?'

Tamim was silent for a moment. He twisted a rare smile. 'Of course not. The English I have always found most trustworthy.'

'You should live down our way,' McCabe said.

Gulbadin handed him some tea. The tall one, Sadiq, came and sat by him.

'You have problem?' he asked, indicating the way he was holding his head.

Another English-speaker? Well, well, he *was* in educated company. 'Concussion,' McCabe told him, simulating a hard blow to his head.

Sadiq tilted McCabe's chin and thumbed back his eyelids, studied his pupils, then leaned back and raised one finger. 'How many?'

'Too many.'

Cool fingertips probed the nape of McCabe's skull.

'Here?'

'Exactly there.'

Sadiq turned him a little and began to massage.

Gulbadin asked McCabe through Mazloumian how the war was progressing. McCabe mumbled that he hadn't a clue, that he'd been working in the field with a resistance group.

Khan spoke for the first time. Which group?

Mazloumian translated.

McCabe shook his head. He wasn't saying.

Mazloumian said, 'You can talk freely. This is Ghoram Khan, the resistance leader. He is asking for a reason.'

McCabe had heard the name. He regarded Khan curiously. Yes, it was there in the eyes, the unrelenting quality. He should have noticed. A little more introverted, less lit, possibly, by ideological conviction than most, but he had met them all and recognized in Khan the one – perhaps the only one – denominator common to the resistance leaders of his experience; that of being resistant. More profoundly, organically, *dynamically* immovable than rock.

McCabe sighed. He still did not speak.

Khan understood and did not press him. He changed the question. Did the group have a resident contact here in Kabul?

McCabe said he didn't know.

Mazloumian spoke confidentially. 'If you are being discreet please do not be. You see his condition. Yasir is crippling him with punishment. Any day now he may be taken back for interrogation by the Russians. We have a plan to help him escape. But it needs outside help and he will not trust the guard who is our messenger with information of where his men are hidden.'

'Good for him.'

'Unfortunately, not good for him – or us. We have suggested he name a – how do you say? – third person. Someone the guard can pass the message through. But Khan says he has no connection in the city. So we are at a stop. There is nothing we can do. We are in despair for him.' The lawyer waited anxiously to see if he had anything to contribute.

The last thing McCabe needed was to get caught up in these men's problems. He had enough of his own.

'What's wrong with the Lily? Put it in their hands.'

Mazloumian looked at him oddly. 'You know of the Lily?' He sighed. 'My friend, they do not advertise. They are very secret. We have no way to contact them.'

McCabe shrugged. 'Pass a message through their information network, I don't know.'

Mazloumian flickered his dark lashes and shook his head. 'Network?'

'The channel used by their informers.'

Mazloumian seemed not to have heard of it. He conveyed the suggestion to Khan.

Staring penetratingly at McCabe, Khan levered himself upright painfully and placed each foot with great care on the floor. He appeared about to speak but, catching Tamim's eye, frowned and remained silent.

A curious atmosphere of constraint filled the room. Mazloumian, the most forthright, was first to break it.

'This channel. Do you yourself know how it may be used?'

McCabe cursed himself. Ayesha had warned him, 'You will please keep this amongst yourself,' bless her syntax. Khan, though, seemed genuinely in a bad way, something the fair doctor would have been the first to respond to. What was the Lily for, anyway, if it wasn't to keep the wheels of resistance turning? Especially the big wheels. Even so, this was none of his business.

But, okay, suppose he *did* tell them – where would that leave him? A lone wolf with no back-up, just the hope that the CIA would rescue their boy. But they could also wash their hands of him, to avoid complicity. If so, this Lily information was his sole asset, blue-chip stuff, not to be squandered.

He said, experimentally, 'What's in it for me?'

Mazloumian shook his head. 'For you?'

'If I tell you – what's it worth?'

'You can do this?'

'As one desperate man for another.' McCabe frowned at Khan. 'Yeah, maybe.'

'And . . . you want payment?'

'Suppose . . .' McCabe squeezed up his eyes and put the words together slowly. 'I help you get him out . . . and when he goes, I go with him?'

Mazloumian said cautiously, 'You want me to put this to him?'

'Go ahead.'

McCabe studied each face in the fading light as the lawyer addressed the court. Tamim would look any gift horse in the mouth, he guessed. But Khan should have been loosening the tourniquet on his expression just a notch. Some factor was bothering him. Perhaps that this was some kind of trap? Well, good. A thinking animal. One that, once they were outside, would know just where to go . . . McCabe could see a whole new scenario shaping.

Only when Tamin finally bobbed his head did Khan consent.

Mazloumian returned his attention to McCabe, his whole manner sparking.

'So tell us, please, how we may do this!'

'The system is the same for each city. It has to be from a call-box. Dial operator enquiries but with an eight in front. When someone answers, you say "Lily". They'll say you have the wrong number. You don't hang up, just wait. After maybe two minutes they switch you through to a radio transmitter and you pass your message.'

Mazloumian spread his hands. 'So simple?'

'ABC.'

'May I ask how you, a foreigner, knows this?'

'No.'

'But it is the truth – you swear it.'

'How could I hope to escape if it wasn't?'

'Then I thank you, my friend. You have our deepest gratitude.'

The lawyer explained the instructions to the others. He leaned across and peered at Tamim's wristwatch – the only timepiece, it seemed, in the room.

'Half an hour,' he told McCabe. 'Our man, the guard we most trust, begins his duty in half an hour.'

He got to his feet and began to pace, like a man mentally rehearsing his lines.

McCabe looked at Khan. He was pulling his feet up, shifting his hips further back on the bed, grunting. When he had got his back against the wall, he closed his eyes as if the effort had exhausted him and withdrew into himself.

The others busied themselves quietly. No one spoke.

The sky outside had turned gradually from yellow to green. The background cacophony of the prison faded for a moment as a flight of gunships came over, pounding the air. Far off, McCabe thought he heard thunder. But it wasn't that kind of sky. So it had to be gunfire.

The minutes dragged like hours. Hafiq was sitting cross-legged, his back against the wall. Head cocked at a shard of mirror in his hand, he was trimming his beard with a pair of nail scissors.

McCabe had noted the Pathan vanity – the *kohl* around the eyes, the oiled hair. The younger ones had a girlish something. Yet all were incredible fighters.

There was a sudden disturbance on the balcony outside the room, shouts, curses. Someone thumped against the door. Then came a cry of pain.

He saw Hafiq freeze and gather himself. But the scuffle diminished, terminating in a cackle of maniacal laughter. The Pathan relaxed again and continued to trim his beard.

Yes, Hafiq was something else. A swashbuckler. One who would kill just to show his mettle, then enjoy a good laugh about it.

Mazloumian took a chair and placed it under the window. He climbed on it and pressed his face to the bars so he could watch the yard below.

Gulbadin hoisted himself up and lit the samovar. The whole room leapt with the spurt of the match.

In a short time the arclights came on in the yard. The reflection crept down from the ceiling.

Mazloumian gave a hiss and got down off the chair. He spoke in Pushtu, then in English. 'He is there. Wish me luck.' He paused, looking around.

No one spoke.

Mazloumian shot Khan an encouraging look, hesitated, then left the room.

When the door closed everyone but Khan moved, drawing towards each other as though released from a spell. Tamim nodded at Hafiq. Hafiq tucked his mirror and scissors away in the folds of his clothing. One moment he was sitting there, the next he was gone after the lawyer on silent feet.

Tamim was speaking to Sadiq. Sadiq, after a moment to marshal his scant vocabulary, said to McCabe, 'Mazloumian – he speak good English, no?'

McCabe shrugged. 'Pretty good.'

'He—' Sadiq groped. 'How he speak? You say, "accent"? How is his accent?'

McCabe thought. 'Painstakingly learned, I'd say. Just something about . . .' He looked at them.

Every face was turned towards him.

'Yes?' The word was clipped, urgent.

'I thought he was your friend.'

'It is important, please – your answer.'

'A Russian accent, yes.' McCabe examined their faces curiously. 'Why didn't you stop me?'

'It is okay, McCabe. It is okay, please.' The surgeon motioned him to remain calm. He explained to the others what McCabe had said. This loosed a verbal torrent. When it had stilled, Sadiq said in English, 'We were not sure.' He tapped his temple. 'Khan, Tamim, they think . . . but not sure. Now you make us sure.'

'It's a great time to tell me.'

'Not your fault.' The surgeon raised his hand. 'We wait.'

Majid got on the chair and looked down into the yard. The others watched him in silence. He had to stand on tiptoe to see out. Presently Tamim asked him a question. He shook his head. Apparently there was no sign of the Armenian.

'Abd Rahim?'

That must be the guard. Majid shook his head again. No sign of him either.

McCabe looked on, arms folded. The escape was down the drain. Now what was he going to do?

After a time the door opened and Hafiq came back, the breath hissing in his nose. He went straight to the samovar and felt it to see if it was nearing the boil.

The others waited anxiously for him to speak. When he did not, Tamim put an impatient question. Hafiq answered thickly.

There was a murmur, the word 'Allah' repeated.

McCabe waited.

The surgeon said, 'Mazloumian – he not go to guard. He go straight to Yasir.'

'That's nice.'

'He not arrive Yasir,' Sadiq went on. 'Now there is a dead man in the small house where is made the electric light.' He added consolingly, 'The Lily's secret – it is safe, still.'

'It always was,' McCabe told him. 'You think I was born yesterday? He died with a headful of horseshit.'

20

THE EARLY sun shone guilelessly from a baby-blue sky. Its light and dense shadow among the old fortifications overlooking the city reflected darkly from Yasir's glasses.

'I made a point of not telephoning, Colonel. Seeing as this was—'

'Who was responsible?' Yakushev demanded quietly, contriving not to show his intense frustration, even sorrow. Mazloumian was the second top agent he had lost in his duel with Khan. His abilities had been exceptional, his cover cast-iron, for Yakushev had recruited him personally from the ranks of the Afghan legal profession – by means of some ruthless persuasion, it is true, having to do with the well-being of his family in Soviet Armenia. For all that, the laywer had served him well, and in the least enviable of environments. Someone must have penetrated his cover.

'I don't know who did it yet, Colonel.' Yasir squeezed up his face and spread his mouth, like a man under a strong light. 'But I will find out.'

'One of those room-mates?'

'I'll have it for you. I delayed putting the screws on them till I'd seen you. I never like to barge in on a security set-up before I check.' Yasir went on talking, using his hands and voice and authority to dispel any suggestion that the murder resulted from slackness on his part.

Yakushev lost interest. He couldn't stand the man. He built a church over his nose and mouth with his fingers and gazed absently along the barrel of the noon gun, beside which they were standing. He was thinking that his other man in the Choukha could probably find out how it had happened more quickly than Yasir. He probably knew already. But did it matter now? Mazloumian was dead, the cause academic. The next act was already scripted – the back-up man would have to take on the Armenian's role. What remained to be done required nerve but no great subtlety.

Yes, he would have to pass him fresh orders before tomorrow. Not through Yasir: Yasir did not know his identity, nor even that he existed.

Yakushev sighed inwardly. It was all very complicated and becoming more so. But the big dividend was within sight now. The Lily. Waiting to be plucked.

Yasir had stopped talking and was standing, belly out, waiting for his response.

Yakushev said, 'The KGB – have they been around at all?'

The *non sequitur* threw Yasir for a moment. 'Not so far as I know. Why should they be?'

Yakushev glanced down towards the lookout vehicles he had posted – one by the turning off the main road alongside Baber Shah Park, the other on the river bridge immediately below them. Their job was to see that he had not been followed here and that this meeting remained undisturbed. So far there had been no signal from either of them. He was still, he guessed, a jump or two ahead of Repin and Organskiy.

'If they do come . . .' Yasir hitched up his paunch uneasily. He was wrestling with the spectre of having to mislead one Soviet security organ at the dictate of the other. 'If they do, and they ask about Khan, what do I say?'

'You don't say. You don't see them. You're not available.'

'How? If they just walk in?'

'By having just walked out the other way. Avoid them, Governor. For the next twenty-four hours.'

'Twenty-four?' The dark glasses came to rest on Yakushev uncomprehendingly.

'I am going to order an execution.'

'I don't understand.' Yasir looked away, as if seeking an explanation among the battlements. He looked back so sharply that his cheeks shook. 'Khan?' He looked dismayed. 'You're – you're not giving up so soon, Colonel, surely? I've hardly begun with him yet!'

'To take place at noon tomorrow.'

Yasir looked sulky. 'Very well.' He turned and paced for a moment, his beads clicking. 'You'll send the transport, of course, detail the squad, the place. I'll have Khan ready for you.'

'Not just Khan,' Yakushev said, right off the top of his head. 'Every man in that room.' He needed to include his own man, and the larger the party, the less any suspicion would centre on him.

Yasir stopped and stared at him. 'You can't do that! Uh – with respect. The others are civil prisoners, Colonel. Outside your jurisdiction.'

'It will be arranged, Governor, quite correctly. Make a list of their names. How many of them are there, by the way?'

Yasir counted on his fingers. 'Including Khan, seven.'

'Well, make the list and submit it, *by hand*, to General Naqaswar of Khad this afternoon. I'll see that he issues the necessary authorization.'

Yasir, though mollified, was actually shocked, Yakushev realized. He watched a new respect surface slowly through the grossness – the sort of respect a man like the ex-sergeant reserved for the rare person who was an even bigger bastard than himself.

The organization of Khad bore more resemblance to the KGB than to the GRU. Its officers were recruited from the privileged classes, not the lower echelons, as in the GRU. General Naqaswar was no exception. His proud antecedents and military staff background were obvious from the cut of his civilian clothes and his almost British appearance: grey moustache and hair, clean jawline despite his years. His attitude to his work was British too: however unpleasant, it was justified by the needs of his country. Only a certain darkness under the eyes told of his haunted nights and the alienation of his wife, who abhorred what he did to keep her and the four children in the manner to which they were accustomed.

Yakushev shook his dry, firm hand in the leathery office that overlooked a section of the *lycée* gardens. Aides bustled about. Ali Jangalak advanced a chair for him. Yakushev sat down, elbows on knees – like the gardener, he couldn't escape the feeling, come to ask the master's sanction to cut down a tree. Overtones of upper-classdom, even among wogs always made him uneasy and aggressive.

'Well,' Naqaswar spoke in Pushtu for his benefit, though

Dari was his accustomed tongue, 'what can I do for you, Colonel?' Yakushev scowled at the aides till the general motioned them to go and only Jangalak to stay. This was protocol – a fact that Yakushev had anticipated.

Yakushev watched the door close, then said, 'Now, are we or are we not secure, General?'

It was a hostile beginning. Naqaswar took it like a gentleman.

'We are secure, Colonel.'

'So you've found your informer at last?'

The general did not flinch at the barb. He opened a drawer of his desk and held up an object the size of a thick coat button. Jangalak passed it over.

It was a bug.

Yakushev was staggered. The implications of the Lily having such technology were immense. It was of Japanese manufacture, requiring activation from a nearby source, a power and monitoring unit.

'Where was this found?'

'Here in this office.' Naqaswar indicated one of the wall-light brackets. 'As I understand it, it must have shifted position and shorted the flexes. Our electrical engineers found it. We immediately swept the whole building.'

'Did you find any more?'

'No, just the one.'

'And the monitoring unit? Presumably you searched the street, the surrounding buildings?'

'We searched where we could. We found nothing.'

'Where?'

'The army barracks opposite, the Ariana Hotel, the *lycée* . . .'

'But . . .' Yakushev swept a hand to the north and west.

'Embassies, Colonel,' Jangalak put in. 'Egyptian, Chinese, Turkish.'

Yakushev palmed his brow. 'Then why didn't you call us? Electronic intelligence has equipment that could have detected the beam. At least we could have found out the point of origin.'

Naqaswar looked surprised and regretful. 'We are not, I fear, very well up in such matters.'

But the Lily was! It was astounding. Unless one of the foreign powers was the culprit. The trouble was, it was too late to find out which – and he needed to find out, because GRU security measures had been based upon the enemy's zero technological capability. Electronic intelligence had swept the schoolhouse automatically upon occupation but not since, so far as he knew. Just one bug in there could account for the recent leaks. Or in Dolin's office, or the mess – those Afghans in the kitchen. Worse still, in army HQ itself. It put at risk every single security measure he had taken to protect Harvest.

Yakushev strove to conceal his dismay from the two Afghans.

'Well, at least you found out who put it there, I hope.'

'One of the cleaners, we believe,' Naqaswar replied. 'Though we have yet to find him. He dismissed himself two weeks ago without warning.'

Two weeks! Yakushev was deeply relieved that Khad knew nothing about Harvest and so could not have discussed it.

Naqaswar and Jangalak were regarding him curiously. Yakushev got out a cigarette and lit it, blowing out smoke, watching it rise to the ceiling. He steadied himself with an effort.

'I want a firing squad, General,' he said at last. 'An Afghan firing squad. Twelve absolutely trustworthy security troops, plus NCO.'

Pale brown eyes fixed on him. 'You do not trust our army?'

He softened his reply. 'Not for this. Ghoram Khan is a charismatic man. Having to shoot him might overtax their loyalties.'

Out of the corner of his eye he saw Jangalak start.

So did the general, who said, 'So after all that, you're going to shoot the rascal. He still wouldn't talk?'

'After all what, General?'

Naqaswar avoided his eye. 'No doubt you have had him under interrogation?'

They're not so stupid, Yakushev thought. They know about the barbecue. 'Talk or not,' he rasped, 'would you expect us not to shoot him?'

'I suppose not.' Naqaswar upended a pencil, pursing his lips. Presently he nodded. 'Very well. I think we can provide you with the men you need.'

You fucking better, Yakushev thought, if you value your roubles.

'For when would you require this firing party?'

'Eleven o'clock tomorrow morning. The execution is scheduled for noon.'

Another start from Jangalak.

'To take place where?' The general was scribbling a memo.

'Beyond Bagrame, the quarry beyond the airport. Map reference 69213430.' Yakushev repeated the reference clearly, twice, not looking at Jangalak.

'You wish us to supply transport?'

'One truck. Sufficient to carry the squad and seven prisoners. We will supply the supervising officer. He'll have his own jeep.'

'*Seven* prisoners?'

'Ah yes. You'll be receiving a list of the other six later today. They are all proven subversives and under the power vested in me I have ordered them shot. Only problem is, they are held in civil custody, so the execution order must come from your office, General. If that is not inconvenient.'

Naqaswar eyed him warily. 'I don't know about inconvenient, it is certainly irregular.'

Yakushev shrugged. 'A freak of circumstance.'

'I will require their case histories, of course, before giving my signature.'

'You have my word that they are what I say they are.' Yakushev's voice hardened. He was in a hurry to end this and get away. 'And that amounts to an order, General. I refer you to the pursuits of war clause – 46(b), I think – in the collaborative agreement signed by Babrak Karmal and Leonid Brezhnev in March 1981.'

Yakushev watched pride wrestle with embarrassment on the patrician face. Naqaswar could not recall the clause (with good reason; it was a bluff), but did not want to display his ignorance in front of his liaison officer.

His eye strayed to the telephone. He said evenly, 'Is General Dolin at your headquarters?

'No, he's out of town. Due back tomorrow night.'

'After the execution. I see. So until then you are officially in command of the directorate?'

'Yes.'

Naqaswar straightened his blotter minutely with both hands, then looked up.

'In that case, very well, I will sign the order.' There was no mistaking his reluctance or the sarcasm in his tone as he asked, 'Is there anything else you require?'

'Yes,' Yakushev said. 'The firing party will be placed absolutely under my orders, I trust?'

'For the period of detachment, yes. Why?'

'I would like them appraised verbally of that fact, General, if you would be so kind. And told to report to me in my office for my detailed instructions before proceeding to collect the prisoners.'

'Where are they held?'

'That is one of the details I will give them.'

Naqaswar frowned. He said slowly, 'This is all very . . . secretive, Colonel. May I know the reason?'

'Khan is the reason. If word of his execution should leak – just one word – there could be a move to rescue him. So I'm making this a high-security operation, General. I ask you to do the same. I cannot stress the need enough.'

'I see your point.' Naqaswar eyed Jangalak. 'Ali, not a word, please, outside this office. The firing squad will not be told what they are being assembled for. I will leave their entire briefing to you, Colonel Yakushev.'

Yakushev thanked him. He slapped the arms of his chair and stood up. Jangalak moved ahead of him to open the door, his handsome face expressionless. Almost painfully so, Yakushev noted.

'You know . . .' Naqaswar's voice sounded behind him, almost sadly. Yakushev paused at the door impatiently. The general was standing by the window, his stature revealed as surprisingly short for a Pathan. 'I think I'm almost going to miss the old devil. Of course he deserves absolutely to be shot. But as a man fighting for what he mistakenly believes in . . . one cannot help admiring his spirit.'

Yakushev clenched his teeth. They just couldn't tear themselves away from this racial thing.

He said dismissively, 'Leave it like this then, shall we – I shoot him, you put up the statue.' He strode out.

The street shimmered under the almost vertical sun. Jangalak paused on the steps of the Khad building to put on his dark glasses. Yakushev stood on the kerb, beckoning his jeep. He appeared distraught. Jangalak could guess why. He was distraught himself, for the same reason. He had purposely avoided informing the Russian of the bug's discovery. But at last it was out – with the inevitable conclusions that the Russian would draw. He cursed Naqaswar, though he knew it was not his fault. The general had no idea what was going on, or that Jangalak had installed the microphone himself.

The GAZ had come squeaking to a stop along the kerb. The Russian got in. Jangalak crossed the pavement hesitantly, as though he had just remembered something.

'Colonel, do you want me for an hour? I have got to go to the gold market. It is my sister's wedding in a few days.'

It was true. And Yakushev had met his sister. Jangalak never took liberties with the Russian's intelligence.

Yakushev stared at him as if he were a stranger. He flapped his hands, dismissing him, as the jeep roared away.

Jangalak watched it down the street, knowing the Russian was on his way to ransack his own headquarters from cellar to roof for bugs. And he would find them.

The rear flap of the jeep was up and he could see Yakushev silhouetted beside the driver. He saw him lean to one side, looking towards a car parked across the road.

If there had been a woman in it, Jangalak would have thought nothing of it. But there were three men. He was instantly alerted.

If his instincts were correct, this was another serious blow. How serious, he would have to work out later, because it was twenty to twelve already. He started to walk towards the river.

As he drew level with the car, a casual glance revealed that the occupants were Afghans. *Kullah* caps, Western jackets. The two in front were sharing a newspaper. Jangalak knew most of the GRU's resident operatives, but these three he did not recognize. They appeared not to be aware of his existence. He realized he *could* be wrong.

Passing on, he paused at the *lycée* entrance to glance round, as if checking that nothing was about to turn in. But yes, the man in the back had got out and was keeping pace with him across the road.

He felt a flutter in his chest. He had guessed some day it would come to this. He was a staff officer with no field experience, while these men were obviously GRU-trained. He had barely fifteen minutes in which to shake them off, and he must keep going towards the bazaar. To live with this afterwards, retain his liaison position, he must not appear to deviate from his avowed intention.

As he strode along he cast about in his mind for a relative, friend, anyone living in the area for which he was making. His family's apartment was across the city. His brother had been posted to Masr-i-Sharif. His tailor? No, he needed someone living in the bazaar itself.

The answer came to him even as he spotted the taxi parked outside the Mines and Industries building. He crossed the road to it, dodging between the crazy traffic. This brought him on to the same side as his tail. He cast no glance towards him. The taxi, he found, was booked and waiting. Jangalak got straight in and flashed his Khad card. In moments they were speeding towards the Pol-i-Hesti bridge.

Jangalak positioned himself so he could see through the driver's rear-view mirror. He was just able to make out the car stopping momentarily to pick up the man on the pavement. Now here it came, speeding in pursuit.

Immediately past the mosque he directed the cab round into the crowded market-place that was the entrance to the Chahar Chata bazaar. He got out – unhurriedly, because the car was close behind and he did not wish to alert its occupants to the fact that he knew they were there. He paid and moved away amongst the motley shoppers who choked the foot-passage. Vendors squatted under umbrellas and makeshift awnings, surrounded by junk, antique weapons, silver, shoes, carpets. The crowds sauntered and fingered and bargained and passed the time of day. It was rapidly approaching noon.

Jangalak suddenly knew that he would never reach Yussuf's house in the minutes available, certainly not in the way he intended, across walls and backyards. He also had to find the place, then convey to his family's old gardener that he was after a change of clothes.

There was a large crowd ahead. Jangalak pushed his way through its fringes. Pipe and drum noises were coming from its epicentre, where a skeletal fakir was wandering entranced under an arc of weights supported on skewers dug into his flesh. On impulse, Jangalak changed direction, circling swiftly behind the throng.

He glimpsed his two followers, craning their necks. He removed his hat first, then his uniform jacket, loosening his tie as he moved along, still circling, keeping the crowd between them.

He caught one further glimpse of them, staring about them jerkily, then he was ahead of the crowd, moving back the way he had come. He ducked into the first clothier's.

One flash of his card had the proprietor's scared attention. In less than two minutes he had slipped a long shirt, *shalvar* and *chapan* over his army trousers and exchanged his shiny shoes for slippers. He took a red bandanna from his jacket pocket, shook out the folds and stuffed it in the back of his waistband, then he folded his hat and shoes into the jacket and told the man to keep them safe until his return. He clapped a *kullah* on the back of his head, paid and melted into the crowds outside.

Shuffling now, without even a glance around him, he joined the growing surge towards the mosque. Five minutes later, he and several hundred worshippers were assembling in the huge inner court.

When eventually all knelt and hitched up their *chapans*, the red kerchief became visible, but not noticeably until all bowed their foreheads to the ground.

Then, amid rank upon rank of white posteriors inclined to the sky, the bandanna flamed, bright and solitary as a poppy in a snowdrift.

Afterwards, when prayer was ended and all arose, a pale youth approached Jangalak. He drew him away and along a columned hall soft with carpets to an anteroom where the *mullah* waited.

There, Jangalak passed on the news that Ghoram Khan was to die.

21

'SO NOW he is to die? I tire of his disasters!' The Lily sounded overwrought. 'A thousand pieces on the board and yet we finger this one again, again, and still he clings to jeopardy as a goat to its cliff!'

The seven mullahs kneeling in the dimness before her murmured in sympathetic unison.

'Nevertheless,' Dhost said, 'he is our Judas ram. It is too late now to select another. We must save him.'

'You dare tell me "must" when I, with my third eye, can see into men's souls?' Her fierce movement inside the *chaderi* gave the effect of a tug of wind. 'Has Khan opened his heart to the *schurawi*, ask yourself? No, he would sooner die. But would Colonel Yakushev let him die before he has opened his heart, ask yourself? No, *he* would sooner die. Therefore, we have a trap. Are we going to play with traps, each seeking to outwit the other and lose ourselves in one small stand of maize, while the reapers bring in their mighty Harvest? Ask yourself that.'

'We have been through this before,' Abdalis muttered. 'You will not let him die. We all know it.'

Dhost found himself for once in agreement. 'We cannot afford to lose him, Soul of Aminah.'

'Good Dhost, who is more concerned with losing Khan than Khan? And who better equipped to save him?'

'We do not know how he is equipped now.'

'Does he not have a force of men, thirsting for his order as a forest thirsts for rain?'

'What if he cannot contact them? At least we can assist him there.'

The Lily fell silent. She was debating.

'Oh, very well. Send a runner to Do Rish. Breathe into their ears the place and time of execution, warn that it is a trap and that they must meet it with a superior trap.'

'At once, Soul of Aminah!' Dhost's lofty body unfolded itself.

'Wait!'

He froze.

'We are but begun. What of the photographer?'

'They have shut him in the Choukha,' said Mirdad, the red-bearded one.

'I need him. Arrange his escape. How is Massud holding in the Panjshir?'

'Well,' cried Sawar, the youngest mullah. 'He is at Do Ab. The *schurawi* have advanced from Rokha with a force of tanks, but—'

'How great a force, beardless boy? A platoon? A company? A regiment? A division?'

The youth spread his hands, abashed. 'The report did not say. I cannot know.'

'If they were wolves upon your flock you would know!'

He managed to stutter, 'Two, certainly, have been destroyed.'

'Two from a thousand! And what of the remaining?'

The young mullah, in confusion, beckoned towards a clipboard held by the oldest. He took it and arose, extending it to the Lily.

'These are their deployments, these their reserves.' He fetched the cresset-light and, his hand shaking, removed its perforated cover so that she could see to read. 'As of yesterday, Great Soul.' He added, 'But tomorrow, how will we monitor them, if this fresh news from the Khad major is true: that the *schurawi* know of our hidden devices?'

The Lily pondered a moment. 'We and the *schurawi* are not two carpets but one. Our threads intertwine. When one is stressed, the other will know. Every ear must be ready to catch and report each whisper, all stealth abandoned now. Many will be caught and sacrificed. It will be their glory. You hear me, Dhost?'

'I hear, O Soul.'

'Now silence while I read.'

Sawar returned to his knees, to watch the shrouded figure in awe. The others sat back on their bare heels, eyes solemn beneath snowy turbans, bodies spare under sleek robes. These were Allah's generals.

When the Lily had finished, she cast aside the clipboard with a moan. Head forward, she began to rock, back and forth, back and forth.

She slowed gradually. Her voice lifted eerily.

'Their reserves are too fat. We must slim them. They have but a handful of days now before their move and a great stillness has come over them. They gather their legs under them before leaping like the locust. We must spoil their balance or when the day comes they will swarm to victory. Abdullah Sikkim – his force must sever their main supply artery north of Jabal Os Sara. Hafiz Beg – he must break out of the Dagh encirclement, spreading south and west into the hills. Ahmed Rahim – he must blow up the dam at Girishk. This must be done swiftly.'

The mullahs exchanged uneasy glances.

'Order it. I have spoken!'

No one moved. Dhost ventured, 'But they have not sufficient manpower, Sacred One.'

'They have the power of Allah. How does the ocean erode the rocks? It ebbs, fool, it flows. The Russian rocks shall become as dust – I, the Lily, swear it!' She added, 'And when you have relayed my orders, we will talk again. This time of the *chabnameh* – when they are to be distributed.' A hand fluttered from the midnight of her robe. 'Go now.'

They backed away.

As the curtain fell to eclipse the last face she leaned to replace the cover over the cresset, grunting with her pregnancy.

She no longer acted. She was what she claimed to be. She could barely detect any stirring of her old self now, her trusting open-hearted, gay-sad Russian self. It had died there in the cave, together with her dutiful, though always uneasy complicity in the most grandiose exercise in political cynicism in the history of the world – the Soviet communist system. In that moment, Islam had risen to fulfil her need. And even her need was Pathan, not Russian – vengeful to a pitch she would never have believed possible in herself. The stronger, wilder culture had rushed in to fill the vacuum. At least, in retrospect, that seemed the only explanation. Pathans wished, so they invented; invented, so they believed. Now, therefore, she *was* divine. The child in her belly *was* the reincarnation of the Prophet. The need had grown to conviction during her dreaming time. Ah, the dreaming time . . .

First the Sabre. She felt it cut a bright arc of pain; her pulse stopped at the void's edge. She clung there while things and nothings had their breathless war. But now the Flower, growing slowly – a tip, a tongue, frail in her soul's field, but hungering for light. Her rage sustained it. 'Thy dawn, O Master of the World, thy dawn – the hour the Lily opens on the Lawn . . . !' It opened. Her breath took trembling root. And now, the Face. A young face, grey with pain but coming and going gently, lifting her head. Now there was water from the supply stored in the cave. Now a perception of horror between the fluttering of her lids. Now the darkness and chill of night. It moved around her, touching her nakedness with leafy fingers, the face beside her, its child mouth twisting with every move. Now the face was sinking, sinking. It lay as drowned among the rocks in the moon's light, staring up through the flowing shadow.

She raised her own face then and howled. The hills howled with her, *Am-in-ah, Am-in-ah!* She was a wolf and they her pack. They bade her come away and she ran with them. Sometimes there were clouds, soft and blooming. Birds shrieked, then were silent as she came near. She lay with her face in icewater, numbing the pain. She heard voices, but they were in her head. When the night came, she howled as she wandered. Suppose he were close and rode past? Each tree became a horseman, galloping in the wind.

The goats munched audibly in the dry stillness. A dog came and looked at her and backed away. Then a man, staring at her as she lay naked, curled under a bank like a fox. He knelt and said a prayer, then shrank across the hill with fearful glances.

An orchard, a village. Why did they stare and jeer, walking backwards before her? Their cast pebbles bit her body like tiny fish. She retired to a rock from where she could see the huddled roofs against the valley's shadow, and wept. The sun went down, but the rock retained its heat. She clung to it as a swimmer from the deep clings to the hot sand. When her howling had weakened to a whimper, she slept.

In the morning there was food beside her – the crust of

cream, bread, mulberries, a bowl of water such as one would leave for a dog. She drank it like a dog and in its mirror saw a face. It was neither human nor animal. If filled her with fear and fury.

She did not leave the rock. It was her home. Though some watched her from afar, none came near. Through the day she picked grasses and leaves and made a bed. When night fell she covered herself with the rest of what she had gathered.

The next day there was more food. The sun climbed. A mullah came.

He stood tall against the light that hurt her eyes and asked her her name.

'Aminah,' she said. She had searched her mind and found nothing else.

The mullah was silent and she perceived his thought: Aminah was mother to the Prophet.

'From what tribe do you come?'

'Quaraysh.' She surprised herself. 'But my town is Mecca.' She did not know if it were so, but the voices had whispered it.

'You lie,' the mullah said in a harsh voice. 'Where are you truly from?'

'From this – this!' She shouted, and threw dust at him. 'Can you deny it?' And she laughed crazily. Then she said, '"I swear by the Day of Resurrection, and by the self-reproaching soul – does man think We shall never put his bones together again? Indeed, we can remould his very fingers!"'

The mullah stared at her. It was from the seventy-fifth *sura*. He paced around her, slowly, then walked away.

'Flee! Flee!' she shouted in mockery. More of the same *sura* rushed through her mind. '"Man would ever deny what is to come. 'When will this be?' he asks, 'this day of Resurrection?'"' She stood up and screamed, '"But when the sight of mortals is confounded and the moon eclipsed; when sun and moon are brought together – on that day man will ask: 'Whither shall I flee?'"'

The mullah's pace slowed a little, but he kept walking and was presently lost to view.

She sat down again on the rock and asked questions to which there was no answer. Were the prompting voices her own? If so, where had she learned these words and why was she saying them?

Presently a woman carrying a bundle came up from the village. She approached with her face averted and dropped it and ran. It contained clothes.

Pola dressed herself. A part of her rebelled at the outer covering, but she forced the *chaderi* over her head. She gazed out through the black mesh, feeling as if some final bond had been severed. There was deep sadness in this, yet fierce resolve.

Later the mullah returned. He sat before her and for the first time she saw his face. It had the chiselled brow and nose of a carving. The fine beard was brown and glistened; also the eyes, as he said to her: 'If you know what you say, repent from this heresy. If not, I cannot help you.'

She said, 'This rock speaks no heresy. Can you help this rock?' And she danced around it.

He watched her in silence, frowning.

She said, 'Or that tree?' She embraced it. She pointed to its branches. 'See? It gives fruit. Allah is in the tree.'

'Allah is in all things,' said the mullah severely.

'A woman may also bear fruit.' She sat down.

His manner became more thoughtful.

She said, 'Would you hunt mice when there is a lion at the door?'

'Woman, you speak in strange riddles. What is their meaning? If they have any.'

She said, 'Is it not clear? Shall we not first slay the lion?' She sprang up and began to shout. 'Strike at its heart! Wipe it utterly from the face of the earth! Shall we not do *that* before ridding ourselves of the mouse?'

The mullah regarded her with eyes narrowed as she stood, her breast heaving. He was beginning to comprehend.

She moved to him slowly. She hung her arms out from her sides, palms forward, the pain in her head pounding to her raised pulse, and said in a terrible voice:

'In my belly is a sword.'

She walked away and stood where the ground began its plunge to the valley. Somewhere in her, she knew, was a purpose, though she did not understand it.

The mullah seemed in turmoil. He arose and approached her haltingly. Then with a last stride he was beside her, following her gaze towards the west, towards Kabul.

'If . . .' his voice shook. 'If you are touched by God . . . then touch *me*!'

He knelt.

Pola turned wonderingly.

Not, even now, fully understanding, she touched him.

Others came to her at the rock. His fellow mullahs from neighbouring villages. The place was in Nuristan, where the war still was little more than a distant throbbing beyond the hills, an occasional caravan of refugees. They sat amongst the grasshoppers and butterflies and tested her. Then they would debate amongst themselves. The talk was not all secular. Gradually it became a conspiracy of beards.

Memory returned to her, slowly at first, like water filtering into her mind's footprint, then rushing to fill it with horror and fury and grief. She began to understand the motivation governing her every word and move – and it was inspired, perhaps literally. Was it possible for the subconscious mind alone to devise so convoluted a revenge? Or was she indeed the tool of godly power? True, she had steeped herself in Islamic teachings, but only to counter the prejudice in Bab-el-Hawa. Could her indoctrinated mind accept the possibility of divine intervention? She was sure, though her mother had been devoutly Russian Orthodox, that it could not.

Anyway, what did it matter? The goal, the outcome, remained the same. The problem was: she had conceived her plan in temporary madness but, now that she had recovered her reason, could she sustain it?

Her memory was her strongest asset. She knew the Koran by heart and could use it to confound their doubts and support her predictions – always obliquely, of course, because if the mullahs suspected she was sane, she would lose her hold over them. For to them the word 'touched' meant touched by God.

Her understanding of the Russian mind they saw as part of the miracle. That she spoke in technical terms of weapons and formations increased their awe and surmise. But, with the exception of Dhost, these were simple provincials. Harder to convince would be the learned doctors of holy law in Kabul. Sooner or later, word would reach them; she hungered for that day.

At last, as the snows began to fall, it came. In defiance of the weather and the Soviet stricture on travel, a Dr Hassan Wakil

Djassin arrived. His lay profession was, fittingly, that of high court judge. He brought with him another doctor, this one a specialist from the Kabul Institute of Medicine.

By now the weather had forced her from her rock. A house had been set aside for her. There, in private before the sessions began, the specialist took of her certain tests. These he carried off to work on at the *malik*'s house while Pola faced Djassin and the assembled mullahs. Dhost was on tenterhooks.

He need not have been. Her performance was inspired. Again that word. The Prophet himself was never so bewildering – which was saying a great deal.

Djassin, true to his calling, evinced little, but she sensed that he was more than intrigued. Prompted by Dhost, he was weighing the possibility that her extraordinary madness presented. But that was before the arrival of the latecomer. He entered unobtrusively, the snow glistening on his black turban and robes. Straight as a ramrod. A shadow within a shadow. It was Abdalis!

She had assumed he was dead, along with her beloved and all others of the valley. In shock, she watched him as he found a space to sit.

To his eye, of course, she was just a female shape. But to his ear . . . Very soon she saw his attention sharpen. He tilted his head, listening. It was her accent, she realized, faint though she knew it to be.

His guttural tones began to feature in the examination. His questions, though innocent-sounding to the others, were pointed. She parried them, sometimes with analogy, sometimes with crazy irrelevance. It was not enough. Presently he suggested that the deluded creature be made to show her face.

Dhost protested and was upheld by the worthy doctor of holy law. But then Abdalis voiced aloud his suspicions. This caused a sensation. Dhost demanded that he be made to withdraw his slander and leave. Now, however, the judge's own suspicions were aroused. He asked 'Aminah' if she would consent to unveil herself.

Her answer was that she would do so only in accordance with custom – which was before her Lord.

'But your Lord consents,' Abdalis replied slyly. 'He always allowed you free will in this matter.' He was referring, of course, to Khan.

'Then my free will should be respected,' she snapped.

'But what is your objection?' Abdalis persisted. 'That to unveil yourself is a breach of God's law?' He was remembering the day of the *jirgah* when he suffered a public defeat on this issue at Khan's hand. 'For it is not. And we are all holy men, not lusters of the flesh.'

Others echoed his demand and Pola saw that he was gaining supporters. Suddenly her whole plan was in the balance. She marshalled all her intellect for a reply that would ridicule and silence him before this company, once and for all. Horrifyingly, nothing came to her.

Now fierce argument arose. She could see the judge steeling himself to announce a ruling.

He was forestalled by the return of the specialist. He leaned over Djassin confidentially.

'It is positive,' he murmured. 'She is with child.'

There was no more questioning. The following day Djassin and the mullahs left. The snows closed in, building around the village a wall of whiteness and silence.

Pola waited. A month passed. A brief thaw unlocked the passes for a few days and brought a message addressed to Dhost. It told him to bring to fruition what he had started. He was to form a war council of holy men, with the woman as its nominal head. The *Ulemas* of every city had volunteered their support. This was to be an exclusively Islamic movement, with members of the lay populace involved only as minions. Its object was unification of the resistance, its rallying standard the second coming of the Prophet. Limited private finance was available. A list of required equipment should be delivered to Dr Djassin. A high degree of secrecy must be established and maintained. Those who sabotaged by doubt (such as Abdalis) should either be eliminated or absorbed into the organization where they could do the least harm. *Allaho akbar!*

There was no suggestion that the *Ulema* believed she was what she claimed to be. But the concept offered itself as a unifying factor and, all else having failed, they were giving it a try.

She didn't care. It provided her with the opportunity her body and mind screamed out for – to bring the Russian army to a mortifying defeat.

22

THE DAY of Khan's execution began as a saffron rent in the overcast. The air was so still that the echoes of the horseman's hoofbeats reached Do Rish a full ten minutes before he came galloping out of the greyness.

His arrival roused few, but some women were already down by the stream with their jars and canisters. They stared curiously as he slid from his sweating beast and came down to them. Some hurried away, covering their faces. The oldest and boldest remained. They answered his query with pointing fingers.

The messenger clambered back in the saddle and rode on between the adobe walls and down the track beyond the houses into the bowl-like valley that sheltered their fruit trees. Here, in man-made holes within a cliff of sandstone, dwelt Khan's remaining hundred men.

The messenger, careless of the weapons pointed at him, sought out their leader – an old warrior with one eye and a foul tongue, named Nour Palawar. After sketching the Lily sign in the dust, he told him that Khan was to die at noon.

That Khan was alive even was heartening news. That he was soon to be snatched away, unthinkable. But why had word reached them so late? The place of execution was a full eighty kilometres from this spot, and dawn's left hand already in the sky.

The messenger made no explanation. He was exhausted. He had done his job. The rest was up to them.

Every inch of the GRU's offices – the messhalls, kitchens, washrooms, even the scattered living quarters – was being swept by Electronic Intelligence crews. Not content with negative signals, they balanced on ladders, checking every ceiling and the outside of every window frame.

So far, three micro-bugs had been located – in Dolin's office, Yakushev's, signals (but not cyphers) and in the officers' mess.

Dolin was going to hit the roof when he got back tonight, Yakushev thought. Like himself, he would play back every blessed word he had uttered in recent weeks, especially concerning Harvest. So would Solkholov, when he found that two hidden microphones had been located in Front HQ.

Yakushev had despatched a signal to Dolin to give him and Solkholov the opportunity to make any necessary adjustments to Harvest while they were still in personal contact with the Baluchis. He did not mention his own conclusion as to the culprit or culprits. Let the bastard sweat that one out for himself, lay it at the door of the KGB, a foreign power, or whoever. The Lily remained his own private pigeon for now, the ace he would play when the time was right. And that time was getting more right every minute.

The Khad firing party arrived exactly on time – eleven o'clock. Yakushev met them in the car park, taking with him the Russian officer detailed to supervise the execution – none other than the bluff Spetznas captain who had commanded the massacre of the *jirgah* at Kerala. His name was Medevev.

The NCO in charge of the Afghan party brought his men to attention and saluted. One look at the squad told Yakushev that Naqaswar had done him well. From their smartness and bearing, he guessed they were the pick of Khad's security troops – handsome, hard-eyed men in peaked caps. Flashes of red on their uniform. White gloves, even. He told them to stand easy.

Turning slightly, he glanced up at the whitewashed upper windows. He could see Jangalak's peephole, but whether he was watching he could not tell. His office had been swept and searched, of course, but so had everyone else's. If he was innocent he would have no idea that he was even under suspicion; his vanishing could have been the fault of the surveillance. The proof would soon be to hand, but until then the liaison officer retained free access to this, the most sensitive premises on the whole army front – a thought that prickled Yakushev's spine.

He commenced his briefing. He watched the Afghans closely

for their reaction, but evidently they had been forewarned by Naqaswar that this job would be outside the normal line of duty. Their faces remained like granite. Likewise Captain Medevev's. But he had already been briefed, and equipped for his role by Special Services.

When Yakushev finished speaking there were some questions, after which the NCO ordered his men back into the truck. Yakushev eyed Medevev. Medevev eyed him back.

'Keep a watch on them,' Yakushev murmured. 'They look all right, but . . .'

'I know. They're still Pathans.' The captain filled his large lungs with air. 'Well. All we need now is the place of execution.'

Yakushev shrugged. 'I leave it to you. Anywhere except the quarry beyond the airport.'

There was no forewarning, just the multiple thud of boots along the balcony. The door of the room crashed back. Eight guards crowded into the narrow space.

McCabe's first thought was that it was a search. But they were all made to stand with their faces to the wall while their hands were cuffed behind them, except for Khan, who had been beaten again that morning and could not comply. He was made to kneel on the bed. After a short altercation his wrists were secured in front of him, and Hafiq's released and refastened in the same way. Whereupon Khan was hoisted on to his back, and his arms pulled down to lock round Hafiq's neck. They were ordered to march.

The prisoners crowding the balcony fell back from the swinging clubs as the procession passed, then thronged to the rail to watch it emerge from the stairwell. The jeers and jabbering died slowly as Medevev stepped into view from behind the waiting truck.

A Russian? McCabe saw Khan become alert in spite of his suffering. His black eyes found Yasir, who was watching from the shadow of the wall, his dark glasses luminous in the reflected light of the yard. The governor's cigar-chewing and bead-clicking froze as Khan's gaze fastened on him, then recommenced slowly and more ostentatiously.

They were herded aboard the truck. As McCabe slid along to a forward seat under the canvas, his last view of the

Choukha was tier upon tier of silent faces. The absence of any sound was eerie. Something was going on that he did not understand.

The soldiers got in last, filling the rear seats, some squatting with their backs to the tailgate, automatic weapons at the ready – ten . . . eleven . . . *twelve* enlisted men and one NCO. Then he knew.

But, no, hell, it wasn't feasible! The driver was pulling the rear flap down, securing it. McCabe consulted the other faces in the green twilight. Khan's expression confirmed his fear.

McCabe's insides took a cold plunge. War reporters could catch a bullet or bomb fragment any time, you couldn't flash your press card at hurtling metal, but by and large, when it came down to it, their role was respected by both sides. *So long as they stuck to it.* But he had not.

The jeep and truck motors whinnied to life in tandem. The prison gate moaned. The passengers lurched in unison as the vehicles started down the hill.

Hafiq, never a man to curb his outrage, began to harangue the soldiers. His manacled hands gestured towards Khan. Did they not realize who they had been ordered to execute? He hammered the name at them to get it through their skulls – with mounting fury as he elicited no reaction. So they knew they were to murder a noble resistance hero, yet still sat there like fat-tailed sheep, obedient to the last whim of their godless shepherds? Where was their manhood, their pride, their faith, their *blood*? Were they not Pathan? Was Khan not Pathan? If they had not the stomach to mutiny against their orders as patriots, then they should do so as brothers!

By this time, Tamim and the politicians were adding their voices to the furore. What was it, they demanded of the soldiers – the higher pay, the security for their families, that kept them in thrall to the regime and its Russian masters? They could rest assured that ample compensation would be provided – lump sums for every man who mutinied.

The bribes became so tempting that the rigidity at last began to buckle. The NCO ceased barking at the prisoners to be silent and snapped an order to his men to stiffen up. He came to his feet and moved along the truck; bracing himself one-handed, gun levelled in the other, his clean-cut hard young face dark with anger. He warned the prisoners to shut their mouths or he would put a bullet in the next one that opened.

The auction faltered to a stop but Hafiq simply switched his tirade to the NCO, labelling him coward, traitor to the land of his fathers', lackey of Marxist imperialism. He hawked his disgust and spat on the gleaming boots.

McCabe braced himself for the roar of the gun. But they were moving in dense traffic. Hafiq had read his man and the odds. The gun jerked savagely and whipped him across the temple. Blood sprang. Hafiq absorbed the shock with the muscles of his neck. Up swept his manacled hands to grasp the barrel behind the foresight. Twisting it away from him, he wrestled for possession of it, at the same time turning his man. Khan swung a straight-armed, two-fisted blow to the fellow's kidneys. As the NCO arched, McCabe stamped at the back of his knee. The man hit the deck, but still clung to the gun. Hafiq quickly stamped on the weapon, pinning it to the floor.

Now, as one, the prisoners redoubled their efforts to subvert the enlisted men. Alas, too late. The spell had been broken. The soldiers came lurching along the truck, swinging their butts. The handcuffed prisoners could do little to defend themselves. Only a sudden right turn, which collapsed the squad on top of those seated on the left, preserved them from a more severe beating.

When the meteor shower had abated and his eyes recovered focus, McCabe perceived both guards and NCO seated back in the rear end, every weapon pointed their way.

They remained like that for the rest of the journey.

They were off the metalled surface, climbing steeply, jolting, bouncing. The prisoners clung to the side, torsos strained forward, searching each other's faces in the green half-light for the smallest glint of hope.

McCabe, in these last moments, found himself no longer a part of them. He clung still to the possibility that he had been included by mistake, but how to establish it, with no knowledge of either Pushtu or Russian?

Oh Jesus, come on, Khan, he thought – or have they beaten it out of you – the leadership thing, the flash of what they least expect? UNITA's Tom Mdobi had had the president's phone number tattooed under his watchstrap. *Call it, just call it!* he'd kept challenging the Cuban firing squad. No one had dared. But they hadn't dared shoot him either. In Somalia, Kafta of the 'expendables' had struck up the Internationale in the execution truck. When he had got all the Marxist Ethiopians singing it, he took a backwards dive through the tattered plastic. But he misjudged the verge. They shot him as he lay half-conscious in the roadway – still all singing lustily.

But Khan just sat there, gazing into nothingness with slitted eyes. Marshalling his energies for a final break, or just remembering past faces and places? McCabe couldn't tell.

The truck lurched to a stop. No one moved. Presently the flap went up, revealing the broad, sun-reddened face of the Russian officer. If his expression was anything to go by they could have just stopped for a beer on their way to a football match. It provided a tiny straw of hope. McCabe grasped at it.

The soldiers piled out. They indicated that the prisoners were to come out one at a time – the nearest first. That was Gulbadin.

He stared round at them all with a woebegone expression and obeyed wordlessly. The seat was wet where he had been sitting and his trousers were stained darkly down both legs. Two of the soldiers hustled him away.

Through the open flap McCabe could see the city about a mile away, glinting in the noonday heat. They appeared to be on a deserted, rock-strewn plateau.

He slid to the end of the seat. 'You speak English?' he asked the officer. The man ignored him. His shoulders were grasped and he was pulled out on to the stony ground and marched away.

Ahead, he glimpsed a ruined building with a long, whitish wall, in front of which were ranged what looked like sawn-off telephone poles. Gulbadin was being secured to one of these.

His last doubt shattered, McCabe nearly broke his neck yelling back to the captain that he was British, press, that there had been some crazy mistake and there'd be hell to pay when the international media heard about it.

The captain made no sign that he heard. McCabe began to twist and kick. He dropped to his knees. The soldiers lifted him. He made himself heavy. They dragged him, bumping, through the rocks. He reached round with his pinioned arms, groping to get hold of one of their weapons. They cuffed him and kneed him on.

'Will you listen a minute? Will you just –'

They rammed him up against a pole. A length of cord was passed round the chain of his handcuffs. He struggled all the way, bursting with outrage. But they got it knotted eventually and left him.

Gulbadin looked ghastly. He was shouting to the officer, reeling off a list of important names. They were bringing someone else out, McCabe could not see who. Now another – four soldiers this time. It was Hafiq, snarling abuse at them. Now Khan was being carried and dragged. He wasn't resisting, just talking to them quietly. The soldiers appeared perturbed, but they tied him to a stake nevertheless. And then they were all there, in a row.

McCabe watched, his insides a void – how many times had he filmed it happening to other poor bastards? – as the squad formed into line, marched, and halted at intervals.

Everything seemed to be sinking. He thought, *Ayesha, Mum, Dad.* His parents would never know, because sure as hell, the Russians would keep this one under their hat. He loved them. *Oh damn, he loved them.* They'd been selfish, sure, but mixed-up, vulnerable, and he hadn't helped by cutting out on them instead of trying to heal the rift. He understood now why they had divorced. If only he could *tell* them that. A last few minutes together – tell them that it was all right, that he understood.

Ayesha, he loved her too – was that crazy? All right, it was always the girl of the moment when he was close to death. Someone to hang his hopes on. Anyone. That snapshot of Angie – he had held it in his hand for what seemed like a lifetime when those SU-24s had shot his camel and it had pinned his legs, and stared at it the whole time they were strafing back and forth, back and forth. And he had hardly known the girl. But Ayesha . . . He hardly knew her either but she came through very strongly. Like a pang of need inside him.

The squad lined up facing them now, range around twenty paces. White fucking gloves! Khan, his poor bloody feet stuck out in front of him, was sitting with his back to the pole. The surgeon was quite a man, just his throat showing the tension.

'Aim!'

You didn't need to understand the lingo to get that one. The Russian officer was standing away to one side, like some goddamn coach on the touchline. School. High summer in England. The chestnut trees heavy with their pink candles. Picnics by the river, Dad and Mum loving each other then. And Sammy. Oh, Sammy. Wagging and barking. Then watching him die. *Dear God, please don't take my lovely dog!* And here he was at God at last. They said you always came to it in the end. He'd never believed it. He'd never got to God before – not for himself. But here it was. Now he'd know, wouldn't he?

'Fire!'

The crackling automatic blaze lit his mind, tore into his body, shattered, blinded. The whole of life was there, then wasn't. Leaves were falling, or was it blossom? He was going away. No emotion. Just a lonely light diminishing in blackness.

23

THE LILY was a grey, fuzzy tongue with black speckles and a golden stamen. It had forced up the stony ground in making its entry to the world; the way, McCabe couldn't help thinking, the egg-cup used to break sometimes through the crust of his mother's apple pie.

Something was happening to his hands. They were being released from the pole. He felt the cuffs open. There were tumbling voices, exultant. He raised his head from the ground.

The firing squad was releasing all of them. Gulbadin, next to him, was weeping uncontrollably. No one seemed to be hurt.

McCabe stared uncomprehendingly towards the vehicles. There was a single body beside them, covered with blood.

Khan, Hafiq and the Afghan soldiers were embracing emotionally.

McCabe had died. In his mind he had actually died. The shock brought fury before relief.

He went and looked at the body. The burly Russian officer lay face down. To judge by the mess of blood on his camouflage jacket, every man of the firing party must have turned his gun on him. Even as he looked, a couple of the soldiers grabbed the corpse by the arms and began to drag it towards the building. Hafiq, all white teeth, was hoisting Khan on to his back. He stopped the men as they passed, turned the body over with his foot and spat on it. The soldiers pulled it round behind the wall and left it.

The prisoners and soldiers gathered by the transport, all deeply moved. Hands were repeatedly raised to faces in the ritual cleansing movement. Khan looked very strange. His eyes had their inside-out look, almost blind. McCabe felt . . . born again? Not quite. The thing that had almost been done to him

– that *had* been done to him – lodged irrevocably in his psyche, colouring everything.

The surgeon was smiling at him. He came over and squeezed his shoulder.

'They not have the' – he tapped his chest – 'heart to do it. To kill Khan. Now' – he spread his arms – 'we go. Everyone go. We – you, me – we are *mujahedin*.' He laughed.

'Go where?'

'Ah,' Sadiq indicated Khan, as if to say, he will decide.

Hafiq had deposited the leader on the bonnet of the jeep and was pointing at the ribbon of road that skirted the plateau, sweeping his arm southwards. He was prescribing a course of action. The Khad soldiers were agreeing, nodding, casting uneasy looks towards the town. It was clear that they wanted to get away from the scene of their defection with all speed.

Khan appeared to be only half listening. When Hafiq finished he shook his head and spoke.

An incredulous murmur coursed through the gathering. This was followed by a storm of protest from every quarter, none so emphatic as Hafiq. He poured out his objections.

Khan remained adamant.

McCabe glanced at the surgeon, who appeared dumbfounded.

'Khan is going back,' he muttered.

McCabe blinked, not sure that he understood.

'Back to Kabul. We go on and wait. He will come later and go with us. After he has done what he must.'

'Done what?'

'Killed Yasir, then a Russian officer – Yaku—' Sadiq foundered on the name.

McCabe felt no surprise. In the light of all that had happened, it even seemed logical. Hafiq continued trying to talk Khan round. The leader sat like rock.

Presently the surgeon said, 'Hafiq tells Khan he cannot go alone because he cannot walk. And he, Hafiq, refuses to go with him.'

The implacable determination in Khan's reply needed no interpretation – it was so close to McCabe's own emotions. The sudden hunger overwhelmed him to film it all – suck it all in, spit it all out in a visual bellow of exultation and fury that would be heard to the ends of the earth. He guessed it was the post-trauma thing recurring. But with a difference now. Like Khan, he had a focal point for his anger. One that he could *do* something about. And would, given the means. He would create the means!

'Khan says that, if he must, he will go on hands and . . .' The surgeon tapped his knees.

Admit it, admit it, McCabe chided himself. You were wrong, you self-righteous bastard. A camera *is* a gun!

Khan looked round till he spotted a soldier of approximately his own build and told him to take off his uniform. He began to unbutton his own stinking jail shirt. The man didn't look too keen, but complied. Hafiq tried to stop him, but Khan froze him with a look.

McCabe grasped Sadiq's arm and drew him to the jeep.

'Tell him,' he said, 'that I'll go back with him.'

As they drove down from the plateau on to the main road, Khan turned and watched the truck feed away into the south-bound traffic. The rear flap was down, concealing its motley occupants. Until it was posted as definitely missing – which would not be for at least thirty minutes – it was just another army vehicle amongst many. By which time it should be tucked away safely at the rendezvous.

As the jeep gathered speed he faced back towards the city, rehearsing what he would do. Khan thought always in pictures. Bab-el-Hawa desecrated, his family and Pola locked in horror in their cave, were the frame. The picture now was the location of particular hills and streets and houses, and, within those, three faces – Yasir, Yakushev and Solkholov, the last less distinct but staring from his headquarters as a giant through a dolls' house window.

Coupled with these images were timings and an instinct that warned him of the folly of what he was doing, but also of its necessity. He knew he must purge his spirit of vengeful turmoil before it robbed his mind of clarity and purpose – vital now as the battle approached its climax.

Beside him was an unexpected ally – a presence directing the vehicle with rare and comforting precision through the thickening traffic. He wore the NCO's uniform, and the stripes of rank pricked the edge of Khan's vision as he stared ahead.

Already they were in sight of the old fortifications. The walls descended the rocky slopes in steps and where they met the roadway was the city entry point, heavily guarded.

Khan adjusted the peaked cap that tended to slip on his shaven head. The smart tunics contrasted with their unshaven faces and this, he feared, would mark them. As would the bloody rags that bound his feet. On the other hand, their upper sleeves bore the red and white flashes of Khad security and this, he hoped, would preserve them from a formal challenge.

The stream of traffic was slowing now, building up at the checkpoint. Khan assured himself that the Kalashnikov was cocked and the catch off, then stood it upright between his legs in military fashion. McCabe carried just the sergeant's pistol. Out of the tail of his eye Khan saw him loosen the holster flap. Khan took out the soldier's pay-and-identity book. McCabe passed him the sergeant's. The photographs were of poor quality and might just pass, with their beards' assistance.

As they rolled forward slowly through the exhaust fumes, Khan saw that the soldiers manning the checkpoint were Afghan. The Afghan army taught obedience before initiative, smartness before perceptiveness. At a checkpoint, this was in one's favour. Though the BMP, with its machine-gun levelled at the traffic, was not. Nor were the two leather-coated Russians talking to the officer in charge.

Khan tucked his feet high under the dashboard as a corporal with clicking black boots stepped up to the vehicle, hand extended. Khan placed in it both identity books and asked him the time. This diverted the man's attention to his wrist, effectively breaking his automatic sequence.

Khan kept one eye on the Russians, aware that they were watching them, also that his ally held the jeep still in gear, his foot poised.

As soon as Khan heard the time he registered consternation, remarking that they would be late at Khad headquarters. This drew the corporal's gaze to them and not the books.

Torn between curiosity at their appearance and sight of their flashes, the man obeyed his military instincts first and drew himself up smartly. Khan took the books straight back out of his hand.

McCabe lifted his foot and the jeep began to move. But one of the Russians had noticed the breach of routine. He remarked on it to the Afghan officer, who at once started forward. But, though he glanced at the jeep, his annoyance was directed towards his corporal. McCabe was increasing speed. The Russian appeared in two minds whether to stop them himself, but already they were approaching the point of no return.

Khan held himself absolutely still.

He heard no shout from behind them, just a low chuckle from the driving seat. Its restraint deepened his respect for his ally. That his own overall picture remained intact was all that concerned him. Now they were actually inside it, a part of it, moving visibly, in his mind's eye, through the streets to its centre. Khan did not, unlike many tribespeople, actually fear the city, but he mistrusted it – its odours and ugliness and unnatural density of population. And never so much as now. Every halt in the traffic had him fingering his gun.

McCabe seemed to entertain no such trepidation. He kept craning his head at the buildings, glancing along side streets. 'Hotel Istalif?' he asked repeatedly, pointing around, spreading his hand. Khan, from deep in his picture, shrugged. But when they reached the big Maiwand intersection he pointed along towards the bridge, whereupon McCabe turned left towards it. Khan gripped the wheel and pulled it round angrily, shaking his head. 'Hotel Istalif,' he told him. McCabe circled the roundabout twice before he understood, then laughed and took the right-hand turn towards the bazaar.

Khan could not fathom McCabe's interest in the Istalif and was in no mood to try. He directed him to the old city, and suddenly they were close to the focal point of his picture, the streets narrowing, dark all at once, with poverty and intrigue swept here from the boulevards, children of four and upwards working alongside their parents in the tumbledown shops, human beasts of burden staggering under enormous loads. McCabe slowed to a wary crawl, progressing thus to a T-junction with a *No Entry* sign, where he stopped. Khan waved him on impatient, into the thronging passages of the bazaar. Hammering the horn, he forced the crowds to squeeze back. Traders, ousted from their pitches by the relentlessly advancing jeep, had to pull whole tarpaulins of goods aside. Fists thumped the vehicle. Insults were hurled. Poor men bargaining for junk as if it were gold jostled each other to make way. A police militiaman appeared from nowhere to pace alongside them.

'Where do you think you're going? Did you not read the sign? Turn back!'

Khan leaned towards him, thumbing his security flash.

'We are on special orders. Begone, brother, or Babrak Karmal will orphan your children!'

The man gave him a hostile but scared look and halted.

Horn beeping, they nosed on for a further fifty paces. Khan's heart had begun to thump. He turned in his seat. He had missed it. He jerked a signal to McCabe to reverse.

Back they went. Then forward and round under a narrow arch, the great, weary eye of a donkey passing within inches of Khan's face, its load buckling their wing mirror. Now they were behind the bazaar street, in a narrow space filled with empty barrows. Khan motioned McCabe to find a space to park.

A man and boy in a lean-to shop straightened from their grindstone to watch as the man in sergeant's uniform got out, came round the vehicle and bent down so that his companion could climb on. Some nearby children tittered and clapped their hands at the spectacle, but swiftly fell silent as they saw Khan's gory feet.

Khan tested the strength of this untried mount anxiously, but only for an instant. The wiry frame that supported him was more than equal to the task ahead. For a Westerner, McCabe was full of surprises, but they were not to be dwelt on. A darkness was rising in Khan's belly and chest. He pointed to a place behind the buildings.

Ducking and weaving, he was borne powerfully through the jungle of hanging merchandise – dried fish, false teeth, bird-cages, sandals. He had been this way but once. If his memory served him, there was a metal welder's . . .

Yes, there was his fizzing blue star. It bit their eyes as they rounded the bench protruding from the back of the workshop.

The back of the carpet merchant's was a dim cave of rugs and prayer-mats and saddle-bags. Entering it, McCabe had to pause to adjust his eyes. A man stood facing them in silhouette against the brightness of the street. Khan dropped a coin into the pot positioned for that purpose. He guided his mount round to a flight of narrow, almost vertical, wooden steps.

McCabe had to pause for breath on the way up. At the top was a long passageway, lit by slits in its outer wall. Khan had never been up here. His sense of direction told him that it extended back over the shops they had just passed. He urged his ally along it. McCabe had to pause again to hitch up his slipping legs. He was tiring.

At the end they came to a heavy old door with metal studs and a small barred window. Beside it was a plastic button. Khan filled his lungs, detecting the faint aroma of incense. He removed his army cap and prodded the button.

The discreet chimes that sounded inside were an unexpected refinement. Mingled with them, he heard the thump of Western music.

Presently the small window opened and a pair of eyes looked directly into his. Unable to see McCabe, who was bending forward, they perceived only Khan's shaven head. A moment later the door was unbolted.

As it began to open, Khan forced it back and spurred his ally forward. He covered the extraordinary man who faced them with his gun.

He was large and heavily bearded, dressed in a jewelled *kullah*, short black waistcoat over balloon trousers, and curly slippers – a costume belonging more to the Arabian Nights than war-torn Kabul. To judge by the man's reaction, their appearance was just as astonishing.

A curtained archway lay ahead of them. The music and incense came from behind it. Khan motioned the man to make no sound.

'Is Yasir Utreb here yet?' he demanded.

The fellow shook his head dumbly.

Khan told him to stay where he was and urged McCabe towards the curtain. As he leaned forward to look through, it was pulled aside.

An obese woman, festooned in finery, stood in smiling welcome. Her smile froze.

Khan told her not to be afraid. This was a security matter concerning one of her clients, not her premises. He beckoned the doorman to enter and stand where he could see him.

The woman seemed hypnotized, but Khan detected a wary intelligence at rapid work behind her eyes. She made an impatient gesture and the music was terminated by one of the cluster of girls staring at them from the divans on the far side of the room – a palatial room, designed like a courtyard with a central fountain.

'By what authority?' demanded the woman, looking at Khan's feet. He could see that she was puzzled that they were bound in rags and not decently bandaged, and that an injured soldier carried by a sergeant should have been sent on such a mission . . .

'What clients have you here?'

She hesitated fractionally. 'None. It is early. But—'

'My orders are to speak with Yasir Utreb – in secret and in private. When is he expected?'

The creature's lipstick gathered in a forbidding blot. 'I do not discuss my clients, their names or their habits. Especially—'

'There is no discussion.' Khan cut her off, at pains to sound like a soldier. 'You will provide co-operation.' He flashed his identification under her nose.

But she was too intelligent. 'Now show me your warrant.'

Khan was in no mood to argue. 'This,' he said, advancing the muzzle of his gun to her lips, 'is my warrant. I understand there is a girl here he favours. Point her out.'

The woman pushed the barrel aside with a bejewelled finger. 'Understand,' she said, 'that I have many important clients. Perhaps your commander is one of them. Perhaps the President himself. You are on protected ground here. So be sure that what you do is within your sanction.' She watched him for his response. Then, seeing he did not waver, called, 'Gabi!'

One of the girls came hesitantly forward. She seemed no more than fourteen, perhaps less, it was hard to see for the cascade of dark hair that masked her face. A slender waif of a child, yet with an air about her of sexual corruption such as Khan had seldom seen. She reminded him of a young animal broken by misuse yet pathetically still obedient to the tricks it had been taught. Her every move was seductive.

Khan said to the child, 'Where will you take him when he comes?'

She raised her slanting eyes to his. With a slight forward thrust of her pelvis she turned and moved away. The provocative yet awkward sway of her hips was an attempt, Khan realized, to conceal the fact that she was lame.

She pulled aside a curtain. Behind it was a door. She opened it and stood there, her hair over her face, staring at the floor.

McCabe carried Khan into the room. There was a brass bedstead. He lowered him on to it.

The room, though ostensibly clean, had the worn look of the back of a taxi. There was a washbasin behind a screen, the ubiquitous portrait of Babrak Karmal above the bed, a table with make-up things, a speckled mirror and padded chair. On the chair was a stuffed toy camel, its button eyes dangling and doleful.

Khan said to the woman and child in the doorway, 'I will wait for him here. If one of you forewarns him of my presence by so much as a glance, I will kill you. Do you understand?'

The woman drew her pencilled eyebrows into a scowl and put her arm round the girl. Neither spoke.

Khan waved them out. He motioned his ally to pull the screen across so that he could not be seen by Yasir when he entered.

McCabe complied, then looked down at him searchingly, clearly wondering how Khan was going to get away with it. He pointed questioningly at the Mickey Mouse alarm clock beside the bed.

Khan indicated how long his ally had to do whatever he had come for – one hour – and signalled him to go.

At first McCabe did not move, but stood calculating whether this would allow enough time. After a moment he gave a fatalistic shrug and left the room.

If he failed to return, Khan realized he would be stranded, with no means of escape. It was a daunting prospect but he was in the hands of Allah. If it was his *kismet* to die here, so be it. So long as it was Yasir's *kismet* to die too, he had no complaint.

Khan tucked his feet under him, clenching his teeth against the pain. At the dead focal point of his picture now, he leaned his head back and closed his eyes, reliving the morning's beating, blow by agonizing blow, reminding himself that Yasir had ordered it knowing full well that this was the day of Khan's execution.

When this outrage had spread its fires into every fibre of his being he drew the soldier's bayonet and laid it on the covers beside him.

24

'SO THEY fell for it?' Yakushev's telephone elbow lifted into the air like an erection. 'What happened? Briefly.'

He listened to Goldanov's beefy voice explaining that a company of Spetznas had waited for five hours in camouflaged concealment around the disused quarry near the airport, since before dawn. Yakushev knew how these men could wait, in perfect discipline, part of the landscape, not a move or a whisper or gulp of water from their canteens. The country there was almost flat, barren except for the spring grass, so there was visibility in every direction. But no rebel force had appeared. By a quarter to noon it seemed evident that no bid was to be made to ambush the execution party. The officer in charge had given the signal to stand down. It was only then, as his platoons broke cover and began to reassemble, that a storm of fire opened up from behind them – so close that at first they thought it must have been one of their own units gone berserk. How the rebels had crept to within a few metres of them without being spotted, they still couldn't figure, but one thing was certain – without their flak-jackets they'd have been cut to pieces. As it was, eight Spetznas were killed. The rest had dived for the quarry, re-formed and returned the fire, while the personnel carriers had circled, still trailing their camouflage nets, and with machine-guns blazing, rode down the rebels where they lay in the grass.

'What kind of force?' Yakushev enquired.

Goldanov said his unit had counted thirty-three dead – a single truckload. They had found the lorry later, parked behind a ruined building one kilometre away.

'No prisoners? Damn. Well, never mind. A splendid victory, comrade! See you for a vodka later?' Yakushev rang off, rattled the bar and asked for security.

So he hadn't been wrong. He was really homing in now.

'Yuri? Arrest Major Jangalak right away . . . Khad liaison, that is correct. Deliver him to the Kollola. Tell the commandant to call me and notify Major Tablian that I want him up here. No hurry. Say, about six o'clock.' He listened to the confirmation, then hung up and turned back to the man beside him. It was Medevev.

'Sorry, where were we?'

The Spetznas captain still wore his gory uniform. One handlebar of his moustache was stained browny-red.

'Well, that was about all. They stood around jabbering for a while. Of course I couldn't understand a word. Then—'

'Yes, nuisance you not understanding Pushtu. But it all worked, that's the main thing. And the capsules functioned.'

Medevev looked down at himself ruefully. 'Right down to the skin. Tacky stuff, too. But I was worried more about the colour and there being no holes. Bastards could have put a burst into me, just like that. Worse – cut my balls off and stuffed them down my throat! I was really sweating till they dumped me, I can tell you.'

'You did well. It won't go unnoticed – once we can take the lid off this, which won't be for a while. So they jabbered for a bit – what then?'

'Off they went. Drove away.'

'You didn't happen to see in which direction?'

'No, I—' Medevev's piggy eyes revealed themselves as watery blue. 'Colonel, you're having them followed, aren't you?'

Yakushev shook his head and smiled. 'Thank you, comrade. You did a fine job.'

'But – what, then? You've got them under air surveillance?'

'Now where will you be going in that?' Yakushev indicated his uniform.

'Uh – back to change.'

'I'd sooner you didn't invite comment. Have someone bring the change of clothing here. And scrub that moustache. And remember this was a security mission. Thank you, Captain.' Yakushev held out his hand.

The captain's grasp was fierce, his gaze full of unasked questions. He didn't click his heels. Spetznas weren't that kind of soldier.

The Istalif was modern and cheapjack. Its three tiers of balconies were of solid concrete painted yellow and blue and angled – presumably to catch the sun – in a way that made them look like half-open drawers, jammed slightly out of kilter. There was no car park, just the square in which the hotel stood, with its parking bay for less than a dozen vehicles.

McCabe drove around it slowly, twice, on the lookout for police or militia. Apart from a number of venerable turbaned characters hobnobbing in groups on the low walls and patches of turf that flanked the paved centre of the square, this part of the city was surprisingly deserted. He backed into a space between an old Peugeot and a Land Rover and killed the motor.

He had picked the Istalif because Sadiq had told him it was where the international press hung out. International these days meaning, of course, the Tass crowd and reps of approved non-aligned nations. But they wouldn't be all mouth and scribble. There was bound to be the odd East European film crew amongst them. So somewhere up there inside those half-open drawers was a movie camera and film. The problem: how to get it. He had forty-five minutes.

A cigarette would have helped. He hadn't smoked in days and it was playing havoc with his thinking processes.

A taxi pulled up at the hotel entrance. Out of it got two, three, no, four black guys. They could have been press but their rounded necks and comfortable bellies suggested a delegation of some sort. Box hats, robes and high foreheads.

Well, no point in sitting about. McCabe got out, crossed and entered the hotel behind them. They went to the desk and he used the diversion they caused to look around.

A few people sat about waiting. Decor lifeless, dominated by the biggest portrait of Babrak Karmal it was possible to squeeze between floor and ceiling. Under its baleful influence the noise coming from the bar seemed like sacrilege. McCabe moved to the glass swing-door for a look.

Yes, there they were, as ever, just like their Western counterparts, hard into the liquid lunch. He peered through the smoke in search of a familiar face. It was not impossible. The same media guys seemed to crop up in every hot-spot. But he recognized no one. He tried to pick out a film crew.

Film people were different, more clannish, a fixed small

group, more often than not including a younger member – the loader-dogsbody, like the thin blond youth with pink eyelids at the table by the window. He was leaning towards his two older companions, listening to them swap stories. The forest of beer cans in front of them was right, the plate of piled sandwiches, longer than normal hair. Though McCabe scanned the other groups, theirs was the only one that tallied. But so what? There was no way he could find out their room number. Unless they had their key on the table. Which they hadn't.

McCabe turned away to see the blacks moving on towards the dining room. The desk clerk was now eyeing him curiously. A security NCO lurking amongst the guests here was about as welcome as a police constable would be back home, McCabe guessed. But hardly as rare. Men in uniform must comprise quite a chunk of their clientele. So the clerk could lump it. McCabe sauntered on, arms folded, as though he were waiting for somebody.

In the dining room, he saw, less than a quarter of the tables were filled. A swift survey of the occupants brought him no nearer a solution. Should he just go on up to the rooms and try his luck? Then he thought, how many rooms would he have to go through? Dozens. And wouldn't the crews with movie cameras have them out on the job?

A glance at the clock above reception showed he had thirty-eight minutes left. The clerk eyed him again as he sauntered back towards the entrance. McCabe ignored him.

The lift door opened, revealing the porter with a pile of luggage. He began ferrying it into a stack just inside the main door.

McCabe looked the cases over. Most were cheap, well-worn. Bulgarian Airlines. None looked like camera equipment. He continued outside and stood on the step.

No one was taking any notice of the stolen Russian jeep yet. But if they weren't looking for it already, they would be soon.

He strolled around the outside of the building. There was a slipway leading to a delivery space round the back – deserted. The rear elevations of the hotel were of plain untextured concrete. They had cut costs on the fire-escapes, too – by not having any. There was, however, a fire exit, with a flight of steps visible inside – a back stairway.

Suddenly hopeful, McCabe strode to the double door and

pushed. But it was solid, designed only to open the one way.

There was nothing else, just the kitchens – at this hour, far too busy. Coming back, he walked across the square and sat on the wall behind the jeep.

Jesus, he needed that smoke!

A taxi pulled up at the entrance and the porter started lugging the cases down to it. A second overblown job stopped behind it and two men got out. One was an Afghan, tall and narrow in an astrakhan hat, the other sandy-bearded, wearing a nylon zip-jacket and sharply creased twill trousers. They leaned over to talk to the driver.

Watching them, McCabe thought there was something familiar about the bearded one, his casual neatness, his serious, rather intellectual good looks. Something glinted between the knitted lapels of his jacket. McCabe leaned forward, peering, but at that moment the two men straightened up and went into the hotel.

He couldn't be sure, but it had looked like a miniature viewfinder. If so, the man could only be a movie director or cameraman.

McCabe crossed the road swiftly and entered the lobby. The two men had disappeared. The elevator wasn't in motion. He glanced in the bar.

There they were, sitting down, with the other three!

After beckoning to the bus-boy, the bearded one launched into explaining something to his crew, pointing across the city, describing something with his hands. McCabe was sure then that he had seen him before, perhaps only once, and not to talk to. The Yemen or Lebanon, somewhere in the Middle East.

There were questions and answers for a while, more visual descriptions, then the bearded one grabbed a sandwich and checked his watch. He said something to the others. His crew began to finish up their drinks.

McCabe became aware that he was being addressed. He turned to face the desk clerk. To judge by his expression, it was no more than an uneasy but respectful enquiry. Was there some problem? Could he help him?

McCabe let him see he was interrupting an official surveillance. He put a finger to his lips, turned the flat of his hand towards him and waved him back to his desk.

The man hesitated, then obeyed. Turning back, McCabe saw now that the two younger members of the crew were on their feet and heading his way. He swung casually aside as they came out. One went to the desk, where he collected a key and joined the other in the elevator.

McCabe watched the indicator stop at the second floor. He glanced around.

Both the clerk and concierge were now observing him with evident concern. He raised the flat of his hand again with a cautionary frown and took to the stairs.

By the time he reached the second floor it was deserted, but faint sounds were coming from along the hall. Moving silently, he presently came to a half-open door. Inside cases were being dragged and voices were speaking in German.

McCabe made up his mind quickly. He drew his gun and was about to enter when he heard them coming out. He stepped aside just in time, holstering the pistol.

They turned towards the elevator, the blond youth first. He was carrying an aluminium box, a smaller one under his arm and a tripod over his shoulder. His companion followed with two more boxes, pausing to lock the door and remove the key. He still did not see McCabe.

McCabe, convinced he had hit the jackpot, followed them. They heard him and turned, but it was just a casual glance.

The light-duty tripod made the camera almost certainly a portable. The size of its box suggested it was a 35 mm, as opposed to an 18. Both were what he wanted. But he had to be sure.

As they reached the elevator he caught them up.

'You speak English?'

They looked round, surprised.

'A little,' the youth said.

McCabe pointed to the aluminium box. 'Open it.'

The two stared at him, his uniform, his holster. An official being officious was not new to them. They were from East Germany.

The older one said something to his companion, presumably for translation into English, but the youth laughed. He put down his load and unfastened the box.

It contained a worn but useful looking 35 mm Arriflex combat camera, plus front bracket with long and short bars, adjustable lens hood and attachable stock for hand-held operation. It was exactly what he wanted. McCabe could hardly keep his voice steady.

'Now that one.'

The smaller box contained a full range of filters. Better and better.

'Now that.'

A multiple power-cell battery and lead.

Magazines – four of them. McCabe stooped and tested their weight and balance. All fully loaded, containing therefore 1800 feet. A card taped to a mag cover indicated that it was Agfacolor.

By this time the Germans were convinced he was looking for drugs. The younger one refastened the last box and spread his hands. 'See? Nothing.'

McCabe made a mental calculation. It was all the film he would need. Was there anything else? Not a thing. He drew his gun.

'Move back to your room.'

They stood blinking at him. The older one demanded to know why.

'I said move it! Hurry!'

The Germans moved, protesting loudly. McCabe ordered the older one to unlock the door and pushed them inside, warning that if they made a sound he would come back and shoot them. He locked them in, took the key and ran back to the elevator.

On the way down, McCabe draped the camera gear around himself, but there was more than he could carry in one journey to the car. It would be only moments, he knew, before the two lads thought of using the telephone.

Downstairs a crowd of new arrivals clustered round the desk. But the clerk was on the lookout for McCabe, and when he saw the camera gear a look of bewilderment crossed his face.

The porter was bringing in the new arrivals' luggage. McCabe grabbed his arm and pointed to the rest of the gear in the lift. The man nodded and went on with what he was doing.

McCabe moved closer and stuck the gun in his ribs. The porter straightened up, dropped what he was carrying and scurried over to get McCabe's gear.

No one else seemed to have noticed, not even the clerk. McCabe watched the porter collect the stuff and hustled him outside with it.

There was a shout from reception. The porter hesitated on the threshold and McCabe saw the clerk, phone in hand, signalling him to stop. The concierge came running out from behind his desk, but, realizing that the thieving sergeant was brandishing a gun, thought better of it.

McCabe hurried the porter across the road. Together they piled the gear in the back of the jeep. Then McCabe vaulted into the driving seat, started up and sped away.

Glancing in the mirror he could see a small crowd pushing out on to the steps. A few were already in the road, waving their arms and shouting after him.

He slapped the wheel in exultation. An Arriflex – fantastic! All the extras – everything he could have bought in a city shop! He just couldn't believe his luck.

As he headed back towards the bazaar, he sobered down. To get the camera he had sacrificed his anonymity. The call would take a while to spread through the channels, he reckoned, but if it reached the checkpoint before he and Khan did, how would they ever get out of the city?

25

McCabe hurried along the upper passageway towards the House With No Doors. As he approached the sounds of high-pitched altercation reached him, a funereal wailing and the to-and-fro tattoo of female heels on marble. He jabbed at the ridiculous bell-push. The place went silent, as if he had severed a sound-track.

After a moment the window snapped back. The man's eyes bulged at him. Some of the wildness left them as he recognized McCabe. He turned away and said who it was. The woman's voice squawked back. There was a stumbling of bolts. The door shuddered open and, as soon as McCabe had entered, slammed shut behind him.

Inside the house the atmosphere was like the aftermath of a bomb blast – a smell, a deadness of air, an evil beyond nature. The mouths of the huddled girls were choked with clothing, their eyes rolling white like cattle before slaughter. The woman was a punctured bag, her finery paste, fingers biting her own flesh. Her mute look led him to the door of the little room.

It stood open against a body that lay open from crotch to gullet. Only a flung arm, a string of beads clutched in the hand, was recognizable. Blood was everywhere – on the floor, furniture, walls. In the middle of it all, on the bed, sat Khan.

It could only just have happened. Yasir must have been late. The woman began taking up where she had left off, screeching at Khan.

'Let him alone.' McCabe shoved her aside and shouldered the door open against the disembowelled weight. Nails like crimson parrot beaks dug into his arm. He shook them away. 'Piss off!' He was looking for somewhere to put his foot that was not intestines.

'You speak English?' The woman was looking at him with amazement.

McCabe reached for the stuffed camel and threw it on the floor to put his foot on. Well, thank Christ, if she understood him, that made it easier. 'Get your man to help me with him.'

'They will close my place, you understand? They will close it down!'

'Bad luck. Get him, blast you. Hey—' McCabe beckoned the bulky fellow. But he hung back, his face a weird shade of grey.

'It must not be closed,' she cried. 'You hear me? *It must not be closed.*'

'Then wrap up the body, get it out, dump it – I don't care what you do.' McCabe had his foot on the camel, straddling the butchery.

'But they will know Yasir came here. Every day he comes.'

'Then tell them the truth – that Ghoram Khan came busting in here. He had a gun – what could you do?' He reached the bed and gripped Khan's arm. His whole uniform was dark with blood. 'Come on, laddie, get yourself together. Let's blow.'

Khan's arm was flaccid. McCabe peered into his eyes. He had gone. He was away somewhere.

The woman was making astonished noises behind him. 'This is Khan? Ghoram Khan? Oh, the fool, the *fool*!' she screeched, then fell silent for a moment. 'Then who are you – the American who makes the pictures?'

That surprised him. 'What do you know about that?'

'Allah, oh this secrecy!' she cried, exasperated. 'Do you both not know what you have done? What place this is? Listen – you must help me!'

'Help yourself. Put Ali Baba at work.'

'You are responsible, you must take the body with you. You must, you must – I order you – in the name of the Lily!'

McCabe straightened up, his attention torn. 'What are you talking about?'

'Do you have—' By stages she was getting herself together, plucking the English words out of the air with her fingers. 'A car – do you have a car?'

'Of course.'

'Wait.' She went to the huddle of girls and pulled one out, holding her there by the arm as she poured out instructions.

The girl protested, still hysterical. The woman struck her across the mouth and repeated the instructions.

The girl nodded, snivelling, and disappeared. McCabe heard the front door open and shut. The woman came back. She was in control of herself now.

'Where is your car?'

'Outside.'

She came into the room. Gathering her robes in tight, she walked round the bed to a curtain. She dragged it aside and in rushed the daylight. She struggled with the window till she had it open.

'Where?'

McCabe pushed his head out beside hers and pointed.

In the distance he heard police horns. Looking for him? The jeep was almost below them, parked among the barrows. Around it was clustered a small crowd of locals. Agog faces lifted to theirs – two guiltily, their youthful owners stepping back from the vehicle. They had been tinkering with the chain and padlock McCabe had removed from the spare wheel and threaded through the handles of the camera boxes.

The woman called down to her neighbours urgently and confidingly, raising her finger to the police horns. She turned to McCabe.

'Bring it closer. Under the window.'

McCabe wasn't slow to get her meaning. 'Do you have any rope?'

'Sheets. Hurry!'

'You'll have to wrap the body in something, and clean Khan up – I can't drive him like that.' McCabe shook Khan roughly. Still he did not respond.

The woman was shouting, 'Ras!' When the big man appeared slowly in the doorway she gave him instructions. He just stood there. She barked at him, and at last he bestirred himself and moved away.

'Got some ammonia? Stick some under his nose,' McCabe said.

'Leave him to me. If not, Ras will lower him. Also the body. We will clean the room, scrub, burn till there is no evidence, and pray to Allah the militia do not come too soon. Go now. In the Lily's name, go!'

McCabe wanted to ask her what the Lily was doing mixed

up with a whorehouse, but there wasn't time. On his way out, he encountered the doorman bringing sheets and a rolled carpet. The woman was shouting at the girls to help.

By the time McCabe reached the jeep the crowd had dispersed. The area seemed drained of all life, save for the salt merchants, who shifted some blocks of rocksalt so he could reverse, then turned their backs. In deference to the woman's warning, they would hear nothing, see nothing.

Again McCabe heard the police horns. Closer.

He called up, 'You listening? It's me they're after – tell Khan that. Tell him to get his skates on!'

The woman's voice was in Khan's ear, her sweat and perfume in his nostrils, yet he remained in a vacuum, drained. The pain was gone. Satisfaction hovered, but the woman's persistence and the image of Yakushev looming through the smoke of Takredi's tortured flesh intruded. At last the repetition of one word summoned his attention – Lily.

The Lily's house? This den of iniquity was the Lily's communications centre and clearing house? Enemy information . . . narcotics . . . What was she saying?

He opened his eyes to find her thrusting a bundle of clothing at him.

'Put these on. Hurry.'

'Repeat what you said.' He could barely articulate. 'You have communication with the Lily?'

She drew back from him, as though realizing she had said too much, and turned to her servant, who was on his knees in the doorway, face averted.

'Quickly, Ras.'

'Listen, woman,' Khan said. 'If you have contact, contact them now. Tell them that I will bring men and weapons, that I only need to know where to bring them and when.'

She nodded. 'I have listened. Now put on the clothes.'

'Now, woman. Tell them now.'

She raised a forefinger waisted with rings. 'You hear the militia? They howl for your friend. Now there is no time. I will call them later.'

'Later I will be gone and will not know their answer.'

'The clothes.' She clenched the paint on her lips and stuck her fists against her hips.

He reached for the bayonet.

She stood for a moment, trembling, sucking her belly away from the blood-dulled point. Then she went.

Khan unbuttoned the uniform. The clothing was evidently the doorman's street attire. Dressed again as a Pathan, how would he now gain access to the Russian enclave? He had conceived his plan in the rush of the moment, without taking into consideration the bloodbath that would result. Nevertheless, he would find a way. There was always a way when Allah pointed. And He was pointing. That this had turned out to be the Lily's house was proof.

The doorman had rolled most of Yasir's remains in the carpet and was tying the ends and middle with cord. Watching, Khan felt no remorse.

By the time he was dressed, the man had secured one end of the knotted sheets to the tubular bundle and the other end to the bed. Khan helped him lift the incredibly heavy, almost liquid, bundle through the window and lower it into the back of the jeep. Khan saw the new pile of boxes, and knew McCabe, also, had succeeded in what he had come to do.

When he turned, the woman was back.

'You are to go to Mir Bala,' she told him haughtily. 'Do you know where that is?'

Khan knew.

'Be there tonight, at the mosque. You will receive further instructions.'

'You spoke to the Lily?' Khan could hardly believe it could be so easy.

'On the little key.'

'Key?'

'That twitters like a bird, O ignoramus. Now go. Not a word more.'

Khan looked hard into her eyes to make sure she was not lying, that it was not a trap. When he saw anger and not cunning, he slung the Kalashnikov across his back and clambered on to the sill.

He lowered himself hand over hand down the brothel sheets into the jeep. McCabe already had the motor revving. He turned around and they drove under the arch. As they nosed forth into the bazaar Khan directed him to the right.

McCabe swung left.

Khan gripped the wheel and pulled on the handbrake. The jeep jerked to a halt. He again pointed right.

'You crazy bastard,' shouted McCabe. 'You still think you're going after that Russian? *Schurawi*?'

'*Schurawi.*' Khan nodded, equally unyielding. 'Yakushev.'

'No way. Too much is enough, old tiger. We're making for the rendezvous.' McCabe released the handbrake and drove on.

Khan reached again for the lever but McCabe held it down. For several moments they matched strength, the jeep weaving through the crowds, vendors and shoppers jumping this way and that. Someone shouted 'Wait!' in Khan's ear as they passed. It sounded like a woman's voice. McCabe wasn't giving in. He accelerated. Khan realized it was becoming too hazardous and relinquished his grip, though by no means his determination. He would get him to turn later, on Jadi Maiwand Avenue. The woman's voice grew faint behind them.

Reaching the street with *No Entry* signs, McCabe made to turn into it, but simultaneously they both saw the militia truck parked halfway along it. McCabe swung back and drove on, scattering a group of rugged-looking men delving into a heap of farming boots. They cleared the way to reveal another jeep coming towards them. It had a mounted machine-gun and was crewed by three militia men. There was no room to pass. Both vehicles came to a halt.

Khan's reaction was instantaneous. He tapped the insignia on McCabe's uniform, then the Soviet star on the jeep, and in a tone of authority ordered the other vehicle to back up.

The militia jeep didn't move. The man next to the driver was a lieutenant and a Pathan – two good reasons why he was not going to be seen giving way in a crowded place.

The only way was to out-rank him. Khan shouted that he was a captain on a plain-clothes mission and they would assist him by reversing to the next turning. McCabe got the gist of what he was saying and drove steadily forward, thumping the horn. But the other vehicle did not move. The lieutenant, peering at them suspiciously, muttered to the man behind him and the machine-gun swivelled to cover them.

Khan levered himself up on to the back of his seat, as if to get out and remonstrate. Instead he lifted his Kalashnikov and shot the machine-gunner dead, then raked the burst downwards across the windscreen. Khan couldn't tell whether the two behind it were hit or not. The bazaar crowd parted, shoving and shouting to escape the field of fire. As they rushed for cover the jeep door burst open and the officer dived out in a sideways roll. Up came his AKMS in a burst that stung Khan's face with glass from the side mirror, causing his own shots to go wide. He ducked and lost balance, falling heavily on his elbow in the road. He felt the wind of someone rushing close past him. The officer was coming to his knees now, aiming straight at him, but the rushing figure reached him before he could fire and kicked the gun up, then took hold of it and tried to wrest it from him. Khan saw that the figure was that of a woman! She was shouting something to the crowd.

'These are resistance men – help them!'

McCabe, with an exclamation, launched himself from the driving seat and ran to her assistance. He clubbed the officer to the ground with his pistol. Then the bystanders closed in and Khan could see nothing save milling bodies.

In no time the alleyway was filled from wall to wall with jostling male humanity. To avoid being trampled on, Khan pulled himself back painfully into the jeep. Still he could see nothing. But there were sounds – the chanting-in-unison sounds men make when they are labouring together – or kicking someone to death. Once aroused, he knew, there was no mercy in his people for the servants of the regime.

Now McCabe and the woman were coming back, talking rapidly together in English, though Khan could see at once from the woman's features and colouring that she was Afghan.

'Khan, meet Dr Salimar!' Despite the drama of the moment, there was a deep glow in McCabe's eyes.

'Khub hasti?' Khan's greeting was solemn, for she had probably saved his life. 'Praise Allah for your coming.'

The young woman lowered her eyes and looked pleased. She said to McCabe, 'Did you not hear me call as you passed? Madame Geneifa sent a girl to tell me you were at her house. I came as quickly as—'

'No time to talk.' McCabe cut her short and made to help her up into the back, his gaze on the road behind them.

Khan knew that he was remembering the militia truck. 'No.' He indicated the other jeep. 'We will take that.'

The crowd surrounded them. For a moment they were all resistance heroes, helping to transport Khan and the boxes to the other vehicle – everything save Yasir's body, which held them fascinated. The woman got in the back. In some wonder Khan saw her check over the machine-gun and ammunition.

McCabe was kicking out the broken windscreen when there was a sudden shouting and pointing. The militia truck was coming! Without being told to, the mob surged into its path. McCabe got the motor started and backed along the alley. The bulk of the throng kept pace, waving their fists and chanting encouragement and slogans.

They reversed the whole length of the bazaar and backed out into the middle of Jadi Maiwand Avenue, bringing both lanes of traffic to a halt. Even then the crowd did not desert them. As McCabe turned the jeep towards the city's southern exit they surged out into the road and ran along the pavements, shouting, 'Victory to the resistance! Death to Moscow!' Cars and trucks added their cacophony of horns. Passengers grinned and waved. It was like a carnival procession.

The expedition to kill Yakushev was no longer feasible. Khan shelved it for another time and thought forward to the checkpoint. With a woman in the back there could be no hope of bluffing their way through.

McCabe was bombarding her with questions as he drove.

'I don't understand about Madame What's-her-name. How did she know you were here?'

'The Lily said I should make myself known to her,' Ayesha told him.

'You contacted the Lily about me?'

'I did it the same day – from Moqor. Wakir and I rode there the moment we knew you were alive.'

'How could you tell I was from that distance?'

'From the way the doctor behaved when they dug you out. They would send you to their Kabul air headquarters, we knew that.'

'So you came on to Kabul?'

'I came alone – by bus. Already the Lily knew you were in the Choukha. I stayed with friends and kept contact with Madame Geniefa, as instructed.'

'You're incredible!'

Militia horns blared ahead of them. Khan looked but could see nothing for the traffic.

'You really did all that for me, sweetheart?'

'For the resistance, Michael.' She leant towards Khan. 'Can you see them?'

He shook his head.

'Let us hope they are beyond the river.'

'Inshallah.' Khan turned to gauge afresh the small face.

'We will soon be at the checkpoint. Are you harmonious with the gun, Doctor?'

'I am harmonious, Ghoram Khan.'

He looked at the black band on her arm and sought no further assurance.

They had long outstripped the crowd. The city traffic had veered away across the bridge. Only the southbound trucks and cars were with them now as they headed towards the city exit.

Khan was still searching in his mind for a solution as to how they would get through when they rounded the final bend. As the checkpoint came in sight the air above his head split with the deafening chatter of the machine-gun. Even Khan was startled by the speed of Ayesha's decision.

The glowing streams of tracer cut above the traffic to spark off the armour plate of the BMP parked beside the inspection point. Ayesha corrected upwards and the Afghan manning the turret machine-gun jerked backwards.

The ground personnel scattered to take cover as the stream of bullets played amongst them. Cars swerved and braked and bumped into each other. The wind through the glassless screen blurred Khan's vision as McCabe pulled out and accelerated between the two lanes of traffic. A crackle of return fire came at them from a sandbagged emplacement to their left. Someone screamed in one of the cars. A cyclist toppled sideways in front of them. The jeep scrunched over his bicycle. Khan raised his Kalashnikov and saw the gunner reel sideways, his weapon spin on its mount. A bus and a lorry were stopped, facing opposite ways, at the checkpoint. There was no way past them and Khan could see no one inside them, save some passengers on the bus's roof, leaping for safety in the ditch. McCabe braked hard and turned the front wheels against a saloon car, trying to push it aside. It wouldn't move. The turret of the BMP was traversing towards them. Khan had not reckoned there would be a second gunner inside. He shouted to the woman, who directed her fire at the gunner's optic. Her accuracy amazed him. The bullets could not penetrate the thickened glass, but their impact was enough. The turret's movement halted. Now Kalashnikov fire was rasping from the emplacement, but blindly, from weapons held above concealed heads. Watching for just one helmet to show, Khan saw the machine-gun twitch on its pivot. He was ready for the man as he rose into view. His own single shot stripped the belt-box from the side of the gun and drove it into the soldier's chest, and he vanished.

McCabe had shifted to four-wheel drive and the car in front of them was hinging aside. They spurted through, mounted the kerb and turned along the inside of the traffic. A man appeared suddenly ahead, frantically trying to haul a whole string of loaded donkeys from their path. McCabe squeezed past them all, clipping the pannier off the last beast. Root vegetables thumped the bonnet and bounded past them. But they were through, beyond the checkpoint.

Ayesha had stopped firing. She was trying to reverse the gun, but was having trouble with the camera boxes; she had seen the BMP's turret gun panning after them. She almost sat on Khan's head before she got her own weapon round – too late. The 73 mm cracked once and an army supply truck behind them came apart, each component silhouetted against the flame, hurling its driver through his screen. The pile-up that resulted created a gap in the traffic, enabling McCabe to cut back into the flow. The BMP was reloading and Ayesha knew it, directing her bursts at its turret. The one-in-five tracer bullets careened away off it, graceful as a fireworks display. When at last the gunshot came, it was wild, bursting in a field beside the road.

They were clear. McCabe raised his fist and shouted like a *buz kashi* rider. Ayesha shut off her fire and, watching rearwards, Khan saw her clear the gun and check the belt-box, then grope around under the cases for a replacement. Tongue clenched between small white teeth, she had it clipped on and the belt fed into the breech faster than even Feizl could have done it.

Our women are capable of this? was the thought that flashed

through his mind. Why have we not made use of them? He shouted through the howling wind, asking her where she had learned to handle a PKMB, but she was peering back along the road. She turned to him sharply, pointing.

Khan saw a machine-gun jeep identical to their own swerving around the pile-up. No sooner were they in its sights than it opened fire.

Nothing graceful about the tracer now as it grew straight at them. But the gunner's elevation was low. Ricochets bounded and snapped past them. Ayesha returned the burst, but the speed at which they were travelling, coupled with the unevenness of the road surface, made accuracy impossible. The jeep gunner seemed to realize this too, for he held his fire and waited for his driver to bring them closer.

Khan peered ahead. They were running parallel to the river. Fields of fresh wheat lay on either side with hardly a tree in sight. Everything was colourless against the glare of the sun. He was looking for the rendezvous – a ruined mosque by the roadside. Through glistening wind-tears he made out a shape. But it was an army truck, veering off into a camp. Camps and depots lay back at intervals among the fields. A signboard flashed past. Now the road was clear. Still no sign of the ruin.

The pursuit jeep was closer, less than three hundred paces now, and gaining. The road was still bad and now there was dust. Both gunners were being thrown all over the place. Both were waiting for a smoother stretch.

Was that the building? No, another camp site, its wire mesh dark against the bare earth, tents, vehicles, a concrete hutment. More fields. More and more. Now a dark blob beside the road far ahead. The river veering away behind it to the east. Yes, that was it!

Khan leaned across and signalled urgently on the horn. He kept hooting. He could see no movement in the vicinity of the ruin, no sign of the firing-squad truck. Suppose Hafiq had failed to find the place? Or been recaptured?

The dome, long stripped of its tiles, showed pale above the gaping entrance. McCabe began to slow, but Khan motioned him not to lose speed. Was that a figure now? Yes, emerging from the inner darkness with a characteristic swagger. Hafiq, beyond doubt. In relief, Khan waved his arm and pointed towards the pursuing vehicle. He repeated the action till they were past. He twisted in his seat to see if he had understood, but the angle of the building masked him from view.

The second jeep came rushing after them. It was approaching the ruin now. Passing it. When it already seemed too late, Khan heard the prolonged burst of fire.

The jeep seemed to stumble like a shot hare. It swerved off the road, hit a rock, somersaulted. It was rolling as it hit the field. A great gout of flame burst from it and obscured it from view.

With the jeep a blazing beacon almost outside the mosque door, Khan knew they had to move on fast. But where to? When both vehicles were under cover in the ruined building, the others gathered around him in hurried debate.

The Khad deserters, the politicians, the surgeon and Tamim were no longer a part of the decision-making. It was up to the resistance fighters to find a way out. But to Khan's surprise McCabe started talking.

Ayesha interpreted. 'You do not mind?' She was shy suddenly, conscious of Khan's authority. 'But this man has much experience of battle. He was in Vietnam, Angola, Beirut, the Jewish war, many, many places.'

Khan was astonished. 'Let him speak.'

'The first thing they're going to do,' McCabe said, 'probably are doing right now, is scramble ground troops in a gunship and come after us.'

Hafiq said, 'Wherever we go they will recognize the jeep and lorry. So we must leave them here, divide and go across country on foot!'

Khan shook his head. 'No, Hafiq, we must keep together.'

McCabe agreed. 'Not necessary. They'll be looking for the jeep only at first, not the truck, not yet. They won't make the connection between what's just happened and their failed execution party, not for some time, maybe half an hour.'

Ayesha added to her interpretation of this, 'Excuse me, then should we not leave the jeep here and all go in the truck?'

Hafiq waved his hand dismissively but Khan told him to show respect. He said to her, 'I will need the jeep tonight, little sister. I am going to Mir Bala. The road is rough and steep.'

This was news to everyone.

McCabe suggested, 'Then disguise the jeep from air observation. Put the top up to hide the gun and broken screen. Someone in uniform ride in front with me. Then we can go in both vehicles.'

Hafiq asked how far Mir Bala was.

Khan said, about six *kro* west of Mohammed Agah, the next town.

McCabe asked Ayesha what the hell a crow was.

She told him six *kro* was fifteen kilometres. And Mohammed Agah from here was twenty kilometres.

McCabe made a calculation and shook his head. 'We'll have to take it in two bites – a short one now, the rest after nightfall, when the gunships have been put to bed.'

Ayesha wanted to get it quite straight before translating. 'Both vehicles?'

'Yes. In convoy, moving nice and slow.'

'*Slow?*' Hafiq scowled at him, plainly resenting this interference from an outsider. 'The gunship will come quickly, will it not? Ten minutes?'

'Less now.'

'Then to go slow is madness.'

'Convoys have a regulation pace, Hafiq, right? If we stick to that pace the gunship won't think it's us. On its first run it will pass us over. Give us just that much more time.'

'Time for what?' Hafiq turned a complete circle, face raised.

'To find a track off the road, pick ourselves a shadowy depression, get out the nets and camouflage ourselves into the landscape.'

There was silence. This was military thinking of a kind they were not used to. All looked towards Khan.

Khan laid a friendly hand on Hafiq's arm to defuse his jealousy. He debated for a moment, then nodded for it to happen.

In the galvanized activity that followed, Ayesha asked McCabe quietly, 'Can I come with you? It is not easy for me alone with men who are not my brothers.'

'Yes, stick with me, sweetheart. I'm not letting you out of my sight ever again! Help me get the top up.' He watched her across the back of the jeep as she complied, smiling. 'You're a sight for sore eyes, you know that?'

'Please,' she said, but with a little tug of pleasure on her lips.

'You stay out of sight in the back here. If we hit trouble I'll collapse the top and you can do more amazing stuff with the gun, make mincemeat of 'em.'

She said softly to the nut she was tightening, 'You have changed, Michael.'

'Too right.' A grim note. 'I've discovered something. Something that should please you.'

'That you are involved with us now?'

'That I know how to hate.' He held her gaze. 'Remember what you said about hate and love, how you can't have one without the other? Well, now you'd better watch out!'

He looked at Ayesha for a response, but her eyes avoided his. She seemed troubled.

Within minutes the jeep and the truck were driving along at a steady 50 k.p.h. They were heading south, the Khad soldier beside McCabe keeping a sharp lookout for a likely track. But there were only rocks on either side now, and time was running short.

Then a few fields appeared among the rocks – scratched there by starving fingers, it looked like, and McCabe remembered the Viet paddies planted under rocket-fire. But no tracks.

Khan was riding out of sight in the truck. He would get the driver to hoot if he wanted to stop. So far, no hoot. No gunship farting past, either.

'Penny for your thoughts, Doc?'

But still she wouldn't look at him.

They'd been on the road for fifteen minutes. Maybe the Russian gunships had been in full deployment when the balloon went up and they'd had to wait for one to come back. It was possible they still hadn't got one. What would they do then? Send out a mobile force, he reckoned. In which case Hafiq would be right: they were crazy to be moving this slow.

Twenty minutes now. It was becoming crucial. The rocks rolled away up into blue, blue mountains. Beautiful, breathtaking, but *no tracks*.

Twenty-five minutes. The soldier was pointing ahead. It was another camp, Afghan for sure out here. They passed the sign at the end of its approach road – a cannon on horseback.

'Mountain Artillery,' Ayesha murmured. At least she was talking again.

They had hardly gone past when the truck horn blew behind

them. McCabe slowed, peering back. The truck was turning along the track.

'What's he up to?'

He scanned the sky sharply, but could see no threat. He backed up, mystified, and turned after the other vehicle. He could hear then that its engine seemed to be missing and popping.

The camp was surrounded by high steel mesh topped by barbed-wire – as much to keep the conscripted Afghans in as keep marauders out, he guessed. Inset was a similarly meshed double gate, shut and padlocked, inside it a guard hut and a handful of fierce-looking guards in side-hats and khaki field uniforms.

Beyond them the camp looked only partially populated, the tents in rows with their side walls up – just roofs on sticks, the only movements a distant game of volleyball and a few men sauntering. McCabe counted six gleaming guns on wheels, old-fashioned 50 mms, only a fraction of their normal complement. The stack of fodder was a giveaway; the two long Nissen huts must be stables.

The truck popped and farted to a stop at the gate. The Khad driver got down, hooked his fingers in the mesh and spoke to the sentry and then the sergeant who came out of the hut.

McCabe looked up at the tail of the truck for a clue as to what was going on, but neither Khan nor any of the ex-prisoners was visible, only the Khad soldiers sitting expressionless.

The sergeant went back into his hut and McCabe just caught the winding noise of a field telephone.

'What can be happening?'

'Wish I knew, sweetheart.' McCabe looked up again, then along the road. A four-eyed American taxi, minted in the chrome age, came jouncing past. Nothing more sinister appeared, but that couldn't last, he knew.

The sergeant unlocked the gate, came out and sauntered around both vehicles, as if to verify their bona fides. The jeep's gaping windscreen clearly puzzled him, but with the top up, Ayesha out of sight and the Khad soldiers looking so spruce in the truck, he let it go. At a nod to the guard the gates opened up.

The truck drove into the compound first and McCabe

followed. The sentries directed them to some lean-to sheds where half a dozen unit vehicles were parked beside what looked like a repair shop. In moments both vehicles were concealed under the corrugated sheeting, safe from airborne observation.

If the savage execution of Yasir had given McCabe cause to doubt Khan's mental fitness, he took it all back. It was beautiful! But what happened now? He told Ayesha to have the gun ready and got out of the jeep.

Six of the Khad soldiers had already swung down from the tailgate and were stretching their limbs. From inside the truck Khan's quiet, authoritative voice told them what to do. Hammering sounds were coming from the workshop, but whoever was doing it was invisible under an old GAZ-66. The soldiers looked around, seemingly for the latrine, but in fact tracing the course of the telephone cable looping in off the road. They wandered round the building, out of sight of the gate.

A moment later McCabe saw them crossing to the long, low hutment that was the terminal point of the cable. They disappeared unhurriedly behind it.

He looked carefully all around. The gunners killing time around camp, if they had noticed, showed little interest. An old camp servant was leaning on a hoe over a small patch of vegetables surrounded by whitewashed rocks. The volleyball game was out of sight from this angle but he could hear the ball thumping. Something else was also thumping. From the Nissen huts came the hoof-stamp a horse makes twitching off flies. As the sign suggested, they used horses to carry guns through the mountains – broken down, of course, into their components. He supposed that that was where the bulk of the regiment was right now – engaged in mountain warfare against some guerrilla band.

The door of the office hut opened and out stepped three officers – two in their shirtsleeves, the third in Russian uniform – their hands above their heads. Behind them, guns levelled, emerged the Khad soldiers.

They prodded them forward about twenty paces, then told the leader to say his piece. He was probably the commandant, tall, beaky and stooping, with a blaze of white in his short black hair. He glanced round at the Russian, who didn't seem to want to know him at that moment, then addressed all within earshot, though it was towards the guardroom that he directed most of what he had to say, letting them know, McCabe guessed, that any heroics would surely get his arse shot off.

Heads jerked up everywhere. The falling hoe squashed a row of lettuces. The guards emerged from their chalet, all looking in one direction like a warren of gophers. They probably didn't give a damn if he got shot or not but they did as they were told: laid down their weapons and stepped away from them.

Everyone came flocking round, to stand hypnotized. The pale-skinned, fleshy Russian officer looked at them sidelong as though inviting them to take action, but what could they do? None of them was armed.

Only then did Khan make his appearance in the back of the truck. Beckoning them all in closer, he identified himself and said that he was taking command of their camp for a few hours; they were going to co-operate fully or get shot. He wanted every weapon delivered here in front of him within five minutes.

The gunners looked at each other and didn't move. The camp sergeant-major, straight as a fencing-stake, called out that regulations forbade the men access to their small-arms while in camp. They were kept locked in the armoury.

Khan demanded to know who had the key. No one answered.

Hafiq vaulted down off the truck, beckoned Ayesha out of the jeep and stripped back the canvas top. The murmur of astonishment that greeted her appearance was silenced abruptly as Hafiq swung the gun on them.

The commandant, scowling, slowly produced the key. Whereupon Khan told the Khad troops to lock up the officers, cut the external telephone cable, collect any radios they could find and put them under lock and key. The gunners he told to disperse and carry on as normal.

It was all over within minutes.

26

It was mid-afternoon when Major Nikolai Zotov himself brought in the first signal.

'We have a fix,' he announced, moving to the wall map. 'I don't know who we have a fix on but' – he measured off the reference and stuck in a coloured flag – 'that's it. Which'll cost you one coffee.'

Yakushev was at his side, peering intently. He read the signal. It did not mention Khan, just gave the code sign, the reference and the time. He nodded to himself. After a lot of bad luck it really did seem as if he had got his game together. But it was getting complicated. He must be careful.

'Black, with sugar.' Zotov took off his glasses and pinched his reddened eyes towards his nose. 'Pointless, I suppose, to ask what you're up to?'

Yakushev triggered the coffee machine. Was Zotov a friend or a spy? He shook his head. 'Too complicated.'

'Yes, don't complicate me any more than I am,' Zotov murmured. 'You know what I'd like?'

'Wouldn't we all.' Yakushev moved back to the pile of reports from his illegals in Baluchistan and picked one up.

'You don't know what I was going to say.'

'Does it matter? A month swimming in the Black Sea, or in bed with your wife, or someone else's? We're privileged to be working on a historical move, Nikolai. The burden falling on us is an honour.' Bullshit, he thought.

'Don't think I'm complaining, Andrei.' Zotov, too, was well versed in the game. 'I'm just cracking up. All this monitoring – neighbouring theatres, newscasts, sorting out what's relevant. There's only so much one can delegate. In the rest of the army all the shit falls on the lowest scum. In our branch it falls on the officers. The academy never prepared me for this sort of decision-making, just taught me how to pass the buck. No, I didn't say that, Andrei. You weren't listening, right?'

'What?'

'You're a pal.' Zotov sat in uneasy silence. 'By the way, General Dolin's flying back, I take it?'

'Of course he's flying. Why?'

'Well, they cut the road. We just monitored it. Three bridges in a row. Same old place. Thirty kilometres this side of Kandahar.'

Yakushev scrawled a note in the margin and laid it on the pile for the general.

'Our Harvest main artery,' Zotov added, as though it was on his mind and he felt it should be on Yakushev's too.

'The engineers'll fix it. They've got a week.'

'A lot has to flow through the artery before then, Andrei. Those rivers aren't dry yet, you know.'

'Some TMM bridging will fix it.' Yakushev maintained his screen of concentration.

Zotov watched him, his mood that of a man picking at a scab.

'They cut the road north of here, too.'

His words took a moment or two to sink in.

'Where?'

'North of Jabal os Sara. One of our supply convoys is blazing up by the pass. Large attacking force. Our tanks and gunships are engaging. I – I'm just wondering if I may be missing something, that these aren't isolated. Coupled with the dam at Girishk, it just struck me that . . .'

Yakushev looked up at last. 'The dam?'

'You haven't read it yet? It's under there somewhere.' Zotov indicated his in-tray. 'According to Herat, they blew it. It's still to be confirmed, but added to this other intelligence we're monitoring . . .'

'Wait a minute.' Yakushev looked incredulous. 'I mean, that's enormous, that dam, a hell of a lot of water!'

'Hell of a lot of explosive, too. I just wondered if this could be a rebel offensive, that's all. I mean, with Harvest so close, and those bugs everywhere. Could they have found out? Are they well enough organized to mount a pre-emptive counter-offensive?'

Yakushev came to his feet, suddenly thoughtful.

Zotov watched him. 'Are they?'

The telephone buzzed.

It was Goriansky to say that General Naqaswar was on the line.

'I don't want to talk to him. Tell him I'm – Say what you like.' Yakushev hung up. The old man was no doubt furious about Jangalak's arrest. Well, he wasn't going to get caught up in that one yet – not before young Ali had been interrogated.

Zotov had barely opened his mouth to continue when the telephone buzzed again.

'Yes?' Yakushev barked into it. 'No, I'm—' He huffed a sigh, but he was curious. 'Put him on.'

It was Vladik, one of the Spetznas staffers, to say that the jeep assigned to Captain Medevev had been reported found abandoned in the Old Town with a body in it – did he know anything about it?

Yakushev's impatience was arrested in its tracks. 'In the *town*?' He glanced round at the flag on the map. 'That's not possible. When?'

'Just reported.'

'There's a mistake.' Then, '*Whose* body?'

'I didn't ask.'

'Why the hell not? Who told you this?'

'Riskin, city security.'

'I'll have a word with him. No action from you. Wipe it from the record. I'll see you get your jeep back.'

Yakushev shot a glance at Zotov, uttered a curse and rattled the bar. He called CS. They told him the enquiry had come from Garrison, their Afghan counterpart. Yakushev got on to Garrison and there was the usual delay, with low-graders asking in limp voices what he wanted, till finally he bellowed and there was dead silence. Down the line came the emotionless voice of their deputy commandant.

'The identity of the dead man?' There was a rustle of papers. 'No, we do not have—Yes, we do.' He sounded surprised. 'Bracelet identification: Yasir Utreb.'

Yakushev stood in stunned silence.

'Are you there, Colonel?'

Murdered? Had Khan come back into the city and risked his freedom to settle a score? How the devil could he? The fix on the map was positive, had to be. Was it possible it referred to only one vehicle and Khan had doubled back in the other?

A chill ran up Yakushev's spine. *The revenge of the Afghan. He* could well be the next target. Khan could be in the building right now. He had got to Rossakov. With the rage that must be burning inside him Khan was capable of coming clean through the wall.

'Can you explain to us the vehicle's mission, who was its driver?' the deputy commandant was asking.

'No,' Yakushev snapped. 'I could, but it would be irrelevant. The jeep was stolen.'

'Ah. The place and time of theft, Colonel?'

'I don't have that information.'

'No? I see. Understand, Colonel, I am not prying into your secret operations, simply we have a murder and a robbery involving a Soviet vehicle and—'

'Robbery?'

'At the Hotel Istalif.'

Yakushev passed a hand across his brow.

'A man wearing the uniform of a Khad sergeant stole some cine-camera equipment from a party of guests. What I am asking is, should we look for the culprit or close our books on the matter?'

'Close them!'

'Thank you, Colonel. Good day.'

Yakushev was replacing the instrument when a shout brought it back to his ear.

'Colonel, while we are connected – we no longer need the gunship.'

'What gunship?'

'CS didn't inform you? Oh, I am sorry. We applied for one on their allocation, but they were all deployed.'

'Hold it.' Yakushev stopped him. 'Why would Garrison need a ship?' He shot another glance at Zotov.

The deputy commandant gave a hurried resumé of the events at the checkpoint.

Yakushev was not slow to recognize its significance in relation to the previous information. His first emotion was of relief. Khan *had* left town.

'How long ago did this happen?'

'Notification reached us at 15.15 hours.'

Over half an hour ago. 'Well, listen. I want you to take no action, understand?'

'But we have already taken it.'

Yakushev's knuckles whitened over the instrument. 'What have you done?'

'Sent out a pursuit force. An armoured car, two—'

'How long ago?'

Pause. The deputy commandant was checking his watch. 'Ten minutes.'

'Do you have radio contact with your force?'

'Do we have radio contact?' he heard him ask someone. 'Quick, man!'

'Yes, Colonel, we have contact.'

'Call them back.'

'What? But why, Colonel?'

'*Do it!* Confirm it the moment it's done. That's an order!'

After he had hung up, Yakushev stood like a man who has narrowly escaped a road accident.

Major Zotov watched his face.

'Going wrong, is it?'

'No. Yes. Could do.' For all the signals officer knew, these calls could well relate to some undercover operation.

'I was asking, do you reckon the *mujahedin* are well enough organized to mount an offensive?'

Yakushev realized he must answer. The question verged on Lily territory, his private preserve. He spread his hands.

'I really don't know. Look, it's not your job to collate, Nikolai, nor mine, we've got enough to do. Leave it for intelligence to figure out.'

When Zotov had gone, Yakushev threw up the window to get some oxygen into his brain. The idea of an offensive disturbed him, but the sudden possibility that his ploy could come apart and Khan escape disturbed him more. As it was, he would have a hard time explaining to Dolin why Khan was still alive. *If* he explained. He was nudging unknown territory – just when he thought he had it all sewn up.

You think you can think like them, he mused, then Khan comes back for Yasir, or this inexplicable robbery occurs and you realize you didn't have their wavelength and never would have.

What else hadn't he allowed for? Suddenly, he wished that Pola was with him. She would have known.

High in the Western Kush, a hundred or so resistance fighters clung like ants to the crags as, with block and tackle, they hauled a shiny new generator and drilling equipment up the sheer rockface, inch by chanting inch.

A scream, high-pitched as an eagle's, echoed across the chasm. The men paused, glancing up to where the Lily's shrouded figure stood silhouetted against the purplish heavens.

'Faster!' she shrieked. 'Faster!'

Limbless and faceless in her traditional robes, she exuded a terror of emotion that set them working with such energy that one slipped and pitched over the edge, whirling like a jettisoned toy, to be swallowed up by the blue maw of the canyon.

Scarcely had he vanished when two others took his place. If they fell, others were waiting. Death was of no concern to them. They were fanatics, volunteers who had lost everything to the Russians, their families, villages, comrades.

Watching them, Pola knew that when the time came they would sacrifice themselves to a man. Alas, perhaps too willingly. They lacked the discipline of soldiers, their combined sense of objective, restraint, cunning. They lacked a leader.

Now, after many setbacks, *inshallah*, one was on his way.

The gunners were dancing. Fangs of flame gnashed at the darkness outside the hutments as they piled various camp articles on the fire; those of their oppression first, the orders board, the wooden 'guns' they had been made to drill with for fear of insurrection if they were allowed access to the real thing. They pivoted and sauntered to the beat of drums, arms lifted, shirt-tails flapping, the thin veneer of their training yielding easily to the instinctive grace of the *norch*.

Their rejoicing had begun in the afternoon. Having seen their officers locked in the detention cells, they had congregated, hesitantly at first, then with mounting confidence, around Khan, to offer him their allegiance, all thirty-eight of them, the sergeant-major last. There were no abstentions. When Khan welcomed their offer they went on a minor bender of destruction. Khan called them back, warning that everything must appear normal for the time being, and put them to work. The guard must remain on guard, letting in anyone who would be routinely given access; once in, they could be dealt with as the situation demanded. What happened if the regiment returned was an imponderable. The staff assured him that they were not due back for at least a week. Khan just hoped they were not shaping answers to please him – a nicety with deadly side-effects in war. He had the camp's main receiver-transmitter reinstalled and a clerk detailed to keep listening watch, just to reassure headquarters that there was no immediate need to send out a signals team to repair the line.

The rest of the men were told to prepare to move, possibly at daybreak. Under Hafiq's supervision they loaded the regimental trucks with ammunition supplies.

Meanwhile the cooks had been given their heads to provide a monumental Ramadan feast for all, and the pitiful bleating of two fat-tailed sheep and a goat being dragged about and slaughtered distracted McCabe as he shot a focus test on each lens of the new camera. There was no way he could check for steadiness. He fancied for a moment that the motor was hunting under load, but couldn't check that either without running off more film than he felt he could spare. It was all a bit unsatisfactory, but at least he hadn't picked up equipment on its way home to an East German repair bench.

For some reason there was no changing bag with the equipment and he had to search for a lightproof cupboard, which he found in one of the officer's sleeping quarters. This was evidently the Russian's, to judge by the gear hanging in there.

While the film was processing, McCabe looked around the small spartan room.

There was an over-exposed snapshot that made the Russian's wife and son look like albinos in a snowstorm, a prayer mat by the bed that showed he had been spending his roubles in the bazaar, a pair of soft, sick-smelling leather slippers and a fat kitbag. McCabe slackened the cord and looked inside.

A black deathshead stared up at him. McCabe pulled it out by its pig snout and a jointed proboscis snaked to the floor jouncing a metal filtration canister. He almost yelled aloud.

It was the ShM rubberized hood. The rest was all there: OP-1 NBC protective clothing, gloves, boots – the Soviet standard anti-toxic-chemicals issue to all troops.

'Ayesha!'

Ayesha came in and stared for a moment, very seriously. She helped him pull the ShM over his head and hard down on to his shoulders. It was like squeezing his face into an inner tube. Now the hooded coat. She pulled the strings, tied the tapes, clipped the clips. He watched her through steamed-up eyepieces, snorting instructions through the tube.

'You are going to try it with the camera?'

'My God!' McCabe suddenly remembered the tank. He drained the developer, flushed it through and poured in the hypo, then put the gloves back on and they went outside to where the camera still stood on its tripod.

One thing he knew straight away: he could never assemble it or lace up the film or set the stop. The American gloves had been more flexible. These, on the other hand, were the real McCoy, guaranteed proof against T-2. He could see through the lookthrough, trigger the motor and pan okay. Given a pre-set stop and focus, he could just about make film done up like this – but for one magazine only. The reload was something else. He would either have to risk exposing a hand or do it under cover.

He tried to find ways to beat it, but could not. Caught in the open with the dust falling, he would have just eight minutes of fully protected shooting time.

When he removed the hood it was as if he'd been under a shower. While the gear was drying out he checked the negs. They were overcooked, but the focus in each was sharp. He was in business.

They were all in business now. Khan, at the head of the long table, looked like a man who had awoken to find himself holding the key to a long-sought treasure. He had firepower, transport, weapons, fifty men here, a hundred more at Do Rish, the means to make real war on the enemy. Ayesha had cleaned and dressed his feet and with every beat of the drums outside he seemed to gain in power and stature.

The feast had helped. Of the enormous mutton curry, *pillau*, curds, dates, only the scrapings remained. Each man knew that that meal would have to last him a long time.

Khan announced that he wanted no one to follow him blindly. This new force must not be an alternative to the Choukha or involuntary recruitment; green wood took too long to reach effective heat, just as dead wood burned out too fast. His gaze was on the politicians, the surgeon, Tamim. If they had doubts, homes they would rather go to, they should say so now.

They shook their heads. The Khad soldiers had already pledged themselves to fight and exchanged their smart uniforms for camouflage jackets from the store. They were all fugitives from communism. Wherever Khan chose to lead, Tamim said, they would follow.

That left McCabe and Ayesha. Khan asked what *their* plans were.

They had already discussed this and come to no conclusion. They could resume their journey to the objective south of Kandahar, but forecasting the site of a chemical delivery was like guessing where lightning would strike.

'We'll hang on a bit,' McCabe told him through Ayesha. 'See what the Lily has to say. Give you our answer then.'

The time now was ten-thirty. Khan was setting out for Mir Bala at eleven o'clock. He was taking a full car in case they got stranded: McCabe to drive, Ayesha on the gun and Hafiq to act as his trusty steed. They would take a radio, so as to stay in contact with the camp, plus provisions, plenty of ammo and, at McCabe's insistence, the camera gear and NBC kitbag. The Khad sergeant had tried hard to include himself but there was no room, and someone of rank had to stay behind to liaise with the gunner sergeant-major and keep the festivities from getting out of hand.

At this point warriors of the Western world would have passed round the booze and raised their glasses in a toast to their leader and whatever lay ahead. McCabe missed that, in this liquorless land. That and a puff of rolled leaf, a fag, hash. Nam had been a high war, a trip both in reality and hallucination, so that sometimes you couldn't tell the difference. But these warriors found their high just in God. It was too simple for the Western mind to grasp. Too dangerous maybe, in that it took war out of the dirty cupboard and sanctified it. While eager now to join in a little blood-letting, McCabe didn't want to die a priest.

At 23.07 hours, seven days before the Soviet Harvest deadline, the loaded jeep drove out of the camp, McCabe at the wheel. It turned south along the road to Mohammed Agah, but it would soon take a cut-off to the west, along a track that zigzagged up through the foothills like the tail of a crazy kite.

Hardly had their rear lights diminished when a kilometre to the north, a pair of in-line GAZ-49B heavily silenced engines throbbed to life. A wheeled, armoured shape rolled unhurriedly into motion.

27

THE TRACK was everything but a road, sometimes running for minutes across rocky serrations that rattled their teeth and blurred their vision, sometimes following a dried watercourse, their headlamps glaring into pockets then lifting away like searchlights. There were hillsides of wild lavender and thyme, with Mohammed Agah a scattering of crystals rotating below them. There were avenues of boulders that revealed their intent faces brightly before darkness released their lights, like greyhounds from a trap.

Again they heard it. McCabe drew up and killed the motor. They listened.

The hills around and below seemed to stir and sigh, sigh and stir. Gradually they fell silent.

'It is our own echo,' Hafiq said, though he sounded less convinced than the first time.

Still no one disputed it. Presently the stink of dead fire came to them. They lost it but it came back. They passed a tattered tarpaulin and a scattering of shell cases, then some mangled small-arms, rusty from the winter snow. The smell grew sharper as they toppled over a ridge.

Below lay a deep gully and the remains of a bridge. In the gully was tilted a fire-blackened horror, the huge muzzle of its gun gaping towards them. One track lay stripped like a giant's discarded cartridge belt. Its innards were scattered along the ravine where the *mujahedin* had scavenged through them. Its machine-gun gone, of course, and no doubt its heavy-calibre shells, to be emptied of explosive.

Hafiq made an exultant sound, urging his resistance brethren on as if the battle were still in progress.

An alternative crossing had been bulldozed, which meant the Russians had continued their advance. Khan stared moodily round at the monster as they rode past it, remembering, perhaps, the circumstances of his capture.

They were on a shoulder now, the trail pulling them back and forth across it, gaining them height. But there wasn't a lot more to gain. The village was close now, its fate becoming more of a certainty with every yard and breath. Not all the winter's snow, nor thaw, nor overgrowth of grass and scent of spring flowers, could erase the odour of death that clung to that hillside.

As they reached the crest, McCabe doused the lights and then the motor. He braked and they sat in silence, peering down at what had been Mir Bala.

'A potter's shop.' Hafiq spat over the side, less ebullient now. 'Each vessel smashed by vandals!'

'I do not understand.' Ayesha turned to Khan in his stillness. 'Why here? Why would they bring you here?'

Khan checked his weapon, releasing the catch. 'Let us find out, little sister.'

McCabe let off the brake and they rolled forward silently. At the first house they got out.

As Hafiq stooped to hoist Khan on to his back they heard the solitary rattle of a pebble.

'Who is there?' Khan demanded.

Air-air, seemed to come the reply. A greenish light grew amongst the ruins. It flowed over and into each successive dwelling, revealing doorways, gaping walls, teetering shapes, before being chased on down by the following dark. Just a patch of moonlight between cloud, but it had shown them a path picked between the mounds, perhaps by goats. They followed it warily.

Their breath told of the altitude. Each wore his blanket.

'There could be mines,' McCabe warned.

They were in a street bunkered by rubble, laced with roofing timbers. They followed the paler thread, ducking, straddling. Hafiq, with his burden, paused frequently to check his footing. The odour of death was everywhere.

Something clinked in one of the houses.

Ayesha became a still shadow, head inclined. McCabe stopped beside her. He could smell the sweetness of her hair.

'We are being followed,' she breathed.

'Could be rats. Keep moving.' He took her arm, feeling its slimness. Together they skirted a great crater.

Hafiq and Khan turned into an alley branching off between roofless walls. McCabe and Ayesha followed. Hafiq deposited Khan on a mound of rubble, then came back silently past them to crouch at the corner.

Ayesha flitted into a doorway, readying her gun. McCabe watched Hafiq's dim shape and thought of the whorehouse woman, her hostility. Who knew whom she had contacted, what the old bitch had arranged, how much of a slave she had become to the commie brass whose custom paid her overheads.

Minutes passed.

There was a sudden scrabble of movement, a thud and a cry. Hafiq's shape had become confused with another. McCabe darted forward to find him kneeling on a man's chest, beating his head against the ground. McCabe drew back his gun-butt piston-wise. Ayesha interposed herself, stooping and peering.

The smell was Afghan, the headgear the flat Nuristani hat favoured by the *mujahedin*, the fallen weapon an old Lee Enfield. Hafiq was snarling, 'Brother of a fox, son of a wolf! I will teach you it is better to be dead than prey upon Hafiq!'

A rush of clothing drew about them. McCabe looked up. They were surrounded.

Something had burst among the stout wooden pillars, and the dome they supported had collapsed. Its rubble filled the small inner court, but the side chambers under the smaller domes appeared more or less intact. A dim light burned in one of them. It was towards this that their captors prodded them.

A curtain lifted aside and a mullah looked out. He wore a portion of blanket wound over his turban and under his chin. He looked cold.

As they.were thrust forward into the light he peered hard at each, unastonished, it seemed, to see one on the back of another and an unveiled woman with them.

'This one *says* he is Ghoram Khan,' lisped the chief captor in heavy dialect, jabbing an unwashed finger at Khan.

'The dog's very doubt is an insult!' Hafiq was outraged, angry at himself. 'Ask him, would I, a hero of the Afghan people, carry a lesser man on my back?'

'That is what we must ascertain,' replied the mullah. He had a high, clipped voice, like the yap of a terrier.

'It is ascertained already,' Hafiq retorted, 'by our very presence in this rats' castle.'

'Rats?' The mullah fixed him with a fierce eye. 'This is holy ground, my friend, consecrated by the blood of innocents – a powerful place, where truth and lies are discerned in the twinkling of an eye!' He snapped at Khan, 'By your answer to one question I will know if you are who you claim to be.'

'I make no claims,' Khan said. 'I am who I am.'

'I will ask it now. Are you prepared?'

Khan glowered at him. 'And if I cannot answer, will it make me more me, or less me?'

'It will make you dead,' snapped the mullah. 'All of you.'

Khan laughed. But he turned his head, gauging how far he would have to reach to seize a gun, for their own had been confiscated. He murmured something in Hafiq's ear as he turned back to the mullah.

'You are alone here, holy man?'

'That is not your business.'

Khan's neck seemed to swell. But after a moment his shoulders lifted.

'Let the question be short. For my man here tires of my weight.'

'It is short,' said the mullah. 'And it is this: *At the hour of dawn, what opens on the lawn?*'

Khan stared at him and McCabe sensed his shock, but also his relief.

'The Lily.'

Holding his gaze, with the thinnest of smiles, the mullah held aside the curtain.

'Welcome, Khan, son of Ahmed.'

'See, dogs?' Hafiq mocked their captors. He snatched back his and Khan's weapons. 'Begone, before I shoot off your tails!'

He strode inside.

McCabe and Ayesha reclaimed their own guns and followed.

The mullah told the men, 'Go, watch the track. Make sure they were not followed.' He went in and let the curtain fall.

McCabe looked around the square chamber. Its walls of natural green pine were carved into ornate panels, so high that the light of the solitary cotton wick dipped in sesame oil failed to dispel the shadows of the domed ceiling. There was a *charpoy* with blankets neatly folded, fat cushions on the floor, a prayer mat, cooking utensils and a samovar.

When Hafiq had lowered Khan to a cushion, he returned to the curtain and looked out, then came back and stood against the wall.

The mullah's gaze darted from him to each of them as he unwound the blanket from his turban and laid it aside. Revealed was a face in its forties, piercing brown eyes, black brows, meticulously clipped grey beard. A face of rigidity and fanaticism.

Khan's mind was wrestling with something he could not fathom.

'The question – was it dictated by the Lily?'

'That you knew the answer is enough.'

'That someone knew to ask it is not,' Khan said strongly. 'It treads so close to my heart – a quotation from a treasured book, read in youth.'

'The reading of all books save the Koran, especially in youth, is heresy,' said the mullah.

'A *rare* book, holy man. Belonging to my father. Translated from another tongue.'

'Twice the heresy then. Let us not speak of it.' The mullah consulted his wristwatch with compressed lips. He struck a match and poked it under the samovar. 'Tea will take a while. Shall we proceed?'

Khan's brow darkened under his turban, but he knew that more important issues were at stake.

'What is to happen?'

'The Lily wishes spoken word with you.'

'Spoken? How can this be?'

'How can anything be?' demanded the mullah, eyes flashing. With a sorcerer's scowl, he snatched aside a curtain to reveal a gleaming black transmitter.

McCabe realized that they were in one of the Lily's high-altitude communication centres. He glanced at Ayesha, then watched fascinated as the mullah knelt and with the quick, almost fearful flick of a horny fingernail switched the set on, then sat back on his heels and made the ritual cleansing movement.

The transmitter came to life, filling the room with static. The static died and the mullah rocked back and forth, raising his voice to the microphone as if in prayer. He was giving a call-sign, as if to God Himself.

Contact established, he turned to Khan and handed him the microphone.

'Press the button and speak. Say who you are.' His eyes were like glowing coals.

Khan frowned and hesitated. 'I am Ghoram Khan, son of Ahmed,' he began, then stopped and asked, 'Whom do I address?'

There was silence.

'Release the button,' hissed the mullah.

A resonant voice of great solemnity filled the room.

'*Allaho akbar. God is Great and Mahomed is His Prophet!* I speak for the Lily, the Soul of Aminah, mother of the Second Coming. She sends you greeting and bids you speak.'

McCabe was watching Ayesha's expression in the hope of deducing something of what was said. He saw her react.

'She,' she whispered. 'He refers to the Lily as *she*!'

'Yeah? Listen, what the hell are they doing talking over open channel? Don't they know the Russians have radio-location units?'

She nudged him to silence. Khan was more confident now, announcing with dignity that he wished to place himself, his friends and full complement of men under the Lily's command. He recited the full inventory with some pride – freedom fighters, Khad deserters, mountain gunners, weapons, transport. 'All these I place at her disposal, to use as she wishes.'

The voice made no comment, just told him to wait.

Silence ensued, marred only by fitful breaths of static. Khan stared at his hands. The mullah remained kneeling with eyes closed. McCabe held Ayesha's gaze, one brow cocked in puzzlement. They must be crazy. Or did the hills screen all this from Kabul? But there would be other direction-finding outfits, if not at Ghazni, then at Kandahar. Didn't they know this? Or didn't they care?

After two minutes, the deep-chested voice came back on the air.

'*Allaho akbar*. I swear by the Declining Day, man's lot is cast amid destruction! Listen well, Ghoram Khan, for this is your instruction.'

'I am listening.'

'The Lily is again with child. But the hour of her travail waits upon history. You, son of Ahmed, and those you trust, including the photographer and doctor of medicine, may approach her and witness a miracle. But of your fighting men, of the artillery and other soldiers, of the weapons and vehicles, she has no need, the forces of Allah being already with her. Dismiss them to the hills and come alone. But the time is not yet ripe. First cleanse yourselves for four days in the wilderness. Then knock upon another door such as that where you are. Its location—'

The voice read out a list of figures.

The mullah seized paper and pencil and copied them down.

The voice continued: 'You will receive further instructions there as to how you may approach and enter the House of the Lily. *Inshallah. Allaho akbar!*'

The transmission ended.

There followed a peculiar silence, each eye seeking another's to gauge his reaction. Khan was puzzled, even chagrined, as to why his offer of men and weapons had been rejected. Hafiq couldn't make it out at all, but he had a strange look, as though someone had just walked over his grave. Ayesha bore the same expression.

McCabe watched her closely as she translated, trying to stay objective. Her medical training was struggling, he realized when she had finished, with a concept that defied rationality. Yet there was no doubt that Islamic faith would elbow out the doubt.

'And Aminah, who's Aminah?' He strove to get it all straight.

When she had explained, he asked her how she felt about it.

She had difficulty finding the right English word. 'Excited,' she said at last.

He thought, oh boy, they didn't miss a trick, did they? It was the biggest load of codswallop he'd ever laid ears on – hence, great! The whole world loved a mystery movie. Spell it out, no one would have wanted to know. They had got it right. Whoever they were. Which opened his mind to a possibility he had not before considered – that the whole concept had been imported. The Afghans were not smart enough to have minted such an idea. Or perhaps the word was not cynical enough. Some Western hand was inside the glove somewhere.

Ayesha was watching him curiously, even anxiously.

'How do *you* feel about it, Michael?'

'Same as you, sweetheart.' McCabe looked serious. 'Excited.' And he was.

The mullah had spread out a map. He and Khan were tracing the coded reference.

'Ghazni,' Khan announced. 'We are to go next to the Sultan Mohamed's Tomb in Ghazni.'

The mullah watched his face intently, as though waiting for some revelation to strike him.

'Four days,' he prompted.

Khan misinterpreted the hint. 'We will need beasts for transportation.'

'They await you,' the mullah said, disappointed, 'at one *kros* distance. For to abandon your vehicle here would bring the infidel upon us. I will send thus far with you a man, for guidance. You may take the map, for it has the secret coordinates.'

The samovar was boiling.

They took tea and talked. But no one wanted to question their host about the catastrophe that had destroyed his village.

It was approaching dawn when they left. The mullah donned his blanket and led them through the debris to the entrance. A few of his guards were out there, dozing, talking, amongst them their guide. Finally, after bidding them god-speed, the holy man caught Khan's sleeve and tugged him close.

'Four days,' he said again. 'Add two to reach the Lily's stronghold. That brings you, son of Ahmed, to the twenty-seventh day of Ramadan.'

Khan stared at him, then he understood. 'The Night of Power?'

'Power, yes! When Mahomed aspired to prophethood. The night of his spiritual birth! Think on it, think on it!'

So saying, he picked his way back in long strides, arms spread like a man on stepping-stones, to his lonely vigil.

28

AT THIS chill early hour the signals office windows were shut tight and blanketed, the night operators huddled over their sets. The NCO circulated watchfully, collecting the completed message forms with unnecessary vigour and delivering them to Zotov's night counterpart at his high desk. The stamp of his boots was an irritant, but it was needed to keep the staff awake.

He paused behind a blond head hunched over one of the R112s, to tell the man to get his hair cut. He checked himself just in time. It wasn't often they had a full colonel operating his own channel at the bench.

'Coming through clear, sir?'

Yakushev jerked a hand at him to get lost. He listened a moment longer, then triggered 'send'.

'What do you mean, *they didn't come back*?' He released the pressel and waited, frowning.

The reconnaissance sergeant's voice was faint but clear in his headphones. 'I mean not past us, sir, where we were hidden below the village. They turned off some way above us and headed south.'

Yakushev brushed ash off the map and moved his pencil back and forth over the mountainous contours.

'I don't see any alternative track.'

'It's not marked, comrade Colonel. It's so small that when we started after them we missed it at first. Hardly more than a goat path, tricky with no lights. I'm not at all sure we can get back.'

'I'm not interested in your recovery problems, Sergeant. I want to know where Khan and his party are now!' Yakushev's eyes were dry and prickly from lack of sleep. The time was almost four. He had waited up until midnight for Dolin's return, only to receive a signal saying that the general's departure from Kandahar had been delayed and his revised ETA was 5 a.m. Yakushev should have gone to his billet then and grabbed some sleep, but he had too much on his mind. The Girishk action had been confirmed – fortunately the dam had only been partially damaged – but there was another action starting, a second heavy ambush, up near Masr-i-Sharif. Added to the Khan thing . . . Was Zotov right? Were they all connected? Well, of course they were connected, bricks from the same kiln, but were they all building to a single climax? His instincts said they were.

'Where is that jeep now?' he demanded.

'At the bottom of a ravine, comrade Colonel – a total wreck,' came the reply.

'What? Are you telling me Khan's *dead*?'

'No, sir, I'm telling you where the jeep is. We reckon they must have ditched it on purpose because they're still on our screen, moving slowly through the foothills, sir, towards the Shekhabad road.'

'I see.' Yakushev pinched the sweat from his nose, deeply relieved. 'Good. Well, keep following, Sergeant.'

'Can't sir, with respect. There's no more track. We're stuck on the edge of a cliff.'

'Position?' Yakushev tried to keep his voice down.

He screwed a dot on the map as the sergeant gave him the co-ordinates.

'Stay exactly where you are.' He pencilled a heavy ring round it. 'I'll get a team out to you. If Khan goes off your screen before they get to you they're going to need his final bearing, so have it ready, *dead accurate*, because if we lose him you're for the penal battalion, understand me?'

He signed off, checked his list of call signs and called the reconnaissance battalion. A helicopter and six-man team with portable tracking equipment were on stand-by there. He ordered their immediate deployment.

After shedding the headphones Yakushev spent a moment wondering about the purpose of Khan's visit to such a remote spot. Apart from ruins, what lay up there? He would get RCN to send a patrol later in the day.

On the way out he stopped to look through the monitoring sheets for further reports of rebel action.

There were two – both in the north.

The din was earshattering. The rotors of every gunship could be seen spinning above the early mist as they warmed the cramps out of their motors. Against this dawn chorus, Solkholov's An-28 VIP transport seemed to land in silence that was flawed only as it burst into reverse thrust.

The marshal and his staff disembarked into their transport. Dolin, followed by his three aides, approached the car where Yakushev was waiting and got in without a word. The aides took the GAZ in front, steeling themselves against noise that was only a few decibels below pain. The motorcade got out fast, the escorts' lights flashing in the mist.

Dolin looked frayed, unshaven; he smelled faintly of vodka. His presence filled the car, nevertheless, with high-altitude static. A head with armies in it, rocket-launchers, massed tank deployments, air strikes, the whole panoply that was gathering to ride to historical victory on the backs of the Baluch near-savages. For all that, he didn't forget to be small.

'You didn't have to come,' he muttered, just to blunt any favour, should one have been involved.

None was. Yakushev had come because the Lily parcel was suddenly coming unwrapped. He was like a jealous husband buttoning his wife's blouse against the gaze of strangers. Unquestionably there was an offensive in progress and such wide co-ordination pointed to a co-ordinator. He would play that down as much as he could. And if he couldn't he wanted to be the first to know.

'It's no trouble, General,' Yakushev reassured him. 'Obviously we have a lot of things to discuss.'

'No trouble?' Dolin cut him off bitterly. 'I should say we have a great deal of trouble. Hidden microphones everywhere. Kailagai Army HQ was stacked with them.'

'Two, to be exact,' Yakushev said amiably, well versed in the reports. 'But the number is unimportant. What is—'

'Well, some at Farah, more at Baghram. The marshal is furious. Holds us responsible. What have you done about it? Who's behind it?'

If there had been any way round telling him Yakushev would have taken it. But he kept it general. 'The *mujahedin*.'

'They wouldn't know which to stick in the wall – the microphone or the recorder!'

'The *mujahedin* are behind it, General.'

'Then who's in front – imported technicians?'
'An educated élite.'
'Educated! You mean ones with shorter tails? How do you know?'
'We caught one.'
That stopped him. The hat came round like a banking spaceship.
'Who?'
'Ali Jangalak.'
Yakushev watched Dolin measure this against his memory of the man, and forestalled the inevitable questions with a swift exposition, diverting Dolin's attention from the circumstances of Ali's arrest to his successful interrogation under scopalomine. Dolin cut him short.
'So they know about Harvest?'
Yakushev hesitated.
'Yes or no!'
'Possibly. It's not certain. But—'
'Jangalak hasn't told us?'
Yakushev shook his head. 'He was just an operative, part of a cell system. He had no access to what went back through those mikes. But current events suggest that they do know about Harvest.'
'All these raids and ambushes, you mean?' Dolin shook his head. 'Unless you know something I don't, I'd say, no, no connection. The marshal is of the same opinion. They're just not that sufficiently integrated.'
Yakushev's flush of relief even encouraged him to push it a little. 'Despite the microphones and 'phone taps?'
'Yes. A few swallows don't make a summer. Forget conjecture, Colonel, concentrate on fact – the fact of whether they know about Harvest. We've *got* to be sure. Not for what the rebels can do to stop us, but for what the Americans could do if they slipped them the word. We need the answer quickly.'
Yakushev nodded and skilfully changed his ground. 'I'm working on it right now.'
'From what angle?'
'Well, I have several leads, but they may take time. All except one. It's a short cut to what you want, but it's going to need your sanction.'
'You have it, get on with it.'

Yakushev was tempted to accept this windfall at face value, but the dangers in it were too real. He shook his head. 'You ought to hear it, General. Militarily and politically, it's a hot potato. So hot that I think we should use Khad to do the dirty work, but there's a problem. Naqaswar is on the warpath over Jangalak and may not co-operate. He hasn't seen the interrogation transcript yet and when he does he may change his attitude, but the one thing that will really swing him is pressure from you.'

'The one thing that will really swing him,' Dolin said through his teeth, 'is a rope. I'll have him stripped and executed!'

Yakushev looked alarmed. 'I'd rather you didn't do that, General. I need him. New brooms sweep clean, I know, but not so clean as an old one fighting to clear his name. If I show him the transcript and you bear down on him hard enough I'm convinced he'll do everything I want . . .' Yakushev's voice faded as he saw Dolin's expression change.

All the impetus drained from the exchange. The big man eyed him thoughtfully.

'Use that word a lot, don't you, Andrei Pavlovich – "I"?'

Yakushev had been watching everything but his pronouns. He forced a laugh.

'Just a figure of speech. By "I", I naturally mean the GRU.'

'I see. Then who is actually handling this – intelligence?'

Yakushev had to admit, 'Not as such. All departments are involved.'

'Then I'll find all this on record?' Dolin sounded relieved.

'I've kept it off the record,' Yakushev said, 'because of those microphones.'

In the grey light the general's cocked head conveyed all the trust and confidence of a rooster eyeing a snake.

Yakushev thought, it's uncanny the way he reads between the lines. Or has he heard something?

The wipers thumped, dragging the glow of the GAZ taillights back and forth across the misty screen. Dolin continued his silent scrutiny. Yakushev tried to break through it.

'As I was about to say—' he began, but Dolin was already speaking.

'Khan – is he dead?'

It was a natural question to ask, but the way he said it made

Yakushev wonder again if Dolin had heard something: not just that Khan had escaped – that fact was now common knowledge throughout the directorate – but the manner in which it had been allowed. Did Dolin know it all, or just part, or was he simply probing? He had to make up his mind fast.

He let his instincts decide, and in doing so gambled his entire future.

'I sent him for execution as you ordered. But he escaped.'

Dolin did not bat an eye. So he knew that much.

'How?'

Now came the real gamble. Until the Khad execution squad were 'recaptured', only the Spetznas captain, Medevev, knew the true answer to that – and he wouldn't talk unless actually interrogated. In the long run, without doubt, it would all emerge. In the short run, with all the preoccupation with Harvest, it probably wouldn't. And Yakushev was interested only in the short run, in keeping Dolin and the directorate away from the Lily long enough for him to locate its headquarters and point the finger at it as the very core of *mujahedin* resistance. Whereupon his every unorthodox and secretive measure would be seen to have been ideological in motivation, courageous in application and justified. He would emerge the hero of the hour, and of the campaign.

How did Khan escape? Through the mutinous desertion of his firing squad, he told Dolin, and watched his face closely.

Again, the general did not bat an eye. He had heard that too. So why had he asked?

'You detailed an *Afghan* firing party?' The emphasis was of censure, not surprise.

'We considered it best.' Yakushev was careful this time in his selection of the pronoun. 'The thinking was that death by a Soviet squad might have elevated him to martyr status.'

Dolin grunted. 'In that case there should have been a covering squad.'

'In retrospect, yes,' Yakushev admitted, relieved. It was clear now that Dolin's knowledge fell short of the truth.

'Was there no witnessing officer?'

'Oh yes. He did his best, of course, but he was completely outnumbered. I forget his name. There will be a full enquiry, General, and a full report.'

(Regrettably delayed by the proximity of Harvest!)

Dolin grunted again. Yakushev felt himself sweating. He started to change the subject, but Dolin talked him down.

'What happened to the cinematographer, McCabe?'

'He's safe. Tucked well away.'

'Where?'

'In the Choukha.'

'Don't lie to me!'

Yakushev stared at him, genuinely startled. 'Well, that's where I put him.'

'So the Norwegians said. He's not there now.'

'Norwegians?'

'Their press attaché called the marshal personally. They'd had an enquiry. I think we can guess who from.'

'They managed to trace him to the Choukha?'

Dolin nodded. 'So you didn't have him tucked away so safely, did you?'

Yakushev had no reply. His mind sped to Yasir, his death. Any connection? If there was, he couldn't see it. He cast his mind wider. *Cine equipment*. For the first time the connection registered. But how could McCabe have got out?

The only possible explanation came to him gradually: that he had somehow included him in the execution party. Was he with Khan now or still in the gunners' camp? Either way, Dolin would have his balls – despite the fact that if McCabe was with the gunners he would be recaptured when their camp was sealed off, and if he was with Khan he was under electronic surveillance. Dolin wasn't really after McCabe, he was after *him*, Yakushev.

'I can't explain it,' was all he could say. 'But I'll look into it the moment we get back.'

They were coming to the checkpoint. The motorcade slowed to a stop.

Dolin sat in absolute stillness, like a man with a weight balanced on his head, while Yakushev wound down the window and established their identities.

When they were through, Dolin said slowly, 'You mentioned something that was politically and militarily too hot for us to handle, for which you needed my sanction. What was it?'

Yakushev said dully, 'It doesn't matter. We can discuss it when we get back.'

'I would like your answer now, comrade.'

Yakushev sighed. 'It has to do with the way the information the *mujahedin* gather from us is passed on.'

'Passed on to whom?'

'Presumably their group headquarters,' Yakushev lied.

'One group? Go on.'

'It is done through the mosques – at midday – the principal mosque in each town.'

'Who says?'

'Jangalak. It means the sufis and senior mullahs are involved. All of them. Throughout the country.'

He felt Dolin sharpen.

'We need to arrest them,' he went on. 'The whole traitorous bunch. Simultaneously.

Dolin sucked in his breath, then laughed. 'This is your prognosis? Incite the entire population to insurrection just as Harvest is about to begin? Aren't you aware that eighty per cent of our Harvest force is Moslem?'

'I can see no alternative.'

' "*I . . . I . . .*" It's exactly as I thought. You'd base an act like that on one man's interrogation testimony without subjecting the recording to expert analysis before full committee? And I know you didn't because you haven't had time. How many sessions did you give him – one?'

'Two.'

'Over what period?'

'Five hours.'

'Hours! Over an issue so important, interrogation should have been over *days*.'

'We don't have days, General.'

'Why not? What can the rebels learn from us now? And what would they do with it? You can feed a monkey caviar, but it doesn't make him a Russian, he stays a monkey.' Dolin pumped himself upright with a breath and faced his front.

He said formally, 'Request for sanction denied.'

They were approaching the enclave. The mist was thinning, daylight strengthening. Life was beginning to stir in a camp facing on to the road.

Yet this was not, Yakushev could see, the normal early

morning routine. Soldiers were standing around outside their huts while the NCOs bellowed at them. Yet they were paying no attention whatsoever. Instead they seemed engrossed in reading scraps of paper that were scattered about the compound. Men were running to escape blows, some falling to their knees as if in prayer. These were beaten and hoisted to their feet. Some fell to their knees again, to be threatened at gunpoint. Through the closed windows of the car came the sound of a shot.

Dolin took notice then, telling the driver to pull in at the gate. He got out and went to the wire. Yakushev joined him slowly.

'*Chabnameh*,' he muttered.

'What?'

'Night letters.'

The unit was the 304b Motorized-Rifle, made up of Turkmen – dark, handsome fellows from Turkmenskaya in the Moslem southern regions of the USSR.

Dolin ordered the guard to let them in. The sentries were in a state of excitement and confusion. They had collected some of the pamphlets, but only one or two of them seemed able to read. As fast as the others clustered round them they were driven off by the guard commander, a ferocious Tartar sergeant. He commandeered all the sheets with cuffings and kicks before ordering a man to open the gate.

Dolin strode in, followed by Yakushev. They took a sheet each, and Yakushev immediately spotted the lily sign at the bottom.

The text differed from the leaflets circulated in the market, and it was printed in Russian.

It read:

Allaho akbar!

Ye Faithful – ask, who is your Master?

ALLAH IS YOUR MASTER!

Others may command your body but Allah commands your soul.

Prepare yourselves to obey Him!

Prepare yourselves for the Day of Resurrection, on which your Prophet will be reborn!

Ask, how may ye prepare yourselves?

By prayer and fasting and purification of the spirit, must ye prepare.

By biding your time. By doing what must be done, patiently, until the moment of the Word.

Ask, how will ye recognize the Word?

There will be none who on hearing it will not know it. It will be heard in all the land, heralding the Miraculous Event.

All who obey it shall dwell forever amidst cool shades and fountains and feed on such fruits as they desire.

But woe unto those that disobey, for they will have cast their lot with the disbelievers!

Woe on that day to the disbelievers! When the stars are blotted out, when the sky is rent asunder and the mountains crumble into dust, they will begone to that Hell which they deny!

Allaho akbar!

Dolin snorted, but his expression was thoughtful. He sent for the security and political officers and asked the sergeant how the leaflets could have been distributed without his or his picquets' knowledge. The sergeant said that if he knew, the man or men would be dead.

Presently the two officers came running, showing signs of having hastily dressed. Both were captains, one a saturnine Georgian, the other a Slav. Dolin told them to parade the regiment immediately and order those in possession of leaflets to surrender them at once or be shot. Every man was to remain on the parade ground while every loose copy was collected. Then the leaflets were to be burned in full view.

'I always warned this could be a danger,' Dolin muttered as they returned to the car, 'using our own Moslems. They're our one Achilles heel. Should all be repatriated.'

Back in the car, Dolin studied his own leaflet again. He tapped the Lily sign and asked what it was.

Yakushev shrugged. 'I have no idea.'

Had it stopped there, Yakushev would have followed Dolin's lead and gone to his sleeping quarters. But when he glanced in at his office the night staff steered his attention to two messages that had just come in from the security offices of the two remaining Moslem camps in the enclave, notifying him of identical *chabnameh* deliveries.

How had they done it? Yakushev paused to wonder. Had some of the Asiatic troops already been subverted? Or had they somehow fired the leaflets in, by mortar, slingshot or something? Even while he was debating this, word came in from Baghram that all Moslem camps there had received a similar quota of *chabnameh*. In addition, a pushtu version had been copiously distributed throughout their Afghan army units.

Sleep receded further with the news from Ghazni base that an officer had shot dead the leader of a group of Azerbaijani soldiers who had refused to get up off their knees when ordered to fall in for the CO's warning address.

When the day staff arrived Yakushev closeted himself with Goriansky to dictate a standing order to commanders of all Moslem units, Soviet or Afghan, on actions to be taken at the first appearance of enemy agitprop literature among the troops. Further news came in of *chabnameh* bonfires burning at Herat, Masr-i-Sharif and Kandahar. Kandahar, the base for the Soviet and Afghan Moslem forces due to take part in Harvest! The Lily was striking uncomfortably close to home.

The very scope of the distribution startled even Yakushev. He took very great pleasure in consigning all these messages to Dolin's desk, to await his awakening.

But there was worse to come. The noonday gun had just boomed across the city when Zotov himself came in, incredulous. Leaflets, he announced, had been reported inside the Soviet Union itself, in each of the predominantly Moslem republics bordering Afghanistan: Tadzhikskaya, Turkmenskaya and Uzbekskaya, as far north in the latter as Tashkent!

The report had arrived from Alma Ata in cypher and so could include a quantity of uninhibited data, mainly concerning the arrest of suspects and shootings. Glancing through them, Yakushev felt an icy constriction of his insides, though he wasn't immediately able to identify the cause.

The scope of the operation, of course, was huge, a quite extraordinary accomplishment when one realized that for the *mujahedin* it wasn't a simple matter of tossing bundles out of an aircraft, but one of road transportation, caravan, smuggling across the border and sheer footslog. The cost probably hadn't been an item: except for paper, all services would be rendered gratis for Allah, so there was no suggestion that this was CIA-sponsored. No, what struck him was that at each of the Soviet cities listed was an army base housing reinforcements and equipment for the Afghan front. An attempt to neutralize these, Yakushev knew, was any general's first move in conducting a counter-offensive. So this *was* a counter-offensive; but that wasn't the point. The point lay in the inescapable conclusion that a general was in charge of *mujahedin* operations. *One* leader. Intelligence would spot it in a flash. Alma Ata too.

Or would they? Perhaps he was looking at it from the vantage point of foreknowledge. Would not their minds go first to Peshawar, to the leaders of the seven resistance movements, in search of an alliance? It was important that he make up his mind, because if the Lily's existence was to be exposed, it must be he who exposed it, he with his folder of facts.

While Yakushev was pondering this dilemma another coded communication from Alma Ata came through for Dolin's eyes only. Full of curiosity, Yakushev had it delivered to the squash club. Minutes later, the general appeared, bleary-eyed and still unshaven, to draft his reply. That was at twelve-twenty.

At twelve thirty-five he sent for Yakushev.

He was seated, head down, at his desk. His hands were interlocked on top of the accumulated reports, forefingers steepled against his lips. He did not look up.

Yakushev waited. After some moments, fatigue forced him to draw up a chair and sit down. Finally Dolin got up and, without a glance at him, turned to face out of the window.

'How many illegals are you fielding in Peshawar?'

Yakushev's spirits soared.

'Politically, militarily, what?'

'In the resistance groups' headquarters.'

'Four.'

'Any reports of an alliance?'

It was almost too good to be true. 'Not a word. Why?'

'You're in contact, I take it?'

'Minimal from this end. But if it's high priority, yes.'

'The highest. I want their explanation of what's happening. Understand me?'

'Yes, General. Right away.' Yakushev rose to his feet.

'I haven't finished. Meanwhile, as a double-check from this end that we're not dealing with some internal phenomenon, I think we should hear what all the sufis and mullahs have to say. Added to what is already going on, this could excite a further Moslem backlash, so I would be inclined to interrogate but *not* arrest them. *In situ*, you understand, without violence or publicity. Just the needle, then let them get on with their work, though under threat – make sure they understand that, and constant surveillance. Put them on parole, as it were. Intercept anyone seen trying to make contact with them. Got that?' Dolin added drily, 'Under these circumstances Khad will not be required to act as a buffer and we can all sleep in our beds secure in the knowledge that they aren't trying to provoke trouble behind our backs. They're for an imminent purge.'

Yakushev remained in front of Dolin. Was that it? It was clear that Alma Ata had hauled him over the coals. He felt like laughing. He couldn't help adding his own personal barb.

'Does that mean,' he enquired innocently, 'that I *do* have your sanction?'

29

CLEANSING HIMSELF before witnessing a miracle wasn't what McCabe had taken the hard-cash advance for, and, as they journeyed, there was more than a passing feeling of playing hookey, indulging his curiosity, when he should have been part of the horror somewhere, his adrenalin pumping, nursing his camera more than his body. Was there ever a guilt like that? Giving you homesickness for a sky with more metal than air in it, throbbing and whining steel and all the modern compounds and fuses, heat-seekers, radar-guided, laser-smart, solid and liquid and plain old cordite-propelled death that burst in your brain and killed you ten times before exploding on a ridge maybe a hundred yards or a mile away.

McCabe had died a thousand times before he crossed the barrier of don't care. It happened back in Vietnam. After which, with death no longer the spectre, his work had leapt in quality and he had slept even on nights when exhaustion hadn't claimed him. It was fantastic. But it was deadly. For the problem was getting back.

He had sacrificed his survival mechanisms for his art and without them he could never lead a normal life. Rehabilitation, they called it. And it was no trick word devised by army shrinks. It was forcing oneself down from an invulnerable high, back into the snake-pit of everyday life, media dominated, consumer orientated, greedy, wasteful and trivial. It was learning again from scratch to accept the shit man spun round himself like a disgusting grub. And it was a quantum leap he just couldn't make. Not without help.

So here he was, on his high plateau outside every damn thing that made the workaday world go round, watching the sun come up on Ayesha's sweet little backside as they tramped through the incredible scenery – and feeling guilty because there was so much peace around. Well, they'd nearly shot him back there. He was involved now, impatient for action.

The others were ahead – Hafiq's gun-toting silhouette spiky against the sunlit distance, the pack donkey behind him, Khan astride its twin, a dark Christ, legs trailing, body moodily nodding, probably still resenting the radio call he had to make before they ditched the jeep, telling the men at the gunners' camp to disband.

They were headed towards Ghanzi, a mere eighty kilometres with four days to get there. By Pathan standards, it was a wander.

Ayesha kept stopping and looking back the way they had come. McCabe would stop beside her and look at the perfect contours of her averted face, the parted lips, the strands of hair straying from their dark flock, and wait for her to look at him. But she would lower her eyes as she turned to move on the way an artiste never looks at the camera. And he *was* a camera.

Perhaps, for a long time, that was all he had been.

But he was changing. And she, a woman, sensitive, in mourning, was aware of it.

The hills were like a continuing island, the sea surrounding them two wide river valleys that would become one huge plain to the south. The sun climbed and baked the valleys till they blurred, like a map spread on one's knees in a car. Up here it was cooler. There was wiry growth, tamarisk, sloes, wild roses, pink and yellow.

They came upon an old man playing a pipe. He was sitting on a rock, his goats feeding peacefully around him. Khan asked him where he lived. He shrugged. Tucked in his headcloth he had two tiny sprigs of herb. He gave one to Ayesha.

The leaves were very green and Ayesha remarked that they smelled of peppermint.

'Boil first the water,' he told her. 'Stir in the herb. Drink it as tea. And Allah will come to you.'

'It is a drug,' Hafiq warned.

'What does it matter?' the old man asked, blinking rheumy eyes at him. 'If Allah comes?'

The hills descended to the main valley with a thread of road and, beyond, a wide, chalky-blue snake of river with banks worn bare by watering flocks. As evening fell, the flocks were there now in their thousands, dotted along the water's edge, herdsmen walking or riding amongst them, women laundering clothes, pack-camels grazing or fetching fodder from afar, all pin-sized and scattered. The black tents with their fire-smoke resembled dark, steaming manure heaps dumped at intervals on the baked earth.

Khan led the way down warily. For the past hour they had heard rocket fire in the hills to the north and there was no cover near the road. They were halfway to the valley when a platoon of gunships came spinning past, their shadows darting across the rocks. Ayesha took cover, but McCabe remained in the open watching them and Hafiq, not to be outdone, did the same. The ships, though, had eyes for nothing but their objective and were soon gone.

Khan led the way across the river to the distant sound of their rocket fire. The water was cool and shallow with only one deep channel. Mirrored in the water, the flocks watched them without alarm as they came through, McCabe floundering around, trying to hoist the pannier nets containing his camera gear clear of the current. Ayesha helped him but Hafiq pretended not to notice.

As they mounted the far bank a venerable herder stood there with a long rifle cradled across his body, his *kohl*-rimmed gaze on their weapons. Having deduced that they were resistance fighters, he raised a sun-wizened hand.

'Are you well? Are you harmonious?'

Khan returned the greeting, to receive another, to which he replied, each as usual prolonging the exchange so as to measure the other. Formality was suspended as all turned to watch the gunships spinning back, returning to base, perhaps to take on another load of death. The old fellow spat.

'Come.' With a deft movement he caught a kid by the hind leg, draped it round his shoulders and led them towards the nearest tents.

Ayesha remained staring intently towards the hills they had descended from. Khan reined beside her.

'What do you see, little sister?'

'All day I have had the same feeling as when we approached Mir Bala.'

Khan turned his mount and raised the army field-glasses. He scanned the way they had come carefully, because he respected both her and her woman's instinct – but could see nothing. He offered her the glasses.

She shook her head. He knew she was thinking that if she saw something where he had not, it would diminish his prowess.

Their host was waiting, their Ramadan feast bleating across his shoulders, but Khan offered her the glasses more insistently, remembering suddenly sharing his glasses with Pola that day on the bluff, and the way she had pressed against him. It pained him now that he had not responded. He thought how strange it was that he could slaughter Yasir like a pig yet such a small arrow could prick his heart.

'Take them,' he told Ayesha gruffly.

But still she would not.

Then suddenly she saw something with her naked eye and reached out for them. As she peered her hands began to tremble. She handed them back quickly, pointing.

'Look there!' she cried.

'And then where?' Yakushev demanded, ringing the reference on his map. The voice in his headphones belonged to the reconnaissance battalion's intelligence officer, and not even he had direct contact with the tracking unit now that it was 'foot-mobile'. Their message came to him via a forward signals unit.

Yakushev frowned. 'Are you sure? They're wandering all over the place. And now you say they've stopped at an encampment.' He checked his watch. It was still a full two hours till nightfall. 'Well, let me know the moment they move on.'

As first light crept upon them, an acid breeze stirred across the rocks, causing the members of the Russian tracking team to squirm and contract inside their kapok chrysalises. But no one awoke. There was no need. If their quarry were suddenly to resume his journey the blip on the screen would start to move.

The duty man sat propped against a rock, hugging himself miserably, his lower half mermaid-like in his sleeping bag. Born and bred in the city of Smolensk, he hated nature's darkness, its *rooflessness*, its uncompromising shapes and eerie sounds. His gaze clung to the illuminated screen-pack as to a letter from home. It was the only civilized thing in the whole landscape. He had mastered its circuitry and marvelled, deducing that it must be a copy of an American device.

The blip on the screen had not moved since yesterday evening and wouldn't for some while, he guessed, judging by the hour the voices and music had finally stilled in the nomad camp below. You could hear practically everything from up here – it was really weird how it carried – babies crying, the river, goat bells.

The lighter shapes were just becoming visible – washing hung on guy-ropes, huddles sheep, folded camels . . . As he watched, human shapes detached themselves from the muzzy dark – women, he guessed, bringing their jars and cans to the water. How could they *live* like that? Well, they wouldn't have to for long, once the guerrillas were defeated and the state could take care of them. So his officer had said.

Rents had begun to show in the night cloud, like patches of rust. He watched them spread, changing hue through orange to yellow. There was increasing movement now in the encampment. A flock of sheep and goats was being driven across the river, over the deserted road to spread out along the hillside, way below, feeding as they went.

The Russian youth shed the warm bag from his legs and, shivering, got up and kicked a boot, then another.

Faces appeared. Watches were consulted.

'They're on the move? What?' The sergeant had his earflaps down, just his Georgian moustache showing.

'There's some sheep coming up, Sarge. Wasn't sure what you'd want us to do.'

The NCO had to stand up to see them. After a moment he let the night-glasses swing, and grunted.

'Just a couple of kids with them.'

'Wasn't sure if you'd want them to see us.'

The sergeant scrubbed his blue jaw, debating.

'With luck, Khan'll get moving presently. There's no way they can warn him without doubling back. If they do,' he shrugged, 'we'll just have to stop 'em. Oblensky.' He stood over a soldier still in his sleeping bag. 'Your turn with the breakfast.'

Self-heating soup, stale black bread, some rancid butter.

Soon the team of four were squatting in the declivity, eating ravenously.

The flock worked its way up the hill, slightly to the right of them. It might have passed by without incident if the smaller of the two shepherds had not circled to toss a stone at a lagging animal. He stood staring for a long moment at the breakfasting men. Calling his companion, he moved towards them with an engaging grin.

The taller one approached a little way and stopped, his gaze alternating between the soldiers and his flock. He seemed shy, even fearful. But the smaller one – he could not have been more than ten – advanced with hand outstretched.

'Cigarette?' he asked in Russian.

'Piss off, lad,' the sergeant said, cursing under his breath.

The child came closer. He was dressed in rags and carried a frayed shoulder-bag, from which poked a stone-bow.

'Cigarette?'

He had an appealing little face, wide-mouthed, sparkle-eyed. He pushed his grubby hand closer.

'Give him one, Oblensky.' The sergeant addressed the horizon.

Oblensky, the only smoker, grudgingly produced his last pack, and scowlingly tossed the child a cigarette.

The small shepherd, delighted, saluted smartly. All smiles, he trotted away, pulling his bag round in front of him, and pausing for a moment to stow the treasure in its depths in such a way that it would not break. Straightening, he turned and tossed something towards the soldiers before running to join his companion.

The tracking team thought the object was a stone, until it rolled to rest at the sergeant's feet. Too late, they saw that it was a Russian RG-42 fragmentation grenade.

Immediately following dawn prayer, GRU officers and agents slipped into the principal mosque of every city throughout the country. Selected for their darker colouring and wearing Afghan clothing, they were largely indistinguishable from the thousands of faithful just leaving, and attracted minimal attention.

They closed the doors, confronted the mullahs, took them to one of the mosque's offices, secured them and injected them with truth compounds. The list of questions to be asked was identical in every instance, prepared by Yakushev himself: *From whom do you receive secret information? How? To whom do you pass it? How? What happens to it then? Who recruited you to do this? Names of all your contacts.* Still no direct reference was made to the Lily.

The first encoded transcripts of the completed questionnaire, Yakushev estimated, would not reach the directorate before ten. Nevertheless, he was in his office by seven, looking spruce and alert. He wanted to clear his desk in good time to give them his utmost attention. He had high hopes of those results, high hopes.

Anxious to find out if Khan was on the move again and heading positively towards an objective, Yakushev ran a licked finger through the tray of waiting papers. Though he went through them twice, he could find no tracking report more recent than last evening's. He told the clerk to get along to signals and jockey them.

He had spotted a memo from the Spetznas halfway down the pile and sheafed back to it. Apparently, their encirclement yesterday of the mountain gunners' camp had been abortive – for the good reason that it was standing empty, totally evacuated. Which meant, Yakushev could only conclude, that the elite Khad execution squad had defected with the rest.

Though disgusted, he had to admit he was relieved. At least that made them unavailable to answer any awkward questions concerning the circumstances of Khan's 'escape'.

The relief was to fade, however, with his perusal of the next two communications. The first was the recce battalion's report of their probe into Mir Bala. 'NCEF' meant no contact with enemy forces. Other than signs of recent occupation, including a severed transmitter aerial, they had found nothing. Well, the wily bastards had seen them coming, hadn't they, and were sitting back behind the crest with all their gear!

The second was the weekly deployment of reserves figures. From the cold statistics Yakushev's experienced eye extracted the fact that, with both the Soviet Asiatic and Afghan army units becoming operationally suspect, the bases were being drained, for the first time since the campaign began, of their white contingents. The ramifications in respect of Harvest were grave indeed.

Could this . . . could this possibly be a part of the Lily's strategy? he wondered.

He was still pondering when the clerk returned to say that, in answer to his 'expedite', the recce battalion had responded with the news that they had lost contact with the tracking team and were investigating. And, as if that wasn't frustrating enough, he laid before Yakushev a host of message slips. More were coming in, he said – notifying the directorate of yet another vast distribution of leaflets among the Moslem camps during the night.

Yakushev was becoming alarmed. What was *happening*? He read of more bonfires, that six Afghan pilots had been executed at Farah, for refusing to bomb civilian targets. But otherwise the camps were reported calm. Dangerously calm – according to several signals, which implied that the troops could simply be following the Lily's instruction to lie low and bide their time.

Yakushev found himself pacing the office. He began, for the first time, to think seriously in terms of counter-propaganda.

He called in his officers. Only one came – the night duty major.

It was not yet eight o'clock, and already Yakushev's ashtray was filled with butts and the room thick with smoke. He told the major to get on to Agitprop. Were *they* awake? If not *roust* them, and order them to prepare a series of ideological propaganda tapes for general broadcast over Radio Kabul, plus Russian language versions, suitably edited to apply to the differing cultures of the Soviet Asiatic troops – all for relay over the loudspeakers that were a feature of every camp.

He even considered distributing his own *chabnameh*, but they would be confusing for the camp security officers and would probably wind up on the bonfires with the rest.

Having got this under way, Yakushev resorted to his coffee machine. But before he could take comfort from a strong, hot cup another message arrived informing him of the fate of his tracking team! It left him stunned.

But at last, thank heaven, the mullah-interrogation transcripts were coming in. Yakushev hoped that they would in some way restore his mastery of the situation.

The results were astonishingly alike. Four of the mosques

visited were plainly excluded from the Lily's network – probably owing to their geographical position – and their mullahs had nothing to divulge. Of the rest, all admitted receiving secret information but said that the men from whom they received it were unknown to them by name. The messages were usually handed to them after noon prayer, the bearer having first identified himself. The mullahs passed the messages to carriers whom they knew by sight but, again, not by name. Only six of the thirty-two mullahs knew that the information went thence to a radio transmitter, but none knew the transmitter's location, save the Sufi in Herat, who said it was installed in the seventy-metres-high city grain elevator. None knew the ultimate destination of the transmitted messages. All had been recruited into this service by written instruction bearing the seal of the Ulema. The list of their contacts was slim indeed. Recognition was ninety-three per cent visual, seven per cent by name, and these probably only aliases.

Yakushev retained hopes of a breakthrough until he had the very last report. True, the operation was not complete; the Herat elevator was being raided, and a lookout was posted at every mosque for the carriers, who, when intercepted, hopefully would divulge the locations of the other transmitters. There was also a handful of names to be investigated and the Ulema to be considered seriously. But so far the operation had yielded few concrete results, and no whisper of the Lily.

'So an alliance based in Peshawar could still be our answer,' Dolin concluded finally.

Yakushev wasn't sure by this time whether to agree or disagree. They were far from alone. Dolin had assembled what he called his committee of seven to debate the results. This comprised himself, his deputy and the heads of the five departments: reconnaissance, Spetznas, intelligence, information and electronic intelligence – the crème de la crème, or, perhaps one should say, survivors with distinction of the awesomely demanding second faculty of the Soviet Army Military-Diplomatic Academy, Moscow. In the presence of such ideological purity and corporate thinking, Yakushev always felt threatened and, this morning, was very much on his guard.

He frowned and shook his head. 'We've nothing to confirm that from our illegals in Peshawar. In fact, our man with Mohamedi's Revolutionary Movement denies it absolutely.

They believe their authority is being usurped by either Gulbudin's Islamic Party or the National Front for Liberation and that it's being done from inside Afghanistan.'

'Which confirms our view,' said Shipov of intelligence, 'that they're all still at loggerheads.'

Shipov, the son of a Kharkov butcher, brilliant but unpolished, had just put the cleaver through Dolin's alliance theory.

With anyone else Dolin would have argued.

'All right,' he said resignedly. 'We have a new co-ordinator. Let's discuss that.'

'Correct me if I'm wrong, Feliks.' The cyphers officer glanced at Dolin, though he addressed Shipov. 'But it seems to me that the structure of their intelligence gathering, though weird of course, is sound. Even professional.' He allowed a pause for correction, but Shipov nodded. 'That, added to this influx of radios and listening devices, makes me wonder if we aren't dealing with the Americans.'

'They couldn't do it,' Shipov told him. 'I mean, get these religious maniacs to pull together. Besides,' he added with a sneer, 'if they were, we'd have read about it in their press.'

'Not by using a figurehead?' The cyphers officer looked unconvinced. 'Suppose they'd brought back some top Afghan refugee? Someone like Mehmed Agah.'

'Agah's a Gailani man,' Dolin replied. 'These mullahs are as mixed in their affiliations as the rest of the population, right, Feliks?'

'Screwed right up, General.'

'To get them all working in the same cause would take a man above all this politico-religious mish-mash. There's no one of that calibre in the West that I know of.'

'No one at all,' Shipov said.

Tripartite discussions between Dolin and his two favourites were par for the course in these debates. Yakushev, as the perennial outsider, was ignored – which nettled him but suited him, because while they were talking he had time to adjust his own thoughts. Goldanov of Spetznas, in the act of taking a pinch of snuff to clear his crushed nostrils, caught his eye and winked. Yakushev smiled back thinly.

Strebitski, the saturnine head of electronic intelligence, added his voice to the triumvirate.

'Then perhaps the CIA set it up through the Ulema. They supply the equipment, the technical know-how, and the Ulema provide the religious authority. Don't they fit the bill perfectly – the one force that could combine the mullahs?'

Shipov pursed his thick lips thoughtfully. 'Not impossible.'

'Would they dare, after—' Cyphers began.

'No, I like it.' Shipov cut him off. He rubbed the double line between his thick brows.

'I thought we put paid to them,' Goldanov growled, stifling a sneeze.

'Mm? Oh, they're still there. You don't destroy the whole core of a country's reaction by severing an arm or two. It just grows more.'

'But we don't know who they are now?'

'We can find out,' Shipov said, then muttered, 'though it might take more time than we've got.'

'Nevertheless,' Dolin said, 'it's an idea worth pursuing. We should do it. And quickly.'

'Not through the regime,' Shipov said.

'No, bypass the regime. The embassy wine and dine the high-ups. They'd be a good place to start.'

'I'll get on to it,' Shipov said.

'Just a minute,' Osipov of information put in suddenly, speaking for the first time. 'I'm remembering something.' Mouth open, he pinched his eyes under his spectacles for a moment.

'Yes, it was in the Jangalak interrogation transcript. He mentions a name . . . "The Lily". Have we pursued this at all?'

Lily? Lily? You could see them all search their memory banks. Yakushev sat quite still.

'The references are oblique,' Osipov continued. 'And they were not taken up by the interrogators, as one would have expected – they were lax there – but it seems to me in retrospect to refer to the organizers of this whole structure. What I'm saying is could "Lily" possibly be a code name for the *Ulema*?'

There was a slightly baffled silence.

It had happened at last. Yakushev knew he had to put his oar in quickly.

'It *could*,' he said casually. 'If it makes any difference.'

Dolin sat forward, obliged to include him in his gaze. He had not read the transcript, for the good reason that Yakushev had 'diverted' his copy.

'Lily? Why don't I know about this?'

'You must have come across the name, General,' Yakushev told him, with no visible anxiety. 'There have been several references to it recently in our undercover reports.' He glanced around the committee, his gaze coming to rest on know-it-all Shipov. 'You've all had copies. Doesn't it ring a bell?'

Shipov said, 'I remember *something* . . .' But the consensus seemed to be No.

'Elaborate,' Dolin said shortly.

Yakushev shrugged. 'It's just a name, a word. I'd already thought it might refer to the command structure we're discussing. But it alters nothing. We're still groping for the identity of this . . .' He looked around. 'If you like, we'll *call* it the Lily.'

Dolin grunted.'Damn silly name. But all right.'

'Of much more importance, General,' Yakushev went on, 'is what these recent flare-ups are doing to our reserve situation. You've all read the figures, I take it?'

'What have they to do with it?' Dolin frowned impatiently.

It was the ideal time, Yakushev realized, for the Lily to have surfaced. With five powerful witnesses present, Dolin would think twice before going to Solkholov and claiming it was his own discovery.

'Would you agree that our Asiatic and Afghan forces are, if not compromised, in the balance? They are our Harvest advance force; without them the operation will never get off the ground. Suppose, just suppose, they receive a final batch of *chabnameh* telling them to revolt . . .'

'In that unlikely event,' Dolin cut in, 'Alma Ata's orders are we crush them, using white troops.'

'What white troops?'

'Our reserves.'

'At the present count, General, that would take every man we've got left, leaving nothing for Harvest.'

There was a brief silence.

'Presupposing,' Shipov said coldly, 'that the marshal is an idiot. Do you think he doesn't know his own reserve figures? And wouldn't compensate? Half of these policing actions could go by the board. He could divert the necessary any time he wanted.'

'As long as the Lily doesn't delay the call to mutiny till the last minute'

'Are you suggesting,' Dolin asked, amazed, 'that this is all planned? Part of the Lily's actual strategy?'

Yakushev shrugged. 'Who can say? But I don't think we should ignore the possibility. Certainly the marshal should be warned of it.'

'And how do you suggest he counter it?'

'Ah. Disarm all the Moslems would be one way.'

Shipov said, 'You're talking about sixty thousand men!'

'And how do you suppose those currently deployed are going to be able to fight the *mujahedin* without weapons?' Dolin demanded.

'Under the circumstances I envisage,' Yakushev replied, 'they wouldn't fight the *mujahedin* anyway, they'd join them.'

This silenced them, but only for a moment. Dolin laughed.

'Disarm the Afghans, conceivably, but our own troops? Have you any idea of the furore it would cause in the republics? If the international press ever got hold of it we'd be the laughing stock of the world!'

'We could become so either way,' replied Yakushev. 'Anyway, this is a command decision and I do think the possible scenario should be conveyed to the marshal.'

Dolin said coldly, 'And *I* think we have quite enough factual problems on our plate, Andrei Pavlovich, without inventing more.'

'Then I ask that it be put on record that I made the request,' Yakushev said, with a lingering look all round.

There. He had staked his claim as an oracle, soothsayer and hero of the hour to be.

But all that, he ruminated afterwards, would be as much use as a snowball in hell if the recce battalion – who had a pair of Antonovs with tracking equipment scouring the relevant countryside – failed to relocate Khan.

30

ON THE evening of the fourth day, Khan and his party halted beside a lone hilltop minaret overlooking Ghazni. They stood in the late stillness without speaking, their throats parched and bellies empty.

How the Russians had picked up their trail after Mir Bala remained a mystery. When they had climbed to the scene of the grenade explosion afterwards, McCabe had been unable to make head or tail of their equipment, which lay in pieces, and, not understanding the principle on which it operated, they could not assess the likelihood of the Russians picking up their trail again.

Seeing no suspicious movement, they focused their attention on the town. Overlaying it was a pastel-blue haze which was part smoke, part dust spun to a web by the departing sun. From the distant north-east the mutter of gunfire was still audible; from closer in, with the peculiar clarity that in other lands precedes rain, came the mutter of goat bells.

Khan's gaze found the small silvery-blue cupola of Sultan Mohamed's Tomb, then spanned the sprawl of the city that had grown vastly since last he had seen it. The tumbledown bazaar district, though, had not changed, nor had the army fort on the hill beyond. Who was in possession of that now, he wondered – the Afghan army or the Russians? He had heard that there was a Soviet base and airstrip to the south of town, too, though he could not see it. Yet despite the military presence and the massacre of four thousand *mujahedin* in 1980 and sporadic tank assaults on the town ever since, the rebels still had not let go. Whole sections of it remained in their hands; he had heard it with pride. But which sections? And was the tomb included in them?

The bells drew closer and, glancing to a flank, they saw a

flock of sheep and goats approaching. An old man accompanied them, his wrists hooked over the stick across his shoulders, like a walking scarecrow. Khan observed him carefully, then hailed him and asked him the situation in the town.

The shepherd unshouldered his stick and beat the air with it.

'Back and forth! Back and forth!' he cried. 'In my youth it was all whispers and songs.' He glared at them for a moment, then turned and marched on.

Khan watched him go, thinking that war had turned his mind. And as he did so a sharp scatter of fire started in the town, followed by a 'crump' and puff of smoke from one of the buildings, then silence. Seeing that the shepherd was continuing, undeterred, in the very direction of the Sultan's Tomb, he said, 'Let us follow.'

Hardly had they begun to move when a winged shadow fell silently across them and an Antonov, with engine cut, passed low overhead.

It was too late to hide. They just stopped and watched it glide on over the town. Presently its motor re-engaged with a hiccough and it drifted away into the distance, curving slowly northwards.

Ayesha looked at the men for their reaction. Khan's was to spur his animal on down the hill at increased speed. McCabe's was a shrug.

'Could be,' he said, 'we just lost our anonymity. There again, could be he's just spotting for the guns. Either way,' he added, 'Khan's got the idea – we do what we have to do fast – and blow.'

The information reached Yakushev the same night. He peered at the signal blearily, at pains to concentrate after consuming too much vodka.

Dinner in the mess had been unexpectedly festive. Marshal Solkholov had dropped in for a word with Dolin and stayed to dine. Word of this had swiftly circulated and there had been a rush back to billets to don best uniforms. In a blaze of medal ribbons and brilliantine, elbows off table, the officers had faced each other like scrubbed schoolboys, politely attentive to the Big Talk generated in their guest's vicinity.

Yakushev, as deputy head, was accepted in that vicinity, though he was sure that Dolin, given a choice, would have had it otherwise. He was well aware of the embarrassment he caused his chief each time he addressed the marshal. It was nothing to do with his good sense or the substance of what he had to say; it was what he stood for in Dolin's and his cronies' self-consciously ideological eyes. He was a maverick. He smacked of 'private thinking', innovation. It was fear, Yakushev knew, that he might outshine them. And in the society prescribed by the architects of communism for their own protection, there was no greater fear than that.

Yakushev mused that they were fully justified in such a fear. Yet, paradoxically, not belonging caused him pain. He wanted both the privilege of rejecting them and the satisfaction of being accepted. Well, he was convinced he would get what he wanted. And Solkholov would provide the key. As Front commander he had the capacity to make or break any officer, even including those in the élite GRU. He would make Yakushev and break Dolin.

He was a large man, or perhaps seemed so because of the expanse of ribbon and braid that spanned his chest and lapels, and the aura of power that surrounded him – the sort of power derived from driving an awesome machine. Tanks and gunships seemed to ripple under the mottled skin. He grimaced, he gestured with blunt hands, he dabbed his lips and raised his glass. It was Harvest-minus four, he reminded them. A toast to success!

His confidence was a salutary reminder of how vast were the material forces under his command compared with the abstractions of the Lily, to which Yakushev had been devoting so much of his time. His plan to ride to personal victory on such an insubstantial back suddenly seemed absurd. To Solkholov this current Agitprop attempt to disaffect the Moslem troops was trifling and in vain, the increased rebel attacks an inconvenience, no more; Harvest would go ahead as scheduled. For a moment Yakushev could believe it with him. But only for a moment. However much Solkholov rippled his guns and armour, he had only so many at his disposal. And these could be swallowed overnight if the Lily's intimated masterstroke were to come off.

He waited till the marshal was well into the vodka before

broaching the subject. He had to do so twice before the reddening eyes focused on him.

Dolin overheard and tried to brush the subject aside, but Solkholov was interested.

'Then your job, comrade Colonel,' Solkholov replied, rotating his glass, 'is to make sure that does not happen! It is a straightforward security matter.'

'And the straightforward solution is to disarm the Moslems.'

From Solkholov's sharp look Yakushev knew that this was the first he had heard of the suggestion.

'And disaffect our allies further? Not to mention our own Asiatic republics?'

'Exactly!' Dolin looked daggers at his deputy.

Yakushev was not to be deterred. 'In the aftermath of the Harvest success, would it be noticed? A little disinformation would repair the damage.' He added, 'I'm simply looking at the alternatives open to us, and they are rather few, comrade Marshal. You don't mind?'

'Feel free,' Solkholov said expansively. He looked around and laughed. A sudden hush had fallen on that end of the table.

'Just supposing we are unable to forestall the fire,' said Yakushev, 'then we must quench it. If our reserves are fully deployed, that might be difficult.'

'Difficult is no problem to you, I hope, Colonel.' Solkholov laughed again. 'Even the impossible takes a little longer, isn't that what you fellows say?'

The gathering responded vigorously.

'I repeat,' the marshal went on, 'that this is a directorate responsibility. One I am confident you resourceful chaps will deal with.'

'With respect, comrade Marshal,' Yakushev reminded him, blinding himself to Dolin's signals, 'you have our Spetznas on standby. With no forces at our disposal, how are we to shoulder that responsibility?'

'I think we've had enough of that subject, Andrei Pavlovich,' Dolin warned, dead-voiced.

But Solkholov said, 'No, he has a point. I cannot answer it. Not at this juncture.' He smiled at Yakushev disarmingly. 'Sorry.' He added, 'Such details are not my business, but I suggest that if you make it impossible for further subversive literature to be distributed, the problem you envisage will never arise. Too simple?' He looked around at his audence, who nodded too readily to have been listening with their minds. If he read in their expressions an eagerness to dissociate themselves from Yakushev's temerity, he made no concession to it. He raised his glass. 'Enough shop talk, comrades.'

'Thank you, Marshal Solkholov, for your patience,' Yakushev murmured and dutifully raised his own glass.

That he was studiously ignored by almost everyone from that point onwards did not greatly disturb him. He had slipped past Dolin's wall and planted his oracular flag on higher ground.

He excused himself early and returned, a mite unsteadily, to his office, where he consumed quantities of coffee and played back the exchange in his head, till a growing roar broke his concentration. He knew it to be fighters and bombers on the move from Baghram and Kabul to take up their Harvest stations at Kandahar. At the same time, synchronized to coincide with gaps in US orbital infra-red surveillance, massed convoys were taking to the road.

He was seated, listening, when the night clerk presented him with the message that dissipated the last clouds of his crisis of confidence.

He was back, as the Americans would say, in the 'ball park'. The only problem, now Khan was again back in his sights, was to keep him there.

31

BEFORE THE sky became light enough for orbital photography, the last echelon of armour and squadron of planes had vanished under camouflage like sly tails under rocks. Other denizens of the night had done their work also and departed, becoming once again herdsmen, camel drivers, well-diggers, innocent in the forgiveness of Allah but leaving a trail of death – a two-man picquet here, a whole guard detail there, throats cut, severed wire strands clawing the sky, *chabnameh* scattered where waking hands would encounter them.

The Hour is nigh!

I swear by the Day of Resurrection that Allah is watching and has marked each of you well!

By your actions of that Hour he will judge which of you in truth believes and which does not. Those who do not He will cast upon the fire. They shall endure mounting torment. As for those who obey the call, theirs shall be gardens and vineyards, and high-bosomed maidens for companions, a truly overflowing cup!

Ask: By what actions will He judge me?

By those you have been taught, and by refusal to raise your hand against all brothers of the Faith. Though ordered, you will refuse. Yea, unto death you will refuse!

Ask: When is the Hour?

It is near. First will come the word. Prepare yourself to receive it. Hearing it, you will obey it and no other, lest you be committed to Hell!

The bakers read them first, firing their ovens, angling their copies to the tongues of flame. Then the cooks, one holding aloft a smoky lantern while another reads and others peer.

Now a man returning from the latrine, stumbling perhaps over a body. He stoops to feel its coldness, then snatches up copies and runs. Into the barrack hut – 'wake up, wake up!' – a copy per bunk, sleep banished more swiftly than by any reveille. Asiatic faces honed to obedience, purged by propaganda, yet vulnerable still to the awe of their fathers. *Fear of God*. But half of them have never entered a mosque. The new culture ridiculed the old. Cosmonauts spanned the seven heavens: had one of them caught even a glimpse of God? And was not the army itself hell? But after demob, and they could count the days to that, they could have all the high-bosomed maidens they wanted, without the pain and uncertainty of a bullet, however glorious that was supposed to be. For all that, it was still there, deep inside them, the spark struck by Mahomed. Though diminished, its weight was of gold on the scales of their mind.

Now the sergeants – Tartars almost to a man, recruited for the ruthless qualities of their race. Lights leapt through the camps, each hut ablaze. A bellow of orders. Who dare disobey? Only a few. Moments were given them to come to their senses, leaving fewer still. The GRU orders were clear: *Instant and summary*. Bullets thumped into chests. Comrades lay writhing, one crying, '*Allaho akbar!* I see them – the fountains!' It was enough. The surge of zeal swept away the guns, the Tartars. Bare-chested men raced through this camp and that. Neighbouring camps were alerted, non-Moslem soldiers rushed to the scene. Some insurrections were quelled, some were not; in some, bonfires of *chabnameh* blazed, in others furniture and uniforms, in yet others whole hutments.

On came the loudspeakers. As per GRU instruction, prepared tapes were to drown out the sounds of conflict with propaganda. At first no one heard. But gradually all violence was suspended. The officers and security troops listened in shock as a resonant voice proclaimed that God was Great and Mohamed was His Prophet. 'This is the Word!' it boomed from the speakers. 'Hearken to it!'

'Surrender your *chabnameh*, for you have read them. Retain your arms, for you will need them. For every believer executed, you will execute a disbeliever in return, no more, no less. Thus will bloodshed abate. Then you will remain calm but unrelenting, for you are now the soldiers of Allah. You will pray. You will fast. You will wait for the Miracle *that will change the world*! The Spirit of Aminah has returned to us. From her loins will spring again the Prophet. Hearken to her voice!'

The camps stood in thrall. In some the tapes had already been stopped and groups of soldiers stormed the intercom centres in a frenzy to restart them. In others, the Lily's voice echoed like the sudden wild cry of a bird.

'I am the vessel upon which all history waits! Yet my hour of travail will be yours, and yours mine. Perceive ye now the meaning of the scriptures? From ye and me together will He come – reborn of our belief! Give great prayer to it! Give, if needs be, your life to it, for life is but a token, a poor sample of the wondrous things to be. Tomorrow my voice will be heard in all the land. Say, *Allaho akbar*!'

A great roar greeted this.

'Again.'

Another roar.

'Again!'

Another.

'Until then. Allah be with us!'

The speakers went silent.

Cars rushed to Front headquarters. Dolin and Yakushev attended the gathering in Solkholov's office. Standing dark-faced behind his desk, the marshal beckoned them forward.

'Explain!' he challenged Dolin.

'We took every possible precaution,' Dolin said, deadpan.

'Clearly you did not or it could never have happened.'

'Within the limits of our capability,' Dolin added. For once in his life he was taking the blame personally, or at least sharing it. He had perceived Yakushev's suddenly enhanced status after his warning last night, and knew, like the old party man he was, that he must side with the one temporarily in the ascendant or risk going under. 'I approved the measures taken and have a copy, if you would care to . . .'

But Solkholov waved the folder aside, his gaze beyond him, brows raised.

'Clearly this could only have been done with inside help.' The gritty voice came from General Organskiy of the KGB. 'Which means those camps are crawling with subversives. Why were they not purged?'

'They were.' Dolin swung towards his counterpart.
'Who by? Not us. Not you.'
'Individual camp security. We hadn't the personnel for so large an operation at such short notice, what with . . .'
'We had.' Organskiy cut him off. 'A simple telephone call could have clinched it. But you're more committed to your own prejudices!'
'What were your political officers doing?' Dolin snapped. 'Don't tell me you didn't know what was going on. You're as much to blame as we.' He turned back to Solkholov. 'If we'd been permitted to disarm the Moslems, all this could have been avoided.'
His sheer effrontery took Yakushev's breath away.
'Had you made the request last night,' Solkholov said drily, 'I might have considered it. Though it would have been too late to implement.' His gaze flicked to Yakushev and back. 'But clearly you were divided on that measure.'
Yakushev suppressed a smile.
'Pity,' Organskiy muttered. 'Had we been consulted, we'd have backed them all the way.'
Dolin said sidelong, 'Easy to say that now.'
'Better now than never, comrade, wouldn't you say? How else are we to learn, if we do not examine our mistakes? And there have been many – too many – in recent weeks: the assassination of General Rossakov, the microphones, Ghoram Khan's escape, *twice*, the news cameraman . . . I could—'
'Look, are we here to sling mud or find a solution – which?' Dolin's sagging jawline was beginning to glow an angry pink.
'Both. If we are to eliminate such inefficiency!'
'And you dare accuse us of prejudice!'
'See?' Yakushev cried suddenly, turning to the gathering. 'We're doing exactly what they want! Permission to speak, comrade Marshal?'
Solkohòlov looked towards him almost in relief. He nodded. 'Tell us what they want, comrade Colonel. You're the only person here who seems to understand what is going on.'
'They want us at each other's throats. This is psychological warfare, Marshal – Islamic style.'
'"They" being presumably this Lily creature?'
'And her staff – advisers, whatever.'
Solkholov made an incredulous sound. 'To be confronted by

a woman in a land where they count for nothing at all sounds like a fiction.'

'We're confronted, I believe,' Yakushev said carefully, 'by an idea. She, and I'm guessing, has been chosen to personify it. I doubt whether she's actually in command, and it doesn't really matter if she is or not.'

'The idea being . . . ? Would you just recap, for the benefit of – uh – those of us who've had their minds on other things?'

'The rebirth of Mahomed.'

'Idiots!' snapped Organskiy. 'They're all mad!'

'Not if it helps them achieve their objective,' Solkholov reminded him soberly. 'Which is what, Colonel? The unification of the resistance?'

'That is the means, Marshal, as I read it – not the end.'

'So what is the end?'

'The sabotage of Harvest.'

There was a startled silence. Dolin looked at Yakushev askance, furious that he was not privy to these deductions, but powerless to do anything but nod to identify himself with them. Organskiy frowned at Repin, who spread his hands, at a total loss.

Solkholov's eyes narrowed. 'They know – you're sure of that?'

Dolin said, 'Everything points to it.'

'Then why isn't it world news? Why go through all this rigmarole when all they need do is whisper in the ear of the CIA and within hours we'd have another Polish situation, only worse, with every kind of capitalist pressure heaped on us, from SALT to the UN?'

Dolin pursed his lips, groping rapidly for a reply.

Yakushev let him stew for a moment, then said smoothly, 'Perhaps because they want to achieve a purely Islamic victory. The fundamentalists hate the US and the rest of the non-believing world as much as they hate us.'

The marshal considered this. 'Sounds in character.' He eyed Dolin, knowing well the cleft stick he was in now that his deputy suddenly had all the answers. But Dolin still commanded the directorate and it was Solkholov who had put his old friend there. Protocol must be observed. 'Do you agree with that, Anatoli Gregorievich?'

'I was about to say precisely that.'

Solkholov swung his gaze round the other faces. 'Then I think we must accept that the Lily is well aware of our forthcoming operations. In which case—'

'One question, Marshal.' Organskiy's ear was angled to an outpouring from his aide, Repin. He nodded. 'Why is all this coming out suddenly? I am not completely without knowledge of what goes on in the GRU' – there was laughter – 'but every word of this is news to me, and it should *not* be. The directorate's job is to keep the Front abreast of developments – via RO Intelligence. But what have we heard from them so far? Absolutely nothing!'

'May I answer?' Yakushev cut in. He turned to face the KGB men. 'We've had a grave internal security problem, as all of us know. If the Lily has managed to find out about Harvest, she can find out about our countermeasures. You've accused us of lax security with regard to Rossakov, Khan, etc. But now, when we rebuild our fences, you complain that you're shut out. You can't have it both ways, comrades.'

Organskiy bristled visibly at being addressed this way by a junior officer.

'Said with respect, I hope,' the marshal interjected, poker-faced. 'You'd better address me, Colonel. You say you've taken countermeasures?'

'Of course. And one of them answers the earlier criticism concerning Khan. He didn't escape. We let him go.' Out of the tail of his eye he saw Dolin's head jerk round towards him. 'We had evidence that if he got away he was going to join forces with the Lily. I took the responsibility of giving him a chance to do it. We have a team tracking him.' Yakushev avoided going into the problems concerning that. 'One can't be certain, of course, but I'm reasonably optimistic that within a few hours we'll have a fix on their headquarters.'

Solkholov looked at Dolin, who seemed stunned, but managed to nod. The marshal raised his meaty hands and clapped soundlessly – a gesture that was taken up in several quarters.

'Excellent! Then we can crush all this Islamic nonsense at source!'

'That's what I've had in mind.' Yakushev lowered his gaze modestly.

'See, Organskiy?' Solkholov chuckled. 'It seems the GRU has not been quite so idle as you supposed.' He turned to the

Air Army commander standing tall beside him. 'The moment the pin goes in the map we'll have an air recce, then a strike.'

This was without doubt Yakushev's shining hour. He was in on the decision-making, the brass assembled to bear him witness, Dolin struggling like a tongue-tied schoolboy to keep up with the class. He replied calmly, 'With respect, comrade Marshal, on the Lily's showing so far, I doubt if it will be that simple.'

'Simple?' Solkholov lifted his chin questioningly towards him.

'The Lily's put a lot of planning and effort into all this. Sophisticated effort.'

'Make your point.'

'I don't think they're exactly going to be sitting around in tents. They could be in caves. Their position will be fortified and probably defended by a considerable force. We're going to need ground troops as well as an air strike – a flying column of some sort, including armour.'

'The air recce will tell us what we need.' Solkholov's reply was brusque.

'Marshal, they have a transmitter. Until it's silenced, the possibility of Moslem insurrection remains a direct threat to Harvest. The faster we move, the less the danger. That means a column ready – on standby.'

Solkholov was staring at Yakushev with pursed lips. There were murmurs from the generals. Had he gone too far in telling the Front commander his business?

'What sort of locale are we talking about?'

'I can't be precise, but south-west of Ghazni, probably in the Kush.'

Solkholov frowned. He pushed his way to the wall map and studied the deployment overlay as his generals gathered round pointing and talking quietly. The marshal dabbed his fingers up the main supply route from Kabul to the Oxus. 'These dispositions must remain. And here . . .' – Masr-i-Sharif – 'And on this side' – from Herat to Kandahar. Someone tapped the cluster of formations spanning the entrance to the Panjshir Valley. Solkholov shook his head with a short laugh. 'We don't want to let *him* out!'

Their attention moved eastwards to the troop concentrations around Jalalabad and the southern Kunar. Solkholov shook his head again. 'We've got to keep a clear run through to the Khyber. In case.'

'We could lose them.' A general tapped a chinagraphed symbol connected by arrow to the air base east of Jalalabad.

'Why not? But armour . . . why are we so tight suddenly?' Solkholov's musing was barely audible. 'You know, looking at this I get the strangest feeling that they've got a Western mind in this Lily organization. And he's good.' Then, after a space, 'Come on, comrades – a company of tanks. Leonid?'

'Presently he returned to his desk, talking over his shoulder. 'How long to move them to Ghazni?'

Two hours, he was told. He checked his watch, then nodded to Yakushev and Dolin conjointly.

'Your advice taken, comrades. You'll keep us closely informed as to Khan's progress of course.'

'Of course,' Dolin said. 'Direct to you?'

'To General Kazinsky.' Solkholov indicated a colleague. 'He will command the operation.'

They were dismissed. Dolin began to move.

Yakushev did not.

'Excuse me, Marshal – did I hear you say the 11th Commando?'

Solkholov was scrawling a memo. He looked up.

'You did.'

'They're Afghan.'

'Correct. Plus a company of their 5th Armoured.'

'Moslem,' Yakushev said.

'Hard-line PDP troops, Colonel. Oath of allegiance, Soviet trained, battle-proven in the Kunar.'

'But still Moslem.'

Solkholov's brow clouded. Dolin had paused and turned, his lips taut. He was signalling his deputy to drop it and follow him. But Yakushev hung back doggedly.

'Our strike force has to be non-Moslem, Marshal. It's vital.'

Solkholov pressed his knuckles on the desk, forcing his shoulders up. Yakushev realized he was going red. Slowly the shoulders eased and the Front commander's gaze moved amongst his assembled brass.

'He has a point. In which case I'll have to think about it.'

'Our Spetznas . . . ?' Yakushev ventured.

'Quite impossible. Now—'

Yakushev lengthened his gaze to the map. 'I see there is a guards armoured division positioned at Ghazni . . . !'

Solkholov just managed to contain himself.

'It's leagured there just for the day, Colonel, on its way to Kandahar.'

'No chance of holding it there another night?'

'Thank you, Colonel Yakushev' – coldly – 'I will let you know what I decide.'

Yakushev hesitated, but even he dared not push it further. He sprang to a smart salute.

'At your command, Marshal.'

He followed Dolin out.

There was a long silence after he had left the room. Solkholov examined the faces of his commanders expressionlessly. After a moment he turned his attention towards the map, the region of Ghazni. He rubbed his chin with a scratchy sound.

Dolin uttered not a word on the way back. Yakushev eyed the general's averted face with curiosity born of exultation. His chief could do nothing to him now without its seeming like vengeance or pique. Solkholov was no fool: he had cottoned on to their relationship well enough, and at any other time would not have tolerated it; he had the power to sack either or both of them on the spot. But with Harvest imminent he couldn't and wouldn't do it, and anyway Dolin had hopped on to his deputy's bandwagon. Now he must stay on it till Harvest was history, or Solkholov would ruin him.

In a burst of exhilaration, Yakushev lit a cigarette, knowing how Dolin hated it in the car. Beware the party, an inner voice whispered. They are less concerned with success than with methods employed to achieve it. But he had already justified his unilateralism on security grounds and they could never disprove that, even with Dolin's testimony. No, he had good cause to exult. His only regret was that Pola wasn't alive to witness his victory.

'I want everything from now on,' Dolin said flatly as he got out of the car and started walking off. 'Everything as it comes in. On my desk. Nothing omitted.'

Yakushev went to his office. His in-tray, growing fuller each day, was formidable now – sitreps from his agents in Baluchistan, directives from Alma Ata outlining security policy in the province following Harvest, for-information-only copies of every damn bit of bumph processed by each of the five departments. On top of all this, his staff actually lined the hall, each wanting a word. He ignored the lot, rummaging until he unearthed a yellow signals slip. He took it to his map.

The replacement foot-mobile team had been carefully briefed and equipped with the dish tracking screen which had a reception area of up to six kilometres – and flown to Ghanzi within one hour and twenty minutes of the sighting. There had been some nail-biting back at recce battalion HQ while a GAZ had raced them from the air base to the hillside where the Antonov had registered its blips. There, they had switched on – and got nothing.

Then began a frantic race around the town's perimeter, all in the dark of course, with cratered roads, rebels on the loose – and still their scan showed nothing.

Was the equipment faulty? Control ordered them to make a cross-country circular sweep five kilometres from the town. They started to the north, lights out, using the moon, It was slow, dangerous going among the rough fields and *karez* wells, but after an hour they got a reading. It came from the direction of the western foothills. It was stationary.

Could their quarry have already reached their objective, or had they simply camped for the night? The unit dismissed the light truck, concealed themselves and waited to find out.

Yakushev received their first report while at breakfast. It informed him that Khan and his party were once more on the move and travelling south-west. Now – Yakushev read the co-ordinates and spread the dividers – they were already thirty kilometres beyond the town. He rechecked that. Astonishing. They really *were* moving – still south-west, skirting the foothills along, roughly, the 3000-metre contour. The altitude was deceptive, Yakushev knew, because Ghazni itself was over 2000 metres above sea-level. Nevertheless, an old hand like Khan wouldn't have sweated up that 800 metres if he hadn't intended to maintain it. That was where he was heading all right, into the Western Kush.

Yakushev had seen those mountains from the Ghazni base: a mighty brown or blue wall – according to the time of day – sweeping up from the inhospitable valley. Somewhere up there, among those blue-black clefts lay a – what? A concrete bunker? His imagination groped through the possibilities while his finger roved the contours. He could see nothing to enlighten him.

But the units at Ghazni base sometimes trained among those foothills. He sent the base commandant a signal asking him to cancel any projected exercises in the area and telephoned Air Army to arrange a ban on overflying, especially by gunship sortie. Nothing must be allowed to deter Khan from reaching his objective with all possible speed.

Only then did he turn his mind to the bulk of his work.

At mid-afternoon several of the tapes broadcast that morning over the Moslem camp speakers arrived on his desk, but there was not time to play them back. He put them to one side.

That evening a memo arrived from RO Intelligence, Front, to say that Solkholov was holding the guards armoured division in leaguer at Ghazni for another day. Yakushev almost burst out laughing. Scanning the distribution list, he saw that Dolin also had received a copy. How he wished he'd been there to watch him read it!

That night Yakushev had his bedding-roll brought to the office. The midnight tracking report, however, said that Khan and his party were halted. He need not have bothered.

So Harvest minus 2 dawned with heavy stillness. Khan was on the move again, still in the same direction. The Moslem camps in contrast were as static as the air itself. No *chabnameh* today. No yelling and rushing about; some praying, but that was permitted for the time being.

Machine-gun posts had been erected outside the wire – ostensibly to prevent further night incursions – but manned by ethnic Russians. They fooled no one. Asiatic music, relayed from Radio Kabul, jangled interminably over the speakers, interspersed with anti-religious propaganda. Despite this, or because of it, an air of brooding hung over the waiting Islamic troops.

With shirt-tails outside trousers, bits of cloth wound round cropped heads instead of fatigue caps, they seemed in small but insignificant ways to be reverting to their pre-Soviet ways.

All of which augured badly for Harvest, which called first for an Afghan response to the Baluchi insurrection. One million Pathans lived across the border in Baluchistan and they would need protection. Tanks and a division of motorized infantry would rush to oblige, and since the Pathans, too, would be actively involved in the insurrection, this force, in protecting them, would pretty soon clash with the 50,000-strong Pakistan Army stationed in Baluchistan. So already the troops of leftist Kabul would send in its SUs and gunships – Soviet manned, but who would know? – and, presently, long-range bombers to attack the principal Pakistan cities. Soviet Moslem troops would join in unnoticed.

The Soviet Union's own role in all this would be that of peacemaker – angry and highly critical of Babrak Karmal for joining in someone else's war when they had an unfinished one of their own to win. The notion that they possessed the power to order Kabul to withdraw its forces was American nonsense, as they would remind the UN. Afghanistan was an independent country with an autonomous regime; the Soviet military presence was purely at the regime's own request. The USSR, hinting that the insurrection was imperialist-backed, would call for a ceasefire – to be supervised, of course, by the non-aligned charade players – and leftists everywhere would applaud.

However, UN decision-making being a procedural quagmire, rapid destabilization along Afghanistan's southern frontier, coupled with heavy insurgent bombing of Pakistan's key cities, would force the Soviets to take international police action themselves. Spetznas para units would overnight capture and secure airfields and other key points and the ethnic-Russian Guards Armoured Division strike through and link them up: Quetta, Kalat, Shireza Kalat, Ocmara – a straight line to the Arabian Sea. They would announce this as the ceasefire line, pour in more troops and aircraft, and consolidate.

Fighting would probably continue along Baluchistan's western border with Iran, but no one cared about the Shiites, who had their hands full enough with Iraq. Negotiations would begin in the UN. The Baluchis would put their case for an independent state. Zia would oppose it, mindful of the untapped deposits of iron ore, sulphur, coal and chrome, not to mention the gasfields. The argy-bargy would go on, while the ceasefire line which divided Baluchistan roughly in half would remain. The Soviet Union would opt for its becoming permanent. After all, Zia would still retain the richer eastern half. The western sector was mostly desert anyway, sparsely populated by primitive nomads. Its capital would be Quetta, but that was a small price for Zia to pay for an end to conflict.

The Baluchis would probably be the strongest protesters, but half was always better than a flea in the ear, which is what they would get if the Soviet Union carried out its threat to withdraw support. By this time, of course, a Revolutionary Baluchi government would have been formed, and the Soviet Union would be negotiating an aid package they could not refuse – in return for nothing more than a corridor to the sea (leased) and use of an existing port, which they would develop on the scale of Karachi and which would include a marine base of huge proportions, offering employment to thousands.

So went the scenario. But it was all balanced, like an inverted cone, upon the initial infusion of Afghan troops to defend their Pathan brethren when the insurrection began. And those troops now were squatting in their camps waiting for the rebirth of Mahomed. Not all of them, it is true. The spearhead motor-rifle, support and supply units had been selected for their loyalty to the regime. On Yakushev's orders they had been cut off from outside contact and thoroughly reindoctrinated. They would probably rally to the flag. But 'probably' was not the most comfortable of words upon which to found so vast an imperialist enterprise.

32

THEY HAD passed gradually beyond all sight of Ghazni, then beyond the hazy glitter of the Russian base, finally beyond the murky smudge that stained the sky above them. Now only the foothills sloping to the plain shimmered below them, veined with erosion.

Khan at long last was back in the true mountains. The pristine stillness, broken only by the soft echoes of hoof and footfall, swelled his chest with a deep sense of exultation, tinged with melancholy for the past. His companions paused frequently for comment and speculation, their voices, even Hafiq's, hushed in the vastness, but he had ridden ever on, in intense anticipation of their objective.

The instruction handed him in silence by the old and crippled keeper of the tomb had borne a solitary coded map reference, nothing more. Khan had known then that they were embarking on the last leg of their journey. He had ordered two things – as much speed as they could muster to carry them clear of the town, and watchfulness. He was remembering the small aircraft.

But, though they had heard rumblings of vehicles and aircraft throughout the night, the day had dawned silent and empty. It was as if the whole world was holding its breath. Doubly wary, they had progressed as fast as the terrain would allow. The stillness had seemed to move with them, surrounding them with its invisible screen. Preserved thus, around noon, they had reached the road.

Though there was a dotted something on the map, its scale and state of preservation had come as a complete surprise. It appeared out of a deep fissure and picked its way back and forth up the mountain. Far below there was little trace of it, just a stretch here and there where the melt-waters of centuries had failed to erase it. But above it appeared almost intact. An ancient road, beyond doubt, cleverly and patiently engineered, each culvert bridged by blocks of cut stone. At the places most vulnerable to landslide, junipers had been planted below the leading edge – gnarled white bones now, with just a frizz of dark green – to bind the road's foundations.

It was eerie, as though they were climbing back in time towards an old, lost mystery of spirit. There were hidden powers, Khan had always known. He had felt them when riding alone, energies and impulses emanating from the air and rocks, glimpses of distant happenings. And a deeper power running through the self, a river, to be dammed and used as they now used the waters of Sorubi – to create miracles. But one needed a key to close the sluices, to arrest and harness that power. Perhaps prayer was that key, or had been once when prayer and man were young. But for ages now, he felt, it had been lost. What if the Lily had found it? *The forces of Allah being with her*. The lodestone. Mightier than all the Russian hosts and their technology.

Whatever the truth, he was relieved to be on the road, no longer dodging rocks and brush with his trailing, aching feet. As, no doubt, were the two weary animals. McCabe also. Though a man of physical hardness, the altitude was beginning to steal his breath. Only Ayesha and Hafiq moved strongly still, their heads raised to the heights expectantly, though a few *kro* still separated them from the dot on the map that marked their destination.

They had puzzled over the dot. It bore no name. Villages were marked with a small square and a name. Spot-heights were marked with a dot, plus figures denoting altitude. There was one of these above them to the east, marked as 4200 metres – a mountain peak still with snow on it. But their destination was just a dot. A mystery.

Each leg of the road now led them closer to a mighty cleft in the rockface. At first it had been an unfathomable black shadow above them but as they drew level they saw it was full of colour. An eagle wheeled by its far wall, a mere speck against the orange and brown and water-melon hues of the limestone.

Rounding a bend in the sheer wall of the cleft they saw that the road followed the wall in a rising curve to disappear into the deepest recess of the concavity. No sign was visible that it continued above. Only when they had traversed the curve did the canyon reveal itself. With walls three hundred metres high, it cut back into the range – a water conduit. Water issued from it now in a silvery fringe which narrowed as it descended to atomize on the rocks far below. Great boulders littered its course and its flood level was prodigious, but the road continued unbroken along a platform of detritus above it.

They paused in awe. McCabe muttered something about the Lost World and dinosaurs. Already they could feel the cold. A moment ago they had been high, now they were deep down in lifeless gloom. It reminded Khan of his own gorge, but this was on a vast scale and serpentine, with no sunlight to show its end. Nor was it blocked purposely with rocks and debris and the decomposing bodies of his people.

They climbed for an hour without once emerging from the gorge. The road never faltered, though here and there they saw distinct signs of renovation, which seemed extraordinary in so remote a place.

McCabe remarked wistfully that they could have come all this way by taxi, and it was true. Hafiq said it was a fine time to think of it.

Ayesha spoke little. She kept her blanket gripped tightly under her chin and still she shivered. Once she stopped, certain that she could hear screams. McCabe told her it was the water-echo, but her senses told her that they were passing through the scene of some terrible tragedy, just as in Mir Bala.

Her mood spread to the others and they went on cheerlessly for another hour and a half. The sky had turned that fathomless blue which heralds mountain sunset. Was it their imagination or were the walls becoming slightly less lofty?

The eastern wall was first to abandon its scowl. They halted, arrested first by the golden blaze of sun on a spectacular outcrop, then by the realization that the outcrop was man-built, finally by the knowledge that this was it – the dot on the map!

The evening was so still they could hear McCabe's camera whirring a hundred feet below them.

'Keep moving!' He was a changed man; the weariness had gone. 'Stick as near to the outer edge as you can!'

Easy to suggest, but the beasts were exhausted and the track a mere scribble up the vertical slope.

The massive edifice, seen from directly below, seemed to reel against the sky. It could only have been a Buddhist monastery, built like a fortress. A thousand winters had come and gone since the Buddhists left the land, but they had only mellowed it to a oneness with the mountain.

Khan was puzzled, even shocked by the absence of life – no sentries, above or below, though there were signs of recent occupation – empty soup cans scattered on the slope, a baulk of timber protruding from an upper parapet with what appeared to be a block and tackle hanging from it.

Twice they paused on the steep climb to rest the animals. On the second stop McCabe came scrambling up to them, gulping the thin air, his eyes excited, eager to reach the top of the track ahead of them and film them as they came up.

There was no terrace, just a weathered doorway set deep in the angle of the wall. Beside it was a rusted iron ring. Hafiq wrenched at it.

Deep inside they heard the merest rumour of a clapper striking metal.

Khan touched the gun across his thighs uneasily.

McCabe focused on the door. Ayesha freed her weapon from her blanket, pulled her headscarf to conceal most of her face, and planted her feet.

The mountains waited, ridge upon backlit ridge to the west; to the north, a sort of headland, then nothing at all for fifty kilometres. Contained in the headland was a small lake with water so blue it could have been dye wrung from the indigo plant. To the east, above the monastery, reared another cliff and, above that, the snow-capped peak; to the south stretched rock bisected by the evil black fissure of the gorge.

The shock of a bolt being thrown made them all jump. There were two more shocks, then the door was dragged back against rubble and a fearsome visage with one trachoma-blind eye glared at them over the sights of a rifle.

Behind him crowded other faces with ragged beards and turbans and the same look of murderous stupidity. A red-bearded mullah parted the weapons and stepped out, greeting them with one hand raised to heaven and the other on his heart. He motioned two of the villains to help Khan from his mount, others to unload the boxes and see to the animals, then led the way inside without having spoken a word.

Darkness, cold and a stench of urine permeated the lower regions of the building. The passageway burrowed through masonry and natural rock alike, revealing side chambers filled with the rubbish of occupation that could not be dumped outside for fear of alerting aerial reconnaissance. There were steps, some leading down, and Khan glimpsed an entrance hewn into the bedrock that looked like a mine.

As they climbed, there were more windows – more light. They were coming to the old living quarters, open cells, some of which were occupied by men like these who escorted them, around charcoal *sigris* huddled against the cold.

Weaponry and ammunition were stacked in the familiar anonymous boxes donated by the Americans via Egypt and China. Fierce eyes glanced round to stare after them, but with never a smile. The man carrying Khan seemed to be all wire and bone. His smell was animal. Were these the 'forces of Allah' boasted by the Lily? They looked like wild men. Khan's lips were close to the tangle of black curls that concealed an ear, and he spoke to him quietly.

'Where are you from, brother?'

'The Kunar.'

Khan knew that he was not a Pathan and not a Nuristani. Nor a Tajik, Hazara, Uzbek or Aimaq.

'From which side of the border – Afghanistan or Pakistan?'

'There has never been a border,' growled the man. 'That is tribal land.'

Khan guessed then that these men were Gujaras – wandering nomad shepherds of evil repute.

'How many of you are there here?'

The man grunted, 'I know not.'

'Roughly?'

'A hundred? A thousand?' The fellow neither knew nor cared.

That they could fight, Khan did not doubt – but with knives in backs rather than face to face, and he doubted if the Russians would be that obliging.

They climbed to a higher level. Then another. At last the passage led to an open portal topped by a lintel carved into five crude stone arches one inside the other. A recurring pattern was discernible on each, painted in pale blue, gold and white. The gold looked like halos but, if so, the faces they surrounded had faded to obscurity.

They passed under it to enter a chamber with mottled brown walls pocked with white. The mottling was age, the brown had been red, depicting the clothing of a succession of Buddhas, the white was bullet-holes. Each likeness had been defaced in the Moslem way, by bullets through both eyes and the nose.

Islamic art did not permit the representation of human form and the elegant figures with naked torsos were unexpected and disturbing. Alien. Though not so alien as the powerful black machines that spanned the long bench beneath them. One was a radio transmitter – twice the size of the one at Mir Bala.

A mullah sat erect at the controls, headphones straddling his turban. He was listening intently, jotting down notes, and did not look round.

Khan saw that Hafiq was bristling and sniffing like a dog at all this strangeness. Accustomed to his devil-may-care swagger, Khan eyed him questioningly, but Hafiq avoided his gaze, squared his shoulders and took a stride after the mullah, who was beckoning them into a smaller chamber. Five more mullahs sat in cross-legged debate around a low table covered with maps and papers. They broke off immediately and their leader came to his feet.

'*Allaho akbar!* Welcome to Qassassin!'

Khan recognized at once the voice in his headphones at Mir Bala. The fellow's stature matched his voice, but even if he had been as big as Takredi he was still only a mullah, hardly a man of war. Mullahs and Gujaras, and the Lily had spurned his offer of a trained fighting force! His gaze strayed beyond the leader – and stopped in shock.

Abdalis!

Or was it his ghost? Leaner, older-looking, an even darker shadow. But there was no mistaking the wrath of Allah in that hypnotic gaze, nor the way he grew jointlessly to his feet. Abdalis waited quite still for Dhost to end the greeting ritual, then stepped forward. But there was no private warmth in his eyes, simply unsurprised recognition.

'Son of Ahmed. It seems we are carried along by the same stream, sometimes touching.'

Never touching, Khan thought. He would have embraced

him, and through him his valley, his loves, his memories, but the mullah's manner repelled the impulse.

'Takredi said that when he found us you were dead!'

'Perhaps I am.' Abdalis's gaze passed over Ayesha without a flicker, to rest briefly, curiously, on Hafiq and McCabe. 'Perhaps we all are. If not, a few hours will rectify the oversight.'

There was never any answer to his theatricality. Khan asked him how he came to be here.

'Evidently I have sinned,' was the only answer he could extract from him, uttered, Khan sensed, more as a jibe at the listening mullahs than to his questioner. Clearly he was familiar with the circumstances that had brought them to Qassassin. He seemed to be holding back, listening almost. Like Hafiq.

Dhost interposed himself. 'I will show you to your quarters.'

'Wait.' Khan gripped the sinewy shoulders of his mount, holding him still. 'Take us first to the Lily, that we may pay our respects.'

'Perhaps later.' Dhost turned them all with his powerful arms and prepared to lead the way.

'Not later!' shrieked a voice. 'Now! Bring them to me!'

Dhost hesitated. Khan saw Abdalis looking at him, a wolfish smile on his lips. Dhost motioned them to stay where they were and strode through to an adjoining doorway. He spoke through the hanging in tones of deep respect, saying there was danger. The new arrivals must be searched.

'Bring them, I say!' screamed the voice. 'Speak not of danger to an immortal, you mumbling idiot. Bring them all!'

Dhost came back slowly, his handsome brow troubled.

'Did I not say she would not wait?' Abdalis demanded in glee.

Dhost's gaze consulted his colleagues. They looked uneasy, but how could they disobey? Clustering around Khan's party, they escorted them to the curtain and told them to lay aside their weapons and remove their shoes.

Hafiq refused.

Dhost turned on him with a look of extraordinary venom. He drew a sword from beneath his robe and laid it against Hafiq's bearded throat.

For a long moment Hafiq matched his scowl. Then with a

short laugh he leaned his weapon against the wall and trod off his *chuplis*.

The sword remained poised while one of the mullahs searched him from turban to ankle, removing the knife at his belt and tossing it to the floor. The curtain was finally drawn aside and they were pushed into the Lily's chamber.

Khan's mount deposited him without ceremony on the stone flagging and fled, his face averted. The mullahs, except for Dhost, remained outside.

In the dimness Khan saw first only the cresset and a jar of smouldering joss-sticks, then gradually the dais. The shadowy figure of the Lily seated in her alcove of spidery hangings grew on his retina like an apparition. She screamed at the other three to kneel.

'Down!' The flat of Dhost's sword whacked across their backs, driving them to their knees.

The apparition ordered them closer.

They crawled towards the divan, Khan beginning to doubt his senses.

'Now confess! Which of you is the traitor?'

In the astonished silence that followed, Dhost murmured, 'But you know which, O Immortal Soul. Did you not . . .'

'Silence!' The Lily, whatever she knew, was determined to have her ritual. 'Strip them!'

Dhost made no move of compliance. Perhaps he was remembering that to display any part of the body was against God's law. However, this was neither the time nor place to protest. He ordered them to strip.

Khan scarcely heard him. His mind was in turmoil, an echo chamber of dead voices, and of one especially.

Hafiq leapt to his feet shouting that he would not strip, not even kneel, before any man – or woman!

The Lily let out a scream of fury. She ordered him to be taken out and flogged.

The curtain was swept aside. In rushed the other mullahs. Hafiq was dragged struggling away.

Khan found his tongue, bewildered by the emotions kindled by his senses. Angrily he reminded her that they had journeyed here of their own free will to aid her in her struggle. Had they expected to be treated like dogs, they would never have come!

'Those who dare question the Lily *are* dogs!' she cried. 'Listen how he howls!'

Hafiq's enraged voice echoed through the building, accompanied by the sound of blows.

She began to sway back and forth, as if in ecstasy or pain. Khan thought either she is mad or this is a hoax in cruel taste. But his body was trembling. Could this be her? If so, what in Allah's name could so have changed her, and why did she not seem to recognize him?

She was speaking again. 'Very well, if it displeases you to strip . . .' she made a conciliatory gesture towards Dhost, one that resolved itself into a pointing finger.

The mullah moved into the shadows and stooped over something – a little box. He returned with a handful of small, round objects. He told Khan, McCabe and Ayesha to each take one in their mouths.

Khan ignored him and demanded an end to this charade.

'Good Khan,' the Lily's voice was suddenly honeyed – and now Khan knew. *He knew.* 'Have faith. There is a path whereby even the blind may meet with revelation. It is called forbearance.' She waited, watching him through the black mesh. 'Nothing here is without good reason, as you will see. Now do as you are bid.'

Khan obeyed. He would have swallowed it, if told to. The other two followed suit. His tongue explored the object's coolness and roundness and smoothness. It was a stone. No more, no less.

Suddenly Hafiq, stark naked, his powerful body whipcorded with fury, was thrust back into the room and forced to his knees.

'Nothing,' grunted one of the accompanying mullahs to Dhost. 'He carried nothing.'

A stone was pushed into Hafiq's mouth also. He spat it out. It was forced in again by Dhost, who gripped his jaw shut until Redbeard had fetched the discarded knife and braced its point under Hafiq's chin.

'The stones will speak of treachery,' the Lily cried. She began to wail, 'Speak, stones, speak . . .' over and over, rocking stiffly, as if in a trance.

Khan watched her in thrall. He would have laughed or wept, but Hafiq's stertorous breaths beside him held him to the harsh reality of it. Hafiq was his brother, being forced – by whom it did not matter – to submit to an indignity. *He carried nothing.* What did they expect him to be carrying? In sudden disgust, Khan spat his stone to the floor.

One of the mullahs pounced on it and held it, glistening, close to the cresset. Immediately McCabe's and Ayesha's stones were extracted and scrutinized.

Now the knife was removed and Hafiq's stone advanced to the light. It glinted but dully. All had been wet with saliva save his.

Khan at first thought it was a different kind of stone. Then he thought, his mouth is dry with fury. Then he thought, fury stimulates the body juices; only one emotion inhibits them. Could his fury have been masking fear?

Hafiq needed no such speculation. Understanding the trick in an instant, he sprang to his feet with a shout, twisted his knife from the mullah's grasp and rushed towards the Lily.

The blade was within inches of her veiled throat when Dhost's sword sliced down through his shoulder, severing his arm. For an incredulous moment Hafiq stared down at his arm on the flagstones – his strong right arm with the knife still clutched in the hand. He made a curious movement with the other, as if to pick it up; though perhaps, Khan thought afterwards, it was to retrieve the knife. There was a swipe of wind as the sword again clove an arc. Hafiq's head toppled from his shoulders.

Khan, McCabe and Ayesha sat in shock in the planning room while a thorough cleaning of Lily's chamber took precedence over everything but the examination of the body. There was no attempt to shield it from their gaze. The mullahs pored over it with no more emotion than a group of tribal women skinning a camel, pulling it this way and that, prying without revulsion into its orifices, searching his sweat-soiled clothes, feeling minutely along every inch of the material. The head was put on a table, the bloodless lips prized apart. Pencils were poked behind the teeth, into the ears.

Khan sat, his pulses thudding, his mind groping for an explanation. Events seemed to have lost all relationship to reality. McCabe and Ayesha were agreed that Hafiq had been provoked into the action that cost him his life. The doctor, red-eyed, her throat so tight that she could hardly speak, kept repeating, 'If I had known it would be like this I would never have come. Better the illusion. Far better the illusion!' McCabe was for cutting their losses and getting out now, while they still had their weapons.

Then at last the mullahs found the homing device they were looking for. Hafiq's left sandal, which had remained overlooked outside the Lily's chamber, had to be held in front of the three of them and its heel prized apart to reveal the small miracle of electronics nestling in its womb, before they could accept the truth.

Even then, they could not quite assimilate it. It was only when Khan thought back to the Choukha that he saw the possible explanation.

His puzzlement and resentment vanished in a flood of relief, though the mystery did not. Why, if Pola – and it *was* his Pola without a doubt – had understood Hafiq's role from the start, had she allowed, even encouraged him to come here, knowing that the device he carried could lead the Russians to her door? If a second tracking party had taken up their trail, they could still be receiving its signals.

If Khan could have walked on his own feet he would have stridden straight into Pola's chamber, taken her in his arms and coaxed from her the whole extraordinary truth. But there was another factor – her refusal to recognize him in the presence of the others. Was it to preserve her own role? If so, he should do nothing to prejudice her position.

Anyway, McCabe was performing strangely with the device, advancing it towards the transmitter. There was a penetrating whine.

He glanced back at Khan in grim triumph, then looked around for a tool with which to deactivate it.

Eventually he beat it to bits on the flagging.

He straightened to face the mullahs, his manner scathing.

'Brilliant! You know what you've done, of course?'

When Ayesha had translated, red-bearded Mirdad nodded calmly. To let the Russians discover their whereabouts had been part of the Lily's plan. The honourable guest was not to worry. Through her, Allah Himself was directing their strategy.

The cameraman rolled his eyes to heaven.

'Whoever's directing it, old tiger,' he said, 'we're as good as dead.'

The mullahs lifted their shoulders. They did not deny it.

Sergeant Berzin had paused in the darkness and was urinating towards the torrent below when Corporal Ezhov called to him that the homing signal had stopped. A glance over his shoulder showed Berzin that the screen, under its hood, still glowed a healthy blue, so there could be nothing wrong with the power-pack. He told him to check the aerial connections.

Buttoning his fly and hunching against the cold, Berzin moved towards the agitated pool of Ezhov's inspection light. The other three trackers were deployed out of sight in lookout positions – the routine when stationary.

Berzin eyed the empty screen, fishing for a cigarette. He was thinking that tomorrow was his thirtieth birthday and this was a hell of a place in which to spend it.

Until a moment ago, the blip had been winking steadily between the same gridlines for – he squinted at his watch – nigh on two hours, signifying that Khan had come to more than a casual halt. They had closed up on his position cautiously, bearing in mind the fate of their predecessors, seeking either a visual fix or to triangulate from a narrow base, and now they had reached the blind-approach limit of two kilometres from source and were stuck. But the apparatus was accurate and Berzin well-versed in its operation, added to which the grid position corresponded so exactly with a feature on the map as to preclude coincidence. The feature, to judge by its cartographic key, was an 'Historical Building, Monument or Ruin' bearing the name Qassassin.

'Comrade sergeant, the connections are good.'

Berzin had rather expected they would be. He watched his smoke against the inspection light and noted that a breeze was getting up, the acid breath of snow in it.

He said slowly, 'Well then, either it's the circuitry or they've discovered our homer and deactivated it.'

Ezhov digested this possibility in startled silence. 'In that case, shouldn't we—'

'Shh!' Berzin inclined his ear to the breeze, He took a drag on the cigarette in his cupped hand, then stamped it out and stood listening. Ezhov doused the inspection light and switched off the screen.

'What is it?'

The water echo made other sound waves hard to interpret. Anyway, whatever had caught his attention had faded. But he did not relax completely.

He told the corporal to contact the relay truck and transmit the fix on Khan's position immediately.

Ezhov moved at once to obey, but could get no return signal. He tried again.

The truck, Berzin guessed, would be parked in the foothills. The range was no problem. It had to be all the kinks in this bloody ravine.

The corporal was trying a third time when Berzin heard it again, this time clearer. It sounded like the tramp of feet. He told Ezhov to switch off. They listened intently.

Yes. Not the munching-toast kind of feet, like troops, but *thudding* kind of feet, a great many of them. Afghan, ambling kind of feet. Some way off, by the sound of it. The gorge, aided by the breeze, seemed to be working as an amplifier.

The lookouts came rushing back.

'Sounds like a damn great army coming, comrade Sergeant!'

Berzin debated. If Qassassin *was* the Lily's stronghold it was not impossible for a large body of men to be in the vicinity.

His team were peering at him anxiously, waiting for an explanation or the order to evacuate. Berzin was loath to retreat without instructions from Battalion. Anyway, it was their duty to observe an enemy force, estimate its strength. The question was, in this blasted ravine, observe from where?

Now he became aware that faint squealings and screechings had joined the growing volume of sound. He felt the hair lift on the nape of his neck. His practised ear knew those sounds as well as his own breathing, and it just wasn't possible!

His men knew too. They stood riveted in disbelief, then a prolonged gust brought to their ears the clatter of tracks and the thunder of multi-horsepower engines.

The truth then was inescapable: a large body of men supported by an armoured force was advancing towards them along the ravine!

Sergeant Berzin and his men grabbed their equipment and fled.

33

DESPITE THE lateness of the hour, the GRU building was lit from end to end like a cruise-liner. Cypher signals were coming in rasping bursts and the office staffs in the vicinity complained so angrily about the to-and-fro traffic that the runners were ordered to take their boots off and deliver in stockinged feet.

Pre-operation time was always more frenetic than even D-Day, everyone anxious for reassurance that all was going according to schedule because if it wasn't there was still time to put it right. But let that opportunity slip and, Yakushev knew, the whole plan could fade into the ground, with the Baluchi ringleaders getting cold feet, and indecision creeping into the back-up arrangements. It was so damn easy, dealing with Islamics, for the fire to go out. They only had to see Allah's hand in a couple of mishaps, and despair spread right through them.

So far, to Yakushev and his staff at the receiving end, all seemed well. But there was another full day to go and the Afghan Moslem troops earmarked for the 'policing action' were still an imponderable, though reports said that the absence of more *chabnameh* and other propaganda was having a stabilizing effect. But where was the recce report on Khan? Since late afternoon Yakushev had been rifling every batch of incoming signals for it. He had hoped it would arrive by nightfall because shortly after that the guards armoured division would be resuming its journey to Kandahar. Firm news giving a fix on the Lily might have convinced Solkholov to stall it at Ghazni for a further night, but now that chance had gone and there was no stand-by force at all.

It was not until 23.35 hours that Goriansky burst in and pushed the message under his nose. The sergeant was in on it now. Everyone in the GRU was in on it. His hand was shaking.

Yakushev perused the signal rapidly. The reason for the delay was a 'break in radio communication necessitating a ten-kilometre backtrack and consequent loss of screen contact with blip-source'. However, here it was – the fix, coupled with some astounding intelligence that confirmed everything he had anticipated. More than everything. They even had armour up there, for God's sake; where had they got *that*? Every step he had taken, every warning he had uttered, his inspired stand against Solkholov yesterday – all were justified.

Yakushev carried the message to Dolin and handed it to him without comment. The general did his utmost to reveal nothing but, watching hungrily, Yakushev saw his eyes widen. Before he had finished reading, one hand was groping blindly for the telephone.

'Front headquarters, Marshal Solkholov!'

It was all Yakushev waited to hear. Dolin could bullshit, strike all the 'as we suspected' poses he liked, but Solkholov knew whom to thank for this priceless information. How he responded to it was up to him; he could even send in the bloody Moslems if he liked. And if they deserted to the Lily, so much the better; that would raise Yakushev's stock even higher – especially if, in the interim, the Lily was neutralized without a shot being fired – assassinated by Yakushev's own agent, about whom he had breathed not a word to anyone! That, however, would be a bonus, and was not to be relied on.

Back in his office, Yakushev just sat for a while, gazing at his reflection in the window and pictured himself for a moment in a large, well-furnished office, holding not a sinecure in the hierarchy but a position of vigour and decisiveness as one of the New Wave, whose energy and pragmatism would sweep away the geriatrics as surely as his counterparts were doing in China at this moment.

He shut his mind to the image. No, it was bad luck to count your chickens. Think first of the things that could go wrong and how to profit by them. There could be no air recce till tomorrow first light. Solkholov and his generals would confer on the results, then order their air strike while whatever ground response they decided on was being assembled. And the Lily – what would she be doing? Making the utmost of every second; you could count on that.

Yakushev remembered the tapes substituted for the propaganda broadcasts to the camps. They should provide the clue.

He slipped one into the tape-deck, triggered the playback and settled back with a cigarette.

It was only as the recording neared its end that he realized it included a short exhortation by the Lily herself.

He listened in shock.

The Lily had dismissed them all except Khan. It fell to the youngest mullah to conduct McCabe and Ayesha on a tour of the monastery. McCabe was in no mood for it. He had eaten nothing for fourteen hours. Ayesha, too, was looking grey. She moved like a sleepwalker, head back, arms and hips slack, swaying slightly as she climbed the many flights of steps.

It was as they returned from inspecting the throbbing power generators, the reserves of arms, ammunition, food stored in the catacombs below the monastery that they caught the unmistakable squeaking rumble of heavy tanks. McCabe shot to the nearest window in alarm. *Already?*

Ayesha hung out beside him. Together, they listened to the sounds swelling and fading on the chill night wind.

The mullah had a rather high, nice laugh like a girl's.

'It sounds very real, yes? You did not see the loudspeakers as you journeyed up the ravine?'

They turned to him in disbelief. McCabe inclined his ear again, but still could detect no flaw in the quality of sound. 'Is he having us on?'

'The Lily wishes those who followed you here to carry home with them reports of great strength.'

McCabe made a distracted noise. 'All this gear, sophisticated communications equipment – who supplies it, ask him?'

The mullah replied carefully, 'Islam is generous. We buy.'

'If it's so generous why don't you buy the real thing – tanks, gunships, rocket-launchers, recruit a proper army?'

'We do not need them.'

'You'll find out tomorrow whether you'll need them!' Hunger sharpened McCabe's temper.

As they mounted to the top level, they did indeed encounter rocket-launchers – the small hand-held anti-aircraft model known as SAM-7. They were being broken out of their boxes and checked by Gujaras before being installed on the roof. Following them up, McCabe and Ayesha saw sandbag emplacements against the more intact parapets and under the changing levels of the flat roofs, which rose in tiers to butt into the cliff behind. Instead of standing free, McCabe realized, the whole building was part of the cliff itself. No wonder it had stood for so long!

The mullah pointed mutely, as if to say, 'See? We are not so unprepared,' but McCabe was not impressed. The SAM-7s were okay for platoon protection, keeping the gunships off – they were used by the Soviet army for that purpose – but they were only tail-shooters. Their heat-seeking heads homed on the plane's exhaust, which meant they could only be fired effectively at a target moving away, and anything over Mach-2 could outstrip them.

He saw Ayesha begin to reel and caught her just in time, holding her steady.

'Look, sweetheart, tell him if they don't rustle up some food soon you're going to collapse.'

Ayesha told him. The mullah murmured apologetically and went below.

'He is going to hurry them. He will let us know the moment it is ready.'

'Come and sit down.' McCabe steered her gently over the roofs and up on to the natural rock. He found an even place and they sat down. He took her hand. It felt bloodless. For once she did not resist.

'Too cold up here? Would you rather go down?'

She seemed either too exhausted or upset to reply.

They sat and watched the Gujaras ferrying up the slender missiles, stacking them in the emplacements – anachronistic shapes against the bright arc of stars, not another living thing for miles, just range after range of mountains.

'Did you ever see a film called *Idiot's Delight?*'

She shook her head.

'I suppose you wouldn't. Hellish old. I must have seen it on TV.'

'Oh?' She wasn't interested in films, only reality.

Except this wasn't reality; war never was. It cut life up into tiny fragments and pasted them back all wrong.

'It was about idiots like us, on the brink of a holocaust.'

She put her other cold hand on his and shivered. He guessed she was remembering Hafiq, the obscene deluge of blood. Not even in a movie would they have dreamed up the Lily. She was a figment of need, he reckoned. Maybe the Allah freaks had fished her out of a madhouse.

'Crazy thing is, I miss the son of a bitch.' He was referring to Hafiq.

'I also.' She added darkly, 'But I think not for long.'

'Reckon we'll all meet again, do you? Among the fountains and fruit?' He was too late to screen out the bitterness.

'It is what I pray.'

He softened it this time. 'See your husband Omar?'

She did not reply immediately. 'Do you not have someone . . . waiting?'

'I used to think my old dog might be. But I guess by now he's gone off to hunt rabbits.'

'But not people?'

'He didn't hunt people.'

'I mean, you don't think people are waiting?'

'Do you reckon they have rabbits up there?'

'Why won't you answer me?' She pushed her hair back, trying to see his face in the darkness.

'Just to make you look at me.'

She just managed to hold his gaze.

'All right, I am looking.'

She waited, her cold hands conveying the tension this induced. Afghan girls were conditioned from birth not to meet the eye of the predatory male.

'Tell me honestly, what do you see?'

'See?' She shrugged, suddenly wary. 'I see . . .' Down went her head but she brought it up again. 'How can I put the way I see you into a few words? Besides . . .' She left the objection unfinished.

'Have a try. I need to know.'

She sighed. 'You are . . . I don't know. A friend. A good friend. But still a stranger.'

'Stranger?' It surprised him. 'How a stranger?'

Away went her face into its Pathan profile. 'I learned your language at university but not your – how shall I say? – culture. The way you do things without God has been a shock. Down inside, where we become Allah, you remain yourself. You are your own direction, your own judge. You try to be fair, but the true workings of *kismet* in all the terrible things you have seen confuse you. But you have to make sense of it and there *is* no sense, not that you and I may understand, but you go on trying, and we do not. That is our difference. And that is what makes you a stranger.'

'Hm. Fair enough,' McCabe allowed. 'That's the way you see me. Now how do you *feel* about me?'

She sat up a little, drawing her hands away slowly.

'I feel . . . what I said. That we are friends.'

'But do you like me, dammit, trust me?'

'Michael . . .' She groped for a moment, then said lamely, 'I know what you are asking and that is my answer.'

'So you do know,' he said softly.

Her gaze roved everywhere but in his direction as she said in a voice carefully purged of expression, 'I know how you look at me sometimes. In the mornings when we wake. When we are talking. But it is normal. We are human. We have certain impulses, certain needs. It does not mean—'

'You say "we".' He pounced on it.

'I speak not good English.'

'You speak bloody marvellous English! But you won't use it to *communicate*. No one can hear us, we're alone – what are you scared of?'

She turned on him. 'Do I have to write it that we are of different worlds? I like you, I trust you, I respect you – why will you not respect *me*, *this*?' She stuck out her black armband. 'Have I not made it clear that I am still part of my husband and the struggle for which he died?'

'But he's dead, Ayesha.'

'That is final only for you, not us. He is watching from above and will not let me rest till I have helped drive the Russians back across the Oxus.'

'Girl, that could be for ever! They never let go, don't you know that? Estonia, Latvia, Lithuania, Eastern Europe – they *never let go*!'

'And we never give up, don't you know that! We will fight them till death!'

McCabe threw up his hands.

'You're high, sweetheart, high on war. You're on negative. Listen – I'll tell you something – there's a switch inside us. Flip it and we change polarity, positive to negative, the fury and hate in us legitimized. War does that. Losing your husband to the Russians, I guess, does it. You'd like to see their entire army slaughtered to a man, right?'

'To a man, yes!'

'Remember the Germans and the Jews? They felt the same way. Negative trip. It's like addiction, hell to get off. You'd like to, but you can't face it, face who you are without a gun in your hand and all that adrenalin.'

'You are saying . . .' she was struggling angrily with his use of the idiom, 'that I am an addict?'

'As one to another, yes. And now the revenge bit is getting a grip on me too. It's time for us to come down, sweetheart, while we can still live with ourselves. Love is the only antidote. The strongest positive there is. A high in the opposite direction.' He paused, peering at her. 'You with me, or do you want me to translate?'

'You speak as if we are all sick!'

'Look around you. All this. What we're doing here. Hafiq. The Lily. It's a mental hospital. Idiot's delight.'

She rose to her feet in a storm of movement. If he hadn't gripped her arm she'd have rushed away.

'We defend ourselves against a monster in the only way we know how and we are sick!' she screamed. '*You* are sick. What happened in Somalia has turned your mind!'

'Easy, sweetheart.'

'Let go of me, let go, you—'

'Not until you hear me out. Please?'

He waited, gripping her till her fury had subsided.

'Okay,' he conceded, 'I overstated. We're both tired and hungry. But one thing stands. When this thing's over, if we're still alive, I'll be going back to London. I want you to come with me. Shh – *listen*. If you decide to come back here afterwards, I can't stop you. But allow yourself that one break from this vicious circle, that's all I ask. Then we'll see where we go.'

She was still fuming. He wanted to tell her that he was in love with her, but he couldn't.

'Will you do that, sweetheart? If not for yourself, then for me?'

She looked, almost in slow-motion, down at her arm and

said through her teeth, 'Michael, you have your answer. It is in your hand.'

Mystified, McCabe followed her eyeline. He released it slowly – the black band.

Pola's heart thumped her ribs. Joy and terror took turns in her breast. In a fever she gazed out at him where his carriers had lowered him before fleeing.

She could see him only as one sees the new moon, by a thin rind of illumination – the hard, dark gleam of a cheek, the cave of one eye. She filled in the rest from loving memory, to find it did not tally. Her Khan had changed. Leaner, and injury to the nose, yes, but the difference lay deeper. He was scarred. Bitterness had never been a part of him, yet it was now.

He came towards her eagerly, his weight on his knuckles, all pain forgotten. She stopped him with a gesture, listening intently. Abdalis was the only one who would dare eavesdrop, but she could usually detect him and he was not there now. So why did she hesitate? From fright, was the answer. From shame of her condition, the physical complication, the confusion of who she was.

'My Pola!' He hoisted himself on to the couch and made to crush her in his arms. She withdrew convulsively.

'No – in case they come – no!'

He laughed. 'Let them come!'

'You don't understand! And we must speak softly.'

'Why? Are you their prisoner?' he asked sharply.

'A prisoner, yes. But yours, beloved, not theirs.'

He looked relieved. 'Then let me see my prisoner!'

'No.' She caught his hand before it reached her veil. 'Soon. Have patience. There are things to be explained before—'

'We're both *alive*, Pola – the rest can come later!'

His joy was overwhelming. She pushed out her hands to hold him away. He seized them and kissed her palms, then held them to his chest, and she could feel his rekindled power, smell the sweat of his journey, leather, the animal he must have ridden. Sunlit memory struggled through her terror. She clung hard to the image of herself he was remembering, but it no longer had substance. It had been so long, too long. She had sacrificed being a woman to become a goddess. She had done it for him, his beloved family and valley, for all who had suffered under the Russian onslaught, for her own father, and, lastly, for herself, her trampled ideals, exploited trust and abused body. But the price had cost her her very identity.

Some of this she had said aloud, she was sure of it by his strange look. She hurried on, clinging to the threads of her lost self, talking as she might have talked, asking about his feet, did they hurt terribly? She had heard what Yasir did to him and had suffered with him, wept for him.

He dismissed the subject. 'He is dead now, and the bones will heal.' He wanted to know about *her*, how she had survived, the change in her. She was an unbeliever and detested all mullahs, yet she was lording it over them, quoting the Koran like a *sufi*! And, even more incredible, espoused to the veil! Did the mullahs actually *believe* in her? How had she managed to fool them?

He was almost laughing, her sombre love, full of joy and curiosity. She tried to rise to his mood but found herself hanging back, even resentful that he was not taking her seriously, that somehow she was being brought to account.

She parried by telling him of the reliefs and agonies she had suffered watching him, his victories and disasters, from her dark tower. She saw the joy slowly fade. He peered at her intently, as if to penetrate the veil.

Why had she not sent word to him that she was still alive?

Because Abdalis had been watching for her to contact him, she told him. 'But I sent you guidance, calling myself the Lily. I hoped you'd understand.'

His head had been too full, he admitted, or too empty.

'Be honest,' she chided him. 'You had forgotten it. The poem? Our last night together?'

He denied it.

'Listen.' She leaned towards him. 'Do you remember on the ridge, when we stood together and you talked of Tamerlane? What a general you were, beloved! But Allah, that terrible time, was not with us.' She added triumphantly, 'He is with us now!'

Why the shadow of embarrassment? Had she sounded so theatrical?

'You should still have let me bring the guns and men,' Khan told her.

'We do not need them. Truly, beloved. Trust me.'

'The whole resistance trust you. You could have had the pick of every group if you had asked – a hundred thousand men!' He added, 'Even though that's no way to fight the *schurawi*. Confrontation is their game. Ours is time.'

'Beloved, there *is* no time. You do not know of the planned Baluchi secession?' She explained quickly what she knew.

Khan frowned. He seemed bewildered.

'The day following tomorrow?'

'That is when it will begin.'

'And you think you can distract them from their purpose?'

'With a miracle, yes!'

'Pola . . .' Words failed him. He clawed the hair of his beard, staring at the cresset. 'The place' – he embraced the monastery with a gesture of concession – 'is well chosen. But to entrust its defence to a few mullahs, a handful of—'

'And to Ghoram Khan,' she cried. 'Who better to infuse them with the will to fight than you, my love!'

He lowered his head and shook it.

'You are a child.' Then, 'If you had called me sooner . . .'

'Just as,' she would make her point now, 'who better than the photographer to record our victory for the whole world to see?'

'Victory? You are dreaming.'

'And who better than the little doctor to perform the sacred service that will be required of her? Who better than Hafiq to lead the Russians to our door? Do you not see? None of it has been chance. And there is yet another to come – the penultimate bead I have threaded on my necklace of death – to descend from the heavens so that Almighty Allah's will be done!'

Khan gave a sigh. 'You cannot change military facts with mystic words, my Pola.'

'Words and *deeds*, beloved. Is not war power? Is not Allah's power greater than all the armies of the Kremlin?'

'If it were, those armies would never have crossed the Oxus!'

'They have been brought here to founder on our rocks!'

'Do you think I haven't dreamed of such power?' He sounded weary. 'But there is a cold reality to things that can't be ignored, Pola. We are such and they are so; words, self-delusion will not alter it. Bitter experience has taught me this.'

'Beloved, listen—' She broke off, giving a little gasp as the child kicked hard inside her. She put her arms around her belly. 'He is so strong.'

Khan frowned impatiently. 'When . . . is it to be?'

She was amazed that he had not made the association. No wonder he clung so stubbornly to doubt! 'It will be when it *must* be. When I have willed it to be! A woman, with Allah's help, has power over these things, did you not know? Especially in the final month.'

She saw his preoccupation give way to calculation, saw it dawn then that it was almost nine months since the destruction of his valley. She watched, in sudden agony, the seed of terrible suspicion take root.

'And do you not know,' she almost shouted to dispel the image, 'what is this month on our calendar?'

'Our' meant Islamic, the Hijra year.

'Ramadan, of course.'

'*Also the ninth month.*' She leaned closer. 'And do you know what is tomorrow? The twenty-seventh, beloved. *The Night of Power!*'

Yes, he knew.

'*That* is when it will be!' she told him triumphantly. 'Now explain to me how it is that the Baluchi uprising coincides almost exactly with that date! Don't you see the poetry, the mystery, the glory of it? The skies alight, the mountains lifting, divine power surging to our aid as the Prophet comes among us again, a tiny ancient child, to lead us and all Islam to victory! Don't you see in it every sign you have ever searched for? Pray for him, beloved. Pray for my baby!'

She waited, shining, confident of his response.

Khan said brokenly, 'Oh, my Pola.'

She recoiled from his sudden compassion as from a snake. But he put his arms around her.

'Don't touch me! No – please!'

'Shh. Be still, beloved, I am here.' He nursed her to his chest as if she were demented.

Appalled by his pity, she beat her fists against him. The more she struggled, the more compassionately he held her.

'It is over,' he murmured. 'Rest still. Whatever happened, whatever they did to you, is past. We are together now. What else matters?' He was stroking her head. Gradually her struggles diminished. 'We will leave here tonight. Disband this folly. Be far away by dawn.'

She submitted to his embrace numbly. Tears of chagrin wet her veil. Suddenly here he was consoling her, talking of love, drawing her into the darkness of himself as in the old days – and it was good, oh yes – but talking of the future, as if, as if . . . the child were just a figment and all the power she had gathered, as the hills gather static charges before a mighty storm, a mere vagary, when in her womb she held a miracle! Had she not wakened at night and heard it screaming, screaming in her belly?

Yet she was so starved of his touch that she rested unresistingly in his arms and let words and memories have their moment: the cottage behind the schoolhouse, his naked body bent over the fire, the black shadows and bearded heights of freedom after the prison of her own land, and gradually, despite herself, she felt the corners of her mouth curl upward, felt him lift back the veil and then the touch and rasp and animal sweetness of his lips on hers. All of life's joy seemed to distil itself in those few seconds in a farewell embrace. Drifting . . . from under her lids she watched him draw back to gaze at her. A reflex stirred deep in terrible alarm. With a cry she wrenched herself away and plunged her face in the cushions.

She felt him grasp her shoulders and try to pull her back to him, but she resisted with frantic strength, mouth open against the damask, tears flowing, her fingers knotting about the cleft gouged deep in her forehead by the glancing Russian bullet. She had seen his eyes, their split second of unguarded horror. His love, she hungered for, but more compassion she could not bear!

Clawing the veil back in place, she screamed for the mullahs to come quickly and remove him.

Saddened, apprehensive of tomorrow, Khan rolled himself in his blankets in one of the cells and wondered if he could ever sleep. If it had not been Pola's creation he would have aborted the whole operation. But it was loyalty to her, not faith in her, that prevented him.

As Khan's exhausted body dragged his brimming mind into sleep, Yakushev remained awake in his office – as awake as he had ever been, his heart stimulated to an unhealthy tattoo from a surfeit of coffee and nicotine.

He had played and replayed the tape till there was no doubt in his mind that the Lily was Pola. It was monstrous, impossible, yet in retrospect it seemed suddenly so obvious that he wondered why he hadn't known it all along. Who but a Russian with security connections would have understood how, with the minimum of equipment, to syphon off vital Soviet intelligence? Or that his own office was the clearing-house for it? And who other than someone who understood the workings of his mind would have gauged his responses to the mounting evidence of the Lily's operation, or known that he would try to use it for his own ends, even *how* he would use it?

The chilling thought then came to him that, through him, Solkholov was now dancing precisely to her instructions. Her objective was the foiling of *Zhātva* – Harvest – and he was advancing straight into her trap!

And that was only the military side. On the personal side she had been just as unerring. In the GRU, where the dissidence of even a distant relative incurred dismissal, the penalty for the defection of one's own wife was absolute. She had built him up deliberately, in order to shatter his career.

The ruthless brilliance of it filled him with fury. Nothing he had done could merit such hate. But forget her motives, what was she now manipulating him to do? What next jerk of his limbs was she trying to trigger?

He caught Dolin, via the internal phone, in the very act of heading for the squash club and bed; it was past one a.m.

Had Marshal Solkholov indicated precisely the measures he intended to employ against the Lily in the morning? he asked him.

Dolin, typically and rudely, wanted to know why.

'Because, comrade General, if you want me to give you everything I get when I get it, you've got to reciprocate,' Yakushev said flatly.

Dolin replied just as curtly that the marshal had halted the guards armoured division on its way to Kandahar and ordered it back to Ghazni. The rest of the plan, so far as he knew, remained as discussed in the marshal's office. Now what had Yakushev got for *him*?

No change, Yakushev snapped, and hung up.

So that was Solkholov's remedy, undoubtedly expected by Pola and in conformity with her plans.

Now what?

Hafiq? He realized now that Hafiq had been Pola's puppet, not his own. Similarly, it seemed likely that she had included her own voice at the end of the tape in order to identify herself to her husband and *only* to him. That was interesting, because she knew damn well that he'd never pass that information to anyone else. But what was her purpose?

To lure him to her personally? No, that would be the last thing she'd do. Her whole Aminah ploy was a bid to meld the forces of resistance through their mutual fear of God. The arrival of her husband, a *Russian*, would kill the mystical image stone dead. So?

So, on second thoughts, was she expecting him to do anything at all? Hadn't she already cut his professional throat? What more was there to do, other than watch him bleed to death?

In which case, whatever he did would come as a surprise, wouldn't it?

This conclusion steadied him. After all, his professional life was a chess game, played not with sixteen but hundreds of pieces, in countless simultaneous permutations and many moves ahead. And that was just for his daily bread. Now his career, everything he was working for, past, present and future, was at stake.

Yakushev took a full hour, working through every possible alternative. When he had made up his mind, he penned a signal direct to Solkholov – to hell with protocol, there was sufficient understanding between them now for the marshal to take serious heed of his advice.

It read, *In view of fresh intelligence, imperative you suspend all action against the Lily until you hear from me.*

Khan awoke after three hours' sleep. He gazed out of the window at the blackness and the torment of stars, then called for his Gujara mount.

Cursing and staggering, the man could barely support his weight at first. Khan called a second man and a third. They must take it in turns to carry him; there was much to be done and quickly.

His burst of automatic fire brought the garrison awake. Khan toured the building, ordering lanterns to be extinguished everywhere, except over the stairways and in essential internal chambers. Eyes must accustom themselves to the outer dark in order to set up machine-guns for all-round defence, Kalashnikovs for short-range fire, PKMBs and Lee Enfields for long. Ammunition reserves to be stacked in the corridors, shielded from incoming fire. Alternative positions designated on lower floors for when air attack made the upper ones untenable. Orders were given for manning, loading and ferrying.

The Gujaras, sleepy and surly at first, were gradually galvanized into a state of readiness. The mullahs meanwhile had assembled on the roof for their devotions. McCabe and Ayesha were already there, setting up the camera.

The solemn procession knelt, facing Mecca, only their turbans showing in the dark, bobbing forward and back in unison. McCabe thought they looked like paper lanterns in a breeze.

The night had been bitter. Still was – Ayesha muffled in her blanket, moody; McCabe cursing his numb fingers. They had scarcely spoken since last night.

'Where does this go?' Her breath plumed in the darkness.

He peered. 'Leave it in the box.' He hadn't been able to find any anti-freeze oil. He was wondering if he would need it. 'They have a fire going below, why don't you go and get warmed up?'

She didn't answer. He could have handled it on his own, but she seemed determined to be dogged.

'Go ahead, why don't you?' He opened up the camera and checked the gate, shining a pencil torch behind it to make sure there were no hairs. He shot her a glance. She kept her eyes on what he was doing, her pupils enormous, as if she were hypnotized by the little light. Her mouth was turned right down. He kept his gaze on her, waiting for her to meet it, but after a moment she turned and moved away.

McCabe laced up, then shut the gate. He gave the motor a flip. It started reluctantly in the cold. But it started. He wouldn't need the oil.

Ayesha was over by the parapet, staring into the darkness.

He joined her, to lean hunched beside her, his shoulder against hers. She did not ease away but she was giving off a sort of smouldering unease that discouraged speech.

Great, he thought. A great way to end it. This was probably their last day on earth.

'Feeling scared?' he said.

She made an impatient movement, but said nothing.

He peered towards the lake. Only the reflected stars showed where it was. Like a hole in the world, with sky underneath.

'I pushed too hard. I'm sorry about that. But I meant every word.'

'It was not the time.' She sounded furious.

'When else was there to say it – how I feel?'

'Did you think I would be grateful? Your patronizing offer!' She was shaking.

'Patronizing!'

'I don't want to talk about it.'

'You little idiot – don't you understand, I love you?'

She clapped her hands over her ears and twisted away.

He caught one wrist and pulled her around, speaking low because of the mullahs.

'Listen, I'll say it just once more. You and I are each other's way out of all this. I need you, *need* you, and you need me. Just come with me to England and—'

'I *have* a country, Michael. It is being invaded. I had a house. My sister and mother died there. A Russian tank destroyed it.'

He let go of her. 'You never told me. I'm sorry.' He clenched his teeth. 'Bastards!'

Her gaze lifted slowly to his. 'Say it again.' She gripped his wrists, exultant, ferocious. 'Say it more. More! You love me, make love to me with the words and the way you say them! Do it, Michael!'

Dazed, he felt her arms go tight around him, her pelvis thrust against his. 'Rape me with words, your hate! Let me feel it inside me.'

With the mullahs praying behind him, he forced her against the parapet in an all-consuming madness and felt her lift to him in sudden rapid traction and the breath explode in her throat. It was over in seconds – a convulsion, no more, their clothing still between them – leaving him cheated.

She wrenched away and leaned, breast heaving, on the parapet.

As control of his senses slowly returned he heard her weeping – a low, inconsolable wail, like an animal driven to distraction.

The stars grew pale. The cooks brought up great platters of *pillau*, *mast*, a dozen dixies of steaming tea. The whole garrison crowded on to the roof and squatted in circles and feasted.

McCabe and Ayesha sat with the mullahs. She neither looked at him nor spoke a word. Khan was delivered late by his three helpers. He, too, was silent, just sat in his own space and ate sparingly, concentrating on what remained to be done.

An awed murmur coursed through the gathering. Looking up, Khan saw a dark shape on the upper roof moving soundlessly back and forth. He could just detect the awkwardness, the uncomfortable thrust of her belly, and his heart went out to her.

Someone shouted 'Ali!' but the chant was not taken up. Abdalis took out his beads, pressed them to his forehead and closed his eyes. 'Drink now of the morning cold,' he murmured, 'for this day we will burn in hellfire for her heresy!'

Those who heard him pretended not to, but Khan said, 'Be still, holy man, or I will speed you into it.'

When the stars had all but faded, Dhost stood up and raised a white thread to the eastern sky, to see if it showed black or grey. If grey, they must end their feast, for the day would have begun.

But no, not yet grey. They feasted on.

Khan saw McCabe move to his camera. He directed it experimentally on to the gathering, then panned up to include Pola. He followed her silent pacing for some moments, then held up a small black box to the sky, as Dhost had done the thread. But its answer was the same. He came back and sat down.

A hush was beginning to spread over the assembly. The mountains stood like iron now against the yellowing sky. 'Thy dawn, O Master of the World . . .' Khan thought. Yes, there was Dhost again, the thread offered, left hand raised to signal the precise moment, while profane fingers groped for last morsels.

But Dhost was looking beyond the thread suddenly, his attention caught by a speck growing towards them above the crags. An eagle perhaps. But no, its steady mutter warned that it was a machine. Nevertheless, he awaited the truth of the thread before he dropped his hand.

The day of the Night of Power had begun!

Khan gave a sharp order. The men assigned to the SAM-7s scattered to their emplacements. The rest came to their feet without discipline, jabbering as they watched the approaching helicopter. Khan ordered them below. Dhost called urgently to the Lily to take cover, but she appeared oblivious, her arms raised towards the ship, beckoning it on.

'Come!' Khan could hear the high pitch of her voice above the pandemonium. 'Come!' He signalled Dhost to fetch her down.

McCabe had swung to the big lens and was using it as a telescope.

Khan called to him. He asked, 'Is it a gunship?' Ayesha was close beside him.

'No, one of their transports. A Hoplite. Or could be a Hound.' He watched it climb to circle high above them, hardly an attack posture. 'Must be a reconnaissance.'

The Gujaras had virtually to be driven below. When Khan looked up again he saw that the helicopter had its lights on and was flashing a signal. It was announcing it wanted to land!

Pola called, 'Let him come. Come, my pretty bead – come!'

Every rocket tube was raised to the sky, but there was no target while the ship's exhausts were shielded by the fuselage. Khan warned the men to hold their fire. No one had a torch to signal back with, but the pilot did not wait. Khan watched the blind belly of the plane start to sink from the sky towards them. He thought quickly of the ways in which it could be a trap. It could contain a bomb, a platoon of highly trained commandos, or simply a sniper with orders to kill just the Lily. Should he shout to Dhost to carry her by force from the roof? He remembered her last night's prophecy, her 'penultimate bead' who would descend from the heavens, and delayed the impulse.

Already Pola's robes were aflutter. Now they were plastered

against her pregnancy as the ship hung like a chattering cyclone thirty feet above them. A cable-ladder snaked to the roof.

Swinging precariously, a single figure came down it, without trepidation or pause. No sooner had his feet touched the deck than the transport lifted away into the sky, to a waiting station.

As the stinging dust subsided, Khan saw that the figure standing with legs splayed, blond hair awry, was Yakushev.

34

'SEARCH HIM!' Khan ordered.

This had to be Yakushev's performance of a lifetime, and he knew it. He pulled out a fur cap, put it on and buttoned his tunic. He had come in full uniform and that, Khan thought, whatever it did for his morale, was a mistake. The olive khaki was the target recognition factor every resistance fighter looked for over the sights of his weapon. To the Gujaras and mullahs, in their curiosity rising from the stairways like prairie dogs at full stretch, it was equal to the red flag.

'Steady,' Khan warned them. 'Let us hear what he has to say.'

Yakushev contrived a sigh of forbearance as he raised his arms.

'It's all right, I haven't come to kill my wife, just discuss her position.' He said it loudly, making sure that everyone heard, and Khan understood then the purpose of his visit and the danger he presented.

Running acquisitive fingers through someone's clothing was a Gujara speciality and Khan saw the Russian's wristwatch, a pack of cigarettes and a lighter disappear into the garments of the searchers. They could strip him to his underwear for all he cared, and Yakushev was too intent to notice. He was scanning every face. His gaze came to rest on Pola, who was standing with Dhost. He measured the way she stood, the bulk under the *chaderi*. Only when he realized the bulk was pregnancy was he sure.

'Pola?'

It was almost an exact replica of their meeting in Bab-el-Hawa. So exact as to generate a shock in Khan. The same tilt of voice, the same wary yet aggressive posture of a man coming alone into the enemy's camp. Had Pola somehow engineered the repetition? If so, she was taking as big a chance as Yakushev himself.

Khan's gaze lifted thoughtfully to the helicopter, lying off to the west, nose towards them, its pilot clearly having seen the SAM-7s. Beckoning McCabe and Ayesha to him, he asked how many troops it could carry.

'Eight,' McCabe told him. 'Armament, let me see . . . No machine-guns or cannon, just the four rocket pods.'

'How many rockets?'

'The usual thirty-two.' McCabe grimaced. '*Per pod.*'

Khan frowned. When he turned back, the search was over, revealing Yakushev to be unarmed. The Russian was making directly for him.

'So who's in charge here, Khan? Not you, you've only just arrived.' Very businesslike and impersonal, his gaze avoiding Khan's bandaged feet.

Khan regarded him in smouldering silence. All eyes were on them, Pola's and Abdalis's included. *Just as before.*

'All right, we have a personal score,' Yakushev conceded. 'But it can wait. This is urgent. It affects you all.'

Khan said, 'Then it is Allah-sent. It has saved me a journey.'

The thick upper lip curled. 'See through just that one vengeful eye, don't you? Always did, always will. You forget that you'd be dead but for me. I saved your life from the firing squad. Remember that.'

'Having first ordered it. I will certainly remember that. And Takredi. Nothing will be forgotten, Russian. *Nothing.*'

Yakushev bared his hate just for an instant. 'Do they know you were her lover? Let's find out.' He stalked on to confront the mullahs. 'Who do I talk to?'

Khan's attention went straight to Abdalis, who was standing slightly back from the others. There was no mistaking the hostility in his eyes as he looked at the Russian, and Khan felt relief. Abdalis was the only other person present who knew Pola's identity. But Yakushev was being directed on to Dhost and did not even see him.

Dhost's hulking figure stepped to the edge of the upper roof.

Yakushev saluted. 'Greeting. I am Colonel Yakushev. I've come to discuss my wife, negotiate terms for her release into my care.'

Again he spoke loudly. Every word was for public consumption.

Wife? Dhost stared at him uncomprehendingly.

'My *wife – her* – the one you call the Lily.' Yakushev pointed behind him.

After the echo had died you could have heard the smallest sound. There was none. The Gujaras just couldn't believe they had heard right.

'I understand perfectly that it's a painful matter – for you as for me.' Yakushev feigned sympathy. 'But we're all men of the world and these things must be faced before too many suffer. She is deluded, I'm sure you know that. She has a sickness. She escaped months ago from hospital, but it was only the other day that I heard her broadcast and recognized the voice. I've come now to take her back with me. She's a non-combatant, a female at that. I'm confident we can come to some arrangement.'

It was masterful. Khan thought that even he would have been tempted to believe it. A sort of tidal murmur started amongst the Gujaras – to be amputated by Pola's shriek of laughter.

'So this is the trick he comes with!'

Dhost leapt heavily to the lower roof and drew his sword.

'On your knees, pagan dog!' He struck him across the back with the flat of it. 'Atone! Atone for such sacrilege!'

Yakushev staggered but kept his feet, turning on the mullah, outraged, but quickly regaining control.

The Lily's laughter took on a tinkling quality. 'No, good Dhost, let him stand – the colonel is too old for athletics.'

'Then let me relieve him of the weight of his head!'

'No, I have brought him here for a reason, Dhost, a poetic reason.'

Yakushev stared at her. He said quickly to Dhost, 'Listen, just ask yourself, would I, would anyone, take the risk of coming here to make a false claim? She *is* my wife – Pola Katyna Yakushevna – and I can prove it.' He delved in his tunic.

Dhost raised the sword in both hands.

It took a lot of courage for Yakushev to complete the move. He produced a polythene folder and, turning his back on Dhost, opened it for the assembly to see. He stepped away from under the sword towards the other mullahs, parading it in front of them.

'You've all seen her face. Compare it with this picture, Look closely.' The shoulder-boards, medal ribbons, full authority.

Khan glimpsed a printed form bearing two photographs, a man's and a woman's with signatures and an official stamp.

'You believe me now?' He searched their faces. 'Of course she was younger then, but . . .'

Abdalis had leaned with the others to look. The mullah frowned, but neither confirmed nor denied. The other faces were blank.

This was clearly a blow to Yakushev. 'Then I can only assume you've never seen her unveiled,' he said and carried the folder back to Dhost, thrusting it into his hands. 'If this means nothing to anyone then you must get her to show herself. I warn you, every life here hangs on this.'

'Give it to me!' Pola stooped awkwardly,

Without a glance at it, Dhost passed it up. She peered at the photo this way and that in the grey light, then uttered a peal of laughter.

'You flatter me – you and your army forgers!'

So saying, she flung the folder far into the abyss.

Yakushev froze. He muttered to Dhost, 'Let me by, I'll prove it to you. If I've lied you may kill me.'

But Dhost remained in his path.

With a hint of desperation now, Yakushev glanced at his wrist and realized for the first time that his watch was missing. He looked to see if the mullah wore one.

'The time,' he snapped. 'What time is it?'

Behind him, however, Abdalis had reached a decision. His mosque voice rang against the cliffs.

'I cannot remain silent.' He waited for the echo to die before each sentence. 'The Russian speaks the truth. The Lily is his wife. I, Abdalis, bear witness to this and to her heresy!'

Consternation ensued. Whereas the Gujaras had mistrusted the Russian's every word, this was confirmation from one of their own mullahs. They surged forward.

'Stand fast!' Khan rode his human mount across their front, though against whom their fury was directed was not clear. The youngest mullah leapt on Abdalis's back and clung there, rather ridiculously, for Abdalis remained stiffly erect. The Lily stood in silence, as if curious to see how far the scene would develop before she intervened. Dhost was too fearful of leaving her unprotected actively to silence Abdalis. Yakushev was striding around, grabbing wrists, looking for a watch. When he found one he raised both arms and bellowed for silence.

'We have three minutes to settle this. *Three minutes!* All right, you know now that what I've said is true. You've been tricked into believing that my wife is some sort of goddess. Well, she is not. Grant me a husband's right to take her back to her people and there will be no attack. That I swear. You can disperse in peace.'

'Peace?' Khan laughed scornfully. 'You fear her so much you will trade peace for her? A "deluded" woman? Or is it us you fear?'

He watched this stiffen up the Gujaras. They needed it.

'If so – rightly!'

'Ali!' someone shouted. The battle-cry spread, compounding into a chant.

Yakushev raised a shaking finger towards the helicopter.

'I came in peace but it will end in violence if you don't let me go, and her with me.' The noise was so great that his words only just reached Khan. 'If in less than three minutes I don't give my pilot the signal to come and take us off – *both* of us – he has orders to attack!'

Only when this had been repeated from mouth to mouth did the noise raggedly abate.

'So let's settle this quickly,' Yakushev said more quietly, the master again now. 'I take her with me, is it agreed?'

Now the silence was absolute.

'It is agreed,' Abdalis said.

But Yakushev ignored him. His gaze was on Khan.

Khan appeared to hesitate. 'Give the signal and we will discuss it.'

'Not before it is agreed.'

What could such a signal be? Khan wondered. The helicopter was lying about two kilometres off. No doubt the pilot was watching them through magnifying lenses. Even so, Khan was certain he could not distinguish Yakushev from the press of bodies on the roof. Therefore the signal would have to be outstanding – a flash of light, a flare. But the Russian had not been carrying a torch. And he must have known he would be searched and therefore would not have dared to entrust his fate to any small apparatus that could be removed from him. What else had he carried?

Nothing, Khan concluded. Other than cigarettes.

Moslems, he thought, if and when they smoke, do so mainly in company, seated at leisure. And the pilot had them in his optics against the darkness of the cliff, the eastern light behind them . . .

'Time's running out, Khan,' Yakushev said tersely. 'Make up your mind.'

Khan had observed who had taken the pack. He was searching for him among the sea of faces. He saw him at last and called him forward. The man surrendered the cigarettes sulkily and out of the corner of his eye Khan saw Yakushev give a start and pat his tunic pocket. It was enough. Khan examined the cigarettes. They were American. They appeared normal. He stuck one in the man's mouth.

'Light it.'

The fellow looked round at his comrades, mystified, but did as he was ordered.

'Puff,' Khan told him. 'Blow it into the air – plenty of it.'

Yakushev could do nothing. The silent crowd watched the plumes rise, luminous against the darkness of the rocks.

Sure enough, the helicopter was beginning to move in their direction.

Khan signalled the men in the nearest SAM-7 emplacements to ready their tubes for a launch.

'No!' Yakushev shouted.

The helicopter came spinning swiftly towards them. Khan watched it come, gauging its distance. Too soon could be disastrous.

'Now seize him!' he shouted, pointing at Yakushev. 'Tie him to that timber. The rest of you, clear back. Right back!'

In moments Yakushev was being dragged, struggling, towards the baulk of wood supporting the derrick, in full view of the approaching ship.

The pilot saw what was happening, realized it was a trap and instantly pulled up. The helicopter's rotor-wind smote the watchers as it banked steeply to avoid the cliff and swung away.

Khan heard the alarms giving the missile-launch tones

behind him followed by a slithering rush from the tubes. Four brilliant tail-fires leapt in pursuit of the veering craft. At Mach-1.5 it was over in seconds. One missile undershot and lobbed. Three homed on the helicopter's momentarily exposed exhaust vents. There was a brilliant orange and black fireball.

The debris, as it showered to earth sounded like gentle monsoon rain.

It was uncanny, exactly as if the last ten minutes had never happened. Had Pola foreseen this from the start? The sun would not shine upon Qassassin until midday, but its yawning light was behind the peak and hazy colour beginning to stain the distance. Wrists lashed to the derrick timber where it canted across the parapet, Yakushev contrived to stand proudly, but his face was ashen. The Gujaras surged around him like children distracted by a new toy. They took his hat, dragged at his blond hair, reviled and spat on him.

The Lily watched. Only when their tormenting began to get overtly vicious did she call a halt.

'Enough, rabble! He is not for you. I brought him here as a gift to the man who has suffered most at his hands – Ghoram Khan. Take him, Khan. Andrei Pavlovich Yakushev is yours. To do with what you will.

The Gujaras stood back – reluctantly but without question. The destruction of the helicopter had somehow banished all doubt from their simple minds.

Yakushev twisted against his bonds to stare at her incredulously.

'Bitch!'

Even Khan was shaken. He knew that hate for her own people ran deep in her, but not so deep as to deliver her husband to him. But then he thought, shocking only when one remembered her former nature. She was no longer that person. She had adopted Islam, the Pathan ethos, with all its traditions of vengeance. And he saw those traditions suddenly anew in her, and discovered their barbarism.

The Gujaras watched, waiting hungrily for what he would do. The mullahs stood austerely; Allah's hand being clearly in all of this, they did not question it. Abdalis was no longer amongst them. He must have slunk away.

Khan ordered his man to set him down. He took his full weight on the broken bones of his feet without a flicker, though the pain was excruciating, and advanced towards the Russian. Someone slipped a knife in his hand.

Yakushev stood rigid, his gaze sober now, not feigning pride or contempt but showing despair. He had gambled all – and come so close. His career was dead already. Bodily death would be mere confirmation. He had no fear of it. But he was human; he had great fear as to the manner of it.

Khan bore his agony to move slowly across Yakushev's front and back, his gaze on him. Yakushev watched with the absolute stillness of a man being sniffed at by a tiger.

Khan examined his vow to kill him as he had Yasir. Could even this dull the obscene memory of Takredi? Could it ever satisfy the fires of revenge that burned in him for this and all the other Yakushevs who had come to take away his land? He knew it could not. Not in Hell itself was minted the special and endless torment they deserved.

He said at length, quietly, 'Gag him, leave him here. No food, no water. Let him be the first, when his people come, to taste the terror they bring.'

He handed back the knife and beckoned his man urgently, for he was nearly collapsing.

There were rumblings of disappointment around him, but they were cut off by a scream from the upper roof.

'Dhost, help me!'

Pola was on her knees, hugging her belly, the breath sawing in her throat.

Dhost, full of concern, raised her to her feet. She clung to his arm, bent and swaying.

The mullahs exchanged sharp glances. The Gujaras gaped. McCabe swung the camera on her and began to film.

At length she rallied herself with a visible effort and faced towards them.

'Every man to his post!' she gasped. 'My mullahs, start the broadcast! Good doctor, come! Our Night of Power has begun!'

35

'YE FAITHFUL rejoice, for the Hour has come! The Hour of the Lily! The Hour of Resurrection! The Hour of *Jihad*!'

Broadcast on the same wavelength as Radio Kabul, these words clashed with an early morning programme of music, until a circuit mysteriously blew in the Kabul transmitter, leaving Qassassin in full command of the national network. In Baluchistan, by prearrangement between the Ulemas of Kabul and Quetta, Quetta Radio interrupted its own programme to relay the broadcast throughout the province.

In Afghanistan most had heard the rumours or read the *chabnameh*, but to the Baluchis, who intentionally had been left in the dark, the news came as a complete surprise. The more sophisticated took it to be a hoax, but the masses responded to the mystic Koranic message in awe. This was a holy event. Certain rules were to be observed. Though *Jihad* against the disbelievers could continue, raising a hand against any brother of the faith during this period was punishable by eternal damnation. This, of course, placed their insurrection against the Pakistanis in temporary suspension.

From the first moments of the broadcast, the regime and the Soviet forces did everything they could to silence it. The results were dismal. Radio Kabul possessed the latest jamming gear, but when Khad ordered its use, the equipment was found to be inoperative. Was it slack maintenance? Khad possessed none themselves so application was made to GRU electronic intelligence. They replied that their jammer trucks were fully deployed. Some were in a position to jam Qassassin, but only locally, in the east and north of the country. That was better than nothing, so orders were issued. But surely the army had tactical RDF trucks standing by on the very borders of Baluchistan? Urgent messages were swapped with Front headquarters, till someone pointed out that tactical jammers operated only on the VH frequency and Qassassin was broadcasting on the long and medium. More confusion.

Dhost and his mullahs exploited this situation, broadcasting mystical prediction and dire warning interspersed with tracts from the Koran. They took it in turns, their voices rising and falling rhythmically, picking their climaxes with all the skill of their calling.

Cypher messages had been pouring into the GRU from their Baluchi illegals and the Moslem camps in Afghanistan. Strict security measures had deprived the latter of most of their radios, but illegals sent news that Zhātva was under growing threat.

Solkholov's ADC came through to Dolin repeatedly, asking where Yakushev was. Dolin learned that he had been back to his billet to change into his uniform, then driven out alone at 4.30 a.m. – destination unknown. Well, said the ADC, the marshal had the whole Lily operation on hold awaiting Yakushev's clearance. Heads would roll if he wasn't found.

What clearance? Dolin wanted to know. What was going on?

Solkholov himself paced and fumed. After thirty minutes of the broadcast he could wait no longer. He ordered Qassassin to be silenced immediately and at all costs – but with the rider that, having taken the objective, the guards armoured division would withdraw and move straight to Kandahar to assume its vital role in Harvest.

'Here they come,' muttered McCabe. He sighted them through the big lens and raised six fingers. They were mere specks in the pristine morning sky, each trailing a thread of vapour.

The roof had been cleared for action. Apart from the SAM-7 and machine-gun crews, only Khan, his four aides, McCabe and, of course, Yakushev, remained.

Khan glanced at the missile emplacements, still in deep shadow from the cliff. For a moment he thought it impossible that these termite mounds, each containing two hill shepherds, with a tube no longer than a rifle between them could provide the smallest defence against enemy warplanes. But he had witnessed their capability earlier and his doubt was only fleeting. He called to them to ready their missiles and remember their group. They were to fire in threes, the first group engaging the first plane, and so on, so as to make the utmost use of their limited supply of missiles.

The planes outpaced their sound until they were almost overhead. There had been no reconnaissance and their first high pass was to determine the lie of the land and identify their objective. They swept over and away in an arrowhead, their rear ends smoking. Khan watched them turn in a steep, wide half-circle, marvelling that they could keep formation. For an instant they caught the sun like knives, then raced cleanly back, perhaps four kilometres to the West. Something in the way they moved told him they were loaded to capacity.

Khan looked towards Yakushev and saw him craning his head after them, working frantically at his bonds. He shot a wild glance at Khan, then saw he was watching and changed his expression to one of mockery. Perhaps he laughed aloud but nothing was audible above the rushing echoes.

Khan got himself to the stairwell where he could observe without exposing himself needlessly. It was too soon for heroics on what he knew would be a long and bloody day.

McCabe remained leaning against the parapet, the camera stock tucked under his arm. Khan thought how calm he looked as he followed the planes round, like a man judging horseflesh. He nodded towards Khan as they turned back towards the monastery and came in for the kill.

Slender cylinders dropped from each in turn before they came storming past, the first two ploughing into the overhanging cliff above. Debris showered them. There were other slamming explosions from the headland beyond, a brilliant flash of flame from the cliff's edge, another from the outer parapet of the upper roof.

Heat-seeking missiles were darting after the now upward veering planes, to be lost in the fog of dust and raining rocks, eclipsed momentarily by McCabe's form stepping unhurriedly into the stairwell to crouch beside Khan.

The planes were lost to view but their after-burning thunder was audible above the echoes as they strove to outpace the missiles. Now was the time they could bag one, Khan thought, while they were still heavily loaded. A great rock had pulverized the sacks of one emplacement. Someone was screaming

'Allah!' The sound of jets diminished as the dust drifted to reveal unfamiliar contours, a small landslide from the cliff. The damage to the upper roof could not be seen. Nor could Yakushev. All was of the same colour in the choking greyness.

Khan knew that the planes had had difficulty with the jut of the cliff, but a distant whine warned him that they were going to try again. The launchers were sliding fresh missiles into their tubes, setting the mechanisms.

McCabe pointed to where Yakushev was peering fearfully out from under the timber. He seemed unhurt but very frightened. Khan, deep in satisfaction, watched him tuck back his head, squeezing himself under the angle of the wood as far as his bonds would allow.

Then the second strike was upon them, barely visible, just the brilliant flashes penetrating the murk, again mostly from the cliff. Great lumps of it began crashing on to and through the roof. Shouts came from below. The cowling trembled, threatened to collapse. Again the heat-seekers, the afterburning roar, all impressions beginning to merge now, into the continuity of combat.

McCabe squatted in the cell where his gear was stored and shook the shards of glass from the filter slide, which had been hit by debris. He could hear the planes regrouping again. They were SU-24s – bomb trucks carrying, he knew, up to eight tons apiece, including air-to-ground missiles, cannon, laser, FLIR, ECM/EW, just about every goddamn device in the book, so Qassassin was in for a lot more shit. Okay, they were having a problem with the cliff but they would get it together soon enough; hell, they could bomb a target blind, by instruments only. All they had to do was programme them right, or guide in some of those missiles by radio.

Khan had ordered the evacuation of the roof and sent the SAM crews down to the northern elevation, where they could make a more protected launch from the window. He was there in the next cell now, giving orders, very calm.

The sky was pea-soup but McCabe could just make out the planes through it, far off and much lower now. Wheeling down towards the distant deck like crows over a cornfield. Three . . . four . . . five . . . where was the sixth? They were clearly into something new.

He selected the thickly laminated Aero-I from the East Germans' filter box and fitted it into the slide. His orders given, Khan straddled an ammo box, set the PKMB sights at 500 and looked out at the moonscape of rocks. The sun's low angle was casting the mountain's shadow on the dust in the atmosphere; spun gold above, underwater hues below.

Without a sound, hugging the shadow like a shark rushing through the deep, the lead plane appeared. First a speck, mere feet above the ravine, it expanded to a monster so fast that Khan barely had time to press the trigger.

Cannon shells thumped into the side of the building, then, as it seemed certain to crash head-on, the plane swept upwards into the sunlight, loosing two bombs. Khan watched them sail apparently straight at him as the men around him plunged to the floor. But the upward thrust of the aircraft had set the cylinders on a rising path and they lobbed harmlessly over the roof to slam into the headland beyond.

Now the second shark was attacking. Khan's gun streamed tracer towards it, as did every other gun in the building. The pilot came straight on through it and released his bombs while still on a level course. He was gone in a clap of thunder, his bombs speeding on like a low kick to the crotch of the building. The double impact was like a small earthquake. Another howling spectre sped past, followed by only a vibration, as if one bomb had struck and not gone off.

The separate rushes merged into a continuous blur, providing barely enough time for Khan's number two to feed in another belt or change the overheated barrel. Men were rushing about in the passageway and breaking open ammunition boxes. One pilot of the five – the sixth had definitely been shot down – started making his runs high, banking to avoid the cliff and slinging his bombs sidelong at the roof. The building shook with each explosion and soon Khan heard the growing stampede on the steps as men abandoned the floor above to take up new positions.

Signalling number two to take over the gun, Khan got up. He blundered into McCabe, who was crouching behind him with the camera, and fought his way up the steps, scarcely aware that he was on his own two feet.

The upper storey was a shambles, ceilings caved in, mountains of rubble with human limbs projecting, some still struggling. He shouted to the few men still up there to go below. As he moved on, seeking others, a plane burst past. The ensuing explosion hurled him on top of a Gujara lying with his eyes wide open and his jaw missing. His tongue moved in a gleaming mixture of blood and dust, as if he were trying to speak. A huge stone lintel hit the floor and fell across Khan's legs, coming to rest only a hand's breadth above them. Dragging himself clear, he could see that his way back was blocked, but gaping beside him was the second stairway. He went down it head first, then righted himself and slid over the debris on his backside. The steps vanished and he fell into darkness, coming to rest with heavy impact.

Mercifully, the rubble was mostly dust. Khan lay dazed and angry, but unhurt – apart from the old injury to his feet. Through a ragged opening he could hear voices – mullahs' voices, raised and sermonizing. He crawled painfully through the opening and blinked up at the five-fold archway. Beyond it, the robed figures were squatting in a circle on the floor, passing the microphone from hand to hand. Each was reading from a prepared script.

' "*Such are they that shall be brought near their Lord in the Gardens of Delight. They shall recline on jewelled couches face to face, and there shall wait on them immortal youths . . .*" '

They could have been preaching in the mosque, unaware it seemed of what was happening, or of the wailing cries coming from the direction of the Lily's chamber.

Khan got to his feet and passed them unnoticed. He found his way barred by the powerful figure of Dhost.

'How goes the battle, son of Ahmed?'

'Is she safe?'

'Aye, safe, but she is in travail and may not be disturbed.'

Khan had to look up to meet the brown intelligent eyes.

'You know how it is between her and me – the truth, Dhost, do you know it?'

Dhost looked at the ceiling, which at that moment trembled with the worst explosion yet. 'I know only Allah's truth and what obtains to it. To all other truths I am deaf and blind.'

'Then you can neither hear nor see me,' Khan said and moved on past him.

He half expected to hear the sword gnash, but only the

increased thunder of attack sounded behind him. Dhost knows, he thought, but will not be distracted from his high purpose.

Coming to the curtain, Khan swept it aside and waited for his eyes to accustom themselves to the dark. As he stood there the building shuddered again and again, the dust sifting down. They are using their missiles now, he realized. They are eating Qassassin away as maggots eat an apple. What will happen when they reach the core? Tottering a little, he stepped in.

Pola, still fully robed, was lying on the divan, moaning and twisting her head. Another figure stood beside her, quite still and staring. Khan saw it was Abdalis. What was he doing here? He was sure Dhost had not permitted him to enter. Perhaps he had slipped in when his attention was diverted. Something nudged his back and Ayesha pushed by with a vessel of water and strips of clean blanket. Her hair was grey with dust. Khan went with her to the couch.

'My Pola . . .'

The veil's mesh turned towards him. The breath hissed between her teeth. Moist hands gripped his.

'Oh. Oh.' She pressed her silk-clad cheek to his knuckles. 'You are safe. I have been in terror for you.'

'How is it with you?'

'It is heaven and hell. My act of will is happening – it *is* happening, beloved!'

'She is coming into labour,' Ayesha said. She kept her gaze down as she laid the things at the foot of the bed, but Khan sensed her shock at their emotion and closeness.

'Prematurely.' Abdalis spoke, sounding distraught. 'Upon this very sacred day. I do not believe it. Yet I begin to.'

'Then serve your penance, Judas,' Pola gasped, 'by usefulness. Tell Dhost to bring an extended microphone.'

'A microphone – at once.' Abdalis no longer questioned her command.

'And a length of rope,' she called after him. Then to Khan, as another missile shook the monastery, 'How do we fare?'

'The upper floors are collapsing. We have many casualties. But the building still defies them.'

'My miracle will preserve it, *inshallah*. Pray for it, beloved – and for me. And remember, whatever happens, I love you.'

'And I you,' said Khan.

'Now go. Stay alive, my love. For the end of this will be our beginning.' Her head came forward as her whole body contracted.

Khan glanced anxiously at Ayesha, but she nodded reassuringly.

'Take good care of her, little sister. If anything is needed, find me.'

As he left, he encountered Dhost unreeling a length of cable attached to a microphone.

'What is her intention with that?' Khan asked.

But Dhost replied, 'I neither see nor hear thee,' and pressed past.

Khan reached the stairway and sank to his knees, the agony in his feet too great to bear. There was another thundering roar followed by a heavy fall of masonry somewhere below him. A face lolled above him. As he crawled up to it he saw that it was his number two machine-gunner. The back of his head seemed part of the wall and the twisted metal of the gun was buried in his chest.

Khan now saw that the inner wall of the cell was gone and the outer open to the landscape. His carriers lay under the rubble, as grey as if they had been turned to stone.

There was another rush and an awesome vibration. His gaze was on the stonework and he saw every block move a little in its seating. He crouched, waiting for the next impact.

It did not come. All sound had stopped, both inside and outside the monastery. Khan continued listening. Very faintly, he heard the planes going away.

The whole top section of Qassassin looked like a doll's house with the roof off, its compartments filled with grit and stones by a destructive child. Tilted against one heap was the timber, which had tumbled through two floors to rest now at a steep angle, pulley end uppermost. Under it, face grey except for a deep gash across his cheek, crouched Yakushev. His wrists were still bound to the stout wood behind him.

He too listened to the planes going away. With a resurgence of hope, he resumed his scraping around the base of the timber with bleeding fingers. He was digging a channel.

When it seemed deep enough, he pushed the headcloth that

had been used to tie him off part of the end of the timber, and down into the channel.

This was enough to release the tension around his wrists. He pulled them free and got to his feet, his body shooting pain in every quarter. Shaking and chafing his hands till the blood returned to them, Yakushev started off in search of a weapon.

Marshal Solkholov stood in the ops room at Front HQ in company with Air Army Commander Karkov, the air LO, Corps Commander Tutin, his ADC, the head of RO Intelligence, two staff colonels and an interpreter. With one ear he was listening to the mullahs' broadcast, and with the other to the one-sided exchanges passing between the air liaison officer and Air Command over the radio link in the corner. Each represented a different side of the picture. The third side manifested itself in the gradual advance of the arrow on his wall map, showing the current position of the armoured column.

Hearing the voices of Qassassin and the sounds of Soviet air attack over the same loudspeaker was a peculiar experience. He could only liken it to listening to a football match, waiting for a goal to be scored. The scoring of the goal would be very simply conveyed – by silence.

Had Harvest been on schedule, Solkholov would have been on his way to Tac HQ near the Baluchi frontier by now. That he wasn't, that he was being delayed by a crazy woman and a bunch of fanatics, infuriated him. Every second that Qassassin remained on the air was costing the Baluchi Revolutionary Council thousands of armed supporters. More important, if the full force of Soviet might could not be heard, over the air, to be wholly effective against these crackpots, the Moslem divisions could be written off as a fighting force. And the resistance would gain kudos and new recruitment, not to mention increased aid from the West.

A woman's voice took over the broadcast, wailing and gasping. The mullahs fell silent to allow her full dramatic impact, and the whole ops room followed suit.

Solkholov turned to the interpreter.

'Is that the Lily?'

The interpreter cocked his head and pursed his lips, listening.

The voice began speaking, in a wild erratic way.

After a moment the interpreter nodded.

'What's she saying?'

'She's swearing by the Declining Day . . .'

'What?'

'That man's lot is cast amid destruction.'

'Hers certainly is!' Karkov said, scowling at the tip of his cheroot.

'Shh!'

'She's saying her hour has come. The Hour of the Lily. That shortly she will give birth to the resurrected Mahomed, that the Soviets are bombing her stronghold, trying to prevent the miracle . . .'

'That'll stir up the Moslem troops!' Tutin muttered gloomily.

'But Allah is disarming their weapons, she says. Fending off their bombs and rockets, striking their planes from the sky.'

'Lying bitch!' Solkholov bluffed a laugh.

Karkov did not smile. He was bending his ear to the loudspeaker. After a moment he straightened. 'Hear that? Bombing's stopped.'

Everyone listened intently. It was true.

'Allah has summoned his bolts of lightning,' the interpreter went on. 'He has smitten the enemy from the face of the earth, every one, that His prophet might be delivered in peace . . .'

The silence in the ops room grew oppressive.

'They've screened out the noise somehow,' the ADC said. 'Clever bastards.'

The moments stretched to minutes, only the Lily's voice audible, rich in agony, fragmented, exultant.

At last the LO leaned forward, touching his headphones, listening. After a few moments he looked up.

'They've disengaged, comrade Commander,' he announced. 'Racks empty. They're heading back to base.'

There was a running murmur of laughter – though neither from amusement nor relief.

'She's no fool,' someone said. 'She used it.'

Solkholov stood incredulous.

'Do you want to know how she goes on?' the interpreter enquired.

'No. No, I do not! Turn the damn thing down.' Solkholov eyed the LO. 'What is their report, their explanation?'

'Tell Sarsov we want it immediately,' Karkov told him.

As the LO passed this over the link, Solkholov took out a red handkerchief and blew his nose. It was a spacer he used when thinking.

'We'll rearm the planes, of course,' Karkov said. 'Mount a second strike immediately.'

'No you won't.' Solkholov glowered at him over the redness.

'What?'

'How long would that take?'

'Thirty minutes.'

'Then you won't. In half an hour she'll have subverted the whole of Central Asia!' In a stride Solkholov was at the map. 'We'll have to use something closer. What have you got at Ghazni?'

'Twenty-ones.'

'Fighters or fighter-bombers?'

'Fighters.'

'We need obliteration bombers – TUs.'

'They're all at Kailagai.'

Solkholov tapped the advance airfield, which was less than forty kilometres from Qassassin. 'Here then – what's here?'

'Nothing heavy – platoon of gunships, half quadron of 11s, reconnaissance and, of course, the NBC team.'

Solkholov was silent. Out came the handkerchief again.

'I have their provisional mission report,' the LO announced.

'Well?' Karkov turned.

'Difficult topography. Direct hits – bombs 50 per cent, missiles 80 per cent. Top of building laid open, structure weakened but still holding. One plane lost to SAM-7 fire, a second with wing damage but operable.'

'Damn!' Karkov muttered. 'Those 24s are like *gold.*'

'That all?' Solkholov demanded. 'What about armour? Estimated strength of garrison?'

'Nothing reported, comrade Marshal.'

'Top of building *laid open* . . . How long to scramble the NBC team and get them on target?'

Karkov stared at him.

'Twenty minutes.'

'Do it.'

'The Moscow directive expressly said—'

'*Do it*, Aleksander Sergeivich. Waste no more time. Plus two support gunships, one with napalm.' He added when Karkov still hesitated, 'I will take full responsibility with the ministry.'

36

PERCHED HIGH on the uppermost ruins with his camera, McCabe turned film on the damage. Across from him, Khan, supported by two Gujaras, was allocating fresh anti-aircraft machine-gun positions, the men extending their tripod mounts and stamping their feet securely into the debris. Others ferried up boxes of 7.62 ammunition. It was all the ack-ack defence left, the SAM-7s having expended their last missile. Custer's last stand.

McCabe panned away slowly to show the mountain panorama, the shadows shortening, the colours bleaching out, sky fathomless, air motionless. Then he noticed the four dots.

They could have been a bar of music. He held them for a space, wondering if they were birds. He felt something happen in his chest.

He cut the camera, thinking fast. First warn Khan.

He shouted to him. His arms flew up and down, his fingers fluttered, he pointed to his throat.

After a moment or two of staring, Khan seemed to understand. He began giving orders.

With shaking hands McCabe unloaded the camera, put on a fresh magazine and laced up. He swung on the zoom, set the stop and focus, checked it all over, then left the camera balanced on the power-pack and sprang down the steps to his gear.

He put the trousers on first. Then the heavy rubber boots, with their laces and clips. The protective mask next – a wipe round the eyepieces with the anti-mist cloth before the struggle to pull it down over his head. Now the OP-1 rubberized hooded coat, the hem straps, waist and hood strings. Next the eight snap-fasteners, and cuff straps, and finally the butyl gloves, clips locked.

Looking out of the window McCabe saw that the planes had passed from sight. Had he time? He would have to make time! Feeling like an alien from space, he lurched amongst the gaping Gujaras and made his way to the transmitter room, where the broadcast was continuing. Dhost barred his way, his expression full of amazement.

McCabe shouted, 'Ayesha!' – his voice sounding in his ears like a foghorn – and kept shouting till she appeared. When she saw him her face filled with horror.

'Tell them to batten every hatch they can – blankets, any tables, heaped boxes, to block the doorways, men to have their blankets handy. You keep right in there, don't come out. I love you.'

She opened her mouth. Perhaps she said something but his hood stifled it. He rushed away.

Before he had regained the roof he heard machine-gun fire. He clambered out to a fireworks display – arcs of tracer lifting to vanish in the direction of the two propeller planes as they circled high, wheeling slowly like vultures. He climbed to retrieve the camera and power-pack before looking round for the other two aircraft. But the helicopters were nowhere to be seen.

Why had Khan not told his gunners to quit the roof? Perhaps he was hoping they would bag the planes before they made their strike. He was there himself, still, arms over the shoulders of two fresh aides, watching the effect of the fire, wishing like hell, no doubt, that he had kept closer rein on the missiles.

Careful not to disturb the focus with the clumsy gloves, McCabe zoomed in and held the prop jobs as large in frame as he could get them. He didn't turn film yet – they wouldn't operate from up there, he was certain, and he needed to conserve every foot of stock.

They were losing height now and turning. Dad's Army planes. Just a couple of SAMs would have cooked them at that speed. How did they know there weren't any left? Obviously they didn't. To take such a risk, the Russians had to be really desperate to stop that broadcast!

Each plane had the red star trimmed in white on the

fuselage, and beside it a serial number. He must get that clearly on film.

Here came the first now – why else would he risk the tracer display? McGabe panned with him and squeezed the trigger.

The L-19 passed harmlessly over. For a moment it seemed to be supported on the columns of tracer fire, like a ball on a jet at a shooting gallery, then the gunners lost it. But its motor seemed to splutter. A puff of brown smoke showed briefly. It went sailing on, but losing height, its motor now definitely missing.

McCabe stayed on it, hoping it would crash, so preoccupied that moments had passed before he realized the sky was darkening. He zoomed out and whip-panned back – and there it was, a greenish-yellow stain stretched above the monastery, descending gently through the air.

Was he getting it? He should have filtered for it, he realized, but too late now. Greeny-yellow, like the sulphurous fogs they used to get in London before it went smokeless.

Panning it down, down, the tracer fire stitching patterns through it. He couldn't think of Khan, whether he had gone below. Couldn't think of anything but breathing regularly to keep the camera steady – he had to suck suffocatingly hard through the bloody filter – but this was it, what he had come for, going on record the best way he knew how!

A spire of masonry swung slowly up into frame, at its base a machine-gunner, teeth bared, pouring fire into the sky. He dimmed as in a dust storm. The fire stopped. He stood stiffly for a few seconds, head back. Then he jerkily took a pace and fell over, got up and fell over again.

McCabe widened the field, aware that the stuff was on him, on the camera, misting his eyepieces. He had no time to wonder if the suit was really proof – other gunners were in his shot. Had Khan left them to die up here as proof of Soviet barbarism?

They were moving around mindlessly, keeling over, struggling on their backs like beetles. Then, as he watched, blood began to pump out of their mouths, noses, ears, *eyes*.

Even McCabe's concentration faltered as he watched it gush forth, as though squeezed out at enormous pressure.

The camera had stopped. It took McCabe a moment to realize he had released the trigger. Only a loud explosion from above reminded him to continue filming. He whip-panned to the sky, too late to record the second-stage rocket-burst but just in time to zoom in on the almost indolently departing plane, then zoom out to show the huge, beautiful sunset cloud of red powder left hanging in the atmosphere.

He followed its drifting descent, and when finally it mingled with the yellow toxin he braced himself to go in tight on each of the afflicted men jerking about amongst the debris. No sooner did the two chemicals combine than the victim began to turn black and visibly start to shrivel. Death came in moments.

McCabe recorded every hideous detail. Not until he was satisfied that the full indictment had been made did he stop the camera. His stomach heaved then. He fought to master it, swallowing, sucking in lungfuls of rubbery air, knowing that to vomit inside the mask would mean suffocation.

Yakushev was lost. This northern part of the monastery was like a maze. Passages and stairways led nowhere. He cursed himself for not having paid more attention to the way he had entered it, but he had been like a dog on the scent as he tracked down the distant sounds of the broadcast, his object to silence it. Only by such an act now could he redeem the error of coming here.

Donning a dead man's *chapan* and turban, arming himself with an abandoned weapon, he had spent several minutes tracking the sound of the mullahs' voices, only to discover that the broadcast was coming from a transistor radio amongst the debris of a cell.

As he stood in frustration the spluttering of a sick aero-engine reached him. Through the torn outer wall he saw an L-19 losing height above the headland. He watched and saw two dark shapes separate from the fuselage. Army chutes opened and they drifted serenely out of sight beyond the headland.

Yakushev was momentarily puzzled by the deployment of such an aircraft at this stage of the attack. Then he saw the shadow spreading across the rocks – and ran. His one idea: to bury himself as deep inside the building as he could get!

There was only one internal passageway in the stretch of corridor. He took it. It led him into gathering darkness, like entering a mine. He hurried on, hands outstretched before him.

The clash of the Kalashnikov against rock was his first intimation that this way was also blocked. He groped for a way through but found none. He saw for the first time the dark rectangle of an entrance a few metres behind him. He retraced his steps.

The room was pitch-black. Yakushev entered it cautiously, probing with each footstep, his breath huffing against the walls. Small. Very small. Some fine rubble in there, like plaster, but otherwise empty. He licked a finger and held it up.

No movement of air. Good. It would have to do.

He slid his back down the wall, laid the gun beside him and felt the relief of crouching with his knees to his chest.

Silencing the broadcast would now have to wait. But once the toxic dust had settled, he would complete what he had come here to do – if Khan, Pola and the mullahs were still alive. And if they weren't, he would still claim he had. One way or another he was going to pull himself out of this even now.

He felt the first explosion through the wall. The sound grumbled through the building like thunder.

'Faster!' Khan told his few remaining men.

For lack of materials to render the lower floors toxin-proof, they were using bodies, piling them to the vaulting. Khan knew that McCabe was still somewhere above, but keeping the chemicals out was more important than any one life. McCabe had become a close ally, and the film would be a loss, but already three of these men had died horrifically in front of him and another two were dying of contamination from simply touching them, showing beyond doubt that the dust was working its way into the building.

Shovelfuls of debris, scraps of clothing and paper were being tamped into the remaining gaps. When completed, that would be two stairways sealed, leaving two more to go.

At this point the first explosion shook the building. It was nowhere near them but he felt the suction of air and saw small implosions of dust spurt from the barrier. He called sharply to his men, who came tumbling down the steps after him to stand staring fearfully at each other.

The explosion was followed by a series centred low down in

the northern region of the building. Khan knew they were calculated to suck the chemicals from the outside air into every part of the monastery. And they were succeeding. He told the Gujaras to find shelter away from the main currents of air.

Access to the northern chambers was complicated, but he had memorized the way. When he got there, he saw a gunship hanging above the lake, storming the surface with its rotor-wind. It was pumping rocket after rocket from the same pod, through the same breach in the outer wall, thereby achieving ever increasing penetration. It had to be stopped at once!

Khan was armed with just the Kalashnikov. He stumbled past the abandoned outer rooms, looking for a heavier weapon. Pola was in his mind, not himself. He would save what he could for her, then, if he felt the terrible spasms, put his gun to his head. Windows and shell holes winked past him; through each he saw the gunship, stabilized in defiance of nature, spacing each missile. There had been a 12.7 machine-gun along here somewhere, the only one in the building, salvaged probably from a Soviet tank.

As he passed one cell a shiny transistor radio caught his eye. But no, not in there. It was in the next cell that he found the machine-gun. Its crew were long dead. He did not look at them but at the gun, its condition, whether there was ammunition in the belt. It was smothered in dust, but who could tell how deadly? He blew it off the handles, gripped them through the tail of his shirt and swung it on to the gunship. Pressing the fire-button – praise Allah, it worked! – he used the luminous stream of tracer to guide it on to the target.

The ship was almost head-on, all eyes like a giant blowfly. The cockpit glass was steeply raked, as was its whole forward shell. The tracer began glancing off it, lofting away into the distance. The ship recoiled, its nose lifting as its rotor hauled it back and to one side – a manoeuvre to present its more heavily armoured undershield. The rocket discharge stopped and the four-barrel gatling gun in its nose turret swivelled to send a crackling stream of fire at the monastery. Khan dived sideways as part of the window frame disintegrated, showering him with fragments. But immediately he was back, redirecting his stream of bullets at the ugly snout.

Almost at once the gun stopped, its belt exhausted. He looked around for the ammunition box and found it under the rubble. Nothing now from the helicopter. Either it was manoeuvring or its pilot had assumed a hit. Yet a stream of metal snapped deafeningly past where his head had been. It had come from behind! He half came to his feet. Turning, he saw a dust-grey figure in the doorway and lunged towards it. His feet could not sustain the move and he fell to his knees. The second burst tugged hard at his headcloth. He smelled the hot breath of the gun.

He half-crawled, half-sprang at Yakushev's knees, toppling him. The Russian – though Khan did not yet realize it was him – turned the gun down to empty it into him. Khan grasped the barrel and wrenched it from his hands. He threw a knee over his chest, straddled him and grasped his throat. Only then did he recognize his enemy.

Yakushev did not struggle, just looked with hatred in his eyes.

This absence of any resistance was so unexpected that Khan eased the pressure of his thumbs.

Yakushev's lips moved silently. Was he trying to speak?

Khan leaned his head closer.

Yakushev's right hand swung up, the rock in it striking Khan's skull behind the ear. Consciousness winked out in an electrical flash and, as Khan slumped sideways, Yakushev heaved him off with a choking cough. Khan came to almost at once, his face pressed to something metallic – the gun. Yakushev was kneeing him, kicking at him, trying to pull it from under him. Khan clung to it instinctively till his mind cleared, then struggled to his feet with it. But it was muzzle uppermost and even as he strove to reverse it Yakushev found the trigger.

Three bullets tore upwards into Khan's armpit, lifting him, turning him around in a spin that ended hard against the wall. He felt his knees start to go and with a huge effort braced them, knowing that if he lost consciousness again he was dead. Somehow he still held the muzzle of the gun. Yakushev had the pistol-grip and was vainly pulling the trigger, while trying to wrench it from his hand. It was either empty or jammed, but the Russian could not seem to grasp this. Khan suddenly let go the muzzle and, as Yakushev fell back, lunged to reach his own weapon beside the machine-gun. Recovering quickly, Yakushev snatched back the cocking handle, aimed into

Khan's gut and pulled the trigger. There was a jolt as the firing mechanism tripped against the exhausted magazine. Khan, with one shoulder useless, was slow in swinging up his own weapon. Yakushev leapt to his feet. He hurled the empty Kalashnikov at his head and rushed from the cell.

Khan saw his bullets spark across the return of the doorway behind him, and again, more brightly, in the darkened passageway beyond. But as he ceased fire, he heard Yakushev's feet beating away up a stairway.

Would he find another weapon and come back? Khan sank to his knees and shut his eyes. Though he fought against losing consciousness with all his remaining strength, he could do nothing to stop it.

McCabe had it all in the can, most of it in one continuous sequence – the planes, make and identification; their delivery method; the behaviour of the dusts and their effect on unprotected human targets from first contamination to death. Only one phase remained to be recorded: the eradication of all evidence that this had ever happened, in itself a Soviet admission of guilt. And it was about to begin.

With a warning whine that had sped McCabe's finger to the trigger, the second helicopter, invisible till this moment, had shot up from behind the cliff and started its run. He had it dead between the tramlines, its markings, the three bomb cylinders locked in its pylons, as it spun straight towards him.

McCabe braced himself excitedly. This had never been filmed frontally. There it was – the release! Even as the first bomb torpedoed through the air he leapt and dropped three metres into the pit of rubble. His knees punched his chest, his breath roared in the mask. With the camera still turning he swung to catch the *whoof* of flame as it burst across the open top of the building, filling each segment, overflowing into passageways, rushing towards him like a river of lava.

He cut and dropped through the hole before the heat of the napalm could melt his suit. Blackened bodies littered the steps. He leapt over them, flying, camera hugged protectively, the other arm extended. He hit the wall of corpses.

Christ! He clawed his way up them, incredulously. They filled the stairway to the very vaulting, rubble and rubbish wedging them tight. He could hear the roaring napalm behind him. He had only seconds. He was scraping away the debris, tearing at the top body – was there ever anything heavier than a dead body? – dragging it by one arm. Daylight winked at him, then yawned. He shoved the camera through first, then crammed his body after it, kicking and struggling frantically, feeling the heat mount against his feet.

He tumbled head first down the far side of the stack, followed by a searing breath that became a liquid sound, then a burning sound. Would the wall of corpses hold back the flood? At the bottom of the next flight he stared back and saw already the brilliant seepage and black smoke. Even as he watched, the bodies glowed, then burst into flame like struck matches. Then through it came!

McCabe floundered down another flight and felt the vibration of the second napalm bomb bursting above. There were men down here, just wandering about aimlessly. He shouted a warning but they seemed not to hear. And Khan – where was Khan? Keeping a sharp watch behind him, he shouted his name through several of the cells. More bodies, one slumped over a machine-gun. He stooped to peer sideways at the face, but no, a Gujara.

As he straightened, the whole wall collapsed in front of him. He never heard the noise. It simply collapsed, vanished, leaving him with a dizzy view of the gorge below.

He froze, staring. A huge serpent of metal stretched back as far as the eye could see – armoured reconnaissance vehicles, hundreds of T-72 tanks, their guns, SAGGERS and missiles straining upward. The foremost already too close to gain the elevation but those behind blasting, recoiling. Shells rushed like express trains towards the monastery.

McCabe reeled away, striving to distance himself from the explosions, thinking, 'Well, that's it – we're done for.' The passageways were growing oven-like. He glimpsed fire already drooling down to this level. It turned, even as he looked, into a flash-flood as the contents of the second bomb came surging after it. The blast of heat overtook him as he ran, almost blowing him along, lighting his way. If the second stairway was in flood too, he knew he would be cut off. But no glow reached him from ahead. It was clear still, its upper flights probably choked by debris. But how long would it hold?

The five-fold stone arch remained intact, but the wall of the transmitter room had been penetrated. Whatever had done it had burst inside moments ago. As he stepped in something soft turned under his boot. He was just able to distinguish that it had been a man, one of the mullahs. By degrees, he made out several others. Dhost was sprawled with his head sideways against the transmitter, bearded lips parted as if he had been listening to something that made him laugh. The dials were still lit; the set was still working.

McCabe rushed in terror towards the inner chamber, shouting for Ayesha. No reply. He snatched aside the curtain and saw that it was still dark in there. That gave him hope. He knuckled his eyepieces and peered, gradually perceiving a scene of such utter incongruity that he stood transfixed.

Oblivious, it seemed, to the mayhem outside, the Lily was giving birth. She did not lie on the bed but, in the fashion of the tribe whose culture she had adopted, crouched on the floor, hauling on the rope which had been attached to a cresset-ring in the vaulting. Her veil and robe were off. She wore a plain white slip gathered about her waist, her hair lank about her convulsed features as she bore down with ferocious strength. Beside her, wholly preoccupied in keeping the baby's head from contact with the floor, knelt Ayesha.

McCabe's first thought was, could he shoot it? But no way. Even with a reflector there could never be enough light. All he could do was contain himself and bear witness.

Gently, gently, Ayesha eased as Pola bore down, knuckles white, on the taut cord. Explosions shuddered and crashed outside. Gently it came, suddenly all of it, Ayesha drawing it out from between Pola's legs. Pola dragged in air to expel it in a great sound of exhaustion and triumph, before slumping to just the hand-grip on the cord.

'What is it, what is it?' she managed to whisper.

'A boy,' Ayesha assured her.

'*A boy!*' Pola's head went back and for the first time McCabe saw the disfigurement of her forehead. She was laughing soundlessly, sweat and tears shining on her face.

Ayesha was working with swift efficiency in the darkness. Pola whispered something. Ayesha relayed it, her back to him, shouting above the barrage.

'She asks if those are Soviet tanks firing, Michael.'

'Yes, thousands of the bloody things!'

At that moment the baby choked and began crying.

The Lily's countenance became radiantly transformed, though whether by his reply or the baby's lusty chorus McCabe could not tell.

'She wants you to call the mullahs.'

McCabe had to break the news that they were dead.

'Dhost?'

'All of them, so far as I can see.'

There was a moment's murmuring.

'Khan?'

'Dunno about Khan. I haven't seen him. But the whole place is running in napalm. If we don't get out of here fast we'll either be cooked or blown to bits. You'll have to help her, I can't touch her – I'm contaminated.'

As he watched the Lily seemed to wilt. She waved her hand weakly, pointing to the outer chamber. She gasped something.

'Then you'll have to do it,' Ayesha cried.

'What?'

'The casket. Under the transmitter.'

'Do what?'

'The casket!' Ayesha shouted. She had the baby on the bed and was wrapping it in a clean blanket.

'For Christ's sake!' McCabe bellowed. But he stumbled out to the transmitter room. Through the shattered wall he saw armoured reconnaissance carriers drawn up nose to tail like traffic in a city street. They stretched to the headland, the nearest still battened against the falling debris and metal fragments of the barrage, the ramps of the farthest already down, their contingents of troops disembarked in clusters.

McCabe peered under the transmitter and saw something dust-covered under Dhost's twisted right knee. He laid down his camera and pulled out a dome-topped metal-bound box about sixty centimetres long.

Ayesha came rushing out to him.

McCabe recoiled. *'Don't touch me!'*

'She says to hurry!' With a gasp of exasperation, Ayesha fumbled the catch and threw up the lid.

'She says it needs a man's strength to be certain. It's for us, Michael. The final act. You say you're a part of us. Now prove it. *Do it!*'

McCabe leaned forward. Even as he did so there was

a stirring in his ears. Daylight leapt once – twice – three times through the wall. The vaulting above fragmented in a succession of rockfalls. McCabe clasped his arms over his eyepieces, feeling his body take punishment and lift backwards.

Even raising his head he could see nothing. Only when he had pushed the rubble off and sat up did the accumulation of dust drop from the glass. Now he could see fog, dim somethings and nothings. Pain was in all of him, but without focus.

'Ayesha!'

She lay propped against the far wall, as if taking a siesta. She looked dead but he couldn't touch her. Couldn't even stir her with the toe of his boot.

'Ayesha, sweetheart?'

The building trembled under his feet like an aspen. Would the tanks never let up? His camera lay smashed. The magazine looked intact, though McCabe didn't even care about that now. He knelt beside her.

'My love.'

The sheen was gone from her skin, the colour from her lips. The excruciating longing to touch her was like nothing he'd ever experienced. With no hands, he was like a fish or a bird.

In the stillness of the small features only the lips moved.

'Do it, Michael.'

It was like a voice from the dead.

No matter what sudden hope it kindled in your chest, such a voice you obeyed.

He groped his way to the casket and peered inside. All he could see was rubble. He dug with his glove and uncovered a handle.

An exploder-box!

Its plunger stood erect, waiting. There were no cables. Now he understood: electronically controlled charges were waiting somewhere to be detonated by a single impulse from this box. But where?

That this was the culmination of the Lily's plan seemed obvious. And only he remained to be the instrument of it. Not just a part – the key role.

But what if her plan were martyrdom? The charges in the building?

Do it, Michael.

McCabe grasped the handle. You've come a long way from your fence, he thought.

'Wouldn't do that,' a voice said behind him.

Dust-caked and bloody, Yakushev managed to hold the gun steady. He spoke without emotion, like a man in a trance. 'Might blow us all up. Just the kind of mad thing my wife would think of.' He peered at the rubber mask for a moment. 'I am assuming you are the cameraman, yes?'

McCabe straightened slowly.

'Where do I find her?' Yakushev enquired. 'Or is she already dead?'

McCabe made no reply.

'If you are not answering from solidarity with these idiots, I suggest you take a look out there' – he pointed outside – 'then decide if you want to survive.' He indicated the transmitter. 'The light is working. Does that mean it can still broadcast?'

McCabe remained silent.

'If so, I can radio the column and tell them to stop firing.'

'Good thinking.' McCabe looked towards Ayesha. She had not moved. Being unable to aid her was a nightmare.

'You see? A little civilized reasoning is all that is needed. But first, where is my wife?'

'Stop the guns and I'll tell you.'

Yakushev seemed to stare right through him for a moment.

He nodded and gestured with the gun. 'If you would move aside just a little . . .'

McCabe complied slowly.

Yakushev sidled to the transmitter. He shoved at Dhost with his boot, waited till he had slumped to the floor, then leaned over to study the controls.

McCabe peered down at his protective clothing. He was almost blind from sweat now, and dust was dust, any toxic contamination indistinguishable from the rest. The cuff of the glove was the most logical trap he could think of.

'Perhaps you understand now,' Yakushev said, flicking a switch and spinning a dial, 'why we – though personally I deplore it – are forced to use – how do you call it? – T-2 on these people. They are incorrigible. Breathe the word Allah in their ears and they will believe any crackpot idea you put in their heads, even be prepared to die for it. You can't reason with them. They are like rabid dogs, so must be put down.'

At this moment, in the inner sanctum, the baby started to cry.

Yakushev straightened and half turned in startlement.

Bending his wrist, McCabe wiped the cuff of the glove across the Russian's facial wound.

'Just like you,' he said quietly.

Yakushev recoiled, uncomprehending at first. Then he understood and clapped a hand to the wound, shaking his head, blinking his eyes, waiting in terror for the first symptom. He made an absent move with the gun that became one of furious intent. He emptied the magazine at McCabe. That McCabe had moved didn't seem to matter. His finger kept tugging the trigger, his gaze roving blindly. Finally his chin jerked up. The gun clattered to the floor. He did a little stiff march in a half circle. Even before he jack-knifed to the floor in convulsions, McCabe stooped and leaned his weight on the plunger.

He stood hunched, oblivious to the hideous sounds issuing behind him.

For a moment there was nothing, save for the terrible rushing and bursting of shells.

Then a faint rumble . . . a succession of rumbles, felt rather than heard, from outside the building.

Rushing to the wall, McCabe saw both sides of the gorge shift a little, lift a little. Boulders leapt in a long line as if disturbed by some supersonic mole. In slow motion then, he watched the whole of both mountain-sides collapse, breaking into their components, outcrop and seam, stratum and detritus, bounding, cartwheeling, slithering, gathering in speed and mass – to thunder down upon the armoured column below, burying tanks, carriers and weaponry under millions of tons of rock.

Incapable of movement, McCabe watched the sky blacken with dust as the echoes roared and grumbled and mumbled away through the Western Kush, to come crashing back and repeat themselves, again, again . . . Till finally silence and almost total darkness reigned above the twelve-mile grave.

37

KHAN CAME to, convinced that someone was branding his shoulder with a red-hot iron. He moved a hand to it and felt torn clothing, blood and the grating of splintered bone. The whole of that side of his body was as slimy as lamp-oil. That he had passed out he could understand, but that the guns had stopped required explanation. He opened his eyes.

Wherever he was lying, the walls and roof had disappeared. By rolling his head he could see down past the shells of the floors immediately below and into the ravine itself.

The gorge had vanished! In its place stretched a chaos of rock that even now shifted a little, settled a little, smoking with dark dusts. Where the ravine had been shallower, parts of armoured vehicles poked through the debris and over these were scrambling scores of Soviet soldiers, clearing rocks, calling down to the men presumably trapped inside. Where the tumble of detritus had not reached, the chain of vehicles remained intact as far as the lake, round which they were parked as tightly as for a *buz-kashi* match or Kabul Army Day.

Khan felt he must be hallucinating, yet knew he was not. He had slept through some cataclysm. But where was he?

By carefully turning his head he discovered he was lying on a wafer-thin section of floor projecting into space. He suspended all speculation and began, gingerly, to push himself back from the edge.

'*Allaho akbar!*' exclaimed a voice behind him.

Abdalis had paused while passing along the passageway, which was now an open gallery.

'I had given you up for dead, son of Ahmed.'

Khan detected no relief in his voice, or acrimony. The mullah's robes were torn, his face scarred and blackened. One hand shone crimson from a wound beneath his sleeve, but his eye was as hard as the nail that crucifies, his posture unrelenting.

He set one foot on the uncertain floor and extended his good hand.

When he had pulled Khan to safety, he clapped his hands imperiously and called down to someone below. Three Gujaras came, dazed and surly. All were wounded but Abdalis ordered them to support Khan and follow him. They protested but endured his command. Abdalis led the way up the steps.

'She ordered me to find you and bring you to her,' he announced. 'Alas, I was trapped by the holocaust. By now she will be deeply anxious.'

Khan said through pain-set lips, 'Have you encountered your friend the Russian?'

'He is no more a friend than you,' Abdalis retorted. 'My loyalty, son of Ahmed, is to Allah and His truth, and no other.'

'He may be looking for her to kill her.'

'Do not fear. Unless it is written, he will not succeed.'

There was heat from the walls and smoke now as they mounted towards the lowest penetration point of the napalm. The stairway took on the aspect of a chimney. Desultory flames still licked the steps. They climbed carefully to avoid the glutinous residue.

'Tell me of the gorge, holy man. Was this her miracle?'

Abdalis nodded. 'Such splendour have I never witnessed, nor rejoiced more. It was a masterstroke. That much I will never deny.'

He moved deeper into the building across the rubble and under the five-fold arch. He stopped in dismay.

Khan surveyed the shambles in shock. He pulled away from the men's support and staggered forward.

'Pola?' he called. 'Pola, are you here?' He peered at the dust-grey bodies till he was reassured that each was a mullah. McCabe's camera lay with its traps open, two severed ends of film protruding. Of the magazine there was no sign, nor of McCabe himself. Yakushev's blackened corpse he recognized only by the plastic-covered medal ribbons showing on the uniform under the *chapan*. He felt brief relief, nothing more, as he struggled on.

Abdalis reached the Lily's chamber before him and confronted him as he entered.

'Prepare yourself, son of Ahmed,' he warned.

The wall was breached and the roof had collapsed. The divan lay broken under rubble, its hangings in dusty tatters. Masonry littered the floor. Pola's head and shoulders projected from under it. Her eyes were not clenched but closed as in sleep, the lips parted, as if uttering a name in peace. All pain and vengeance purged; the turmoil, the feigned vanities and tempers, having gained their purpose, laid to rest. What remained was the simple truth of her – the young woman who had come one day to his valley to teach the children, spirited, courageous.

Khan knelt beside her and with his breath laid bare the alabaster of her skin, with his fingers drew a tress of hair across the obscenity made by the bullet. It was done out of respect, not compassion, for she was not there. No part of her was left in this likeness. Pola, his beloved, had gone, taking with her all of worth in him, all hope, all love.

The many pains in him drew into the one pain. He wept deeply inside himself with not a muscle moving.

Abdalis had searched the debris for signs of the baby, of Ayesha, but had found none. He gazed down now through the wall.

When his throat would allow it, Khan said, 'I thought her mad, but she was a saint.'

Abdalis shook his head. But unexpectedly his voice was not without emotion.

'To you, son of Ahmed, she was . . . whatever she was. To me, she was a heretic. But I see now that she was sent by Allah.'

'Then pray for her soul, holy man,' Khan cried savagely. 'Pray for it!'

Abdalis again glanced out of the gaping wall. He appeared uneasy. Nevertheless, he turned his back on whatever was troubling him, sank to his knees and, without losing his straightness, went through the cleansing movements. Now his body came forward and his forehead touched the rubble that man seems doomed to make of God's creation.

He abbreviated not one word as he recited the *sura yasin*.

At the end he said, 'We have no dim light to place beside her; we must let the light of her spirit suffice. We have no *hafiz* to chant the Koran over her, but she knew our *suras* by heart. And already she wears a shroud, though it be dust. There is no more you and I can do here, son of Ahmed.' And he rose, in the one familiar motion. 'Now we must go. *Schurawi* soldiers are climbing the cliff. In minutes they will be here.'

'Go where, holy man?' Khan asked dully.

'There is a way from here. We will take with us those who are still alive. Come, take my arm.'

McCabe shone the lantern on the cave floor.

'This way. Go easy.' Even though he had done everything possible to shake off the toxic dust he kept well away from her and the baby. The film magazine was hugged to his chest.

Not being able to help Ayesha was agonizing. She was wandering and stumbling like a dreamer, only holding herself together for the infant's sake. That she had been no more than stunned by the explosion was a miracle, but exhaustion, physical and emotional, was taking its toll.

'Suppose there is no way through, Michael?'

'Suppose there is – look on the bright side!'

McCabe was high. Okay, there had been no way of barring the cave storeroom entrance against the Russians, and the cave could end in a blank wall or a crevasse. Yet their guide the night before had indicated that the system ran deep into the mountain, and when he now raised the glass of the lantern, the flame flickered and bent. A steady draught meant an exit.

No, they couldn't lose, not now they had the baby. Wasn't he the Prophet reincarnated? The Lily's lie become truth?

The caves were changing, the lamplight tiny now in huge darkness, just the tips of crystalline spears poking down at them, mirror images beneath.

Suddenly a distant boom reached them. McCabe and Ayesha stood stock-still.

Seconds later a great wind overtook them, flattening the lantern flame, holding it flat for a small age before releasing it.

'Sounds like they blew the whole building,' McCabe muttered.

Ayesha looked at him mutely, then at the baby. Just its tiny face showed, squeezed tight. She sat down on a rock, drooping.

McCabe raised the lamp and peered round through his one clear eyepiece. He was practically all liquid inside the mask and suit and was beginning to feel waves of faintness.

Ahead, the floor of the cavern fragmented into outcrops. Between them were black depressions, which could melt as you approached them or plunge into crevasses. He took an exploratory pace towards the nearest, raising the lamp.

He stood thinking, excited by his discovery, but cautious. It had to be done absolutely in the right order.

McCabe set the lantern on a rock, sat down on the edge and pushed his feet into the water. He tested the depth, feeling the icy chill trickle into his boots.

Leaning forward, he immersed his gloves and washed them one against the other. Then he took the magazine, made sure the lids were clamped tight, and, holding it traps uppermost, dunked it briefly a number of times. The lids weren't waterproof but they would be resistant. He wiped around the traps with his wet glove, then laid the magazine beside the lamp. He looked back towards Ayesha, who was watching intently. She came towards him.

'Will water be enough?'

'There's only one way to find out!' He said it blithely, but he felt himself begin to come down from his high. This was life and death stuff.

She sat down again, closer.

He waded in up to his neck, holding the filtration canister above the water, first with one hand then the other, as he scrubbed himself with the gloves, again, again. He lay down in the shallows and rolled and splashed and rinsed. When it seemed impossible for there to be a grain of toxic dust left on him, he took a deep breath and ducked his head. He scrubbed all over the mask till he ran out of air. When he tried to breathe he discovered he couldn't; the canister had filled. There was no choice then but to tear off the hood.

The cool air on his sweat felt marvellous. He stood inhaling the limy atmosphere of the cave. He was tempted to wash his face but resisted it. He waded ashore and began to strip off the suit, keeping the gloves on till last.

When he stood there in just his shirt and *shalvàr* he pulled the gloves off and flung them into the darkness. He turned to face Ayesha and waited, on tenterhooks.

She watched him, petrified.

A wave of dizziness assailed him. *Jesus!* He hung on to a rock and fought it. Slowly the feeling went away.

After two minutes he relaxed and forced a grin.

'Don't look now, sweetheart, but I think we'll be together on that plane'

She wasn't ready to believe anything yet.

Casually, to prove he was okay, he salvaged the boots and took them to another part of the stream and, after first rinsing his face, washed them afresh, and put them on.

He went back to her, squelching, utterly relieved, and squatted before her.

'Well, how's our baby?'

Ayesha shook her head. She was too overcome to speak.

It was his first clear view of the pair of them. He peered at the tiny screwed-up face with a frown.

'Shouldn't he cry or something?'

'Being born in a battle is very exhausting.'

The incredible nativity scene flashed again in his mind. He shivered and shook his head. There was a purple, bloody welt high on Ayesha's forehead. He cupped a hand to the side of her face and examined her expression closely.

'You sure you're okay?'

'Now you are, yes.'

'So you do care a little?'

He waited, but she did not commit herself further. He helped her to her feet, then fetched the camera magazine and the lamp. As he stood there, juggling the equipment so he could give her as much support as possible, they heard the distinct sound of voices.

The exit was little larger than a foxhole. It emerged on to a steep eroded slope on the other side of the mountain. After the dimness, the sunlight was excruciating. They sat together, squinting, till they could distinguish far below them a vast valley, part lake, part marshland. It must have stretched for thirty miles.

'The dasht-e-Navar,' Ayesha murmured.

Though they stared hard at the thread of road that skirted it, then at the surrounding slopes and heights above, they could make out no sign of movement. What was happening at Qassassin behind them, Allah alone knew. They heard the echo of helicopters, perhaps as they overflew the headland, but hopefully they were far too preoccupied with their rescue operation to search for any resistance survivors.

'You're sure the voices back there were Afghan?'

Ayesha said she was sure.

'All right, I guess it'll be safe to wait. I just hope they don't drink from the stream, that's all!'

He sighed and put his arm round her. She leaned against him. He looked down at the sleeping baby in her lap.

'What are we going to do with him?'

She shook her head, too tired to think.

'Find him a – what do you call it?'

'Wet-nurse.'

The quicker the better, he thought.

He tilted her chin impulsively and laid his lips on hers. Her own parted in a gasp, but she did not withdraw. The softness and moistness came somehow as a shock. Her free hand lifted and curled in the looseness of his shirt, and for an instant he caught an echo of this morning's passion.

'You are squashing Mahomed.'

'Sorry.' He eased back a little as the baby stretched and gave a whimper.

Her passion was still there, but subtly changing. The lips, glistening from his, tightened fiercely.

'As soon as it is dark we will take him to the nearest village. We must guard him, hide him.'

'You – you're taking the Mahomed bit seriously?'

'Of course!' She twisted a look at him, astonished.

He said, 'Come on, sweetheart. The Russian said the Lily was his wife. He wasn't acting.'

'It does not matter if he was. Your Christ was a Jew, Buddha an Indian.'

She was still way up there, McCabe realized. Without him. 'It's any weapon really, isn't it,' he said. 'A gun, a baby, whatever you can hit them with. Well, you don't need it. You have all the anti-Soviet ammunition you need in this magazine, believe me. Let's just concentrate on that, shall we? Leave little Mo to the Ulema.'

She wasn't even listening. She had drawn away from him and was rocking the infant gently, trying to lull him back to sleep. Murmuring to him softly in Pushtu. Her eyes slid sidelong towards McCabe, fiercely protective.

Their expression confirmed his worst fears: she had a whole new mission in life.

The reunion as Khan's party emerged from the caves thirty minutes later was an emotional one. In all, they numbered ten – the sole survivors of Qassassin. They had demolished the entrance from the monastery, Khan gasped. His whole *chapan* was matted with blood. Only his iron will was holding him together. The explosives had been there all the time, he said, laid and wired for just such a need. The Lily, Allah rest her, had thought even of that.

Ayesha cleaned and dressed his shattered shoulder and raw feet as best she could, while Abdalis went down on his knees before the babe and offered up a prayer for its miraculous deliverance.

Khan watched him with pain-clouded eyes. 'Do you believe it, holy man?' he asked the mullah wearily. 'Truly believe that he is our Prophet returned?'

'I believe it, son of Ahmed. From this small twig shall grow the bow that will smite death to our enemies.'

'Inshallah!' Ayesha whispered. And McCabe needed no translation to recognize another nail in the coffin of his hopes.

Now, Abdalis was outlining what must be done next. The sun was growing red above the western mountains and its rays probed the cave entrance. Until the thread of tomorrow's dawn showed white, he reminded them, this was still the Night of Power.

'First we must find one who will suckle him,' he continued. 'And swiftly. Secrecy will be of the essence. So let us take him among nomads, where he can begin his life in simplicity, as in his last incarnation. But the Ulema must be told at once. They will come and pay homage. They will prescribe the manner of his instruction and how the divine power of his spirit may be directed to confound our enemies. But we here, for it is plainly written, will be his mentors – you, Doctor, his foster-mother; you, son of Ahmed, his guardian; you men, his helpers, as the Medinans were his helpers and soldiers in his life before. More will join as the word spreads, till all of the resistance becomes his Sacred Army. The Russians, like the Meccans, will either be driven from the land or remain to pray, their swords become candles at the shrine we will build in our Prophet's name at Kabul.' Abdalis paused, frowning. 'Why, son of Ahmed, do you shake your head?'

Khan said thickly, 'Your studies, holy man, have taught you fine words, but a soldier you are not.'

'You doubt the manner of it?'

'I doubt the conclusion.' He paused to ease his position gruntingly. 'To drive the Russians back will not be so simple.'

'You are tired, son of Ahmed, sorely wounded and in grief.'

'But still a soldier.'

Abdalis contemplated his expression for a moment.

'Where is your standard, O soldier?'

Khan shifted again. 'You know I have none. Save here.' He thumbed his chest.

'Well, you have one now! All will be different.' Abdalis pointed triumphantly to the baby. 'All will rally to it. *All.* The whole of Islam, do you not understand? *A thousand million souls!*'

Khan's restlessness stilled in shock. Ayesha gasped. The Gujaras murmured.

Encouraged by these responses, Abdalis continued, expanding his theme.

'Give it to me roughly,' McCabe muttered, furious that he could not understand.

Ayesha was too busy lapping it up to pass him more than the odd quote.

There she goes, he sighed. The baby would be used, abused, she couldn't see it for the Technicolor. Drop the Bomb! Bury a division of armour! Okay, *he* had done that. But already he was feeling the horror of it. Sooner or later, what she was getting into would reach her, too. Its acid would eat her away. Well, he wasn't going to let it happen. She was his prize for all this – not the film, the cash, the grin and handshake from the President – her!

He gripped her arm so hard she winced.

'So all this, now, is so much celluloid.' He rapped the magazine.

Abdalis was still holding forth. She stared round at him, distracted, then back to the mullah.

'You don't want it, right?'

She glanced round again in annoyance. 'In a minute, please, Michael.'

'Okay, sweetheart.' McCabe thrust the magazine into her vision and braced his thumb and fingers against the cover release. 'If that's the way you want it.' He gave it a slight twist. There were two releases, one for the unexposed side, the other for the exposed. He was threatening to open up the unexposed side, but she wasn't to know that.

All at once he had her attention.

'What are you *doing*?' Her hands shot out and gripped his.

'It's no use to you now, surely? You've got his nibs here.'

Abdalis broke off, scowling at the interruption. All eyes turned to them.

'Michael, are you mad? Of course we need it. And so do you.'

'Oh, I don't know,' McCabe said carelessly.

'Now wait, please.' Ayesha looked confused. 'Michael, your film is vital propaganda for us. You risked your *life* for it.'

He sighed. 'Ah well. You win a few, lose a few.'

'But it is worth to you a lot of money.'

'Well, I won't need it, will I, if I stay here?'

Her eyes narrowed as she sensed the emotion underlying his flippancy. She glanced uneasily at the others, who were plainly agog to know what had suddenly become so urgent.

'What is it, exactly, Michael, that you are saying?'

'Ah. Well. Nothing, actually, that I didn't say last night. Except that I love you. And to give you an ultimatum.'

'You mean,' she said slowly, 'that if I don't come with you to London you are going to destroy the film?'

'You're there,' McCabe bluffed.

'You care enough for me to do that?'

'Well?' He waited. 'Which is it to be?'

She had to grope for words. 'Michael, I am not a person to be forced, you know that. And if I was, the others would not allow it. You are not thinking properly.'

'Suppose they gave us their blessing?'

'They are Pathans. They will not bow to pressure.'

'Put it to Khan.'

'It is nothing to do with Khan. What I do is my own decision.'

'All the same, I'd like his opinion!'

Khan had difficulty in bringing his mind to bear on what the little doctor was explaining with such obvious embarrassment. Astonishment surfaced through his pain.

'Why does he need you to go?'

'He . . .' Ayesha reduced it to Pathan basics, 'wants me.'

Khan looked hard at McCabe.
'Do you want him, little sister?'
'With respect, that is not the point.'
'Indeed it is not the point!' Abdalis interjected.
'I disagree,' Khan said. He had been too recently reminded of that other world, one he had almost forgotten.
'My duty is with the resistance,' she said.
'But do you want him?'
Her gaze fled everywhere but to the man beside her.
'I respect him. We are close. But—'
'Then I think you should go with him,' was Khan's opinion.
'Impossible!' Abdalis snapped.
'The film', Khan's voice, at times, was barely audible, 'is important. So—'
'The baby is more important.' Abdalis's was strong.
'So why do we not assign her the duty of safeguarding its journey to *Engelstan?*'
'She assisted in the birth, son of Ahmed. She has a sacred role to play.'
'She can fulfil that role when she returns. If she wishes. If not, we will find another to take her place.'
'Why go to such lengths when this absurd threat is so easily countered?' Abdalis only just avoided scorn. 'Simply let her *tell* him that she will go.'
'I will not lie to him,' Ayesha said quietly.
'She will do what she is told.' Abdalis addressed her through Khan. 'She is now a servant of Allah. The unbeliever seeks by threat to change what is written. It is our sacred duty, therefore, to thwart him *by whatever means to hand*. She will *tell* him she will go. That is the solution and the end of it.'
Khan thought wearily, he opposes me still in the name of God. Yet there was logic in his words that could not be faulted. Khan waited to see if Ayesha would object again, but she sat silent.
'Very well.' He eyed the mullah and Gujaras warningly. 'But I want no violence. The *feranghi* has served us well.'
'There need be none,' Abdalis conceded. 'Since he bears no weapon.' He added, still without addressing Ayesha directly, 'She is to tell him now.'
McCabe had been observing the speakers closely and was suspicious.

'Well?'

Ayesha continued to nurse the baby in silence, then she turned to him with a smile.

'Michael, the holy man is watching so be careful of your expression. Do you understand me?'

'What's the verdict?'

'I am to *tell* you I will come. I am to lie.'

'Then later they'll stick a gun in my ribs and take the film?'

'I think so. Look happy, Michael, this is good news.'

'Terrific,' McCabe said, a broad grin concealing his puzzlement. 'Did Khan agree to that?'

'Khan is not himself.'

Nor am I, McCabe thought. He cursed himself for not having thought the thing through before embarking on it.

'What happens if you tell them you opt to come?'

'I am to stay. It is the holy man's order.'

'To hell with his order!'

She shook her head.

'Thanks,' McCabe said, 'a million.' He showed his teeth again to Abdalis.

'I am sorry, Michael. Truly sorry. I am flattered and grateful for what you have tried to do.'

'I believe you.' McCabe thought quickly. He lifted the magazine and ostentatiously screwed the lid tight. 'I'm going outside. Tell them it's to work out how I'm going to get you home.'

With the magazine under his arm, he squeezed out through the cave mouth and was gone.

The sunset colours deepened. The Gujaras began to stretch the cramp out of their limbs. It was time to move.

McCabe had been absent for some minutes. He's gone, Khan thought. Unlike Abdalis, who refused to look upon an unveiled woman, he had noted Ayesha's mystification when McCabe left the cave. She warned him, Khan concluded, and he went. Well, perhaps it was for the best.

Abdalis moved out first. The Gujaras helped Khan to his feet and supported him. Ayesha followed with the baby.

They emerged into the evening light to find the mullah standing rigid as a tent-pole, glaring towards an enormous rock. On its crest, still very much with them, sat McCabe,

Buddha fashion. He had a loop of film tied around his neck.

It emerged from the take-up, the *exposed* side of the magazine which he had anchored to the ground with a heap of stones. He meant business this time, as his expression showed.

'Now this is the scam, sweetheart,' he called to Ayesha. 'They go their way, we go ours, simple as that. Break it to them.'

Ayesha's cheeks coloured with fury. 'Michael, this is going *too* far!' She handed the baby to one of the Gujaras and marched towards him, determined to end the fiasco.

'Hold it,' he warned her. 'Think carefully what you're doing.' He leaned back and a few more inches of precious film were drawn through the traps to be lost to posterity. When she didn't stop he leaned further, his body supported on his wrists. The drop beneath him was no more than five metres, but below that was a steep slope that plunged away, seemingly forever. Ayesha stopped with a catch of breath.

He grinned. 'Got the picture?'

'You wouldn't dare. You would break your neck!'

'Maybe. But a spectacular end, don't you think?'

She almost choked on her rage. 'I swear, if you destroy that film I will shoot you.'

'With the same result.' He came back into balance. 'See? Now listen. From here I'll be heading east to Pakistan. You won't need any gear from your old camp or anything, just what you're wearing. We'll buy everything you'll need for the journey home in Peshawar.'

She stared at him for a speechless moment, then turned abruptly to face the men, words pouring from her in an angry torrent.

Abdalis turned his head aside so as not to gaze on her.

'She betrayed us to him,' he hissed to Khan. 'Why else would he act thus?' His scowl deepened. 'Why do you smile, son of Ahmed?'

'It seems his "absurd threat" was not so easily countered. Also that she cares more for him than us.' Then, severely, 'We are wasting time, Abdalis. We must let him take her.'

But the mullah unslung his weapon and called, deep-throated, 'Out of the way, woman!'

Ayesha started to obey, then saw his intention. She registered dismay and planted her feet defiantly.

Khan said sharply, 'Abdalis, stop – that is an order.'

'Have no fear.' The mullah slipped the catch of his gun and took a stride, first to one side, then another, as Ayesha moved to screen him from his target.

McCabe now experienced real alarm. What had started as a ploy was now in deadly earnest. He pushed himself to the very edge of the rock, balancing precariously.

'Tell him to drop the gun or I'm going over, no kidding. And for Christ's sake get out of his way!'

He had scarcely got the words out when a prolonged burst ripped from the mullah's weapon. Ayesha screamed as the bullets cracked past her. Sparks leapt around the traps of the magazine. The film flickered with the impacts. McCabe recoiled in reflex. Too late, he realized that the film had been the mullah's only target. He felt himself going over, twisted, clutched at the brow of rock. Its weathered contour chafed under his hands and was gone. He fell, bouncing once against a protuberance, the damaged film tightening but not breaking as it sprang from the traps. The mullah had failed. McCabe wished in those split seconds that he hadn't. To sacrifice what he had risked so much to obtain had never been his intention.

He hit the slope in a roll. He dug his heels into the shale and tried to check himself, and at least save the bulk of the footage. Someone else had the same idea. A gun blazed at him, spattering him with flints. *Jesus!* He let himself roll on to avoid getting hit, the film spinning out in his wake, leaping, snagging. He felt the razor-slash of its edge around his throat. Then one arm got entangled and he became a human take-up spool, the film winding round him as the ricochets whined past.

The slope eased a little and he somersaulted to his feet. But the bursts of fire had followed him. He daren't stop and now, suddenly, in his fury he thought, to hell with you, the whole bloody thing, and bounded on, a wild cry bursting from his lips.

Whooping crazily, he maintained his headlong rush, till at long and breathless last he felt a jerk as the end of the film broke free of the magazine.

He slithered to a halt, chest heaving, and looked back.

The Afghans were masked from view by the intervening ridge. Film littered the slope as far as he could see in whirls and kinks and ravels, corkscrewing grey and white in the breeze like a single, huge New Year's streamer.

He disentangled himself with difficulty, then cast away the festoons and watched them spiral idly across the hillside. He was bruised but intact.

Well, he had blown it. Lost her, lost his film, lost his mess of dollars. About his only satisfaction was that it served them all right, including Ayesha. When he looked back again, the Afghans had appeared silently on the ridge. They stood in the light of the dying sun and stared down at him.

Abdalis slowly raised his gun and took final aim. There was nowhere to hide. McCabe did not move. Then Khan belatedly must have asserted his authority, because the mullah reluctantly lowered the weapon and hung it on his lean shoulder. Moments later they faced north and began to make their way down.

Their figures turned black and sharp against the glaring sky – Khan supported, moving awkwardly and angrily it seemed, but indomitable, Abdalis the erect finger of a vengeful God, the Gujaras goat-footed. Ayesha was carrying the precious infant. She, alone, looked and kept on looking in his direction. Finally she turned her face away and they shrank from view beyond the shoulder.

Winner take nothing. McCabe sat for a while and watched the sun's rays lift from the vast landscape. Instant cold came with the blueness. He was wearing only shirt and *shalvàr*. He would freeze at this height. But still he lingered – a man marooned between two worlds and an ocean of hostile space to traverse before returning to his native planet, where he would not be welcome.

He heard the whine of the gunships a full fifteen seconds before they lifted into view behind him, thudding the air like monstrous carpet-beaters. Perhaps they could see him, perhaps not. Perhaps in their rage and frustration on their way back to Kabul, they would take it out on even a lone figure sitting on the mountainside. He waited, not in the mood to care.

Their thunder grew till he was in the eye of their storm, the film eddying and tumbling around him in mocking saraband. For a moment he saw himself. It was the perfect end-of-movie title and credits background!

But no. The storm moved on, scattering echoes. They lapped against the rocks, diminished to slippery whispers and died.

The sky beyond the ridge was turning green now. He watched a blob of something silhouetted against it and decided that he really should move on. The blob seemed somehow to be mobile. He guessed it must be an illusion, the day's heat maybe, still rising from the rocks. But curiosity held him there a few moments longer.

He watched it rise laboriously into a climbing figure – that of a young woman, coming towards him!

Khan did not look back, it hurt his shoulder too much to do so, but he was relieved for Ayesha that she had chosen as she had, stopping suddenly and handing the babe to one of the Gujaras, then facing him mutely, with all the turmoil gone and her gaze clear.

She had touched his hand and said simply, 'May you live forever, Ghoram Khan,' then, with a warning scowl at Abdalis, had started back up the slope.

To live forever, Khan thought, would be more than he could bear. But a year would be a boon. Two, a godsend. Three . . . he could accomplish great revenge against the *schurawi* in three. Though it would never, could never, erase the ache in his heart.

They had all but reached the valley when Abdalis paused for him and his helpers to catch up in the darkness.

'I have been thinking, son of Ahmed . . .' He sounded oddly excited, like a man anxious to make amends. 'Suppose the baby were *not* premature . . .'

Khan waited, inwardly still cursing him. He was impatient to bathe his tortured feet in the marsh.

'And it was conceived *before* the *schurawi* invaded Bab-el-Hawa . . .'

He did not complete the sentence but pushed his face close, in an effort to witness Khan's reaction.

Khan suppressed the sudden powerful emotion that seized him.

He said gruffly, 'Suppose it was – what difference would it make?'

'To our project, nothing,' Abdalis murmured. 'But no heart is so brave that it can beat in emptiness.' He turned away. 'I offer it you simply as a thought. For company in life's long and lonely night.'